ALL THE WAY

A Love Story

Stephnie Conn

Copyright © 2024 Stephnie Conn

All rights reserved

The characters and events portrayed in this book are fictitious. Any similarity to real persons, living or dead, is coincidental and not intended by the author.

No part of this book may be reproduced, or stored in a retrieval system, or transmitted in any form or by any means, electronic, mechanical, photocopying, recording, or otherwise, without express written permission of the publisher.

ISBN: 9798326583949
Imprint: Independently published

Cover design by: Art Painter
Library of Congress Control Number: 2018675309
Printed in the United States of America

For James and Joe, the true loves of my life.

CONTENTS

Title Page
Copyright
Dedication
Chapter One — 3
Chapter Two — 10
Chapter Three — 22
Chapter Four — 31
Chapter Five — 42
Chapter Six — 50
Chapter Seven — 59
Chapter Eight — 68
Chapter Nine — 80
Chapter Ten — 96
Chapter Eleven — 103
Chapter Twelve — 112
Chapter Thirteen — 118
Chapter Fourteen — 127
Chapter Fifteen — 136
Chapter Sixteen — 142
Chapter Seventeen — 154
Chapter Eighteen — 159

Chapter Nineteen	169
Chapter Twenty	182
Chapter Twenty-One	195
Chapter Twenty-Two	204
Chapter Twenty-Three	212
Chapter Twenty-Four	225
Chapter Twenty-Five	243
Chapter Twenty-Six	258
Chapter Twenty-Seven	271
Chapter Twenty-Eight	290
Chapter Twenty-Nine	298
Chapter Thirty	313
Chapter Thirty-One	339
Chapter Thirty-Two	355
Chapter Thirty-Three	368
Chapter Thirty-Four	381
Chapter Thirty-Five	390
Acknowledgements	403
About The Author	405
All the way	407

Prologue

Isabella had just sat down to have a rest whilst she waited for him when a bulletin appeared on the television ... *You're watching a BBC News special. Reports of a shooting outside the Palace of Westminster. Outside the House of Commons. A police officer has been stabbed and his apparent attacker shot by police officers. In what is developing into a major security incident outside the Houses of Parliament. These live pictures of Westminster Bridge, where eye witnesses say a car, in the words of eyewitnesses, mowed down several people. Some reports suggesting as many as 12 people injured after a car hit them and then ...*

She felt a surge of adrenaline, and the room spun as she realised that's where they were. Near there at least. She thought she was going to faint or be sick, or both. Oh my God, what should she do? Unsure of what to do, she was at a loss. Her thoughts were such a mess that she couldn't focus.

She rang his mobile. No answer.

She rang again. Still no answer.

She tried Harry. No luck.

The TV continued in the background and she could pick out broken pieces. *Many people are being treated at the scene ...*

She texted them both. Continually.

She rang again. Over and over again.

... at twenty minutes to three, London time.

She couldn't think clearly. She didn't know what was going on. Panic consumed her. Fear and anxiety overwhelmed her.

Her phone rang. It was Bibi. "Have you seen?"

"Yes. Oh God Bibi, that's near where they are."

"What? No."

"I can't get hold of them. Oh God Bibi, what do I do?"

***

CHAPTER ONE

Katy Perry's music was being streamed through the Bose. Thanks to the lively music and the sunlight flooding through the grand bay windows, the pre-holiday vibe was impossible to ignore. Quite a contrast from the previous two weeks, when the rain had been incessant.

As Isabella sorted through the array of colourful garments heaped on her large king bed, she grappled with folding them neatly into her suitcase. Taking a momentary pause, she cast a quick glance at her best friend, positioned on a stool in front of her old chest of drawers, engrossed in spraying and sniffing the assortment of perfumes on display,

She groaned, "Oh shit. What have I got myself into, Bibi?"

"You'll be fine," Bibi replied nonchalantly, taking one long last sniff of Aqua di Parma. "It's only 2 weeks. You'll be surprised how quickly it'll pass by. It's a holiday and you deserve it. It'll do you good to get away. I wish I was coming- wow I would give anything to be going away for 2 weeks."

"I wish you were coming too," Isabella groaned, her voice filled with disappointment. "It won't be the same without you," she added, as she fell onto the only part of the bed not covered in clothes. "What the hell did I say I'd go for, anyway? What was I thinking? Seven other people I've barely met before. What will we have in common? Ingrid's work colleagues. Jesus, you can imagine what they'll be like, can't you? If they're anything like her ... it'll be a bloody nightmare," she wailed, running her fingers through her hair.

"Such a pessimist" grunted Bibi, who, having finished

with the fragrance, moved on to Isabella's leather jewellery case, "Anyway, you've met most of them before haven't you?"

"Yes, and that's the problem."

Isabella Michaels, at 31, was startling to look at. With a full wide mouth and eyes the colour of deep violet; *Elizabeth Taylor eyes* people said. She was successful, elegant and even without a scrap of makeup, unquestionably beautiful. Her long, dark, tousled hair cascaded down her shoulders, giving her a perfectly imperfect, just-got-out-of-bed look. With her unblemished, olive complexion, she radiated a natural beauty. She already had a fantastic suntan, gleaned from many hours playing tennis at the weekends and the occasional evening at her local tennis club. Although, if she was honest, she hadn't played as much as she'd have liked over the past couple of years.

Isabella's best friend, Bibi Javid, at 5 foot 4 inches was a good five inches shorter than her friend. Her thick, jet-black hair framed her face perfectly, highlighting her mesmerising hazel eyes and complementing her radiant Persian complexion, making her undeniably beautiful. Together, they were an unstoppable force, drawing admirers wherever they went on their nights out. They had great fun together; catching up on all the latest gossip, enjoying a cocktail or four. They tried to meet up at least once a week for dinner or drinks, in the pub or just at each other's houses, where they put the world to rights. Bibi watched as Isabella rose from the bed and continued to place the beautifully cut, elegant clothes into her suitcase. She wished she was going too.

Even in a white, cotton ribbed vest and a pair of shorts, Isabella looked fabulous ... and those legs. Bibi watched as her friend packed her last few pieces into her case, ready for her fast approaching holiday, then watched as she slumped once more onto the bed with an enormous sigh.

"Stop it Izzy," she scolded. "You'll have a wonderful time. Stop huffing and puffing–you're lucky. Most people would give their right arm for an expensive holiday to Africa.

Think about it another way. This will be the ideal break from Robert. It will give him some serious time as well. He may just realise what he's missing."

"What are you taking about?" snapped Izzy.

"You said yourself, things haven't exactly been a bed of roses lately. You're far too smart and beautiful to be wasting your time on him. Hopefully, you'll realise this whilst you're away. Everyone else came to this conclusion ages ago."

"You don't understand–he has his good points, you know."

"Really? I'd agree with you, but then we'd both be wrong. He's been a miserable shit lately and has no time for anyone, you especially."

"He's not that bad." Isabella didn't know if she was trying to convince herself or her friend. Her well-known expression, which Bibi was so familiar with, indicated that the conversation had come to a halt.

"Right. I think that is everything," said Isabella, forcing close her suitcase, "I'm going for a shower. Go make us a cuppa - when you've finished trying on all my jewellery, that is. I'll meet you downstairs when I'm finished, okay?"

"Sure" Bibi grumbled.

Isabella wondered if she'd been too short with her friend. She cared, that's all. She didn't like to admit it, even to herself, but Robert had been a shit lately. Bibi was right.

Walking into her bathroom, she leaned into the shower and turned on the tap. She stripped, piled her hair up on top of her head and put her hand under the cascading water to see if it was the right temperature. She stepped in and stretched her face upwards, closed her eyes, and enjoyed the rushing water pummelling her skin. Inevitably, her thoughts turned to Robert.

They had met four years ago in a charming little pub in Windsor. With a wry smile, she reflected on the possibility that this had been an omen, questioning the significance of the moment. It seemed like he could always be found in the pubs these days.

She had been with a group of girlfriends and they were all sat outside, enjoying the warmth of the late summer evening. Chatting and laughing noisily round a grubby old wooden table, they were enjoying an ice-cold bottle of Whispering Angel; the energy flowing easily between them.

Robert had been sitting at a table nearby with two or three friends and she'd noticed him looking over twice.

In fact, he'd spent the best part of a couple of hours watching her, catching her eye at every opportunity.

She'd lifted her sunglasses a couple of times to make sure she was seeing what she thought she was seeing–her eyebrows furrowed with irritation as she silently reprimanded him for his lack of courtesy.

After consuming a great deal more wine, the cheerful banter now even more rowdy, the men eventually made their way over to their table and asked if they could join them "Sure," said Sammy, "the more the merrier."

The guy who'd be staring at her sat down next to her.

"Hi. I'm Robert."

He was better looking up close up and continued to flirt unashamedly with her. He was relatively attractive and funny and she enjoyed his easy-going, friendly personality.

After a fun, wine-soaked afternoon, they eventually arranged a date for the following weekend and that had been that, really.

Things had been so easy back then. So fun. What had gone wrong? She didn't want to go there. Their first three years together had been almost perfect. They'd even casually talked about an engagement. She had a pang of heartache, not only for what was going wrong, but for what had been. And now here she was, going to Kenya without him.

Her thoughts were being drawn back to the present. Exiting the shower, she used a large, fluffy white towel to dry herself before returning to the bedroom. Using expensive body lotion, she covered herself and then sprayed some Jo Malone behind her ears and on her wrists. She rummaged through her underwear drawer and pulled out an ivory string and matching bra. She grinned to herself as she thought of Bibi's teasing about her "gnat bites." Yes, she wished she was fuller up top and yes, Robert had once suggested a breast enlargement–but no bloody chance.

She applied an insignificant amount of makeup; a touch of mascara, a few dabs of YSL's Touché-Eclat under her eyes, some bronzer and highlighter, and a little lip gloss. She pulled on a black Balmain T-shirt and a pair of faded jeans and slipped into her Gucci sliders. Comfort was definitely on the cards.

She put on her favourite ring, earrings and necklace. Finally, she picked up her White Gold Rolex from the dressing table and slid it over her wrist–an uncommonly generous birthday gift to herself after opening her own very successful interior design studio and showroom on the King's Road.

After years of relentless dedication, studying Fine Arts and marketing, she achieved her goal and landed her first job at a prestigious department store in London's West End. First, she began as an assistant buyer and eventually advanced to overseeing her own team of buyers. In a market that moved, she had a discerning ability to choose the best possible merchandise for customers. The fast-paced environment was something she loved, and she stayed calm even when under pressure. She developed strong commercial skills and became more aware of current trends, before joining a prestigious design firm where she soon rose to become one of their most successful interior designers, fuelled by her genuine passion.

Once she sensed the timing was ideal and had confidence in developing her own client base primarily through word-of-mouth, she established her brand identity that reflected her style and values, ultimately launching her own boutique.

After securing the perfect space, she started with minimal tools and gradually renovated the showroom, eventually landing her first commission. In no time, she became a Member of the Chartered Society of Interior Designers and was running a thriving business. With her business booming, she had the freedom to select her projects.

Coming back to reality, she unclipped her hair, bent over and shook her hands vigorously through her hair, then throwing her head back sharply, regarded herself in the mirror "Ready."

As she grabbed her recently acquired, now weighty, rolling Louis Vuitton suitcase from the bed, she descended the stairs and headed towards the kitchen where her friend patiently stood.

"Wow," said Bibi, "You look amazing."

"Thank you, but don't you think I should have had a trim before I went?"

"Not at all. Your hair looks wonderful. It's really grown. Do you want anything to eat before you go?"

"No thanks. In a hurry, I'll snatch a coffee and an apple. I can't bring myself to eat because I'm so nervous. I'll just eat on the flight. Actually, the Uber's here in five. Shit, have I got everything?"

"Passport? Tickets? Condoms?"

"Ha funny. What the hell would I need condoms for? Robert's not coming."

"So, what? But Harry is and that other guy you told me about?"

"Piss off Bibi. Don't remind me about Harry. And don't even bring up the person we shall not name. And for crying out loud, I am still with Robert."

"Just. Anyway, that means nothing. Look at this old woman," said Bibi, pointing to an article in the paper. "She met a Masai warrior and gave up her whole family for him."

"Bibi, just stop," snapped Isabella. "And Christ, I'm not that bloody old. Stop trying to set me up with other people all the time, will you? Just because Robert and I aren't like you and Darysus, not all of us have the same perfect marriage as you.

We can't all be perfect."

"No, but some of us have partners who at least show a bit of interest in us every now and again," responded Bibi, but as she saw the cloud come over her friend's face yet again, she knew she was reaching dangerous territory and added "Look, here's your Uber. I'm sorry, I just want you to be happy, that's all. Now give me a hug."

"I'll miss you Bibs. Now make sure everything's turned off and locked up properly and leave my bloody jewellery alone."

"Love you. Have a fab time, okay?"

"Love you too. And sorry if I was short with you. I'm stressed and always feel anxious when going away. I hate flying." She grabbed her jacket from the back of the chair, flicked her hair from underneath the collar, and picked up her bag. "See you in a couple of weeks."

***

CHAPTER TWO

As Isabella's feet crunched down the driveway towards the waiting car, the Uber driver, not normally one to help customers with their luggage, took one look at her in the mirror and jumped out of his seat eagerly.

"Help you with your bags, love?" he asked.

"Please. Just the one case." She didn't want to let go of her Hermes Birkin, containing her passport and tickets. Knowing her luck, she'd leave it behind–it was probably worth more than the holiday itself.

As she sank into the worn faux leather seat, she found herself staring idly out the window, lost in thought. She spent the Uber ride to Heathrow thinking again about Robert.

He worked as a major account manager for an investment firm in the city. Many late nights wining and dining clients. They were communicating less often. Weekends were their only time together. Was it really good? The prolonged absences didn't bother them initially when they were younger and more ambitious. They cherished every moment spent together on weekends. They spent hours on the phone or on FaceTime. They'd talk for hours, enjoying each other's voices. Laughing at absurdities. But they were becoming more distant. They had run out of things to talk about. The odd text was all that was left.

Robert was charming. Good-looking, dynamic, self-assured, conceited. He effortlessly engaged in conversations with strangers about any topic. He was six feet four and initially took pride in his appearance. After years of indulgence, he was neglecting himself, though. Isabella teased him mercifully about it, but he was acutely sensitive and took offence at the perceived criticism. So *what if we drink bottles of wine at lunch? So, what if my face is red? And for your information, it's not bloated, it's my age,* he'd whine.

Unbeknownst to Isabella, he was also spending thousands of pounds each week in strip clubs, entertaining clients. His excessive drinking was becoming a secret burden, as he feared her uncovering his late-night revelries. Many colleagues had pointed out to him that his late nights were affecting his work during the day, a fact she was unaware of. His usual professional demeanour was slipping away, as his lack of focus became apparent. In his line of work, it was far from ideal. It was clear that things were not going well at the moment.

Her thoughts turned to the holiday. What the hell *was* she doing, going off on holiday without Robert and with practically a group of strangers?

Isabella and Ingrid Sandersson had been friends for years. Together, they had gone to UCL and ended up sharing digs in Camden for a couple of years. Through their mutual support in studying for their respective degrees, they had navigated through many short-lived relationships together. They'd lived uni life to the full, attending dozens of wild and raucous parties. They were a lethal combination throughout their years together and had broken many hearts and had had theirs broken several times along the way. They had kept in touch over the years, even if only by the odd text or email, but when they met up, it was as if they had never been apart.

Ingrid had never had a serious relationship, the longest lasting only six months. She lived in a sensational apartment on the Thames, opposite the Oxo Tower. She was known for her love of socialising and was always a sought-after guest at parties, as she had a reputation for being incredibly entertaining.

Ingrid had telephoned Isabella the previous week, out of the blue, to say she had arranged a holiday for eight to Kenya and one had dropped out last minute. She was desperate to fill the place and would love Isabella to come along if she was interested and able?

"Thanks for the afterthought," Isabella had said. "Why wasn't I invited in the first place?"

Ingrid had squirmed her way out of that one, explaining that she had been going to ask both Isabella and Robert, but knew Robert would not have been able to take time off work anyway and that ...

"Yeah, yeah," said Isabella, "Excuses, excuses. Anyway, I don't want to be the odd one out, Ingy. If it's all couples, I don't want to be the only gooseberry."

"No, blimey, it's nothing like that," said Ingrid. "It's a kind of work thing. All of us are single and you know a couple of them, anyway."

"Like who?" Isabella asked suspiciously.

"Well, of course, me," Ingrid said. "And you'll love Dave, our chief exec. He's incredibly friendly. Fiona and Maddy, you know, from last year's Christmas party? The two girls on our table? You must remember? Fiona's relentless attempts to seduce everyone lasted all night until she eventually passed out on an architect. Maddy's the redhead, the one that pounces on any man she meets."

"She was so rude to me. I hated her. Sounds like a great bunch so far." She said sarcastically.

"Don't be a bitch Izzy."

"Oh, you know me, sarcasm is just one service I offer. You're welcome."

"Well, what about Ewan, a nice young guy? He started a couple of years ago. He's gorgeous and just my type - so hands off. Knowing my luck, he'll take one look at you and Auf Weidersehn Ingrid. But if you fancy a younger man ...?"

"I'll pass, thanks. And the rest?"

"Harry."

"Oh, Jesus."

"Yep. The one and only. The only guy we've both done."

"Wow. Make it sound so much worse than it was. It wasn't a threesome. And I didn't sleep with him, by the way, as you well know."

"Not at the same time, obviously. You know what I mean. By the way, his body's even better than it ever was. Still got tons of money and still as fun as ever."

Although Isabella hadn't seen Harry for years, she'd followed his bachelor's lavish lifestyle on social media. They'd had a short-lived fling at university. It had been fun, but he was not the girlfriend type.

"Ok, who's number eight?"

"Well, here's the thing. Don't say no. Wait until I finish before you say anything. It's Jack Vincent."

"No way," snapped Isabella. "It's a definite no from me."

"Oh, come on Izzy. What's your problem with him, anyway? He's the most gorgeous man ever to walk on this planet. Most women would give their right arm to spend two weeks with him."

"Yeah, but I'm not most women, am I?" she answered curtly. "I just don't like him, okay? He's an arsehole. We rub each other up the wrong way. Anyway, I think *Mr God's gift to women* won't be happy when he finds out that I'm one of his holiday buddies. No, I can't come. You'll have to get someone else."

"Izzy, you're being a dick and on top of that, you're giving up the opportunity to have a fabulous, all expenses paid holiday. Anyway, Jack has hardly ever mentioned you. He probably doesn't even remember who you are," she lied. In truth, Jack asked about Izzy every time he saw her. "Besides, why give up a good chance of getting away from Robert the Drunk for two weeks?"

"Don't you start,"

"Lying in the sun. Drinking cocktails. Hmmm, just think. Come on Izzy, don't let me down. We'll have a great time. It'll be like old times, us girls together. Don't let Jack put you off. There's enough of us so that you don't even have to talk to him if you don't want to. There'll be plenty of us around. Anyway, you may even hit it off? You're very similar, you know?"

"Thanks for that," huffed Isabella haughtily.

And that, more or less, had been that. Ingrid had relentlessly pestered her for days until she'd finally given in.

In all honesty, she was looking forward to getting away, but it wasn't just the long flight she was dreading–she hated flying - no doubt the butterflies in her stomach were because within the hour she'd be seeing Jack Vincent again. But as Ingrid had said, there'd be eight of them. No reason she'd have to spend much time with him. She didn't know why, but he was dangerous. Typical Italian. He came across as moody, inordinately complex and egotistical, but he possessed a tremendous magnetic quality and he awakened potent feelings in her and she didn't like it, not one bit. On the handful of occasions they had met, they'd clashed. Big time. Every little thing seemed to set them off.

Isabella, as well as being very personable, radiated confidence with every word and gesture. She had an amiable, open manner and could put a person at ease with her contagious smile, which could light up a room. On the negative side, Isabella earned a reputation for her stubbornness, short temper, impatience towards foolishness, and tendency to get irritated easily.

She was also never short of things to say, but the New Year's Eve she'd first encountered Jack Vincent had been the exception. For the first time in her life, she'd ended up feeling insecure and ill at ease. For what reason, she still had absolutely no idea.

Ingrid had invited both Isabella and Robert (reluctantly) to join friends at her lavish penthouse for a New Year's Eve party. Isabella had graciously accepted the invitation, but wasn't looking forward to it. Robert insisted he didn't get on with Ingrid, even though they'd only met on a handful of occasions. They just seemed to rub each other up the wrong way. He also complained about the company she kept and just didn't like *those kinds of people*, even though he'd never even met or been amongst *those kinds of people*.

"I just don't like her, okay?" he'd said.

"She's one of my oldest and closest friends," she'd pleaded.

However, as they had received no other better invitations for once, she'd decided they'd be going, even if only for a few hours. She didn't mind driving; she wanted to spend a quiet New Year's Day at home, anyway.

She had purchased a new and exquisite, silver sparkle column dress from a small boutique on Beauchamp Place for the occasion and, combined with some beautiful costume jewellery, she looked especially glamorous. Not that Robert had noticed. Compliments were never his thing.

Robert had already wolfed down several glasses of red wine before they'd even left the house, and she was on edge already. She dreaded to think about what he would be like later on in the evening. She would have to watch him like a hawk. Why did he always do this? Why did he always act worse when meeting her friends?

They'd got lost en route, having a mini argument with Waze and each other and arriving late. The mood between them was increasingly tense.

The party was in full swing when they got there, and Ingrid greeted them cheerfully at the door. A wave of happiness washed over Isabella as she spotted her long-lost friend, despite the tension between her and Robert.

Ingrid ushered them in to her spacious apartment, full of about 80 or 90 noisy, drunk people, a few of whom Isabella recognised. The music was exceedingly loud, and everyone seemed to enjoy themselves. A vast wall of glass occupied the far wall, providing spectacular views of the twinkling lights of the city and the glimmering surface of the Thames below them.

Foil balloons decorated the room and Ingrid had obviously cleared away most of her contemporary furniture to make room for the dance floor, where many people were doing their best dance moves to Bruno Mars.

They made their way through the crowd, over to a pop-up bar on the far side of the room by the enormous window, and Robert ordered himself a double scotch.

"Is it a good idea to mix your drinks, Rob? Why don't you stick to red wine?" she asked gently. "You'll only regret it in the morning?"

"Why don't you stop bloody nagging? It's New Year's Eve. Can't you let me enjoy myself for one night?" he grumbled, before turning away and striding to the other side of the room, leaving her alone.

"Great," she thought, talk about an overreaction.

She helped herself to a mineral water, trying to calm her sombre mood and quell her embarrassment, hoping no one had noticed their little spat. Maybe she had been too hard on him? Luckily, Ingrid came over and, after chatting, introduced her to some other guests.

Over the next few hours, she had mingled with different people and spoke with others she had met before, although it was difficult, seemingly the only one not drinking and battling against the loud music. In hindsight, perhaps driving wasn't the greatest of ideas.

Everyone seemed to be in a jovial mood and she had lost sight of Robert, who appeared to be getting more and more inebriated each time she glimpsed him fawning over every attractive-looking female who stood anywhere near him.

She'd spied him about 11pm, persuading a girl who looked barely older than eighteen to dance with him. She was livid as she watched him paw her and literally drool all over her. Oh Jesus, he was trying to twerk? She tried to ignore him and watch all the other party goers - she could do with a drink herself right now.

She glanced over to the front door and watched as

an incredibly striking, powerfully built man walked into the party. He caught her eye and scrutinised her intently. His dark, penetrating eyes startled her, as if they were drinking her in. She eased when she noticed his charming, ever-so slight, lop-sided grin. There was an instant connection. Almost a recognition between them. She looked away fleetingly. Flustered and feeling herself redden, she composed herself. Then, curiosity getting the better of her, she turned back in his general direction. But he'd disappeared.

A short time later, someone came up close behind her and whispered into her ear in a deep American accent, "I've been watching you. Do you always spend New Year's on your own at a party?"

She turned, and it was him. The man at the door. The most charismatic man she'd ever seen in her life, the one who hadn't taken his eyes off her as he'd entered. His eyes were melancholy, but as he smiled at her, they transformed. "Jack Vincent," he growled, holding out one of his huge hands to introduce himself. He looked like a movie star.

"Isabella," she stammered, holding out her hand to join his, meeting his excruciating gaze with her own and after she'd composed herself, added, "and by the way, I'm not on my own. I hope that wasn't your feeble attempt at a chat up line? My partners over there," she said, nodding in Robert's direction, "Dancing." She did not know why she'd been so sharp with him. She only knew that he frightened her with his intensity.

"Right. Although I'd never have known that guy was with you," he eyed her almost pityingly, "He looks like he's about to go home with her. She a friend of yours?"

"No. But that's Robert. He's always like that. Friendly," she snapped, excusing his appalling behaviour and finding herself oddly defensive. "Anyway, are you always so impudent with people you've just met?" She pulled her hand away sharply. She hadn't realised he'd been holding on to it so tightly.

"I didn't realise I was being *impudent*, but yeah, I suppose I am," he replied, smiling seductively at her. "Especially when someone looks like you. So, what's someone like you doing with such a jerk?"

"You're so rude," she gasped, rolling her eyes.

"What? What have I said?" he was teasing her now.

"Look, I'm having a nice, quiet evening. Would you just mind just leaving me alone?"

"Sure, but hey, we've gotten off on the wrong foot. Can we try again?"

"There's nothing to try."

"Please?"

"We've nothing to say to each other. I don't even know you."

"Well, you could start by telling me about yourself and your relationship with the jerk?"

"There you go again."

He laughed gutturally, "We're not doing very well here."

"I wonder whose fault that is," she sighed, unnerved by his stare.

"Can I get you a drink?" he asked.

"I'm driving."

"Bad call."

"I suppose one glass of champagne won't hurt. It is nearly midnight."

"Be right back."

"I can't wait," she added with more than a touch of sarcasm.

She watched him walk away, took a long deep breath and ran her hands through her hair, trying to gather her thoughts, her racing heart. Isabella Michaels, she sighed to herself. You are acting like a 16-year-old. Why on earth was she being like this? So defensive? He stood out in the crowd. Tall, well over six and a half feet, probably six five. Dark, nearly black hair, cropped incredibly short, with a few telltale silver hairs above his temples. Everything about him was dark and brooding. His most outstanding feature, though, were his dark brown, almost charcoal, soulful eyes. A strong nose and extremely kissable lips. Well-defined cheekbones and a solid square jaw. He direly needed a good shave. His burly frame looked incongruous in his black Dolce and Gabanna tux, his crisp white shirt open, no tie. Pull yourself together, Isabella.

He sauntered back to her, a glass in each hand, and handed her a glass of champagne.

"So, Mr Vincent, are you on holiday in London or do you live here? And how do you know Ingrid?" she fiddled with the rim of her glass self-consciously.

"Jack, please," he smiled at her, his eyes teasing. She blushed again.

"I run a construction company. We're working on a deal together, Atlas? The company Ingrid works for?"

"Right."

"We've done a lot of business in the past, and I've gotten to know a few of them fairly well. David, Harry and, of course, Ingrid. Although I think she felt a little sorry for me, over here and all alone for the holidays, so felt obliged to invite me to her party. I don't know her that well." She wondered if there was anything else to the invite. To their relationship.

"Great view of the city," he added, "Smoke?" he asked, pulling out a crumbled packet of Marlborough.

"Yuck. Disgusting habit."

He put the packet back in his jacket, self-consciously. "And what about you, Isabella? What do you do and how do you know Ingrid?"

She told him about her new company and how she and Ingrid and first met.

He told her about his family back home, gesturing emphatically as he spoke, his hands adding emphasis to his passionate words. About growing up in New York's Lower East Side and his home now in Manhattan, an enormous penthouse overlooking Central Park East. He was third generation Italian American, and she watched him become misty eyed as he talked about his family. She'd met no one whose eyes betrayed their emotions so intently, whose face was so expressive. And his voice. So hypnotic. She found she'd totally forgotten about Robert and was no longer paying any attention to what he might get up to. Jack made her feel like an adolescent again and she felt, to her amazement, in awe of him. She was drawn to him, in a way she couldn't explain, and could hardly bring herself to look away from his entrancing eyes, which had hardly left hers since they'd first met. His inflection, his imposing physical presence, his whole being totally dwarfed her, and she became completely unaware of her surroundings, feeling they were the only two people in the room. He seemed genuinely interested in her and what she had to say and he possessed a rapier wit. She found his candour bracing. She couldn't focus, leaving her at a loss for words. Overwhelmed by him, she sensed a disconnection from her usual self. He must think her an absolute idiot.

"I love this song" he said, as *My Way* played, as people sang raucously along.

"Me too. I love Frank."

"Baby, I can see this is beginning a beautiful friendship."

They continued to chat for what seemed like hours and she groaned as Robert swayed towards them. Someone turned down the music, and the countdown began.

"Ten. Nine. Eight. Seven. Six ... One. Happy New Year." The crowd cried noisily around them, as Big Ben chimed and the fireworks exploded outside.

"Happy New Year's Isabella," Jack whispered into her ear.

"You too Jack."

"What the hell?" he said and grabbed her upper arms, pulling her towards him and kissed her hard on the mouth.

"What the fuck?" screamed Robert, taking a swing at Jack, who sidestepped and sent Robert crashing into the window.

"Robert," screamed Isabella, turning around to face

Jack, "You! What the hell were you doing kissing me like that?"

She turned back to Robert. "Are you okay?" she helped him up from the floor, where he'd crumpled like a rag doll.

"You," she turned back to Jack bitterly, "Just go. Leave us alone"

When she thought back to this first encounter, she felt mortified. Mortified.

***

CHAPTER THREE

"Here's your terminal, love," the driver disturbed her thoughts. 'Penny for them?" he smiled.

"Sorry I was miles away."

"I can see that." He opened his door and stepped out. He opened her door for her, then walked round to the boot and lifted out her case, setting it on the ground before her.

She opened her purse and gave him a tip, thanked him, then walked off towards departures.

"Ave a good un," he called after her.

She turned and smiled briefly and nodded towards him before walking through the doors, lugging her suitcase behind her.

After she had checked in her luggage at the priority desk, she walked through security and passport control up the escalators and made her way to the executive lounge.

Checking her watch, they had plenty of time before boarding. Ingrid had arranged for them all to meet here any time now, so she shouldn't have too long to wait. She scanned round for Ingrid, but it wasn't surprising that she wasn't visible yet. She guessed–correctly, she would still be in duty free. There were a few couples sitting around the lounge, but she didn't recognise anyone.

She sat down on a large, empty, comfortable leather sofa and once again checked her passports and tickets were all safely together in her handbag. She pulled out her iPad and began reading her book.

After about half an hour, she glanced upwards after hearing someone say, almost growl, "Ciao. Finally, we meet again," and looked straight into the enigmatic, infuriating eyes of Jack Bloody Vincent.

His hair had grown considerably since their last encounter, much longer than when they'd last met. He ran his hand through his hair self-consciously and smiled at her engagingly, waiting for some kind of response.

"Oh. It's you" she said. She didn't know what else to say. Yet again, he'd taken her by surprise.

"Good to see you, too." He was wearing a pair of well-worn jeans and a very crumpled, lived in pale-blue linen shirt, his strong tanned forearms visible beneath the turned-up sleeves. She noticed a few faded tattoos. His dark leather boots looked like they'd seen better days and looked like they'd never seen a clean. He was carrying a tatty leather holdall and had a battered brown leather jacket thrown lazily over his arm.

"Can I sit?" he asked, sitting down next to her like he owned the place, before waiting for her response. "You look nice," he commented. She ignored him and continued looking at her iPad blankly.

"Hemingway? A little light holiday reading," he added, with just a hint of sarcasm. "Why *For Whom the Bell Tolls*? I'd have thought *The Snows of Kilimanjaro* more appropriate as we're going to Kenya. Or even better, *A Farewell to Arms*?"

"Nosy. And why would you think that?" she enquired, challenging his scrutiny.

"American guy falls in love with a British girl. Need I say more?" he studied her even more intensely.

"I do not know what you're talking about," she huffed haughtily. "Why are you always so patronising?"

"Didn't realise I was. You should see me with people I don't like,"

"I dread to think." What was he talking about? American guy, falls in love with a British girl, surely … just ridiculous, "Do me a favour Jack, let's play a game?"

"Anything."

"For the rest of the week, don't talk to me."

"Ouch."

To her relief, and before he could say anymore, Ingrid and the others arrived, and not a moment too soon.

"Izzy. Jack. So glad to see you both," Ingrid exclaimed, not sure why Isabella seemed so flustered. She hugged Jack as he rose to greet her, then bent down and gave Isabella a kiss on both cheeks.

"Izzy, you've met up with Jack, that's good. I was worried you'd be sitting here all alone," noted Ingrid.

"Believe me, I'd much rather be on my own," Isabella muttered under her breath.

"Boy, are we gonna have fun." said Jack, "I do not know what your problem is, but I've only ever been friendly with you."

"Jack, you're many things, but friendly isn't one of them," replied Isabella. "Look enough of this crap," she gathered her belongings to escape. He hadn't offended her. He had said nothing to upset her particularly. But he got under her skin. She just wanted to get away from him. To breathe, to think straight. Being so close to him was driving her mad.

"I'm sorry," he said earnestly. He was staring at her again. She felt as if he could peer into her very soul. How could someone she'd literally only met a couple of times have such an effect on her? Could trouble her so much and irritate her so deeply. Just his presence unsettled her. "Izzy please?" he said.

She glared at him. "It's Isabella. Only close friends and family call me Izzy."

"Okay, I'll call you Bella then?"

"Bella? I don't know if I like that?"

"Bella. Bellissima. Suits you."

"Right, let's make sure everyone knows everyone in this unsavoury group," interrupted Ingrid, noticing the tension between this pair yet again.

Isabella welcomed the interruption, as she had already grown tired of Jack Bloody Vincent's presence within just a few minutes. How the hell was she going to manage two weeks in his company?

Ingrid made all the relevant introductions, and they chatted between themselves, before making their way over to the bar, where David ordered a bottle of champagne and Ingrid began introducing Isabella again to everyone.

David Matthews. Despite being forty-eight years old, appeared much younger. He could easily pass for thirty-eight. He had been divorced for three years and even now was still adjusting to life without Amelia, the woman he had thought was the love of his life, until he caught her in bed with someone else. David was chief executive of Atlas Incorporated, the European subsidiary of a world-renowned firm of architects, renowned for their extraordinary and adventurous designs of large office buildings, shopping centres, schools, hospitals and airports. He spent most of his time flitting between offices in London, the States, and across Europe. Many women certainly considered him a catch, but he showed no interest whatsoever in forming a new relationship. He had been on a couple of dates since the divorce, but he just didn't enjoy the dating scene and preferred to focus entirely on work. He found going out to dinner with complete, or essentially strangers, a chore. Long hours, squash, occasionally golf, suited him fine. He enjoyed relaxing at home in Wimbledon, enjoying nothing better than to unwind in the evening with a few G&Ts. He had a head of thick, curly sandy-coloured hair that framed his striking blue eyes. His smooth, stubble-covered skin gave him a ruggedly handsome and youthful look. He was always impeccably dressed, but on this rare occasion, he chose a more relaxed outfit instead of his usual suit. He had the reputation of being a very honest man, but his presence exuded an undeniable sense of authority and power. She imagined working with David, envisioning the sound of his cheerful voice and the positive energy he would bring to the workplace. He seemed to command a great deal of respect from his employees, and she noticed Ingrid seemed fond of him.

Fiona Harrison and Madison (Maddy) Smyth-Collins both headed up the HR department of Atlas. Fiona was small and petite, with a perfectly coifed lob. She had an infectious personality and usually those who met her warmed to her immediately. She evidently always dressed in bright, vivacious colours, which more than complemented her good-natured disposition. Today, she was wearing a shocking-pink cashmere sweater and a pair of skinny jeans and looked chic.

It seemed strange to Isabella that Fiona and Madison were such good friends. Madison seemed the complete opposite of the bubbly Fiona. On the few occasions Isabella had met Madison, she never warmed to her. She always got the impression that she was one of those people that had no women friends and surrounded herself with as many men as possible. She also had a grating voice. Madison always courteously answered Isabella's questions, if not abruptly, but always seemed to regard her warily out of the corner of her eye. She seemed insincere and fake, always trying to impress. Her demeanour around the men, though, was entirely different. She was all fragility and helplessness. Madison was always excessively and heavily made up–way too much contouring. Had she never heard that less is more? Her lipstick always remained perfectly applied and never seemed to fade. How? How was that possible? Her dark red, bottle-enhanced hair was also never out of place and almost clashed against her pale skin. She always dressed in sharp tailored suits, which seemed to match her austere personality, and today was no exception.

Harry Jacobs, lovely Harry, was a fantastic rugby player. Standing tall, his dark and rugged appearance was noticeable. He dressed casually in jeans and a t-shirt. He was gorgeous and had a magnificent bod and Isabella knew he knew it. In fact, she knew it. Oh God, don't go there. Not interested in pursuing a serious relationship, he had never had a love that lasted over 6 months. He worked as Legal Counsel for Atlas, possessing a sharp mind, and spent most of his spare time as a forward on the rugby field. He also spent a lot of time squandering his fathomless inherited fortune in a frivolous manner. Evidently, he didn't need to work at all, but he liked to keep occupied. He had briefly dated Ingrid a few years earlier, following their brief affair at university, and both had invited Isabella to a BBQ he'd thrown one sunny weekend at his beautiful Edwardian home in Richmond. Isabella's heart fluttered with excitement as she fell head over heels for the house, her curiosity piqued about the person behind the interior design. A sense of wonder washed over her as she realised he had done everything himself, leaving her utterly amazed. Ostensibly, he enjoyed browsing some of the finer stores and galleries in Kensington and Chelsea, filling his charming home with significant pieces. There was obviously a lot more to Harry than first met the eye.

Ingrid and Harry had split after a few excitable months and, thankfully, had remained close friends. They both had a similar personality and their outlook on life was similar. They both had known from the outset that there would be nothing long-lasting or too serious between them, but they had both enjoyed what they had.

Isabella hadn't slept with Harry, but they had had a few drunken snogs back in university. Isabella noticed that Harry consistently flirted outrageously with her whenever they met, and she grew fond of him. However, even though she was flattered, she firmly believed that she was just one of many attractive women in his life. Even earlier, greeting each other with a quick peck on the cheek, he practically undressed her with his eyes. Harry Jacobs was 32 years old, drove a top of the range Audi R8 and as far as everyone could tell, had absolutely no intention of ever settling down.

Ewan McCarthy was a young looking thirty. Originating from Glasgow, having moved to London in his mid-twenties, he was feeling a little out of this depth, joining all these senior management on holiday. However, being single and having no ties, Ewan had no hesitation in accepting the invitation to join them on holiday. He worked as a Junior Architect for Atlas, his work was remarkably promising and very individualistic and he definitely possessed a creative flair. He was exceptionally keen to do well in this challenging, multi-national corporation, with his goal, being partner. Ewan had short, cropped, reddish-blonde hair and green eyes. He was about the same height as Isabella, but incredibly gangly. Even in his jeans and t-shirt, there was no mistaking how thin he was. However, he was still very athletic and played football for his local pub most Tuesday nights and Saturday afternoons. He had broken up from his girlfriend of five years and felt this singles holiday was just what he needed to buck up his spirits. Especially with the vivacious Fiona in tow, one of the main reasons for coming away. He had a secret crush on her and hoped that by the end of the fortnight, she will have reciprocated his feelings.

Finally, Jack. 39 years old and the owner of a large American construction company and excellent friends with Harry and David, both of whom he'd known for years. He had started his own business at 23 from practically nothing and it had gradually grown into the small empire it was today, stretching over the whole of the US and in more recent years, the UK. He was now taking more of a back seat in the day-to-day affairs of the company. He had an excellent management team whom he had hand-picked and, more importantly, trusted implicitly, which thankfully left him a little more time to enjoy some of the great fortune he'd made along the way.

He was still the most attractive man she'd ever laid eyes on, exuding an unmistakable intensity and an unwavering old-fashioned masculinity. Everything about him seemed dangerous, dark, and brooding. His sheer physical size and almost exaggerated sense of maleness seemed to dominate all those around him. She also found him inconceivably self-assured, if not arrogant, and they always seemed to rub each other up the wrong way. Isabella was not aware at this stage, however, that she had mis-read and mis-judged him entirely.

As she regarded him closely in the middle of a hard-edged exchange with Harry, noting he'd exchanged his glass of champagne for a large Jack Daniels, she groaned inwardly as he caught her staring at him. He gave her a genuine smile and a wink. Great.

David ordered a second bottle of Cristal and continued to pour and hand out another flute for everyone.

"I'd like to make a toast," he announced, raising his glass with a flourish.

"Oh God. Here he goes," said Ingrid.

"Be quiet, Ingrid," he ordered affectionately. "All I want to say is here's for a fantastic holiday. I hope we all have a great time, with plenty of sun, sea, sand and most of all ..."

"Sex," shouted Ingrid.

"You can't take her anywhere," said Harry.

"You can always rely on Ingrid to lower the tone," said Fiona.

"I was going to say fun," said David.

"One more thing," said Ingrid to everyone, "No shop talk, ok? David. Harry. Jack," she nodded at each of them.

"Sure, sure," each mumbled.

"Okay, let's party," said Ingrid as she gulped down the rest of her drink.

Isabella stood to the edge of the group, observing them all, joining in their friendly chitchat now and then. And totally unlike herself, she was withdrawn and uneasy and she was sure it was because of the unnerving effect Jack Bloody Vincent had on her. She glanced at each of them individually, whilst sipping her own drink, trying to avoid Jack's occasional and officious eye contact.

"So, Isabella" asked Madison, smiling with her teeth, rather than her eyes, "I understand you're a shop owner?"

"It's actually an interior design boutique. I'm a designer." Wow! Here we go. That didn't take long.

"I've been told that you did up a friend of a friend's place recently," offered Fiona kindly. "It's apparently out of this world."

"Thank you, Fiona. Who was it, do you know?" and she continued to chat with her about her company.

Jack surveyed her with an amused expression on his face. Hell, he admired this woman, but she always seemed so defensive and hostile. Was she always like that, he wondered, or was it just him? He also wondered if she was still with that jerk he'd met at Ingrid's party. He decided that maybe he'd need to tread a little more carefully around her.

The PA system interrupted their chatter.

"Right, let's go, that's us. Last call," exclaimed Ingrid.

They finished their drinks and gathered their belongings, before making their way to the gate and, ultimately, their plane.

***

CHAPTER FOUR

"Oh gosh, I'm dreading this. I don't enjoy flying," exclaimed Isabella to no one in particular, whilst they walked hurriedly through the walkway to the awaiting aircraft.

"Don't worry baby, I gotcha," joked Jack, smiling his engagingly handsome smile, whilst attempting to take her hand in his own.

"I'm good," she huffed indignantly, shaking his arm off her own. "Anyway, hopefully I'll be on the other end of the plane to you."

But she wasn't. To her utter dismay and distress, she ended up with the seat next to him in business. Ingrid was sitting with David. Fiona and Madison. Ewan and Harry. None of them were willing to trade places with her. Unfortunately, the flight was full, so she found she was going to endure the next 9 hours with Jack Bloody Vincent.

"I don't bloody believe this," she hissed, throwing a look of pure frustration at Ingrid, running her hands through her hair vigorously.

"Do you want this one nearer the window, or this one, honey?" asked Jack.

"Honey. For fuck's sake," she gasped.

"Shh," hissed Ingrid. "will you two stop acting like a couple of children? You're at each other's throats the whole time. If you don't stop it and start acting like grown-ups, I'll give you both a slap," Then whilst stowing her bag, whispered to Isabella, "What's the matter with you Izzy? I've never seen you act like such a spoilt brat."

Isabella merely glared at her friend in response and took

her seat, noticing there was a good deal of space between her and him, thank God. She fastened her belt and gazed out of the window, anything to avoid having to turn to her left and the unnerving presence next to her.

After a short period, they began taxiing towards the runway. The flight attendants checked everyone's seat belts and prepared the aircraft for take-off. The flight soon began its ascent, and they were on their way to Mombasa.

Isabella leafed through some of the in-flight magazines, feigning interest, and fiddled with her screen. She got herself comfortable, took out her earbuds, put them in, and began looking for a film, hoping to have a little nap.

"Can I get you anything from the bar, madam? A glass of champagne, perhaps?" enquired the flight attendant.

"No thank you, I'm fine," Isabella replied.

"And what about you, sir? Can I get you anything?" She smiled. Isabella noticed the change in her voice, as the pretty, but heavily made up flight attendant eyed Jack in admiration, fluttering her eyelashes at him shamelessly. She was obviously drawn to his magnetic presence. Isabella was willing to bet that he has this effect on all women.

"I'll have a Scotch please," said Jack.

"There's a surprise," voiced Isabella under her breath scathingly.

He merely regarded her curiously out of the corner of his eye, a slight smirk on his lips.

The attendant unfolded his tray and placed his drink in front of him. "If I can get you anything at all, please just ask for Sandy," she smiled and turned to serve Ewan and Harry.

"*Please, just ask for Sandy,*" mimicked Isabella in a high pitch tone. "How obvious."

"Jealous?"

"Not on your life."

"Lighten up Bella. I'm on vacation. Maybe smile? Not drinking again? Are you on the wagon or something?"

"I had a glass of champagne earlier." She added, staring

nonchalantly out the window, before turning to him and adding, "I do like a drink for your information. I'm just not dependent, that's all."

"And you think I am? Jeez," he asked, "What are you, my shrink?"

"Oooh, touched a nerve."

"Man … I'm only having a damned Scotch. I can't even smoke the entire flight."

"Great. That'll help with the mood." She added frostily.

"Me. What have I done?" he said, holding his hands open and gesturing with his palms up, showing he had nothing to hide. "The only one always in a shitty mood is you," he said.

"You started this," she snapped.

"Here you go again. Fuck, you're goddamned nuts,"

"I wonder why? Now enjoy your drink and leave me the fuck alone."

So, he did. He let her sulk and watch her shitty chick-flick.

She couldn't concentrate on the movie at all. She was conscious of him sat so close, taking sip after sip of his drinks, wiping his mouth lazily with the back of his hand. God, he smelled good.

Her thoughts drifted to the last time she'd bumped into him. Ingrid had invited her for drinks one evening earlier in the year to celebrate her recent promotion. Coincidentally, Isabella had been visiting a client's premises in the City on that day, so could take up her friend's invitation to join a small party in the West End for a bite to eat and a quick drink.

As she had to drive home later that evening, her car filled with sample books and swathes of material, she stuck to a couple of glasses of Bucks Fizz whilst chatting to Ingrid and several of her friends and colleagues. It was a fun crowd.

Eventually, she finished a latte, glanced at her watch, before tapping her friend on the shoulder "Look, Ingy, it's been great, but I must get going. It's been a long day and I'm shattered."

"Okay, if you're sure. Thanks for coming. It was great to see you–sorry if we didn't get time to chat much."

"I've enjoyed myself, thanks. Congratulations again," and pulled her friend in for a hug.

As she was preparing to depart and saying her farewells, her phone started ringing. She fumbled around in her bag, trying to find her mobile, "Isabella Michaels, she said into the phone, sitting at a vacant seat to her left, "Shit." She mumbled, having missed the call. She was just scrolling through to see who had called, when somebody sat in the seat next to her. Personal space. She put her phone back in her bag and just as she was about to get up and leave, she turned to the person who'd sat down next to her and took a sharp intake of breath. He was just as devilishly handsome as she could have even dared to remember.

"Isabella, right?" he smiled.

She just stared.

"Jack. Jack Vincent? We met at Ingrid's New Year's Eve Party a while back?"

"Yes. Yes. I know," she stammered, "I'm just leaving."

"You can't stop for another drink? My treat?"

"No. Really, no. I can't I'm on my way home."

"Shame. If I'd know you were coming, I'd have tried to get here earlier."

She merely regarded him.

A server interrupted them. "Can I get you a drink, sir? Madam?" he enquired.

"I'll have a Scotch. Isabella?"

"I really must be going."

"Five minutes?"

She paused.

"Please?" he smiled, raising his eyebrows in anticipation.

"Okay. I'll have a mineral water please," she asked the server, who promptly departed to fetch their order.

"So, how are you?" enquired Jack.

Damn, he was gorgeous. "Good. Good thanks. You?"

"Yep. All good. You look great," he added, drinking her in, before continuing, "Here on business. Seem to be in the UK more than the States at the moment."

Once again, she lost the ability to speak.

"You look so good."

"Yes, you just said," she mumbled.

"So, are you still with the jerk?" he said.

"If you mean Robert, yes. Not that it's any of your business."

"Shame." he stated.

The server returned and handed them their drinks.

"Isabella ..."

"Yes," she whispered, as he viewed her intently.

"That night we met ... Did you ... Did you feel ...?"

All she could feel at the moment was the heat from his leg next to her own.

"Look Jack, I must be going, thanks for the drink." She stood up, downed her drink, and put her glass on the table.

He grabbed her hand before she could move. "We could have something here, right? I mean, you must feel it?"

"I do not know what you're talking about."

"Bullshit, you felt it. I know you did."

"Jack, you don't even know me. I've only met you once, for God's sake. You've got your signals crossed."

"Look, I'm over here for a few weeks. Meet me for a drink. Maybe dinner? Can I get your number?" he pleaded.

"No" she stated.

"Because of the jerk?" he smiled.

"Wow, your ability to annoy me knows no bounds. Impressive."

"You don't like me?"

"No comment," she got up, "I'm leaving" and she turned and walked straight into a server carrying a tray with a bottle of red wine and 4 glasses. The noise and the mess were phenomenal, as the glasses smashed into smithereens across the floor and the bottle of red wine landed ... Oh shit. All over Jack.

He cursed and mopped himself with a napkin. "Goddamned woman."

"I'm sorry," she hissed. "It was an accident." And before either of them could say anything more, she turned and ran out, leaving Jack and the rest of the crowd staring after her in astonishment.

Isabella had fallen asleep to the immutable drone of the plane and after what only seemed like a few minutes, but was much longer, she sensed someone place a blanket carefully around her shoulders. "Hmm" she murmured, stretching her arms and legs and opening then rubbing her eyes.

"Comfortable sleepy head." It was Jack. Oh my God, she realised, as she attempted to pull herself together. She must have been in a deep sleep. How long had he been watching her? Was she drooling?

"Feeling better now you've had a sleep?" he enquired.

"There was nothing wrong with me in the first place," she grumbled, running her fingers through her mass of hair.

"Here's the attendant with something to eat. Hungry?" he asked.

"Famished. And I'd love a glass of water."

"Pardon me?" he smiled at *Sandy*. "Can we get another scotch and a glass of water, please?"

"Sure, no problem," she smiled back.

"Actually, can I have a glass of red wine as well, please?" Isabella asked her before she left.

"Oh no, red wine? Do I need to move?" asked Jack, teasing her.

"Funny." she said dryly.

Sandy returned with their drinks and some dinner.

"Your Scotch Sir and for your ... err," she glanced at Isabella's ring finger, "your girlfriend, red wine."

"Thanks, but I'm not his anything," griped Isabella.

"You certainly seem to have quite an effect on all the women you meet," she added to Jack, taking a sip of her wine.

"Not all women," he replied, gazing at her.

She ignored him and ate her food.

After she had finished, he asked her, "Tell me. Why are you coming to Kenya with us reprobates?"

"Speak for yourself. The others don't seem too bad. To be honest, I do not know why. Last minute, fill in for Ingrid."

"And the jerk doesn't mind?"

"No, why should he? We trust each other. Anyway, Rob's incredibly busy in his job at the moment and couldn't have taken the time off anyway this time of year for a holiday. I've been working so hard lately, and Ingrid wore me down. Eventually, I just decided what the hell and here I am. And will you stop calling him the jerk?" she added as an afterthought.

"Well, I'm glad you're here. Honestly, though, I can't believe you're still with him. I know if you were with me, I'd never let you go on vacation alone. I wouldn't let you out of my sight."

"Well, thank God I'm not with you, hey? Not only are you undiplomatic and extremely rude, you're obviously possessive. Nice qualities Jack. No wonder you're single. What are you? Some kind of control freak?"

"No, you misunderstand. I just think he's crazy for letting someone as beautiful as you out of his sight for two weeks. He must be mad." And he turned and talked to Ewan.

Beautiful. She couldn't believe he'd just said that. Especially after the dreaded wine incident. And why did she feel like she was naked every time he so much as glanced at her?

After a while, he turned back around and started talking to her about Africa. They had a real, proper, civilised conversation.

Thereafter, the flight was relatively uneventful and whilst the others slept for most of the second leg of the journey, Isabella and Jack talked for hours and hours about every subject under the sun. Their connection grew stronger as they realised how well they listened to each other, how interesting their conversations were, and how much they had in common.

She told him about her friends and family, her childhood, her parent's painful divorce. It broke his heart to know she was an only child and had distant relationships with her parents, especially since he had such a tight-knit family.

She also told him about Robert, leaving out the more negative parts (no more ammunition needed) and her love of interior design and how happy she was now she had her own business. As she described her own design studio, he leaned forward with genuine interest, captivated by her words. "... I wanted my showroom to surround the customers with an ambiance of refined opulence and contemporary charm, allowing them to explore a superb array of meticulously curated displays of the finest furniture, décor, and accessories."

He expressed his admiration for what she had accomplished and praised her style, recognising the exceptional work he had witnessed, "Google," he said.

"Have you been stalking me?" she giggled. Thrilled that he'd taken the time to peruse her success.

He opened up about his childhood, about his sisters and brothers and the rest of his seemingly enormous family, with countless nieces and nephews.

She found it intriguing to learn how he had turned his once small, local company into the industry leader it is today. Vincent Construction had grown from a fairly small local residential contractor to the full-service commercial contractor it was now. His company had a solid reputation, and he took great pride in their accomplishments. They operated out of 4 offices around the US; New York, LA, Chicago and Dallas, ensuring they could effectively bid and manage projects throughout the States. They had a wealth of experience and expertise and they had a professional, highly qualified team of staff, thoroughly dedicated to the company and its projects.

"Sorry, I sound like a brochure. Am I boring you?" he enquired, as he noticed her yawn.

"Not at all. Sorry, I'm just tired. I'm fascinated, honestly." She laughed, as he noticed his frown and asked him how he knew David and Harry.

He explained how he met David and Harry many years earlier. His company had worked on a few projects with Atlas' US subsidiary of Architects and Engineers.

Vincent Construction had opened their first European subsidiary a couple of years back, which was proving very successful and again involved a great deal of input and liaison with Atlas.

He mentioned his hobbies to her. With a deep passion for baseball, he delighted in attending Yankees games. He told her about his favourite foods and his favourite restaurants whilst in London. She learnt he stayed either at Harrys when convenient, or at his favourite hotel on Park Lane. During his visits to England, he had done a fair bit of sightseeing. He told her he especially loved the Cotswolds, the quaint towns and villages around Broadway and the spectacular countryside. He had also spent time in Cornwall and Scotland, and other places, but longed to spend more time driving round and exploring the countryside and had yet still to go across to Ireland.

It turned out they both loved music, from rock and pop, to opera and classics.

"What have you been listening to today?" she asked.

"Swing. Sinatra," he said.

"Oh yes, you love Frank. Me too," she swooned.

"That voice," they both said together, then laughed.

"I do a mean rendition," he said

"No way." She giggled. "I'd love to hear that. Why Sinatra?" she asked.

"Why not? No, in all seriousness, I grew up listening to him. My mom and dad are huge Sinatra fans. We grew up with him. The guy was a genius, that voice. My biggest regret? Not seeing him live."

"Me too," she sighed.

Everything was fine, talking about music, movies, animals, but then everything went AWOL when they got on to religion, politics and worst of all, when things couldn't get any more heated, children.

"I'd love to have lots of children someday, probably because I'm an only child. I then plan on giving up work entirely and devote my life to caring for my children," she stated.

"Is this with or without the jerk?" he asked mockingly.

"You're always so bloody derogatory." She said in retort, "that's none of your business."

"Why? I can't believe that someone like you, an intelligent woman, who's built up her business from scratch, would give it all up and throw it all away to have some damn kids. I can't understand people's obsession with children and their need to pro-create. Isn't the world full enough already? Children are a constant source of annoyance. They're expensive, persistently seeking attention and …"

"Oh, you're right. My mistake. I forgot that your degree in everything qualifies you to judge everyone else," she then added.

"Touché."

"But you talked so fondly of your nieces and nephews." She exclaimed, shocked at his negativity.

"That is different. I've seen too many happy, well-accomplished, loving couples split a few years after having children. I'm not gonna go down that road."

"Don't be ridiculous Jack. That's not the children's fault. What a sad, lonely old man you're going to be, actually, are. Congratulations, you've officially won the hypocrite of the year award."

They continued to argue, neither willing to back down, but he was adamant he wasn't having any children.

Isabella was again fuming by the end of the conversation. He was so dour and pig-headed. What a chauvinist. Anyway, what did she care? She'd always known he was an idiot. The classic case of too much ego, not enough brain cells.

The conversation died then, the atmosphere frosty again, so they spent the rest of the flight dozing. Now and then, he tried to break the ice and enquire if she was okay, or if she needed anything. But she just mumbled her responses until he gave up on her.

***

CHAPTER FIVE

When the plane finally touched down in Mombasa just before 9.00am local time the following morning, Isabella was dreadfully tired. She wished she had got some proper sleep, instead of wasting all that time idly chatting to Jack Bloody Vincent. Just as she was warming to him after all, he had revealed more of his true, selfish colours and re-fuelled her dislike of him.

They all disembarked together, somewhat dishevelled and in varying states of sobriety. Excluding Madison, of course, who still looked immaculate. How? Even her suit didn't have any creases. How was that possible? On the flip side, the 90s called and wanted their fashion back.

They were all excited about having finally arrived at their far-away destination and what was in store for them over the next two weeks. The extreme sticky heat and humidity encircled them and tickled their senses as they crossed the tarmac. They were chatting between themselves, pondering what was in store for their trip.

Jack lit up a cigarette. "Man, I was dying for this," he exclaimed, as they made their way towards the arrivals hall inside.

"What were you two chatting about all night back there," enquired Harry, as they all stood in the queue in passport control.

"Nothing of any importance," responded Jack sourly, wondering why Isabella was once more giving him the cold shoulder. Damn, she was a pain in the ass.

"Well, Isabella, you certainly don't look any worse for

having had no sleep, you gorgeous girl and for having to sit next to and hear the views of *God's gift to women,*" said Harry and playfully pushed Jack in front of him.

"Fuck off, man" drawled Jack.

"Did I hear you trying the old Sinatra line?"

"Screw you" hissed Jack.

"If that was a line, it failed miserably," snapped Isabella.

They all passed through passport control with no real delay and waited around to collect their luggage from the carousel. It was humid and clammy, and there were dozens of people wandering around.

"What a shithole," commented Madison.

"Rude." Said Isabella, not caring if anyone could hear her or not.

After having retrieved their belongings, Harry lifting her suitcase onto his trolley. They made their way to a large, distinctly run-down, green and yellow minibus waiting for them outside the terminal building.

The heat was brutal and all around them, people were milling around them back and forth. It all seemed so hectic.

The men helped the ladies with their luggage–they were all weary after the long flight.

"Talk about travelling in style. Who arranged this heap of shit?" said Harry.

"We're in Africa Harry. What did you expect? A stretch limo?" snapped Ingrid.

"I agree with Harry. I didn't pay thousands of pounds to ride in a rust bucket," added Madison.

"Oh, for God's sake. Will you two be quiet and get on the damn bus?"

"Let's hope the hotel's better," hissed Madison under her breath.

Isabella climbed aboard and sat next to Harry, who kept touching her knee and hand with his own, at any opportunity. She noticed how huge his arms were and how sexy he looked as he smiled at her and she found she was enjoying his company.

He was funny, charming and made her laugh constantly and she couldn't help but compare him to the unpredictable, abrasive Jack Vincent.

She also noticed that Jack kept turning around in his seat to glare at them from time to time and his rage was almost tangible, which did nothing but turn her against him even more. She also noticed his chain-smoking again. This man was revolting.

En route from the airport to their hotel, there was a spicy, sort of smoky, smell of burnt wood or spice in the air– something exotic she couldn't name, but it smelt like Africa. They bounced and jolted down rough streets, jerking their way through twists and turns of the city until they reached reddish-brown muddy roads, covered in potholes and Isabella couldn't believe how poor and shabby everything looked. They drove past many unremarkable buildings, with their faded and flaking paintwork. Groups of young men conversing under trees, trying to stay out of the morning sun. Men and young boys leading herds of goats along the roadside. Old men were fast asleep on benches, seemingly oblivious to the already searing heat. Women walking languidly along the dusty paths, dressed head to foot in bui-buis and brilliantly coloured kangas, fresh produced wrapped in ketengis balanced on their perfectly still heads. They drove past schools where children played in their brightly coloured school uniforms. Dozens of stray, skinny, filthy dogs just milling about or routing through piles of rubbish.

Although the sparse towns looked full of only concrete, mud and rubbish, the panorama was tropical and charming and a world away from London.

Intermittently, she'd see a sign in Swahili and to her surprise could interpret a few words, after she'd spent the last week or so on Duolingo. However, most of them were for Coke or Fanta.

They eventually arrived at the Likoni ferry, where there were dozens of people dawdling along the roadside, others riding old, rusty bicycles. Children waved excitedly at them as they drove past and when they finally came to a halt, a crowd of people surrounded their bus. Their driver advised them to remain seated, as there were a lot of pickpockets about. He also advised them to ignore the begging children, who were standing around the bus offering them bags of monkey nuts and other bits and pieces for sale through the windows. Other people just grouped around in fascination, smiling and waving at them.

The bus eventually made its way onto the packed ferry. Fiona began taking photos with her phone to capture some of the excitement and atmosphere of the moment. One man alarmedly waved his arms and moved away, and the driver, speaking in stilted English, explained that according to some tribes' belief, their souls could be stolen if their photo was taken.

Isabella decided she wasn't staying on the bus. It was too hot anyway, and to the dismay of the others, she climbed off. She walked straight to the front of the ferry and stood amongst the locals, who were staring at her in fascination. She might understand why the others were uncomfortable, having never been in a third world country before. The crowds seemed oppressive, but she had already fallen in love with the hustle and bustle of it all. The smells, the heat, the colours. Making sensible choices was the key to keeping yourself safe. Was this a sensible choice though?

She stood next to a young family, who had obviously been to market. They were carrying between them a large basket, piled high with delicious mango, papaya, sugarcane and vegetables.

"Jambo" she said to the little children, staring at her with wide-eyes, one of whom was carrying a little white kitten, "Habari yako?"

"Nzuri sana" he replied, upon his mother's urging. They all continued to stare at her.

She looked out across the brown water, wondering what

was in there–crocodiles? hippos? She turned back towards the bus and noticed the others were waving at her frantically, urging her back onto the bus as they were nearing the other side of the river bank.

Just as she was about to return to the bus, she saw Jack jump out and head out pointedly towards her, his face puce with rage. He grabbed her hand in a vice like grip and snarled, "Are you crazy or something? The driver told us all to stay on the darned bus. You're gonna get mugged or your purse stolen or worse. Now do as you're told and get back on the bus."

"Don't be so melodramatic," She hissed, "And let go of me, you arsehole" and stormed off, wrenching her hand from his, head held high, back to the bus, "How dare you treat me like a child?"

"I will, if you stop acting like one," he growled, as they climbed the few steps back on to the bus.

As their bus left the ferry terminal, they thankfully left behind the smell of exhaust fumes caused by the dense traffic. The streets were bustling with pedestrians, vehicles, and street vendors, where the enticing smells of grilled meat, fried snacks and other local delicacies being prepared on the roadside wafted through the air. The area was alive with activity as people went about their daily routines. Numerous small shops, kiosks, and open-air markets lined the streets. Isabella could again smell the wood smoke from cooking fires, which gave a rustic and homey aroma to the air. The urban environment gradually gave way to more suburban and then rural landscapes, where the air became fresher. She could smell the earthy scent of soil and the slightly sweet fragrance of vegetation. The buildings became sparser, and she started to see more greenery and open spaces; local villages with traditional houses made of mud and thatch, and more modern structures. As they got closer to Diani Beach, she noticed the signs for the resorts, hotels, and tourist attractions along the road which were lined with tall palm trees and tropical plants.

Here, the scent of the sea became stronger. The salty tang of the ocean breeze was refreshing and invigorating.

They arrived a short while later at their elegant hotel and beach club, apparently one of the best on the coast, which offered all the latest modern facilities, combined with traditional African architecture. It was in luxurious surroundings landscaped with fragrant tropical flowers; frangipani, hibiscus and bougainvillea, adding sweet floral notes to the air. The resort, by all accords, offered a variety of activities, including all-inclusive water sports, two sparkling swimming pools, a well-equipped fitness centre and health spa, floodlit tennis courts (perfect), shops, conference rooms and business centre. There was a choice of different restaurants, all providing a dissimilar ambience and cuisine, including one offering an authentic Kenyan buffet and another offering local, freshly caught seafood. In the evenings, there was regular entertainment, including live tropical bands and traditional African dance shows, a nightclub, and a casino. To top it all, the hotel overlooked the awe-inspiring Diani Beach. Miles of glorious palm-fringed, brilliant white sand, lapped by the warm, crystal-clear, turquoise Indian Ocean.

As they stepped off the bus, a delightful, refreshing cool breeze embraced them, whispering through the coconut palms and providing relief from the scorching sun. Having collected their cases, they walked as a group into the open, spacious reception area. Huge pillars rose skywards from the marble floor to the high thatched roof above. There were enormous electric fans on the ceiling, anything to bring down the temperature. Lush green plants and exotic flowers in full bloom surrounded ponds filled with strange, multi-coloured fish. Little huddles of cane furniture with sumptuous, comfortable cushions were arranged on the floor, and Isabella longed to lie down on one and remain there for hours, amidst this paradise.

There was a group of tourists gathered together,

chatting animatedly amongst themselves near the entrance, obviously waiting for the four black and white zebra-striped jeeps that had just pulled up behind their bus.

They all checked in and started sorting out their luggage. Jack lifted Isabella's case.

"I can manage thank you," she snapped haughtily, although then promptly handed her case to a waiting porter.

"WHAT. THE. ACTUAL. FUCK. IS. THAT," shrieked Madison, "A Snake?"

"For god's sake Maddy, it's a fucking lizard. We're in Africa. What the fuck did you expect?" shouted Jack. "Fucking women, man. I give the fuck up," and turned on his heels.

"Well, that was a lot of fucks," wailed Ingrid, embarrassed by both Jack and Madison.

The porters led them back outside along a tropical pathway, which snaked the main building, pointing out various things along the way. They were all shown to their respective state-of-the-art suites-all had their own, except Fiona and Madison, who had opted to share.

"I hope there's Wi-Fi," exclaimed Ewan. They all groaned.

After the porter unlocked her door and entered, Isabella received a room tour from him and thereafter gave him a few Schillings tip. She then turned up the air conditioning and collapsed onto the huge double bed. Grinning inanely at herself, she examined the large airy room and gazed at the glorious sunshine pouring through the window, encompassing nearly the entire wall, fronting the lush, tropical gardens. Outside this, there was a fair size patio, with a couple of garden chairs, overlooking the luxuriant grounds and a glimpse of the Indian Ocean. To her pleasure, she noticed the room, not only offered air-conditioning, but a mini-bar, tea and coffee making facilities and, yes indeed, Wi-Fi. She jumped up and helped herself to a small bottle of mineral water from the fridge.

When she opened the wooden sliding doors, instead of

finding a wardrobe, she was surprised to discover a bath in the middle of the room. As she slid open the doors on the other side of the bath, she was greeted by the sight of a stunning, pristine marble bathroom. The locals' living conditions were a stark contrast to her own, and it made her reflect on the disparities.

Exhaustion and exhilaration overwhelmed her simultaneously. Desperately in need of a sleep, but eager to get out and explore the abundant surroundings. Not a minute to waste.

In the confines of her mind, she pondered. She could sleep later on that day and, in the meantime, try to adjust to the time difference. She wanted a dip in the pool and wanted to feel some of that brilliant sunshine on her skin.

She opened her suitcase and rummaged around for one of her bikinis. Having found one, she then put away some of her clothes in the drawers and wardrobe. First, she placed her valuables in the safe, then she piled her thick hair on top of her head. She put on a black bikini (ouch; it left little to the imagination), her sunglasses and a slinky cover-up. She looked incredible, already tanned and in extremely good shape.

As she neared the glass window, she opened the door that led to the patio. As soon as she locked the door behind her, the heat and humidity bombarded her senses. She walked down a few steps, feeling the harsh Kenyan grass tickle her bare feet in her flip-flops. She shortly reached the cobbled-stone path, winding through the bougainvillea and other tropical, aromatic flora and eventually arrived at the large, kidney-shaped, gleaming blue swimming pool. In the distance, she could see the glimmering cerulean ocean. The view was spellbinding.

***

CHAPTER SIX

A man shading underneath an umbrella saw her coming. "Mwanamke mrembo," he said, handing her a towel.

Beautiful lady. "Assante sana," she replied, smiling at him.

The poolside was already bustling with people in different positions of relaxation. Some were lounging on the sunbeds, seeking refuge from the heat under the shade of palm trees scattered throughout the garden and pool area. Placing her towel by the edge of the water, she discarded her cover up. Gracefully wading into the shallow end, she swam across to the far end where the waters grew deeper. After swimming a few lengths in the refreshing water, she came to rest with her elbows on the side, her chin in the palms of her hand. Squinting, she observed a little group of children splashing noisily in the smaller pool to her right, regarded the lush gardens surrounding them and then looked back at the hotel itself, enjoying the hot, piercing sunshine on her face. She was relieved that she'd remembered her sunglasses, as even with them on, she still had to squint to keep out the powerful sun's rays.

To her delight, she noticed an acrobatic group of monkeys playing high in the trees and coconut palms on the other side of the gardens. Some were walking safely along the branches of the trees; others were swinging from tree to tree, which to the human eye looked unbelievably hazardous. She then noticed some of the larger monkeys had even wandered into the garden and were trying to steal food or scraps left lying around the tables and beds under the trees. One was very fortunate, it seemed and had found a half-eaten banana and scampered away to show off his prize. The pool guy went running over, trying to chase them all away, and they screeched.

She turned her gaze and noticed Harry jauntily coming down the steps to the poolside. He glanced around and noticed her more or less immediately, waving at her as he did so and walked towards her. He slumped down next to her, plunging his feet into ice-cool water.

"Isn't this paradise?" he said. "You were obviously just as keen to get out here and explore as well. The others are probably resting after the long flight?"

"Yep, I suppose so. I was too excited to wait in my room, as lovely as it is. I just wanted to get outside and get some sunshine. There's plenty of time to rest later," she said as she turned around and gracefully lifted herself out of the pool. As she sat beside him, she inquired, "Do you want to grab a couple of beds or go for a swim first?" she asked.

"Jesus Izzy. That bikini is practically obscene. Cover your arse, woman," he commented mockingly, and patted her buttocks.

"You don't look too bad yourself," she said, nudging him with her shoulder. It was true. His toned body was stupendous, and he looked fantastic.

On their way over to a couple of unoccupied beds in the shade of an exceedingly old baobab tree, he couldn't help but notice the admiring glances they received as a couple from people lounging poolside.

"Drink?" he asked her, whilst attracting the attention of one of the waiters hovering nearby, placing his towel down carefully, then lying on top of the bed.

"Please. I'd love something refreshing. Say an orange juice?"

"Oh, come on Izzy. You're on holiday, have something a little stronger."

"Okay," she smiled, perusing the small colourful

cocktail menu on a little rattan table beside them.

"I'll have a Pina colada, please," she asked the waiter.

"Vodka and Coke for me, please. A large one buddy," asked Harry.

They both settled back comfortably on their respective beds, soaking up the sun's rays.

"Here, put this on," he said, handing her a bottle of sun cream.

"Thanks Harry."

"Unless, of course, I can oblige?" he smiled.

"I can manage thank you," she said.

"Your room okay?" he asked.

"Perfect. The whole place seems sheer luxury, don't you think?"

"Just what the doctor ordered. I plan on doing nothing but lie about in the sun, eat loads and drink loads."

"Sounds like a plan," she said.

They chatted comfortably for a while, enjoying the sun and each other's company. Their drinks arrived, and they drank them greedily, finishing them straight away, so Harry ordered another round.

"You know Izzy, I hope I'm not overstepping the mark, but I couldn't help but notice the friction between you and Jack. You shouldn't take everything he says to heart, you know. He's a great guy. We've known each other for years and you couldn't hope to have a more loyal friend than him. Most of the time, he's teasing, you know."

"Harry, I'm an excellent judge of character and can decide for myself. I don't think he and I will ever be friends. He's always smoking and drinking and, well, basically, I just don't warm to him."

"The guy likes to have a drink and insult people, but he always does it with a smile on his face."

"Oh, so that makes it okay?"

"Just try to give him a chance, Izzy. You would like him if you got to know him, and I believe he's more than smitten with you."

"You must be joking. We can hardly bear to be in each other's company."

"Jack is Jack. Just give him a chance."

"What are you, his agent? His pimp?"

With a shake of his head, he smiled at her. He began telling her about how he knew Jack and amusing her with humorous tales. He painted an alternative picture of the Jack she knew. The genuine warmth in his voice revealed the exceptional nature of their friendship, surpassing the realm of mere colleagues. Maybe it was only her that thought he was a smart-arse?

"Does Jack have a girlfriend?" she enquired casually.

"Why? You interested?" he said.

"No way. Just curious."

"I don't think there's anyone serious."

"So, there is someone?"

"I think he dates on and off, but definitely nothing long term."

"There's a surprise. A few hours in that man's company is enough to put anyone off for life."

"Izzy, that's not nice."

"No Harry, he's not nice."

"You're wrong, you know?"

"I don't think so."

Changing the subject, Harry then told about his rugby achievements to date and made her laugh with his stories from the locker room.

As they lay in the sun chatting, Isabella noticed again how amicable Harry was, and boy he looked incredible in his swimmers. He was personable, friendly, and seemed more than interested in her. He was exceptionally witty and, if she was single. Stop it Izzy, that's the cocktails talking.

"What are you thinking about?" he asked, noticing her staring at him.

"Nothing really," she said shyly, feeling herself blush,

embarrassed he'd caught her unawares.

"Admiring my wonderful body, hey," he said.

"Something like that," she giggled.

"Doesn't surprise me."

"Oh, do shut up Harry."

They lay quietly and comfortably together, occasionally cooling off in the pool.

"Any plans later?" she asked, as she rose from her bed and lifted her legs over the side. She patted her arms as she felt them burning.

"We're meeting for drinks in the cocktail bar near the main lounge at eight," he said. "We're just eating in one of the hotel restaurants tonight and might visit the casino afterwards, if there's time."

"Great. Before we go out, I think maybe I will have a nap. I'm worn out. I slept little on the plane."

"Yeah, I noticed you and Jack were engaged in a heated debate for most of the journey. What were you talking about?"

"Nothing of any importance."

"He does like you, you know."

"If that's like, I dread to think what dislike is."

"See you later Izzy."

"Bye Harry," and she turned and walked back up to the room.

"By the way," he called after her, "you look good enough to eat in that bikini. You'd better get a move on before I catch up with you and do something we'll both regret."

"In your dreams Harry. Now have another swim and cool yourself off."

She returned to her room, smiling to herself, and began the dreaded chore of unpacking the rest of her clothes. She folded her underwear and smaller items of clothing into the little drawers of the wooden dressing table and hung her glamourous, exquisitely cut dresses, jackets, and trousers in the wardrobe.

Beautiful clothing was her only downfall. Despite her usual preference for classic designs, she boldly incorporated more flamboyant pieces into her wardrobe when she felt brave enough. And as for accessories, Rob was always going on at her about her many handbags and sunglasses. What? You can't have too many handbags and sunglasses.

She slid the empty case into the back of the wardrobe and, after unloading all of her toiletries in the bathroom, she took a quick shower. Ouch, maybe she had overdone it in the sun, she thought as she glanced at herself in the mirror.

After drying herself on a soft, white towel emblazoned with the hotel logo, she wrapped herself in a fluffy dressing gown, lay down on the bed, and fell asleep.

She awoke listlessly several hours later. It was seven thirty. Shit.

She walked into the bathroom and regarded herself in the mirror, noticing again she really had caught the sun earlier. She turned on the tap and splashed cold water on her face and brushed her teeth.

She ran her fingers through her still damp hair, applied a little subtle make-up and sprayed herself with perfume.

Okay, what to wear? She sifted through her clothes, settling on a beautiful Missoni one-shoulder long dress, in their instantly recognisable zigzag knit and a pair of strappy heels. She looked fabulous.

By now it was just gone eight o'clock and she made her way to the bar, where the others were sitting around waiting for her, enjoying an apéritif.

"Pheeewww." whistled Harry, "You look stunning Izzy." Whereupon the others agreed and nodded in greeting, with varying levels of enthusiasm, "Drink? Are you ready for more cocktails?"

"Please Harry, I'd love one."

"Another? Have you two been drinking already?" asked David.

"We met up by the pool earlier," explained Isabella, "And

may have enjoyed one or two," she smiled.

"I thought you'd caught the sun," stated Ingrid. "Us lot were too busy snoozing. Nice out there?"

"Wonderful" said Izzy.

"Amazing," said Harry, "Views were outstanding. Especially Izzy in her incey wincey teeny-weeny bikini. Man Alive. Needed to keep jumping in the pool."

Some laughed, others – Jack and Madison remained deadpan. In fact, Madison looked at her disapprovingly. Tosser.

She noticed they'd all dressed neatly for dinner and were enjoying themselves, sipping delicious, vibrantly coloured cocktails, decorated with exotic fruits. They certainly made a handsome group. Ingrid, Madison, and Fiona were wearing dresses, but the men opted for less formal attire, yet they all looked refreshed.

Jack had changed into a pair of black jeans and a short-sleeved, tight fitting black t-shirt, which only seemed to accentuate his deep tan, ripped abs and remarkable good looks. She couldn't help but notice that he was also regarding her, a mischievous twinkle in his eyes. However, she was relieved when he decided to stay quiet for a change.

She stood chatting with David and Harry for a while about one of their latest projects near Docklands. A huge development of luxury 4 and 5 bedroomed apartments overlooking the Thames, a joint venture apparently with Jack's company, promising to be one of their most dramatic buildings to date. It would apparently provide fantastic views over East London.

"Well, are you three going to stop talking shop and let us all go through to dinner? We're on holiday, remember? No business," declared Ingrid, grabbing Isabella's arm and leading her into the dining room. "I don't know about anyone else, but I'm absolutely starving." Everyone followed them into the soft, candlelit dining room.

Isabella found herself sandwiched in between Harry and Ewan around a large circular table and spent a delightful couple of hours being flattered, told ridiculous jokes and being made a fuss of. It did her the world of good. She could hear Jack's customary brisk, staccato manner over the other side of the table in heated debate with David, Madison, and Ingrid and was glad she had chosen the "lighter" side of the table.

She enjoyed a beautiful cut of steak and vegetables, followed by a crème brûlée and a side of fresh fruit. There was a seemingly never-ending supply of surprisingly good red and white wine, paid for on this occasion by Harry. They were a noisy group, and the conversation flowed freely.

Several hours later, they retired outside to enjoy a coffee. Madison practically draped herself all over Jack, thrusting her rather accentuated and provocative cleavage towards him. The dress she was wearing certainly left little to the imagination and Jack certainly seemed to enjoy the attention and unwavering flattery, cigarette in hand obviously. Isabella found, to her astonishment, that she felt a little unsettled and irritated. She couldn't be jealous, surely? What did she care?

However, she continued to enjoy herself enormously and felt quite tipsy. Okay, a little more than tipsy, she felt pissed. She soon forgot all about Jack and Madison and reciprocated Harry's advances and was flirting with him shamefully.

They were all thoroughly enjoying sitting outside in the balmy African evening, listening to the successive orchestra of the crickets and the intermittent chorus of frogs.

They felt pleased when the in-house band returned to play some local Benga music, which all added to the profound, laid back atmosphere. Harry grabbed her hands and led her to the dance-floor, where she swayed languidly. The others were quick to follow, apart from Jack, obviously, who regarded her unrestrainedly.

Following a lively evening of drinking, dancing, and engaging conversation, they all wearily made their way to bed in the early hours of the morning. Isabella collapsed onto the bed, feeling the weight of regret for indulging in a couple of whiskies at the end. She knew she would suffer the consequences in the morning as she drifted into a sleep intoxicated by the drinks.

***

CHAPTER SEVEN

The following day, after only about five hours of sleep, her head pounding and her eyes bleary, she wandered down to breakfast, to find only Fiona and Ewan had surfaced.

She smiled and nodded at them, and then walked over to a long buffet table that offered an impressive array of fresh fruit, cereals, pastries, as well as various chefs offering omelettes and crepes made to order and even a nearly full English.

She poured herself a steaming cup of strong black coffee and filled her bowl with a refreshing mix of fresh fruit salad before joining the other two.

"Good morning, you two. How are we this morning?" she asked, sitting down at their table.

"Not bad at all," said Ewan, "Considering. I walked past Harry's room and could hear him snoring his head off."

"You, Fiona? And Madison?" inquired Isabella.

"I'm okay-ish. Maddy's still out for the count. Anyway, how do you look so bright and cheerful?"

"I certainly don't feel it, believe me."

"Look Izzy, sorry, we don't mean to be rude, but we've just finished and we're about to go for a walk on the beach. We can wait if you like and you can come with us?" asked Fiona.

"No, I'm fine thanks. I'll just enjoy a quiet breakfast and then I'm going to find the gym. This place is so big I can't remember where it is. You go, enjoy yourselves."

"Ok, we'll probably see you later," and off they went.

That is nice, thought Isabella. Those two certainly seemed to have grown quite close over the past twenty-four hours. They'd had a great time last night, and she wondered if they were into each other?

She looked around at the other tables nearby. Lots of couples. Honeymooners, she presumed.

"Isabella."

"Jack." Great.

"Mind if I join you" he asked, sitting down next to her.

"I'm just about finished, actually."

"Crap. You have finished nothing. Stay for a while?" His stubble had grown even more, his face looking even darker than usual. He obviously rarely shaved. His hair stood in disarray and his eyes appeared red. She didn't want to hang around and face one of his mercurial moods.

"You're looking a bit worse for wear," she commented.

"Mm" was all he could offer in reply as he continued to tuck into his plate of bacon and eggs with gusto, occasionally downing his coffee.

They continued to sit in silence whilst she finished her coffee and he finished his breakfast, followed by an enormous glass of freshly squeezed orange juice.

"Ahh," he moaned, smacking his lips and running his hands over his bristly chin. From his shirt pocket he pulled out and lit a cigarette from his crumpled packet and began puffing away earnestly. "That's better. I feel more or less normal now" and he pushed his empty plate away from him, "Refill?" he asked, nodding towards her empty coffee cup.

"I'll get it." She felt awkward.

"I'm going anyway," and he snatched up her cup before she could say anything further. He returned seconds later with two steaming mugs of black, delicious Kenyan coffee. "Careful, it's hot."

"Thanks" she mumbled.

"You seemed to enjoy yourself last night with Harry," he stated gruffly.

"I was. He's good company."

"Hmph" he snorted.

"Fun."

"He's a great guy."

"I think so."

"So, you don't dislike all men then?" he commented.

"No, not ALL men," she uttered.

As they both reached for the sugar bowl, their hands brushed against each other. She delicately held her hand around the basin, feeling his firm grip as he covered her hand with his own. His bottled-up volatility was palpable, and she could feel it radiating off of him.

"Look Isabella. I need to talk to you," he stared at her with an impenetrable gaze, his magnetic and intense eyes locking her own, until she flushed and had to look away.

"You do? What about?"

But before he could say any more, they noticed David, Ingrid, Harry and Madison making their way towards them.

"It's not important. It can wait," he snarled, letting go of her hand finally.

They completed ignored each other for the rest of the breakfast. The others were totally unaware of the frosty atmosphere between them.

Afterwards she found the small, but well equipped and air-conditioned gym and did a light workout for about half an hour. She questioned why the churlish Jack Vincent had something so important to say that he hadn't already said, but she dismissed him from her thoughts. She hoped he would not go over old ground again.

Feeling much better and a lot more refreshed, she returned to her room to shower, before heading to the pool for a quick dip and a bit of sunbathing.

She had only one thought on her mind. Avoid being alone with Jack at all costs. She had absolutely no idea what he wanted to say, but whatever it was, it was of little or no concern to her.

One by one, the rest of the group appeared around the

pool and they all spent an enjoyable day together, lying by the pool, lapping up the luxurious surroundings and having the occasional swim in the pool to cool off. They made an attractive group, but Jack just couldn't take his searing eyes from Isabella and she responded, by doing her utmost to avoid getting close to him. His quiet simmering disturbed her.

They talked about plans for the rest of the week and Harry surprised them all by announcing he'd chartered a plane for their trip to Nairobi. They were stunned, but excited and he assured them it would be the ultimate relaxed journey.

"Apparently," Harry said, "they assure us total flexibility regarding timing, routing, and accessibility to airstrips that are not serviced by scheduled flights."

"Trust Harry," mumbled Jack, "There's people dying from malnutrition and he charters a jet."

As the sunset, an organiser in the hotel arranged an impromptu game of water polo amongst the guests, which they all took part in and thoroughly enjoyed. Isabella found herself on Jack's side and she was sure that his many bumps into her weren't entirely accidental.

"Will you stop using my shoulders as a prop to jump up on?" she yelled. Then a short time later, "Ow. You bloody idiot. That bloody hurts." She rubbed her arm and tried to wipe away the water that stung her eyes.

"Sorry, baby, got a bit carried away."

"You can say that again. Do that again and I'll smack you back."

"I believe you would as well," he said.

"Damn right I would," she snarled, giving him the middle finger.

"Guys. This is supposed to be fun," intervened Ingrid.

"Tell Mike Tyson that," snapped Isabella.

"I'm sorry baby, really?" he came towards her and rubbed her sore arm, "I'm sorry okay?" and at that he picked her up and threw her over his shoulder and literally kissed her on the arse.

"Nice ass," he whispered to her, as she screamed blue murder.

They had dinner that evening at the hotel's Italian restaurant. Isabella was amazed by Jack's impeccable Italian, but they all had a good laugh when they realised the waiters couldn't comprehend him.

Isabella enjoyed a delicious Aubergine Parmigiana and a green salad and the rest all tucked into pizza, pasta, salad and other gastronomical delights, all accompanied by some more palatable wine.

They then had a flutter in the hotel casino, as they had not made it there last night.

They all wandered in and broke off into little groups. Isabella sat with Harry at the Roulette wheel and after he'd explained what she had to do and where she could place the chips, she found she was thoroughly enjoying herself.

"This is so much fun," she giggled.

Sometime later, a man of middle eastern appearance joined them at the table and began placing piles of the equivalent of $1,000 chips everywhere. Isabella laughed and whispered to Harry that he made her little $1 chips look relatively insignificant.

To her dismay, the man heard her and handed her one of the $1000 chips and said, "Please. Beautiful lady. Place it for me?" After a little gentle persuasion, she accepted and placed it on red seventeen.

The croupier spun the wheel and said, "Black eleven."

"Oh my God, I'm so sorry," she said to the man, apologetically.

"Hakuna Matata. No problem," he laughed and walked off to the bar.

"Hell." Harry whispered, "He's going to offer me a thousand quid for your body next."

An elegantly dressed, older lady, sat next to Isabella, leaned in towards her and explained that the gentleman was the owner of many large hotels along the coast, and in the UAE, and thought nothing of spending thousands of pounds in the casinos.

"How wonderful." exclaimed Isabella, laughing in amazement, then she turned to Harry and playfully hit his arm. "A thousand pounds? Is that all I'm worth? At least Demi got a million dollars."

She glanced over and saw that Jack, with Madison again adorning him, was holding court with Fiona and Ewan and they were all playing and making a great deal of noise at the Black Jack table.

Ingrid and David were at the bar chatting with a German couple.

Isabella returned to the game in hand and, having never played Roulette before, couldn't believe her incredible luck. After a short while, she found herself $650 richer and was having a phenomenal time. Harry ensured she was never without a glass of wine and was the perfect gentleman.

"Don't get too confident," he said, "beginners' luck."

"Sore loser." She said. But he was right. She progressively kept placing bets and lost again and again until she'd lost all her winnings. She couldn't believe that she could steadily win each time, her pile of chips growing around her and then watched as little by little they slipped from her hands. However, she didn't feel disappointed. She just felt exhilarated and wanted to play more, but Harry persuaded her enough was enough for one evening.

They all walked back outside to the main bar area and Fiona, David, Ewan and Ingrid called it a night, made their excuses and went to bed. As they walked towards some unoccupied seats, Jack sidled up to Isabella and whispered in her ear.

"I didn't do that, did I?" he asked.

"What are you talking about now?" she snapped.

"The bruise on your shoulder?"

She was wearing a champagne satin slip dress and a

fairly large bruise on her left shoulder.

She glanced briefly at her shoulder and challenged him. "You know damned well you did. You were like a bull in a china shop and I told you time and time again to back off as you kept hurting me."

"I'm so sorry," he whispered. "I was just playing."

"You always are Jack. Your problem is you don't listen."

Before he could say any more, she sat on one of the large sofas. Harry came and sat next to her and put his arm around her shoulders comfortably. Madison and Jack each pulled up a huge comfy armchair and sat opposite them.

Again, they all had had a lot to drink by now and were laughing and joking amongst themselves (well, not Madison obviously), whilst drinking glasses of Baileys. It had been another very relaxed, warm, comfortable evening and Isabella still felt on a high from her excitement at the Roulette table and was chatting cheerfully to Harry about it.

Jack stared over at her, his raw envy plain to see and asserted, "I'll have to take you to Vegas down the road Bella, you think this was good? You'd love it there. It's like you're on another planet. The lights, the noise, the slots, it's fun man."

"I'd love to. It's been my dream to go to Las Vegas, to see more of America, really. Although I don't think you and I would be the best people to go together. It'd be like a title fight at Caesar's palace."

"Crap." He looked quite hurt and Harry wondered what they were talking about. He hadn't noticed her shoulder.

"Well, you can have Las Vegas," sneered Madison. "So tacky. Give me Monte Carlo any day."

"I don't think he was asking you," said Harry. Ouch, thought Isabella.

"Touché. I was just saying I didn't like the place."

Jack wasn't giving up. He continued by offering her a personal tour of Caesar's; perhaps a show at the Hilton; venture downtown to the Golden Nugget, "We can try visit all the Rat Pack's haunts too, that'd be fun."

"What's the Rat Pack?" asked Madison.

"You don't know who the Rat Pack is?" he said, "Google it."

"I guess that'd be good fun," admitted Isabella. "I'd like to see The Sands?"

"Gone baby. It's now the Venetian," Jack said.

"That's a shame. I'd love to have seen the real Vegas," she sighed.

"Drive around in an open top Caddy."

"I don't think so," she said nervously.

He was regarding her broodily and a little too seriously for her liking. She tried to make a joke of it and put all the banter down to too much alcohol. He was eyeing her with such fervour. He seemed to have a confident intensity and exuded a manic energy and sexuality and it scared her.

Unable to withstand Jack's intense gaze and Madison's disapproving glare any longer, she turned to Harry to ask a question. As she did so, she noticed Madison whispering in Jack's ear, her voice low and seductive, captivating his full attention. Her perfectly manicured nails grazed up and down his legs while she laughed at his jokes. With her constant compliments and ingratiating behaviour, it was clear that she was a sycophant. Feeling the weight of it all, Isabella got up and informed everyone that she needed to get some rest.

"I'll walk you to your room if you like?" offered Harry.

"Thanks, I'd appreciate that." And off they went. As they walked away, Harry placed his hand in hers and they headed towards her suite.

She glanced back over her shoulder to wave goodbye and saw Jack scowling at them, not knowing he was thinking to himself, that much to his distaste, Harry and Isabella certainly made an impressive-looking couple and wishing for the first time in his life, he was Harry.

"Well, goodnight Harry," she said as they reached her room finally, "thanks for being such good fun and brilliant company tonight. I've enjoyed myself."

"Me too. Shall I come in for a nightcap?" he smiled. "I don't fancy turning in just yet."

"Oh Harry. I'm exhausted and I dread to think what kind of nightcap you have in mind." She said.

"Isabella. What kind of man do you think I am?"

"Harry. That's the problem. I know exactly what kind of man you are. Goodnight" and she kissed him on the cheek and shut the door behind her and leant against it, smiling to herself.

She was just about to head into the bathroom when she heard a couple walking past her room, giggling. She opened the door, thinking it was Fiona and Ewan and was going to bid them goodnight. But to her astonishment, she saw Jack and Madison disappearing into his room in fits of laughter.

She shut the door and felt sick to her stomach. Jack and Madison? Then again, she wouldn't put anything past either of them. Wow, Jack and Madison. She didn't even want to go there.

After she'd washed and undressed, she untied her mosquito net and climbed into the clean, crisp white sheets and smiled to herself. God, Harry was attractive, but she could never see him as anything other than friends. So handsome, but such a terrible flirt.

Now Jack Vincent. What the hell was he doing with Madison? She dreaded to think. And why did she care? If he wasn't so simply awful ... and then she fell asleep, her last thoughts of the irrepressible Jack Vincent.

***

CHAPTER EIGHT

They spent a few glorious days lying by the pool, swimming and walking miles along the paradisiacal beach, trying to avoid the almost too persistent hustlers and vendors; unable to resist any longer, she surrendered and splurged on a stunning jade necklace.

They all attempted the exhilarating water sports offered by the hotel, each showcasing their varying levels of expertise in water skiing, snorkelling, and windsurfing. With great enthusiasm, Harry coordinated a game of beach volleyball with the local lads, creating an atmosphere of fun and excitement. Even though they fell short by a few points, their laughter filled the air, contagious and unrestrained. Everyone joined in except for Madison, who stood on the side lines watching. No matter how many excuses she made, she couldn't deny that her preoccupation with her hair and nails was the true reason behind it all.

They also organised a mini table tennis tournament and, much to Isabella's chagrin, noticed that after a few warm up games; no one wanted to play with her, or be on her side.

"You're absolutely crap," said Jack, but she enjoyed herself all the same.

Jack and Harry were fiercely competitive, engaging in a relentless battle.

"It's only a game, for God's sake," screamed Fiona at them. But Jack came out on top, much to Harry's disappointment. He didn't enjoy losing.

"I thought you were a tennis player, Bella?" asked Jack.

"I am. I don't know why I'm so useless at table tennis.

Anyone want a game of doubles? Maybe I will impress more at real tennis?" she asked.

"As long as you're better than you were at table tennis." Jack teased, "I'd love to be your partner. Harry? Anyone else? Fancy making it a foursome?"

"Sure Jack, I'm game. Ingrid, can you play?" enquired Harry.

"Me. Unquestionably shite." She responded.

"Well, as you put it so eloquently, perhaps I'll find another partner. Fiona? How about you?" he asked.

"I'm not bad. Not good, but not bad," she said.

"You'll have to do. But I warn you, I don't want to lose twice in one day," grumbled Harry. They bid their farewells to the others and made their way to the tennis courts.

"Your shoulder better?" enquired Jack.

"Hadn't given it another thought," said Isabella.

"I'm sorry, okay?" he said solemnly.

"There's nothing to be sorry for. Really, forget it."

They'd been getting on well over the last few days, so both of them said no more.

To Isabella's embarrassment, one of the hotel's employees offered to be a ball boy. She felt sorry for him, having to run about after their mis-hit balls in such intense heat, but Jack persuaded her it would be okay and it would be a way for him to supplement his appallingly low wages.

They began with a brief knock around and Isabella found Jack a very accomplished player. He was also a generous partner, and they made an exceptional team, winning the first set, six, one.

Fiona was okay, but not up to Harry's high expectations, and Isabella and Jack were in hysterics at their arguing and cursing at one another.

Not surprisingly, Jack and Isabella took the second set six, love and the final straw came when Fiona hit Harry over the head with her racquet whilst trying to reach a high volley.

"Shit Fiona. What are you trying to do, kill me?" he

bawled, rubbing his crown.

"It was an accident you bloody pig," she screamed, "anyway, it's your fault, you shouldn't have got in my way."

"Well, I don't want to play anymore. I've had enough," he grumbled.

"Oh, don't be such a spoilsport, you baby," said Isabella. But Harry and Fiona didn't want to continue. Jack decided it was too hot for a game of singles, so the foursome made their way back to the hotel. They undoubtedly delighted Henry, the ball boy, by giving him the equivalent of $50 for his help on the court.

Whilst Harry and Fiona walked in front, still arguing amongst themselves, Jack turned to Isabella and remarked, "You're quite a tennis player."

"You're not too bad yourself," she smiled.

"And you look fantastic in those shorts."

"Ditto."

"Wow Bella. Are you flirting with me?" he said.

"Now that would be telling."

An easy friendship was developing, after all. The animosity had cooled, and they seemed to have developed an unspoken truce. It made life easier all-round.

The group decided to charter a yacht the next day, ensuring they had a professional captain and a dedicated crew of two. They'd chosen a spectacular day, and they sailed out into the dark, choppy waters, past the coral reef, so those that could, and wanted to, could try a bit of snorkelling. They then moved on to some deep-sea fishing. There were plenty of rods and bait, but only Harry, David and Ewan fancied a go, whilst the other basked in the piercing sun.

"Isabella, your back is burning," noticed Jack, who was lying next to her. "You want me to rub some lotion in?"

"Umm," she mumbled unsurely.

"Come on, it's only suntan lotion. I won't bite," he grinned, unscrewing the lid.

"Go on then."

He began rubbing the cream over her back and shoulders, "You've burnt, you know?"

"It doesn't hurt. It's probably just red."

"It will later," he was kneading her shoulders firmly.

"Okay, okay, I'm done. I asked for sun cream, not a massage."

"Okay, done. Can't blame a guy for trying. Anyone else?"

"Me. Me. You can rub me up and down any time, Jack," said Madison suggestively.

"There's a surprise," whispered Ingrid to Isabella, "*You can rub me up and down anytime, Jack*" she imitated Madison's breathy voice, "what a creep," and they both watched as Jack gave Madison a back rub.

"I think I just felt some sick come up," said Ingrid.

Having decided to call it a day, the three valiant fishermen made their way back a short while later. However, their adventure was far from over as they were greeted by the breath-taking sight of a Whale Shark, its massive body gliding gracefully through the water just a few yards from their boat. Ewan's terror was evident as he urgently demanded that all fishing rods be returned and that no one else dare set foot in the water.

"It's perfectly harmless man," taunted Jack.

But Ewan refused to be swayed. "Yes, but who knows what other creatures are lurking out there, bloodthirsty sharks," he grumbled as he walked away. He settled down beside Fiona, who was relaxing on a vibrant yellow beach towel, coated in glistening suntan oil.

They spent the rest of the day and early evening lounging around on deck, basking in the sunshine and, for those eventually brave enough, diving and bathing in the abyss below of the Indian Ocean.

Isabella was a fair swimmer but the deeper dark blue waters unsettled her. It was true what Ewan had said.

You didn't know quite what was below you. And then Jack and Harry started kidding around. First Harry pretended to get a cramp, then Jack shouting that something had grabbed his leg, so she clambered back up the steps.

"Isabella. I'm joking." He said, grabbing hold of her leg, "Come back in."

"No chance. Get off my leg Jack."

"Party pooper."

There then followed an early evening picnic that Ingrid had arranged with the hotel staff, washed down with bottles of ice-cold Tusker beer. They all gathered round and watched the magnificent sunset. Isabella was totally oblivious to the fact that Jack hadn't taken his eyes off her all day, but a few of the others had.

The next few days rushed by in a blur of nonstop activities. They sailed out in a Dhow, a battered little fishing boat, to explore further the coral reef and try their hand at snorkelling and scuba diving. The other more accomplished divers braved the deeper waters again, where they could study the incredible marine life in the frigid waters, but Isabella and Fiona stayed in more shallow waters where they could stand safely and still touch the seabed. Isabella ultimately had a superb time once she'd adjusted her goggles and snorkel to the correct position, swallowing no further mouthfuls of revolting, salty seawater. The two girls still saw diverse shoals of varicoloured fish, an eel and several starfish, amongst the sadly, ever-depleting coral reef.

The next day, opting for a couple of taxis, they arrived at the somewhat faded and flaking, yet still enchanting, city of Mombasa. They ventured around the old town with its winding lanes, mosques and cramped aged houses, which sloped gently down to the harbour, haggling with the vendors and buying souvenirs for friends and family back home. They wearily sauntered, in the scorching midday heat, downtown, with its wide and busy streets, throngs of people everywhere.

Matatus, with countless people hanging from the sides, roared past them on the busy road. It was just a hive of activity.

They spent their evenings drinking and enjoying delicious food in the different restaurants, both in the hotel and in the local area and neighbouring hotels. Isabella avoided being alone with Jack like the plague. There was definitely something bothering him. She knew there was something on his mind, so she tried her best to ignore him and stay at a safe distance. She ensured she wasn't sitting next to him at the dinner table and ignored many of the more personal comments directed at her. However, he was hard to ignore. She could hear his low voice vibrating, deep and sonorous, even across the other side of the room. The aura of raw masculinity that surrounded him was almost tangible. He could make people flinch with his bracing comments or vulgar swearing, itching for an argument, yet on other occasions he would sit back, merely observing those around him, taking it all in.

Isabella and Harry seemed to have paired off, but under her strict instructions, that they were friends only and would be nothing more. She found Harry thought provoking and comical and he made an excellent confidante and she wanted to remain this way. It was like having a gay best friend who wasn't gay. He respected her views, but pestered her to relent to his wishes and let their relationship become more, but she tried to explain as gently as possible her reasoning. Well Robert, for a start. She felt sure that a couple of the others thought there was more to their friendship, but as long as she and Harry knew the score, it was okay by her.

One night after dinner, again accompanied by bottles of excellent wine (so much alcohol and too much drinking every night), in the grillroom, they went to a large and busy club in one of the neighbouring hotels. Isabella looked especially enticing in a black, fitted, part-boned and strapless knee-length dress from Prada. She was wearing high-heeled black strappy Manolo Blahnik's and looked like she'd just stepped off the cover of Vogue. It was one of those outfits that made you feel glorious and she was so glad she'd worn it for the club. The other girls all wore cocktail dresses too and the men, all except for Jack, who was his perpetual scruffy self, had all tried.

Whilst David made his way to the bar and bought an enormous round of drinks, the others located a large empty table.

"Oh no," Isabella groaned, when Harry pointed out there was a karaoke for a couple of hours before the DJ started properly.

"Right. We all have to do it," pronounced David, returning with a tray of drinks and shots.

"No," shrieked the girls in unison.

"How common," stated Madison, "I've never been to a karaoke in my life."

"There's a first for everything," said Ewan.

"I can't sing. I sound like a parrot being strangled," screamed Ingrid.

"It doesn't matter. Everyone has to do it or else," maintained Harry.

"Or else what?" challenged Isabella.

"Come on, don't be spoilsports. We're on holiday," pleaded Ewan.

"Or else ... the forfeit is ... jeez, help me out here, guys," pleaded Harry.

"Whoever doesn't sing has to strip naked and run across the dancefloor," said Ewan.

"Sounds good to me," said Jack.

"You bastard," said Fiona.

"This isn't fair," wailed Isabella.

"Sounds fair to me," said Jack. Don't sing. Don't sing. He thought to himself.

"Shit, I wish I'd stayed in tonight," cried Isabella.

"What? And deprived us all of the sight of you in that dress," quipped Jack.

And that was that. They chose their songs and David went first. He chose *Copacabana* by Barry Manilow and when he finished, they all stood up and were clapping and whooping.

Ewan and Fiona did a sweet, but tuneless rendition of Aretha Franklin's *Say a Little Prayer*. Neither could sing and they kept getting their words wrong, but ended up enjoying themselves immensely.

Ingrid did her best Madonna with *Like a Virgin*. She sounded awful, but was a good sport for at least trying on her own, and her dance routine was hilarious.

Harry chose Ed Sheeran's *Castle on a Hill* and was excellent. Isabella, along with everyone else, were astoished and couldn't believe their ears as his voice filled the air.

Then it was Isabella's turn. They had to physically push her up to the mike.

"Jack. What are you doing?" she shrieked as Jack jumped up and joined her on the stage.

"I've changed yours so we can do a duet," he smiled.

"No," she wailed.

"Look, stop making a scene," he hissed, "the song's starting."

And he grabbed hold of her free hand and started swinging.

"No." She groaned, as the opening bars of Bobby Darin's *Things* started.

They were brilliant. Jack had a husky, gravelly and powerful voice and Isabella's was soft, but perfectly in tune and complemented him.

"You guys were brilliant." Crowed Harry upon their return.

Everyone was patting their backs and congratulating them.

"Didn't they make a fantastic couple?" exclaimed Ingrid.

"Didn't they just." Added Madison bitingly.

"Your turn Maddy." Said Harry.

"Not on your life," she backfired haughtily.

No one pushed her. No one suggested she do the forfeit, they didn't particularly care if she took part or not.

"Okay, one more shot," said Jack a short time later. He downed his drink.

Although there were several hundred people in the room, few of them wanted to have a go at singing and they were all getting a bit fed up with the DJ's in-between tuneless renditions of old-hat party songs.

Jack mumbled something to Harry and then swaggered up to the booth and held a long discussion with the DJ, whilst a couple of young girls sang a tuneless pop song.

Eventually, he took his place at the microphone.

"Here he goes." said Harry, "Go get 'em, ol' blue eyes." He roared.

"But his eyes are brown?" commented Maddy.

"He's going to sing Frank Sinatra?" gasped Isabella.

"Just wait. We're in for a treat," said Harry.

Jack tapped the mike and pulled over a bar stool.

"He looks like a bloody professional." said Harry.

"He looks like a bloody prat," quipped Ingrid.

Jack took a slug of his Jack Daniels and then viewed his large audience. "This one's for the most beautiful woman in the room. You know who you are," and he polished off his drink as the big-band music of *Witchcraft* began.

"Who's he talking about?" asked Ewan.

"Can't you guess?" said David.

Madison looked pleased with herself.

"Maddy? That's not who I thought he was talking about." whispered David to Harry.

"Me neither," he responded grumpily.

Jack began singing and had them all mesmerised. His delivery was impeccable. He knew all the words, not needing the screens or the lyrics, his diction sensational. He was a cross between Frank and Michael Bublé.

At the end, the place erupted and shouts for more. More. Prompting Jack to remain where he was. He loved every darned minute of it. A waiter brought him another Jack Daniels from which he took a slug. She watched as he removed a cigarette from his packet and shoved the rest back in his shirt pocket. He started to light up, but the staff rushed over and protested, so he tucked it behind his ear.

"Thanks. I'm enjoying this," he said sexily into the mike.

Show-off. Thought Isabella. She was utterly shocked by his sheer arrogance. His bravado.

"He thinks he's Frank Sinatra." said Harry.

"Someone get him the hell down from there," retorted Ingrid.

"He's only just begun." bellowed Harry.

Thereafter followed *'I Get a Kick Out of You'*, followed by *'One for my baby (and one more for the road)'* and then a rousing rendition of *'My Way'*, whereupon the entire crowd joined in.

"Surely, he's done now," said David. "Let someone else have a turn," he yelled.

Then they heard Jack's voice again, 'To the lady who knows who she is, or at least she should do by now. I've changed my mind ... *this* is our song,' and he perfectly started to sing, *All the Way*.

He was incredible, even though he'd had a lot to drink by now, as had they all.

Isabella watched as he stumbled down from his stool, still singing and jauntily begun ambling towards them, patting people's hands as they held them out for him as he walked past. He grabbed a trilby from an old local's head, who stared after him in astonishment as Jack placed it on his own head.

"Oh shit. What's he doing now?" Isabella whispered to no-one in particular and groaned.

"Yes. What is he doing?" shrieked Madison, who glared viciously as she watched Jack get down on one knee and take Isabella's hand in his own as everyone around them cheered.

"... *but if you let me love you, it's for sure I'm gonna love you, all the way ...*"

"Oh. My. God" shrieked Ingrid.

Isabella felt mortified. But what could she do? All eyes

in the room were upon them. He was serenading her. He sang beautifully to her, not letting go of her hand and his eyes locking onto her own. As the song ended, Jack rose to his feet. Everyone was cheering. He walked over to the old man and returned his hat and thanked him, then returned the microphone, ordered a round of drinks for his table and rejoined the group.

"Well, fuck me," said Ingrid.

The evening didn't end there. They stayed whilst the DJ played tune after tune, whilst everyone danced. Jack stared despondently into his glass of whiskey and Isabella sat on Harry's knee in the seat next to him.

"Excuse me beautiful," said Harry as he lifted her up. "Men's room is calling."

Shit. She was on her own with brooding, moody *HIM*, just as the music changed to something slower.

"Come on, my turn," growled Jack as he removed the drink from her grasp and placed it on the table. He took her hand and swiftly pulled her to standing and led her to the dancefloor. He drew her roughly into his arms and held her tightly as they danced together. As the music swelled, they drew closer, magnetised by an electric attraction. Each movement was deliberate, yet tantalisingly slow, as if savouring every fleeting moment of this closeness. Their gazes locked, sparking a silent conversation of desire and anticipation. Her hands explored, tracing the contours of his muscles, igniting a fire that burned with each tender touch. The world faded away, leaving only the intoxicating rhythm of their movements, a dance of passion and longing that spoke volumes to all around them without a single word.

He eventually broke the silence. "You've been avoiding me?"

"I haven't" she lied.

"Stop playing games Bella" his lips grazed her ear, as he pulled her even closer.

She tried to break free from his grasp, but it was fruitless.

"You know how I feel about you," he whispered.

"Don't be ridiculous Jack. Just leave it."

"Don't be ridiculous? You just don't get it, do you?"

"Leave it Jack. Now. I mean it. Do. Not. Go. There."

"Look, forget about it. Let's just dance. Pretend we're Fred and Ginger."

She'd had far too much to drink to argue with him any further and found she was thoroughly enjoying being wrapped in his huge, solid arms. He smelt divine, and she felt safe and at home. She rested her head against his muscular chest and remained comfortably in his arms. She didn't dare turn around and look at the others.

As the song ended, she abruptly pulled away from him, without so much as looking at him, and returned to her seat.

"Fuck this shit. I'm going back to the hotel," mumbled Jack to no-one in particular and walked out without saying goodnight, but still giving Isabella the most ferocious glare.

Isabella shrugged her shoulders. "What the fuck did I do?" she protested.

"I think it's more a case of what didn't you do," answered Harry.

Madison's face was like thunder, and she followed Jack out ten minutes later.

***

CHAPTER NINE

The following day, after a late breakfast, the girls were enjoying a day of pampering in the hotel's spa and beauty salon. Whilst lying around in various states of repose, Fiona confessed to having spent the night with Ewan.

"Oh, my God. Give us the gory details then, you little tart," chuckled Ingrid.

"We did it all night long. I can barely walk." Fiona shrieked, and they all fell about in fits of giggles as they bombarded her with questions.

They were giggling and laughing about the men they were with and all men-except Madison, who was pretending to read an old dog-eared edition of Cosmopolitan, whilst waiting for her freshly painted, dark red fingernails to dry.

"So," said Ingrid to Madison, "Looks like you'll be sleeping alone for the next week, whilst Fiona *the holiday shagger* here, spends the night with Ewan."

"What makes you think I'll be sleeping alone?" said Madison, with a wicked glint in her eye, glaring at Isabella, "There's a certain American I wouldn't mind getting my freshly manicured talons on ... again," she added. "We're getting very close, you know?"

"Really?" the others asked doubtfully.

"Not after that display at the karaoke," said Ingrid.

Isabella didn't meet Madison's challenging stare and carried out laughing and joking with the others. No one picked up on the 'again' except Isabella. It made her feel sick. God. How could he go *there*? She knew there was something going on behind everyone's backs. She'd seen them.

"You know, I think I might have developed more than just a crush on a certain David Matthews," revealed Ingrid. "Shit, I shouldn't have drunk already. I shouldn't have said that. I take it back. He's my boss,"

"No way. He's not your type?" cried Isabella.

"Izzy, you're my friend," she wailed. "David would be good for me. Opposites attract and all that. We're very different, I know, but we have that spark, you know?" said Ingrid.

"I know what you mean," replied Fiona, "that unmistakable, electrical, sexual chemistry. Like me and Ewan and, without a doubt, like Jack and Isabella. You guys are literally combustible."

"What the hell do you mean, Jack and Isabella." screeched Madison, bouncing rapidly back into the discussion, "She detests him, don't you, Isabella? Don't you? You're always fighting."

"Of course," protested Isabella, not sounding too convincing, to either herself or the others, "He's egotistical, infantile, hot headed ..."

"But hot as hell," said Ingrid "And anyway, everyone with a vagina fancies Jack."

"Fancy him? Don't be ridiculous. I'm 31 not 12," snapped Isabella.

"Fireworks. That's what you two create. Seen nothing like it. I wish you'd just sleep with him and get it over with," added Ingrid.

"Ingrid. I have absolutely no intention whatsoever of sleeping with Jack Bloody Vincent." Isabella admonished.

"Well, he wants to sleep with you. More than sleep with you."

"Honestly. Were you born this stupid or did you take lessons?" she grumbled.

"Ouch. You must admit, though. Fabulous body. It's the forearms that do it for me. I love a man with tattoos. He's so well built," commented Fiona, "Did you see him yesterday by the pool, no top, just his low-slung jeans? Did you see his abs, his sexy 'V' and hips?" she continued.

"Mm" muttered Isabella.

"And well endowed," panted Madison.

"How the hell would you know?" said Ingrid. "No, it's his voice. Did you hear his voice? It was all for you, you know?" nodding towards Isabella.

"What are you talking about now?" Isabella groaned, infuriated as she found herself once again being dragged into a conversation about Jack. And yes, how the fuck did Madison know?

"The way the guy came over to you and was singing to you. Just to you. I wish Ewan did that for me," signed Fiona. "Yep, he's in love with you."

"You're mad. Anyway, one small thing you're all forgetting, whilst trying to fix me up with Jack, Harry, and God knows who else, I'm in a relationship, remember? Remember Robert? Right, I'm off for a hot tub," and she turned and left them all with something to think about.

"God, she loves herself, everything is about her, the virtue signalling ..." started Madison, behind her departing back.

"If you're going to be two-faced Maddy, at least make one of them pretty," snapped Ingrid.

"Well, if I looked like that, I'd love myself too. I mean, have you seen her in that thing that dares to call itself a bikini? She's essentially got all the men in this hotel drooling after her. In fact, I was probably Ewan's second choice. Okay, maybe third," Fiona said.

"Well, if you ask me, I find her stuck up and prudish," added Madison.

"Oh, shut up Madison. Remember when we asked for your opinion? No, me neither," snapped Ingrid, "And anyway, if anyone around here is stuck-up and prudish, it's certainly not Isabella." And she got up and followed in her friends' footsteps. As an afterthought, she turned back around and added, "and as for you and Jack, I don't think so."

Lying by the pool later on another hot, cloudless afternoon, Isabella jumped up and tied her sarong around her waist and said to no-one in particular, "I'm going for a walk along the beach. I'll see you all later."

"I'll come with you, you can't go on your own" countered Jack, and he jumped up briskly, took hold of her arm and marched her off before anyone else could join them or she could utter any objection. He gave Harry a glare as if to say, don't even think about it.

They walked in complete silence down a few un-even stone steps onto the pristine white sand, their feet sinking where they stood, the fine granules trickling between their toes. Miles of beach stretched out in front of them, practically deserted-sunbathers deterred from lying down because of the constant attention from the beach traders.

"You can let go of my arm now?" she stated.

He did so without comment.

They walked along, side-by-side, the sun on their faces and the ever-so slight breeze whistling around them and after they'd walked a fair distance, some of the infamous beach sellers came running up to them.

"Jambo." They cried, forming an eager huddle around them.

"Jambo." Replied Isabella.

They were trying to sell them Kitenge cloths, woodcarvings, sandstone ornaments, leather goods and beaded jewellery.

"Wewe ni mrembo." one young man said and said with his friends.

"Asante sana," replied Isabella and they stared at her in amazement. "Ndiyo, Ninaweza kusema Kiswahili" and then Isabella continued to explain in stilted Swahili that they were not interested today, but would come back before the end of their holiday to buy a few souvenirs.

"What did they say?" said Jack as they carried on up the

beach. "And how the hell did you know?"

"They said I was pretty. And Duolingo. I'm a fast learner."

"And boy, are they right. Thank God you put this thing on," he said, grabbing hold of her sarong, giving it a tug, "And covered at least your bottom half."

"Why?" she asked.

"Why?" he said. "Have you looked at yourself in the mirror lately? Bella, don't you realise the effect you have on most of the men here? Actually, I'd say all the men here. You're stunning."

"Please." She said and playfully and pushed him with her elbow.

They continued to walk along the glistening white sand in silence, now and then stopping to pick up a small shell or look under a piece of seaweed. They made their way to the shoreline and paddled in the crystalline, invigorating water.

"This sure beats the office," he sighed, looking out towards the horizon.

"You can say that again. It's idyllic, isn't it?"

"Glad you came?" he asked.

"Definitely, the break has done me the world of good."

"Not missing the ... Robert?"

"A little," she lied. If she was honest, she hadn't given him a second thought. Not even a text. He hadn't texted her either though, he hadn't even checked she'd arrived ok. Yeah, thanks for that. No, I'm fine. Dickhead.

"You realise this is one of the first times we've properly been alone this vacation," he whispered. "If I was even suspicious, I'd say you've been avoiding me."

"Of course, I haven't," she lied again. "I've been having such a good time, that's all. We all have."

"I've noticed. You and Harry seem to be quite a couple."

"Like you and Madison, I suppose?"

"No way. She's not my bag at all." He said.

"Oh yes? That's not what she thinks," she teased.

"She can think all she wants."

"And just what is your type, Jack? A catch like you?" she teased, her warm eyes sparkling with wit.

"It's a long list. Are you ready?" he said. "Someone intelligent, warm-hearted, funny, irresistible. The exact opposite of Maddy, I suppose,"

"And there's been no one serious?"

"Not really, no. I'm picky, I guess. At my age, I'm still waiting for the *one*."

"If the *one* really exists. Do you believe that? Do you think we each have a soul mate?" she breathed.

"I'd like to think so," he replied just as quietly.

Out of the blue, he turned to face her with such pent-up passion and emotion; she felt herself go dizzy. How could he have this effect on her? One minute she loathed him, the next minute ... don't they say there's a fine line between ... don't go there? And why did he make her feel so self-conscious and tongue tied, but before she could say anything, he did.

"Look Bella. This has gone on too long. It's driving me crazy."

"What is?" she asked, puzzled. She tried to avoid his gaze and watched her feet as the waves rushed up to meet them.

"I've wanted to be alone with you ever since we got here, just us. Ever since our conversation on the plane., ever since that darned New Year when we hit it off. Are we gonna just pretend there isn't a connection between us?"

"Humph," she murmured derisively and crinkled her nose in disgust. "I thought we'd been getting on well the last few days."

"I want to know more about you. Hell, I want to know everything about you. What you like. What you don't like. Your turn ons. Your turn offs. But fuck. Harry has glued himself to your side and I can't get near you. What's going on with him? Plus, you've been giving me the cold shoulder."

"That's all crap Jack. Anyway, you look like you've been having a whale of a time with Madison's constant attention-

ooh, Jack, your muscles are so big, and who knows what else you've been up to together?"

"What are you talking about?" he sighed.

"What's changed Jack? Do you no longer find me ... what are the words you used to describe me? Let me see now," and she counted them off her fingers, "Difficult, spoilt, irritating, and condescending?"

"Ingrid, the bitch. She told you," he said. "And yes, you're all of those things and more, believe me."

"You bastard."

"Look Bella. You may be difficult and spoiled and in complete disagreement with everything I say or do, but I've met no one like you in my entire life. Sshh. Be quiet," he put his finger gently to her lips. "Let me speak. Even though you turn everything I say into a disagreement, you're also the most beautiful and extraordinary woman I've ever met. Yes, the biggest pain in my ass, too. I've never been jealous in my goddamned life, but I could kill Harry for being the one getting closer to you." He paused then, whilst he took in her look of absolute astonishment, then continued "And also, it's been hell being so near to you and not being able to talk to you alone, to touch you, in fact, to spend all of my waking hours with you and you alone. Now, what do you have to say?"

Isabella gaped at him, open-mouthed, still in a state of shock, with a look of utter bewilderment on her face.

"Well?" he asked.

She eventually stammered "I ... I, uh, I, don't know what to say, Jack. I did not know," she denied.

"Don't Bella. Of course, you know how I feel?"

"Really. I don't know what to say?"

"In that case, say nothing," and he pulled her convincingly towards him and kissed her hard and with increasing passion on her mouth. She felt his tongue probing hers, sending shivers throughout her entire body. He wrapped her in his arms, so tightly, she could hardly breathe and his mouth was so hard, yet so soft against hers, she could feel teeth cutting into her flesh and his unshaven jaw rubbing against her chin. After what seemed like an eternity, he drew back and released her and searched her eyes with his own.

"Why did you do that?" she gasped, holding down the corner of her sarong as it blew in the wind.

"Why do you think?" he said.

"I don't know. I don't even know if I like you."

"Bella. I know we hardly know each other. I know you're in a fucking shitty relationship. You probably think I'm being stupid, but I think … no, I know, I'm in love with you. Completely and utterly in love with you." Still gazing into her eyes, he took hold of her hands tightly.

"Jack please. You don't know what you're saying. A few minutes ago, you were the last man on earth I expected to say that. I know you wanted to talk to me. But that."

"Come on, Bella really?"

"I'm practically engaged to be married. We live together," she implored.

"The guy's a jerk."

"You don't know him."

"It's true. Look, I've never seen you on your phone? How often have you spoken to him since you've been here? Texted him?"

"I don't know? What are you, the text police?"

"See."

"All WE do is argue. Hot and cold."

"Our feelings are all mixed up. Christ, my entire head's fucked up. I've never felt like this in my life, and I know you feel the same."

"You know nothing, for Christ's sake. Now, please let's get back. We need to forget this ever happened. Fucking love me. What the fuck are you on?" and she turned away from him, trying to gain a few seconds to compose her thoughts. She began walking back toward the hotel, finding her progress slower than she'd hoped, because her feet kept sinking into the powdery sand. "Fucking sand," she screamed.

He chased after her and stood in front of her to block her way. She stepped to the side to move round him, but he moved again. "Bella, please. I can't bear this. Just give me a fucking chance? Even one night? What do you want me to do, beg?" he pleaded.

"Don't be ridiculous." She kept walking.

"Come on baby, please?"

"Just leave me alone."

"Please?" he implored. "We'll make our excuses tonight? Just give me a few hours of your time, so we can be together alone for once?" he smiled at her, "And if after that you still feel the same and you still have this insane antipathy toward me, I promise, I'll leave you alone and we'll never mention this again. My heart will be broken, but ..." He smiled, his sentence unfinished.

"Jack."

"I've seen the way you look at me. You must ... I'm almost positive you feel the same way?" He waited for a response, but there was none. "Harry? It's not him, is it?"

"Harry? It's got nothing to do with bloody Harry. I'm in a committed relationship with Robert. And as for you. It's you."

"And?"

"It's you, or us I mean, shit I don't know what I mean. You drive me crazy. You stand here and tell me you love me. Ha," she shrieked, "It's the most stupid thing you've said yet. You're not just a clown, you're the whole fucking circus."

"Its true Goddammit. All I want is you. All I want is to spend some time with you. Fuck the others. Just you and me? Please?" he rubbed his hand over his face and through his hair, he looked tormented.

"It's the heat. It's gone to your stupid head."

"Stupid head." He threw back his head and laughed at her, "Isabella please. I'm deadly serious. Tonight, meet me at nine back here on the beach. Then I swear if you don't change your mind, we'll never talk about this again, okay? No-one needs ever know. You can forget it ever happened."

He watched her deliberately and when he saw her falter slightly, said again, "Please? For me? You don't have to say or do anything, just listen to what I have to say, ok? We can go for dinner? A drink?"

"Okay, okay, but I can't promise you anything. I'll meet you, you can say your piece, then I don't want to hear any of this shit again. Are you clear?"

"Crystal," he smiled.

She walked up the steps in front of him and went straight to the relative safety of her room. She was in a daze. What on earth had happened? She'd been having a totally remarkable, relaxing holiday and now he'd turned her entire world upside down. Robert? What about Robert? He didn't give a shit about her, did he? Shit. What had she done? She had agreed to meet another man after he'd professed his love for her. What the absolute hell.

She lay for ages on her bed, her mind whirling. Twenty to the dozen. Why had she agreed to meet him? How could she get out of it? What had she done? She couldn't back down now. He'd never leave her alone.

Eventually, she finally picked up courage to text Ingrid. She felt terrible for lying.

"Sorry Ing. Too much sun. Staying in tonight xxx."

"No problem, babes. Hope you're okay."

She then tried ringing Robert, hoping he'd pick up, but he didn't. Shit.

Afterwards, she had a long soak in the bath, trying to quell her waves of anxiety. She knew how he felt about her, really. She lay there thinking back to the other night, when Jack had come over and was singing to her. It was quite obvious to all then that he had feelings for her. It was the most romantic thing anyone had ever done for her. His voice. And the way he just kissed her before, on the beach. Oh my God, I'm screwed, she thought.

She washed her hair and let it dry naturally. Thereafter, she changed into a beautiful new floral, floaty dress from Erdem, which clung to her magnificent figure. She looked feminine. She wrapped a baby pink pashmina around her shoulders and stepped into some pink strappy Jimmy Choo's. Okay, not very practical for the beach, but they looked great. Anyway, she was only staying for a few minutes to explain. Explain what exactly she had absolutely no idea.

Just before nine o'clock she strolled down to the beach to meet Jack for their clandestine tryst, after first having downed a large glass of white wine from the minibar to calm her nerves.

Her hair was blowing around her face and shoulders in the breeze, and she held her heels in her hand. She saw him leaning against the wall, his face a mixture of longing and concern, waiting patiently for her, smoking a cigarette. Surprise. Surprise.

He was wearing a loose, crumpled shirt and a pair of old cargo pants. He smiled at her, then threw away his half-smoked cigarette onto the sand.

"Fancy a drink?" he smiled, picking up a cold bottle of Rose and 2 glasses, before making his way towards her. "You look amazing."

She smiled at him. "Thanks. Nice to see you tried too?"

"What? These old things" He smiled slowly, then took hold of her hand firmly and led her onto the beach in silence. There was a heady sense of spices in the air and palm trees were swaying ever so gently in the breeze, which all captured the magical African night.

He gripped her hand and led her down to the water's edge, where they strolled, the only light from the moon above and behind them, the lights of a nearby hotel.

"You know it's not safe to go out on the beach after dark, don't you?" she said, breaking the silence.

"With you? Or in general?" he teased. "Let's sit here and have a glass of wine?"

They sat down and he poured her a glass first, then his own, and they sat companionably, sipping their wine.

"You look beautiful," he said.

"Thanks. Not really beach attire."

"I hope your dress doesn't get ruined."

"Nope. It'll be fine," she replied, taking a sip of her wine. "It's only sand-it'll brush off."

They made some small talk for a while before he faced her carefully.

"Okay, here goes nothing," he said, lighting up again. "I'm in love you. Have been since the first time I met you. I haven't stopped thinking about you."

"In love with me? Don't be ridiculous."

"Really."

"Lust maybe."

"Well, there is a bit of that too," he smiled. "When I heard you were coming, I knew it was fate. I know you're in a shitty relationship. I know he doesn't deserve you."

"And you would know that, how?"

"Ingrid," he stated bluntly.

"Wow. Thanks for that, Ingrid." She grumbled.

"I know you're with him purely out of habit, and I know he's away all the time. He drinks too much,"

"That's rich," she interrupted, nodding at his empty wineglass.

"He has little respect for you. You need someone who adores you. Who chooses you and only you? Someone who can give you the world."

"And that's you, I suppose? How dare Ingrid tell you anything? Talk about my private life? To you, of all people. A practical stranger. I'll kill her."

"Bella,"

"You hardly know me. Come to that, I hardly know you. How can you say you love me after barely knowing anything about me? Know nothing about me?"

"When you know, you know. You're *the one*. I've spent

my whole life looking for something. Someone. And you're it."

"I can't believe you're saying this," she gasped, taking a large gulp of her wine.

"I've been thinking about you ever since we met at the New Year's thing."

"But I'm a pain in the ass, remember?"

"You still are. A pain in the ass. A tremendous pain in the ass. But I want *you*."

"Jack," she groaned.

"Do you love him?"

"I ... We ... We live together. We've built a life together."

"That's not what I asked?" he said, his frown deep.

"It's complicated. Look, I can't do this. I'm sorry, but I have no intention of getting into any kind of relationship with you, platonic or otherwise. Is that clear?"

"We'll see," he smiled. "Look, let's head up to that little hotel up there and we can have a meal and a few more glasses of wine. I'll ditch this stuff. It's gone warm, anyway. We can talk about whatever you want to talk about and we can get to know each other more. I want to know everything about you."

"God. I'll give you one thing. You're certainly persistent. Dinner and that's it ok, no promises?"

"No promises. Come on, you," he said, taking hold of her hand and pulling her up from the sand.

Leisurely, they strolled up to the hushed and charming little hotel and made their way to the bar outside, adorably lit with candles and twinkling lights hanging from the trees. The staff showed them to a small table in a secluded corner, with one side opening out over the ocean. They could hear the waves lapping on the shore and felt the cool breeze whistling through the palms in the garden surrounding them. Jack ordered a bottle of champagne and a seafood platter.

"It's beautiful here," she said, for something to say, perusing their surroundings.

"Excellent choice for our first date."

"Jack."

She could call it whatever she wanted. A feeling of contentment settled in his heart as he savoured the moment of being alone with her.

"And by the way, you really do look beautiful tonight," he said, as he watched her sip her drink and play with her hair self-consciously. "Can I ask you something?" he said, smiling at her.

"Yes? You rarely ask permission."

"Are you always so darned argumentative?" he teased.

Their waiter arrived with the platter of seafood; Indonesian king prawns wrapped in filo pastry, served with chilli sauce; fried red snapper with tamarind sauce and pad Thai and jasmine rice.

"I hope you are hungry," he said.

They ate in comfortable silence, and he continually topped her glass. When they'd finished, well, she picked, he finished. He took hold of her hands across the table and gazed into her eyes.

"Bella, baby. Let me lay it on the line here. I have no intention of hurting you. I have met no one like you. As I said earlier, you're the one. My one."

"Jack, you just don't get it. I live with someone, or have you forgotten that minor fact?"

"Yes baby, so you keep telling me. But never once have you said to me, Jack, I'm in love with someone else. I don't want to spoil our evening talking about him. I don't want to put any pressure on you. But I mean what I say. I can't get you out of my head."

"I don't know what to say? I'm so confused."

"Can I take away your plates? Are you finished?" asked the waiter, interrupting them.

"Yes, thanks. And another bottle of Veuve please?" ordered Jack, lighting up a cigarette.

"Jack? Another bottle? Really?"

The bottle arrived, and he poured them both a drink,

"To us and our future," he said, clinking her glass.

"Jack."

"I'll wait Bella. As long as it takes."

"Jack."

"Okay, okay. Can't help a guy for trying."

They chatted and laughed and drank their way through the second bottle. She never drank this much. But although she was unnerved just by being in his presence alone, she felt at home with him, too. Beneath his gruff demeanour, he harboured a genuinely thoughtful and caring personality. He seemed totally at ease in his surroundings and oblivious to anyone but her. Why did she feel so comfortable with him? Had she misunderstood him? Maybe he was right? Maybe they had something? He was definitely the most attractive man she'd ever laid eyes on. It was such a challenge for her to meet him directly in the eye. Her feelings made her scared. She knew she was wearing a mask. She didn't dare tell him, but her feelings mirrored his completely. Jesus, how much had she had to drink? What was she thinking about?

Impulsively, as if reading her thoughts and catching her off guard, he leaned towards her and stroked the side of her neck, brushing her long hair behind her ear, sending shivers down her spine, "You are the most beautiful woman I've ever seen," he whispered, "I'm going to say this only one more time, I love you. I won't push you. I will wait for you. Fuck, I'll wait forever, if that's what it takes. But don't throw this, whatever this is, away. We've got the rest of our lives to be together. Sort your shit out. I promise I'll wait."

He looked at her with such longing and tenderness; she felt tears sting the back of her eyes. No-one had ever uttered such words of devotion. She didn't, or couldn't, say anything, as she fiddled with her empty glass. She only knew that she had never felt this way about anyone, either. The realisation hit her like a physical jolt. She loved him, too. She could no longer deny it to herself. But she kept her thoughts to herself, for now. She needed time to think.

The hours flew by as they chatted amicably, but she found herself tired and yawning.

"Come on you. You're tired and cold," he said after settling the check. He led her down to the sand once more. He put his arm around her, seeing her shiver, as she wrapped her shawl around her shoulders.

"I guess I should have worn something more practical," she giggled. "I didn't expect to be out this late, though."

"I'm glad you didn't. I wouldn't have had an excuse to put my arms around you," and he squeezed her even tighter to him.

Finally, they reached the hotel steps, and he walked her back to her room. He didn't ask to come in, he just held her close for a long while, not wanting to let go and then simply brushed his lips tenderly on the side of her mouth. She loved the feel of him, the tickle of his unshaven jaw, the smell of him and then she felt him stroking the back of her neck and heard him breathe "Goodnight Bella," as he turned and walk along the path to his room.

***

CHAPTER TEN

The next morning, she woke early with a fuzzy head. What the actual fuck had happened last night? Her mind was awhirl. What had she said? What had he said? She could still hear his voice and feel his powerful arms holding her tightly, his touch on the back of her neck. She could picture the little creases in the corner of his eyes when he smiled. The way he was constantly running his hands through his hair when he was troubled or just out of frustration. The way he rubbed his coarse jaw and mouth with his rough hands and stroking his stubble when he was looking pensive. She thought about his hard, toned body. His overwhelming presence, the way he made her feel, so secure and, most of all, she thought about the way he had kissed her yesterday. Was it only yesterday? He'd literally taken her breath away, and now he had captured her heart.

    She wished she could stay in bed, but she knew they had to leave early, as they were heading to the capital. Whilst she showered, she went over everything he'd said to her yesterday, over and over in her head. How was she going to face him? How was she going to face the others?

    She reached for her khaki shorts, slipped a small white t-shirt over her head and stepped into an old battered pair of hiking boots. She pulled her long hair out from underneath her top and tied it into a high pony and then packed a small bag containing a few outfits and other essentials, ready for their excursion. Even dressed casually, she still looked fantastic. Nobody would believe she'd had only a couple of hours' sleep. As she walked towards the door, she noticed a small scrap of paper lying on the floor. She picked it up, unfolded it and realised who it was from. *Bella. Thanks for last night. I meant everything I said and more. However, I won't put any more pressure on you. It's your call. Remember, I'll wait–as long as it takes. Jack.*

She tucked the note in her back pocket and felt queasy at the thought of seeing him, but wearily made her way down to reception and found all the others waiting for her, all except him.

"What happened to you last night? Headache better?" asked Madison icily, raising her eyebrows in judgement.

"A little better, thanks. I just needed an early night."

"Well, you don't look like you've had much sleep," she commented, regarding Isabella with a look of utter contempt.

"Yeah, thanks for that," grumbled Isabella.

"Madison, what *is* your problem?" interrupted Ingrid, who also received a look of disgust.

Isabella retrieved her black sunglasses from her bag and put them on, ignoring Madison, not wanting to engage.

She also noticed Harry regarding her, a hurt expression on his face. Fucking hell, that's all she needed. Everyone was pissed off with her.

"Right. Everyone here? Great. Let's get on this bus and go find us a plane," said Jack, arriving suddenly, looking unusually cheerful, wearing his worn denim jeans and crisp white t-shirt, rucksack hanging carelessly from his back.

"What happened to you last night?" asked Harry.

"Work," he offered simply.

They set off on their journey. Isabella staring out of the window, as the now customary hot air and aroma encircled her head and tickled her senses. In and out of the window, the smoky scent carried faint hints of the surrounding grassland. The scent, reminding her she was far from home. The sultry breeze had stolen her worries and raided her of all her woes.

As they wove their way to the Airport, through streets

and neighbourhoods, she surveyed the land around them as they travelled the dusty roads. She watched shanty homes and shops, roasting fires and people sauntering by on the roadside. Everywhere was already alive, even at this early hour. She eventually dozed off into dreams of both Jack and Robert.

They arrived at the tiny airstrip not that long afterwards and boarded their jet to Jomo Kenyatta International Airport. The sun had not long risen over East Africa and they were all silent as they enjoyed the glorious views from the little oval windows.

Upon arrival in Nairobi, a driver was waiting for them on a mini-bus, ready to take them into the city and to their next hotel. They drove along the busy roads, again in silence. What the fuck's going on? thought Isabella. Everyone was so fucking quiet.

The city centre was thriving, and the volume of traffic and honking of horns by people in shabby, old cars stuck in jams amazed them. Their driver told them to keep their windows rolled up and doors locked, as there were a lot of thieves among the busyness and dust of the city.

They arrived at the hotel, an oasis of calm, where they merely checked in and dumped their bags in their respective rooms on the top floor. As arranged, they met a short time later in reception, all except Jack.

"Where's Jack?" enquired Isabella, as casually as possible.

"He had to work. Again," answered Madison, with a look of sheer triumph on her heavily painted face.

Bitch. Thought Isabella.

"An urgent call from NYC," confirmed Harry, "Hopefully something he can sort out over the phone. If not, he'll have to return to the States. He's hiding in one of the conference rooms."

"I hope he won't be too long," said David.

"Never mind, we can enjoy ourselves all the same," said Ingrid. "Come on, let's explore," taking Isabella's arm in her own.

Isabella tried to mask her disappointment. Shit. She didn't even have his mobile number.

They walked outside into the surprisingly now cooler air and walked opposite to the tourist office, where they collected a few brochures and maps and picked up some ideas of where and what to visit.

Nairobi was certainly a compelling place, with enormous vitality and buzz, with a fascinating variety of people. They relished exploring the bustling and vibrant central market, immersing themselves in the artful display of fresh produce; then wandered around the exhaustive historical exhibits of the National Museum; they climbed to the top of the Kanu Tower, where they enjoyed a light lunch in the revolving restaurant and enjoyed spectacular views over the city and lastly, they strolled along Kenyatta Avenue.

As the sun went down over the city, they returned to their hotel and enjoyed a brief rest and shower. Isabella thought constantly of Jack. She wondered where he really was. Was he avoiding her? She had missed him today. She hoped he hadn't left. But wouldn't that solve everything?

That evening Harry had booked them a table at a Japanese restaurant, which was apparently one of Nairobi's finest. Thankfully and to her relief, Jack had re-joined them, after having solved the problems back at work and there was no need for any more of his intervention, leaving him to enjoy the rest of his holiday in peace.

The restaurant was indeed excellent, both impeccable service and food and they had a fun evening. Fiona and Ewan made some of them feel a little uncomfortable, as they were practically eating each other alive in the restaurant. Isabella and Jack avoided sitting next to each other, just in case anyone else picked up on the extreme sexual tension that had developed between the two of them. He had kept his word and had put no pressure on her. He'd tactfully kept his distance, but the few times he'd stood near her or brushed accidentally against her, the atmosphere between them was recognisably electric.

"You okay?" he'd mouthed at her from across the table.

She nodded in response and smiled at him, then laughed out loud as he unsuccessfully tried to mask a yawn and tried to act as if he *was* interested in Madison rambling on and on about her father's career in politics.

The following morning, they embarked on a journey just over an hour west of Nairobi to Lake Naivasha, one of the jewels in the Great Rift Valley, where flocks of graceful pink flamingos had settled on the grassy shores. Isabella couldn't help but notice Jack's delight at the tranquil and incredibly scenic surroundings and he seemed in his element, snapping away with his camera, oblivious to those around him.

They ventured back to the charming county club for lunch alfresco, where they all sat on Adirondack style chairs around a large wooden table beneath the shade of the grand acacia trees. Later, the men had a dip in the swimming pool, whilst the women stayed chatting in the cool, before their short drive back to the hotel.

They all retired early, as they had another early start in the morning. Isabella felt utterly drained, unable to summon the energy to even open her eyes. but whilst she lay there in the dark, she thought about what was going on with Jack. What lay ahead? Why hadn't he tried to talk to her again? Had he changed his mind or hadn't he been as serious as he first made out? Was he regretting what he said? Then again, what about Robert? She felt a sense of relief and satisfaction when Jack didn't approach her again, didn't she? Would it be obvious to the others? Thank God he hadn't mentioned the other night. She was disappointed he hadn't mentioned the other night again. Oh, how her mind was whirling.

They met whilst it was still dark in the early hours of the morning, where they were all excited and avidly expecting a balloon flight over the Masai Mara, site of the one of the largest and most spectacular animal migrations in the world. They travelled by bus to their destination, where they enjoyed a hot cup of coffee in the crisp dawn air. The crew partially inflated the balloons and then ignited the gas burners, filling the balloon with hot air, which began rising above the baskets. One at a time, they clambered into the baskets and were soon ready for take-off. Isabella, Jack, Ingrid and David were in one, and Harry, Ewan, Fiona and Madison were in the other.

The balloons lifted off just before sunrise and, once airborne, the prevailing winds blew them across the vast landscape. It ranged from grassland to woodland. Apart from the hiss of the burners, the flight was magically silent. Their faces lit up with joy as they witnessed a magnificent array of wildlife; buffalo, a herd of elephants, lions, zebras and giraffe.

They watched in astonishment at what looked like thousands of wildebeest, as they made their way to another part of the savannah, throwing up clouds of orange dust as they ran elegantly across the plains. The aeronaut controlled the height of the craft by regulating the flow of hot air into the balloon, occasionally descending over the plains for a closer view of the animals. Jack was in his element, as were they all really, and was taking many photographs of the superb view, clicking away animatedly. At one stage he paused just to stare with his naked eye at the many animals which had congregated around a nearly dry waterhole.
He then stood closely behind Isabella and she could feel his breath on the back of her neck. She longed for him to put his powerful arms around her once more, desperate for his touch.

"Beautiful, huh?" he commented.

"Spectacular," she sighed, as he moved around her and began snapping away with his camera again.

At the end of the flight, the crew treated them to a champagne breakfast, complete with flowers, china and crystal, all arranged tidily on a linen-covered table cloth, placed under a convenient acacia.

"That was amazing," exclaimed Harry.

"I agree. It was one of the best experiences of my life," replied Isabella, the others nodding in agreement.

It was hard to put into words what they'd just experienced.

***

CHAPTER ELEVEN

After they'd collected their belongs and checked out of the hotel, they piled into another mini-bus and headed to their next destination.

Isabella spent her time once again staring out of the dirty, dust-covered windows of the ancient bus. As they exited the city and its environs, she watched as the barren but glorious landscape and the extensive wilderness of Kenya pass them by. She saw a tall, regal Masai warrior leading a herd of cattle in the open grassland and wondered where he had come from. Where was he going to in the middle of no-where?

They stopped at a colourful little marketplace in a small, busy town to fill up with petrol. Small, shabbily dressed children quickly approached the bus, holding out their dirty little hands, smiling and waving at them eagerly through the windows, hoping for any small rewards they might receive. Through the window, Isabella handed a small and poorly dressed little boy her unopened litre bottle of mineral water and watched his face light up with sheer joy and wonderment.

"Asante sana," he cried as he turned around and ran off through the market square, holding up the bottle of water for all to see, shouting and laughing at his prize, whilst his friends chased excitedly after him. Isabella couldn't believe that a simple bottle of water could warrant so much pleasure. The look on the little boy's face was a glorious sight and brightened her day significantly.

A few hours into the journey via the Mombasa/Nairobi highway, along the Great Rift Valley, their driver, Samuel, a highly trained and knowledgeable safari guide, pointed out the tallest and most beautiful mountain in Africa, Kilimanjaro, capped in snow, far away in the distance. Jack and two others asked Samuel to stop the bus so they could get out and take a few photos, which he was keen to oblige before getting underway.

They arrived at their lodge in the western sector of the vast Tsavo National Park several hours later. The lodge looked wonderful and seemed more than comfortable. The staff checked them all in and directed them to their rooms. Everyone had noticed that Ewan and Fiona had now elected to share and Madison, to her gratification, found herself alone.

Isabella explored her glorious little room, furnished with pretty cane furniture and decorated with attractive jungle and floral prints. Despite its simple design, the room provided all the modern comforts. She texted Bibi back home. *Just arrived at safari base camp. All good. Miss you.*

She threw open her balcony doors and viewed the superb savannah surrounding her. Interspersed with groves of acacia, stretching for miles and miles, with large, imposing hills in the distance. Just below to her right, a water hole. No animals at present, however, a few herons, a marabou stork, pelicans and other smaller birds were drinking from the water's edge.

Directly underneath was the pale blue, inviting swimming pool, which looked tempting in the tropical sun.

Suddenly, the balcony doors next door flew open, interrupting her thoughts. She heard Jack say to her, "Amazing, isn't it?" He was leaning against his handrail, only a white towel covering his lower body. His tanned torso and hair still wet from the shower. His taut, dark skin glistening with water. Wow, yes, and that V.

"Africa?"

He regarded her sexily. "What else?"

She flicked her hair, turned and walked back into her room, closing the doors behind her, grinning to herself, not able to banish the image of him stood there, tanned, solid, muscular, dripping with water, wrapped only in a white towel. Fucking Adonis.

"There are only a few wooden slats between you and me, you know," he called after her.

"Don't even think about it," she laughed.

She read a little more of her novel and took a quick nap. Her dreams only of Jack this time. She showered and dressed for dinner. She took more care than usual in getting ready, applying her negligible make-up carefully, a little more lip-gloss than usual. Her hair looked shining with health and highlights from the sun, tumbling right down to her lower back. She changed into a short, black Herve Leger dress and a pair of black, ridiculously high Louboutin's. The finished result was phenomenal. With her honey coloured tan, she looked like a model.

As she made her way down to the bar, she bumped into Harry in the corridor.

"Madame. May I have the pleasure of escorting the most enchanting woman in the corridor to dinner?" he quipped, taking her arm and placing it in his own.

"I'd be delighted sir," she laughed back with him and they walked downstairs to the bar.

Jack and the others had already positioned themselves around a small table, and he grew furious when he looked up and saw them arriving together, arm in arm.

Madison looked delighted. Which soon changed as she heard Jack say, "Wow. Now that's what a call a statement. You look incredible, Bella. My God, you look like a supermodel, doesn't she, Harry?" he added through gritted teeth as he rose to greet her.

"You look good enough to eat," he whispered huskily into her ear, as he kissed her cheek, "God, you smell good enough to eat too," he added.

"Most definitely. Stunning." Replied Harry.

Ingrid and Fiona fussed over her shoes and dress and

Isabella returned the favour. They, too, looked sensational.

"You look like Bradley Cooper's ex," said Ingrid.

"Who's that?" asked Fiona.

"Irina Shayk."

"I don't think so," said Isabella.

"No really. You do," said Ingrid.

"Isn't she a Victoria's Secret model?" asked Ewan.

"Woo. Get you," said Fiona.

"I know my Victoria's Secret models." He said.

"Oh God, I bet you have a poster in your room," giggled Fiona.

"I'm not saying," he said, "Although, yes, I'd love to see Isabella in wings to go with those heels."

"Me too, believe me," added Jack.

"Oh, for God's sake, can we all stop drooling over *Isabella* and get something to eat?" snapped Madison, absolutely fuming. "I'm starving."

"My sentiments precisely," murmured Harry, slugging back the brown liquid in his glass.

There was a frenetic, busy atmosphere in the dining room. Noise levels were high, making conversation difficult. Throughout the entire taster menu, Isabella observed Ingrid and David being engrossed in deep conversation once again. Despite her previous thoughts, they made quite a good-looking couple. She chuckled to herself as she watched Fiona and Ewan all over each other again like a rash. At least they were oblivious to the oppressive and uncomfortable atmosphere between the rest of them. Again?

She threw back large glasses of chilled white wine to give her more courage to face the piercing, angry stares of both Jack and Madison. What the fuck was their problem? Hell, she'd only walked into the room with Harry. No one had caught her performing a blow job on him in the men's toilets.

"Blimey. We've done nothing but eat and drink ourselves rotten this holiday," said Fiona as they made their way to the indoor/outdoor lounge.

"Yes, but isn't it great?" added Ewan as he flopped down on the sofa beside her.

They'd chosen a wonderful seat around an enormous fireplace, complete with roaring fire, built entirely of volcanic rock.

Isabella plonked herself down next to Ingrid, but to her annoyance found herself directly opposite Jack, who had barely taken his savage eyes off her all night. Tosser, she thought to herself, pissed by now.

They ordered liqueurs and Jack asked the waiter if he could smoke.

"No problem," replied the waiter, so Jack lit up.

"Can I have one of those?" asked Isabella.

"You don't smoke." Shrieked Ingrid, as the others looked at her as if she'd asked if she could murder Father Christmas.

"Sure." He grinned and handed her a Marlborough.

The others watched in amazement as she smoked an entire cigarette. They also watched as she went a little green, too.

"Izzy," moaned Ingrid.

"What?" she challenged.

"Right. Let's liven up this party," said Harry. "Shall we play a game of truth or dare?" ordering a round of shots for everyone, even though they were all already quite intoxicated.

"What are we, twelve?" asked Ingrid.

The girls all grumbled and groaned.

"We'll have one turn each," he continued. "Okay, who wants to go first? Nope? No takers?"

"This is so childish, wailed Ingrid again. "You're a lawyer, for Christ's sake."

"Ok. David?" asked Harry, "Truth or dare?"

"Fuck off Harry," said David.

"Ingrid? Truth or dare?" asked Harry again.

"Dare," she challenged.

"I dare you to polish off the rest of the shots left on this table," voiced Harry.

"Call that a dare. No problem," she muttered, before picking up and downing the dregs in everyone's glasses.

"Ew," said Isabella, before they all cheered and applauded Ingrid.

"I'm gonna be sick," she slurred, wiping her mouth with the back of her hand.

"This is so infantile," remarked Madison.

"Maddy. I think it's your turn," said Ewan.

She glared at him.

"Well? Truth or dare?" he asked.

"Truth" she snapped.

"Is it true that you're the office, bitch?" he asked innocently.

Everyone stared in astonishment. His nerve.

"Screw you, you little Scottish twerp." Madison shot back.

"Ewan," hissed Fiona, whilst the others said nothing and merely stared into their glasses.

"Okay Jack, your turn mate?" intervened Harry, before things got out of hand.

"Fucking great." Jack mumbled, "Here I am. President of a multi-national corporation, playing fucking truth or dare, like I'm at a frat party." He lit another cigarette in succession and glared at them through narrowed eyes, removing a stray piece of tobacco from his tongue with his thumb and forefinger, challenging them to take it further.

They were receiving some snooty glares from the other hotel guests seated near them. They were getting obnoxious.

"Okay. Isabella my love?" said Harry.

She narrowed her eyes, trying to focus and trying to scowl.

"Truth or dare" he challenged.

"Dare," she slurred, almost incoherently.

"I dare you …" Harry started.

"To snog the person you fancy most in this room," shrieked Fiona, "And they don't have to be in our group!"

"And no bullshit." Said Ingrid, staring at her friend directly, wondering if she would dare.

Isabella looked at them all one by one. She looked around the entire room at the other guests. She was feeling exceptionally worse for wear, but simultaneously, outstandingly brave and not at all like herself. Shit. Should she go for it? What would everyone think? What would he think? She toyed with the idea for several seconds, whilst they all regarded her intently. She could see Madison's hackles rising. Fuck it. She was no longer in control of her actions and sod it. She was on holiday.

"Now," she said, rising unsteadily to her feet, "I want you all to know I'm pissed" she slurred. Would she dare? She started heading towards the bar.

"Where are you going?" asked Jack, baffled.

"Well, there's this guy at the bar ..." she smiled slyly, before turning back around and heading towards him. They were all watching her, unsure of what she was going to do next. She ambled around the table and stopped in front of Ewan, and pretended to bend down before him. She looked at him sexily, twirling her hair between her fingers.

"What the fuck?" said Ewan.

"Only joking," she said.

Jack was scrutinising her every move. She headed towards him, hitched up her already short dress and sat astride him.

The others gaped at her with open mouths.

She tossed her long hair over one shoulder and uttered, "Here goes nothing," her inhibitions shot by now and she pulled his face towards her and kissed him fully on the mouth. He groaned. She didn't stop. He groaned even more. She caressed his jaw before running her fingers gently through his hair. She felt his brawny arms clasp her upper arms and instead of pushing her away, pulled her towards him firmly. They momentarily forgot they were in company. They were being watched. The others went absolutely fucking mental.

She finally wrenched herself away from his grasp to come up for air. Regaining her composure and she returned to her seat, as if absolutely nothing had happened. She looked round and tried to gauge the others' reaction. Madison's' blood was boiling. Good. Serves her right, the stuck-up cow. The others just looked shocked. Jack stood there, mouth agape, unable to utter a single word for the first time in his God damned life.

"Well?" she challenged them all. "It was only a dare. Stop looking so fucking pious, will you?"

"I think we'd better call it a night. Everyone's had a little too much to drink," said Harry, shifting in his seat.

"Speash for yourself," slurred Isabella. "I don't wanna go to bed."

The rest all said their goodnights and started heading to their rooms.

"Come on Izzy. We've an early start in the morning and our jeep is coming at 5am," said Ingrid.

Jack remained where he was until the others had gone. "What the fuck was that?"

"What the fuck was what?" she replied innocently.

"Come on, you know exactly what I'm talking about. What was that?"

"A dare."

"It was more than a dare."

"Okay, it was a kiss," she confessed playfully.

"It was some darned kiss."

They sat in silence, oblivious to all those around them. Oh fuck. What had she done? She couldn't take it back. Fuck.

"Riish zack, I'm going shoo bed," she rose shakily.

"Come on, you." He laughed and half carried her through the reception area, whilst she groaned and mumbled incoherently all the way. He didn't let go of her. She wrapped her arms around his neck. Oh God, he felt so good.

Halfway to her room, he stopped and pushed her against the deserted corridor wall, "I apologise in advance for what I'm about to do, but oh my God Bella, you drive me crazy." And he kissed her with such force and desire, holding her, caressing her, she became unaware of her surroundings, unaware of anything but him.

Another couple walked past them, tutting their disapproval, prompting them to break free.

Her legs nearly gave way. She didn't think she could walk any further. She felt dizzy, short of breath, but it wasn't just the alcohol, it was him.

They reached her door.

"Where's your key?" he asked.

"Bag" she managed.

"Okay, come on baby," he literally picked her up and put her on the bed. He removed her shoes and her dress. He tried not to look at her tiny lace underwear.

"Jack," she hummed, "I think I love you too."

He pulled down the covers and tucked her in.

"Jack, please. I really do. I think I love you too."

"I know baby, I know," he kissed her on the forehead. "Goodnight."

"Jack don't go. Stay."

"Not a good idea, Bella. You've had way too much to drink. You do not know how much I want to stay, but not now."

"But I love you, I really do."

"Goodnight Bella."

And he left before he got himself into big trouble.

***

CHAPTER TWELVE

She woke about 2am, gagging for water. She reached for her nightstand and thankfully found a bottle of water, which she downed in one. Oh my God. My head. Oh, my God Jack. She looked down and noticed she was in just her underwear. Oh my God. What. Had. She. Done.

Jack. Oh my God. He invaded her thoughts. What was going on? What had happened? She groaned as she thought back to earlier, just a mere few hours ago. Her stomach was in knots, and she did not know what to do. Robert? Jack? Was he a fling, a holiday romance? Did she really love him? Did he really love her? Why didn't he stay? Thank God he didn't stay.

She fell back asleep and the alarm clock woke her in the middle of a deep, drink induced sleep at four thirty the following morning. It was pitch black, and she reached for the light switch.

She sat up and put her head in her hands. She felt like shit and then it all came flooding back. How on earth was she going to face them all? The shame.

She got up and took a couple of Paracetamol, showered, dressed, and made her way down to reception. Mortified. Absolutely fucking mortified.

There they were. All stood around the enclosed entrance to the lodge, mumbling to each other, waiting for the safari bus to arrive. They were all half asleep and probably all still drunk.

They saw her arrive and greeted her with varying levels of enthusiasm. What must they think of her? Madison ignored her.

Isabella couldn't bring herself to look at anyone in the eye, after what had happened the previous night and stood silently on her own.

Jack was leaning against the wall, fiddling with one of his camera lenses, dressed in crumpled shorts and another faded t-shirt, a huge camera and binoculars around his neck. She couldn't see his eyes because he was wearing a pair of Ray Bans.

When the bus finally arrived, they all climbed aboard and she found to her joy (and horror), she was sitting next to him. She didn't care what the others thought. She wanted to be near him.

"You okay?" he asked.

"I guess," she groaned, "I'm sorry about last night."

"I'm not. I kinda enjoyed myself," he smiled sexily. "Here, drink some water."

"You didn't stay?" she asked before glugging down the cold drink.

"No chance. I would not take advantage of the situation. Believe me, I wanted to though."

"Wow. Didn't peg you for a gentleman."

"There you go, you see. Although it was damned hard seeing you in your underwear. And yes, you looked like a Victoria's Secret model lying there, without your wings."

"Oh God, I dread to think. I'm mortified."

"Don't be," he said, "Although I can't get the image of your black, lacy, almost underwear out of my head."

"Stop." She pleaded, putting her head in her hands.

They drove for miles through the green and gold grassy plains, every now and again one of them squealing in delight at the innumerable sightings of the majestic wildlife.

They saw herds of impala grazing; the males standing about 3 feet high, with their long black horns distinguishing them from the females, their tails flicking back and forth, glancing round cautiously.

The landscape was adorned with majestic giraffes,

reaching up their long necks to delicately pluck leaves from the acacia trees, while nearby, herds of zebra grazed on the meagre vegetation and brush.

With their phones and cameras in hand, they snapped countless photos and filmed an array of captivating moments.

They came to a halt along the dusty track, as Samuel spied another safari bus returning from the long grass, which had taken a diversion from the main road. After a loud but brief discussion in Swahili between the two drivers, from which Isabella only picked up the word 'Simba', Samuel followed the tracks left by the other vehicle and eventually came to a rest close to a clump of trees.

"What's going on?" asked Ewan.

"Simba. Over there, you see?" asked Samuel, pointing.

"Oh my God, look!" shrieked Fiona.

They all clambered to their feet and there in the undergrowth, they watched in delight and wonderment as four little lion cubs, jumped, tumbled and rolled about on top of one another, in and around the relative safety of the trees, in the middle of the savannah.

In the distance, on a raised part of the ground, Samuel also picked out and pointed towards their mother. They could just about make out the sleek, elegant, but dangerous lioness, not too far away from her precious cubs, always watchful of her domain.

They were all incredibly excited by this unique experience, seeing and being able to get so close to these remarkable creatures, undisturbed in their natural surroundings.

After an age, they moved off as slowly as they could, trying to make as little noise and disturbance as possible to these extraordinary creatures.

"Wasn't that fantastic," said Isabella, itching her nose, "I never imagined I'd get so close to lion cubs in my life."

No-one replied. Jack just smiled.

Over the next couple of hours, they saw buffalo; a lone ostrich running strangely through the long grass; oryx gnawing away at the grass and bushes around them and adding to their joy, an incredibly rare white rhino, flanked by her calf.

They also watched an enormous lion lying sleepily in the shade of a large tree, not too far from the roadside. They were so close they could look right into his eyes. The white fur under his eyes and around his muzzle, along with his short scruffy mane, was easily visible to them. His body bore many scars and wounds, suggesting he had engaged in multiple battles throughout the years. They were all ecstatic when he opened his mouth for a slow yawn and they could make out the sheer size of his incredibly powerful jaws and enormous teeth.

As they were heading back, they were all discussing their trek through the wilderness. Ewan naively pointed out that he'd expected to see every species of animal there and then, milling around them, as they drove past, like on the TV. He hadn't realised how interminable the plains were and, in fact, they were lucky - you could drive for hours seeing nothing.

"I thought it'd be a bit David Attenborough. You know cheetahs and leopards catching and eating their prey in front of us. There was no commentary either?" he joked.

In that moment, one of them caught sight of a group of lions peacefully dozing under the shelter of the trees. Once again, they brought the bus to a halt and eagerly captured countless photos of these breath-taking, magnificent creatures. One of the larger lionesses sat up sharply, her ears perked and her tail swishing in agitation. A smaller one, seemingly intrigued, followed her every move. Then another. They stood still, like sleek statues, staring at something ahead.

"Jesus, something's happening," said Ewan.

"You might get your David Attenborough after all." Said Harry.

"No." Wailed Isabella.

"What is it? Bella, what's wrong?" Jack asked her anxiously.

"There. Look," she pointed to a young wildebeest, injured, ambling along the road ahead of them, lost from his herd, unaware of the extreme danger he was in.

"Do something," squealed Fiona.

"Shit. Look at that," said David.

Within the space of a split second, the four lionesses were off. Silently and stealthily, one moved to the right, one to the left, all in separate directions. Encircling their prey. They crouched low to the ground, their senses alert. The wildebeest picked up speed, but to no avail. He was no match for the big cats. Within only a matter of seconds, like a pack of Velociraptors, the lionesses were upon their prey, tearing at the raw, tender, young flesh. The animal was dead almost and the rest of the pride arrived seconds later to share in the feast.

"We should have saved him." Cried Isabella, as her bottom lip trembled. They all watched as the pride tucked into their banquet, their muzzles now covered in bright red blood.

"Yeah right." Said Harry.

"You gonna go out there and save him?" said Ingrid.

"They gotta eat too," offered Jack kindly, rubbing her thigh, trying to offer her some comfort, then put his arm around her shoulders.

Harry started singing *the circle of life ...* and they all started laughing.

"Dick," said Isabella, shifting in her seat.

They were all filthy from the red earth. It was in their clothes, their hair, on their face, but Isabella had never felt better. She had thoroughly enjoyed herself and felt exhilarated. It was even more enjoyable because she'd spent the whole time sat next to Jack. Touching Jack. As the jeep bounced and lurched along the unmade roads, they'd kept knocking into each other. She could feel his hard, thick, muscular legs pressing against hers, the soft, dark hairs on his legs tickling her own bare skin.

After this day together, feeling his closeness, all she knew now, at this moment, out in the wilds of Africa, was that she wanted Jack Vincent more than anyone or anything in this entire world. She didn't care what the others thought. This time belonged to them. She forgot all about Robert and knew deep within herself that things had died between them months, if not years ago. She had reached her decision.

***

CHAPTER THIRTEEN

On their return to the lodge late afternoon, just as the dazzling sun was lowering in the sky, they saw a family of warthogs dining on a patch of succulent grass and a little further on again, a group of baboons, who peered intently into their jeep as they drove at a snail's pace alongside them.

Some of them felt a tad let down because they had spotted no elephants or other species of big cats, but they reassured themselves that there was always tomorrow.

As they pulled up outside their lodgings, they were all filthy and exhausted and in desperate need of a good shower. They all said their goodbyes and started making their way to their respective rooms.

Jack and Isabella remained behind the others as they all traipsed wearily along the hallways. They didn't need to say anything to each other, but something unspoken had passed between them and they realised that they no longer wanted, or could be apart any longer. The surrounding air crackled with desire.

They climbed the stairs together, hand in hand, and eventually made it to her room. She unlocked the door, and he followed her inside. The shutters were already closed, and the room was in relative darkness, but they didn't even turn on the light. They threw their bags on the floor against the wall and he started kissing her passionately. He pushed her backwards onto the bed and fell on top of her, pulling at her clothes, while she tried to tear at his too, kissing each other hungrily all the while.

They were eventually naked, their bodies totally

entwined, their hands running lazily all over each other's bodies, exploring each other frantically. He kissed her lips, her eyes, her ears, her neck as she groaned. Then he moved down to her breasts and she could feel his tongue teasing her, biting her gently, until she could bear it no longer and grabbing his hair in her hands, moaned. "Jack, please. I can't bear it any longer. I want you now." And with that, he entered her with such urgency and longing, she felt she would burst. He continued to kiss her fervently, his body full of strength, hard, raw. He held her too tightly, all the while pushing and probing, forcing his way deeply into what felt like her very soul, biting her neck, pulling at her hair.

"God, Bella," he groaned as he ultimately came inside her.

They lay there wrapped around each other, dripping in perspiration, for what seemed like ages, just holding each other, gazing at one another, neither wanting to be the one to pull away first.

"Well," he said breathlessly, as he relaxed his grip on her, wiping away sweat from his brow, "What the hell happened there?"

"Jack" she breathed.

"Wow, man."

"God, we're both filthy," she groaned.

"Good, huh? What changed your mind?" he asked.

"Nothing changed my mind. I hadn't really decided. Something just told me I wanted you. It just felt right," she sighed.

"It felt more than alright," he said, grabbing hold of her again, pulling her towards him. Their longing gazes met again, igniting a fire that had been smouldering for hours. He traced the contours of her face with gentle fingertips, each touch sending shivers down her spine. Their lips met in a fervent embrace, a union of souls long yearning for one another. Lost in the moment, they once again surrendered to the passion that consumed them, their bodies entwined, taking things slower this time, taking the time to get to know each other's bodies more intimately, not giving in to the desperate urgency of last time. Time stood still as they became one.

Afterwards, as they dozed, they knew they had found a home in each other's arms. She felt him touching his lips gently on her forehead to wake her. "Time to wake up sleepy head," he said, reaching for a glass of water on the bedside table.

"No … I'm so tired," she wailed, but she didn't mean it. How could she sleep with *him* lying naked next to her? "But oh my God, I need a shower."

Just then, there was a knock at the door.

"Isabella? Isabella, are you in there?"

"Shh," whispered Jack, covering her mouth with his hand gently. "Say nothing. Hopefully she'll go away."

She felt awful ignoring her friend, but did as he asked and remained silent, until Ingrid must have finally left.

"Oh God, I feel terrible. She'll know I'm in here."

"Don't worry about it baby," and he started nuzzling her neck again.

"Come on, we both need a wash," she laughed, as she extracted herself from him and walked into the bathroom to fill the bath generously with hot water and bubbles.

"God, you're gorgeous," he said, as he wrapped his arms around her.

"I look like shit," she said.

"Never."

They got into the bath and lay there soaking, rinsing off the day's dust and dirt.

"Oh my God. Look at the colour of this water," she squealed. "We should have had a shower first."

"Who gives a shit? Come here, you," and he once more pulled her towards him, lifted her up and sat her astride him, penetrating her deeply once more.

"Oh … my God," she groaned.

In the darkened bathroom, the steam rising around

them, they sank into the warm embrace of the less than fragrant bath. Their eyes locked, filled with longing and desire, as they leaned in, lips meeting in a hungry kiss. The water lapped urgently against their skin as they explored each other's mouths with fervour, tongues dancing in a sensual rhythm. Hands roamed freely, tracing curves and eliciting moans of pleasure. In that moment, nothing existed beyond the two of them.

As the water turned practically cold, they took it in turns to have a shower, wrapped themselves in the hotel robes, then returned to the bedroom and sat on the bed.

"Hungry?" he asked.

"Ravenous."

He picked up the phone and ordered room service.

A bottle of champagne, 2 steaks, 2 fries, and 2 ice-creams arrived shortly afterwards, which they wolfed down, as if they'd never eaten before.

"Oh my God, that was delicious," she breathed, swiping the last of his fries, before wiping her mouth with the back of her hand.

"No, you're delicious," he grinned sexily and grabbed her once more.

"Jack. Not again," she wailed, as he made love to her once more.

Afterwards, they lay there again for hours, wrapped in each other's arms, chatting and giggling, kissing each other, touching each other, enjoying each other.

"God, you're beautiful," he moaned.

Every so often, they stopped and got up to use the bathroom, or top up their drinks or grab some snacks from the minibar. But then got straight back into each other's arms.

In the early hours of the morning, they eventually fell into a deep sleep. She lay in his arms, head on his chest, satisfied. She'd forgotten, as had he, they'd had a dinner reservation with the others that previous evening.

Her phone rang and woke them both the following morning. She reached over and swiped her screen. "Hullo," she drawled, her heart lurching at the prospect of who was on the other end.

"Hi. It's me," said Ingrid. "What happened to you and Jack last night, or need I ask?"

"Umm. Nothing. I mean. Oh, shit," she pleaded at Jack imploringly with her eyes and shrugged her shoulders as if to say, what do I say?

He merely leant over her from behind and began kissing the side of her neck and nibbling her earlobe, drifting down towards her shoulders, "Jack," she cried, trying to muffle the phone with her hand.

"Isabella. What the fuck?" said her friend down the phone.

"Look, can we talk later?" asked Isabella, as she heard her friend's sharp intake of breath at the other end.

"Tell her we're kinda tied up today," said Jack, loud enough for Ingrid to hear. "We're busy. They can go on safari without us."

"Sorry." Was all Isabella could cry, before hanging up, she turned to Jack and was just about to voice her doubts about what they'd done, what they were doing, when he kissed her hard on the mouth and before she could resist, he made love to her again, hard.

"Shit. Don't you ever give up," she wailed.

They spent the next few days in bed, dozing for a few brief hours at a time, but essentially just getting to know each other more and more, both mind and body. They talked for hours and hours on end and sometimes just lay in comfortable silence, alone with their own thoughts and fears. While she slept, he sat and watched her, feeling a love for her that surpassed any he had felt before. It was unbelievable to him how much he cared for her, and how fortunate he was that she had finally reciprocated his feelings. He was in love with her-of that; he knew.

Neither wanted to venture outside her room, leave their own safe little haven. All they wanted was to have more precious, quality time together. They existed entirely on room service and each other. They had missed the other excursions, but they didn't care.

They went outside occasionally to sit on the balcony and watched as the golden sun dipped low on the horizon, casting a warm glow over the vast expanse. They would stare for ages into the plains and the hills in the distance, pointing out wildlife to each other at the serene waterhole; herds of zebras and antelopes gathered to quench their thirst, their movements graceful against the backdrop of the African landscape. The sounds of the savannah surrounded them, the distant calls of wildlife blending with the rustle of the wind through the grasslands. With a gentle breeze caressing their skin, they watched side by side, hand in hand, simply gazing out at the breath-taking scene before them. The colours of the sky painted a masterpiece of reds, oranges and purples, reflecting off the still surface of the waterhole like a mirrored canvas. In the distance, silhouettes of acacia trees stood tall against the fading light, adding to the ethereal beauty of the moment.

One particular night, as they stood there, enveloped in the tranquillity of the wilderness, his heart swelled with a sense of awe and reverence for not just the natural world around them, but for her. In that magical setting, their love felt as timeless as the African plains stretching out before them. He hoped they had forged an eternal bond under the vast African sky.

"Wait there, two seconds," he told her.

Intending to organise a surprise, he instructed her to wait outside on the balcony. He went inside, closed the door and made a phone call indoors, in private. He re-joined her, and they watched together as a handful of animals took refreshment at the waterhole. A short time later, there was a knock door.

"More room service?" she asked, smiling at him.

"Kinda. Listen, can you wait in the bathroom, until I call you?"

"What are you up to?" she said, as he directed her patiently by the shoulders to the bathroom.

"Wait there" he ordered.

"Okay, you can come out now," he called a while later, and she returned to the bedroom dressed only in one of his large t-shirts, baggy on her. He was smiling. He told her to shut her eyes once more and took hold of her hand and led her onto the balcony.

"Open them," he exclaimed.

She gaped in astonishment at the dozens of tiny little candles placed all over the balcony. Some cushions lay on the floor atop a picnic blanket, amongst a scattering of rose petals. He told her to sit down, and she obeyed, looking in wonderment at the flickering candlelight. He went back inside and returned carrying a large silver tray upon which sat a magnum of champagne, two glasses and a dish of fresh oysters, mussels and other fresh, choice seafood and some just-baked crusty bread.

"You truly are amazing." She said before kissing him hungrily on the lips, "This is just perfect."

He poured her a glass of champagne and they lay together, enjoying the food, savouring the moment and staring out at the darkness and the million twinkling stars above, where the night unfolded like a celestial tapestry. The air was crisp and clear and as the horizon faded into a deep indigo hue, while above the heavens above shimmered with an otherworldly brilliance.

He went indoors to fetch her an extra blanket as the temperature changed, and as she sat between his legs, her back resting on his chest, he held her tightly as they regarded the clusters of stars painting intricate patterns across the sky.

He pointed out the constellations that whispered

stories of ancient myths and legends. He talked about the Milky Way, which stretched like a luminous river, weaving its way through the celestial expanse, casting a soft, ethereal glow upon them below. It was a night neither of them would ever forget.

Getting up at the crack of dawn, they sat and watched the sunrise together. The distant roar of lions echoed across the plains, mingling with the calls of birds and the rhythmic chirping of insects. There was a sense of peace, as if the entire universe had admired the beauty of the African sky. In that moment, time seemed to stand still, and the world felt infinite and full of possibility. Everything was perfect. Too perfect?

"This is heaven, don't you think?" she asked, as the beauty of the nature before her ignited her soul and filled her with a sense of wonder that transcended words.

"Absolutely. I never want to go home. I never want to leave you," he murmured, "this is my heaven. My reality."

"But it's not, is it Jack? We have to re-join the real world eventually."

"Fuck that," he groaned, "I want you all to myself."

"Jack, we can't. It's our last night tonight. We have to see the others some time."

"I'm not sharing with you anyone, least of all Harry," he added, pulling her into his arms sharply.

She sighed. It wasn't only Harry that bothered her. How was she going to face everyone? After much persuading and cajoling, he eventually returned to his room to wash and change.

His departure gave her some time to think about what had happened over the past seventy-odd hours, and now she was on her own, her mind went wild. Her thoughts turned to Robert. Back to Jack. To the others. Back to Jack. What was she doing? What had she done? Was she making a huge mistake?

After showering, she changed into a charcoal silk cheongsam with intricate embroidery and paired it with matching kid slippers. While continuing to stare at herself in the mirror, she piled her hair on top of her head and pinned it. She looked stunning. She was glowing, radiant. Her bare skin showed a tan, and her eyes had a renewed sparkle. It was *him*. She couldn't believe she was looking at the same person as a couple of days ago. How had she got herself in this predicament? There was certainly no going back now. Was there? Isabella Michaels. What the fuck have you done?

***

CHAPTER FOURTEEN

She made her way down to the bar, where the rest of their group were waiting, enjoying an apéritif. Shit, where was he? Why hadn't they at least come down together? Now she had to face them alone.

"Good evening everyone," she called, as brightly as she could muster, "So sorry to have missed out on everything over the last few day," smiling as boldly as she could. She took an empty seat amongst them.

Fiona was the first to greet her. "Great to see you Izzy. You look wonderful. Even more so than usual, if that's at all possible. And Jack? Where is he?"

"Oh, for God's sake, I think I'm going to vomit," said Madison.

Harry smiled at Isabella and walked over and gave her a big hug. "We've missed you Izzy," and he whispered into her ear, "And yes, where is Jack? I'm as envious as hell."

The others all greeted her more enthusiastically than she'd expected. David told her all about their adventures across the Shetani Lava Flow to Amboseli, as well as the animals she had missed out on during the remaining safaris near the border of Tanzania.

Jack appeared at last, cigarette in hand. He didn't give a shit about rules.

"What's up?" he called, nodding to everyone, "Bella? Drink?" he took hold of her hand, pulling her from her seat and led her towards the bar. The look on the others' faces was a picture.

"God, I missed you," and he kissed her on the lips.

Without looking, she could feel the others' eyes burning into them.

"Shit Jack, I wish you'd been here when I arrived. I didn't know what to say. I was so embarrassed. It's so obvious what we've been doing and I think if I'd have turned my back, Madison would have put a knife in it." She wailed.

"Ignore her baby. She doesn't matter. Nobody matters, okay? It's me and you."

"Okay," she replied, although not wholly convinced.

He sensed her hesitancy and added, "Look. We've done nothing wrong. We've fallen in love. You look amazing, baby," he growled sexily, drawing her towards him and nuzzling her neck.

"You've done nothing wrong, you mean? They all know I've got a boyfriend back home."

"Bella baby. That's over. History, what matters now are you and me. All the way, baby, all the way."

"Okay," she whispered, and kissed him on the cheek. "Ouch. You need a shave, Mr Vincent."

"Ya think doll face," he teased, "Now let's go eat. I'm starving," and he led her back to the others.

Despite his seemingly generous gesture earlier, Harry slouched in his chair, sulking. He was finding it hard to accept. He hardly responded to questions addressed by Isabella or Jack. Likewise, he didn't join willingly in any conversation whatsoever with the others.

Madison was openly hostile and completely ignored Isabella, not even willing to glance in her direction.

Ewan and Fiona sat huddled together in a world of their own and even David and Ingrid seemed disapproving of Isabella and Jack's behaviour. Or was that just Isabella's overactive imagination?

They were consenting adults, for God's sake. Anyway, Ingrid practically encouraged them to get together.

Only Jack seemed completed oblivious to the uneasy

atmosphere around him. He was on cloud nine. He kept telling rude jokes and making inappropriate comments whenever there was a pregnant pause and was oblivious to the fact that no one appeared to be laughing.

Isabella had never seen him more alive and animated. The frown, which she found so sexy and caused his brow to furrow, the one he'd been wearing since arrival in Africa, had disappeared.

He was incredibly tactile towards Isabella throughout the meal and kept constantly reassuring her by giving her an affectionate glance, squeezing her hand under the table and asking her if she was okay.

"You okay, baby? You're silent," he observed and gave her hand a tight squeeze.

"I just wish this was over." She sighed.

The conversation had drifted towards marriage.

"My marriage break-up was one of the worst things I've had to endure," said David wretchedly.

"At least there were no children involved," stated Harry.

"There is that, I suppose," said David, "but you don't think of that. She never wanted kids. You just find it so hard to deal with the betrayal and humiliation. I thought I'd never be able to trust anyone again."

"At least you're young enough to start again. Look at Susan and Geoff, from finance. They had two kids, been together thirty-odd years, and a woman, he ran off with his dental nurse, 20 years younger than him as well."

"It's always a younger woman," stated Fiona.

"I can't stand home-wreckers," said Madison, "or people who have no morals, people who are unfaithful come to that. I think it takes a certain person, don't you think?"

"It depends on the circumstances, I suppose," said Ewan. "Not everything's always cut and dried."

"Well, my view is what goes around comes around. Karmas a bitch. Don't you agree … Isabella? You've gone quiet. What are your thoughts on cheating?"

"Um ... I ... I ... don't know," she stammered, put on the spot.

"Funny that." Madison added snidely.

"Madison. Uncalled for" snapped Ingrid. She'd have given her a nasty look, but she already had one.

"Ignore her, honey," said Jack angrily. "Madison, I think you've had too much to drink and you've said about enough for one night."

"Me. Ha. That's rich. I have done nothing wrong."

"I'm going to bed, I need some rest" said Isabella, rising to her feet.

"Rest. Ha. You've been flat on your back for the past few days." spat Madison viciously.

"Enough." roared Jack.

Isabella glared at Madison across the table.

"Yes?" Madison screeched nastily, meeting Isabella's glare.

"If you have something more you want to say to me, Madison, just say it."

"I don't have to say anything. Go to bed. I've had enough of you and your holier than thou attitude, *miss butter wouldn't melt.* And now look. Just how many men have you slept with on this holiday? Jack? Harry? Any more?" she hissed viciously, looking around the room.

"How dare you?" gasped Isabella. "You don't know what you're talking about."

"Oh, is that so? Isn't it simply a case of whilst the cats away ... and boy, have you played?"

"Madison. I said enough," snarled Jack through gritted teeth.

No one else said a word. Not a fucking word.

"Well? Is this what you all think?" whispered Isabella, tears welling in her eyes. But before anyone could answer, she added, "Well, you know what? I couldn't give a flying fuck. And as for you, you fucking bitch, you can go to hell," and she threw the rest of her white wine straight in Madison's stupid, puce, face, turned on her heels and marched away.

"Bella," she heard Jack call after her. The others stared after her in astonishment, open-mouthed.

She ran as fast as she could. As she was nearing her room, she heard Jack running to catch up with her, calling her name.

"Bella. Wait. Slow down."

"Wait? Are you insane?"

"Ignore her. She's jealous as fuck."

"Jack. No one stuck up for me. No one said a word. They're all thinking what she's thinking. They all think I'm a whore."

"Don't talk shit."

"Don't tell me I'm talking shit, you arsehole. This is your fucking fault. God knows what they're saying about me now. Just go away. Leave me alone."

"Shit Bella. Screw them."

"Don't you think you've caused enough trouble already by screwing me?" she hollered. As soon as she uttered the words, she wished she could take them straight back when she saw the pained expression in his eyes.

"Goddamn it. It wasn't entirely one sided, you know. You didn't make any complaints. What the hell have *I* done? Why're you taking this out on me? I'm on your side, remember?" he was shouting at her now.

"Just leave me alone." She cried.

"It was my belief that we had a clear understanding. I thought something had happened here. I've spent the best few days of my life and I leave you alone for a couple of hours and what the hell's changed?" he was yelling at the top of his voice, holding her arms in a vice like grip, "I just can't figure you? What's going on in that damned head of yours?"

"Look Jack, I need to be alone?"

"Oh, don't start with the *Bette Fucking Davis* crap."

"Don't be sarcastic. I need space. I need to think about what the hell I'm going to do. With this holiday. With the rest of my life. Now please, just go."

"Space. Goddamn it. Here we fucking go again. Are all British women as frustrating as you?" he yelled.

"Thankfully not. Now goodnight," and she rapidly opened her door, slammed it and disappeared inside before he could reach her, hoping that was the end.

But it wasn't. She heard him slam his fist against the door violently. "Shit. I'll never fucking understand you" and then, gratifyingly, he turned and walked away.

She spent a restless and resentful night alone. Resentful towards other people. Resentful towards the situation. She lay awake, tossing and turning, mulling over what she was going to do and her options. God, what must the others think of her? How could she ever face them again? She had lots of decisions to make, but now she did not know what she was going to do. What line she wanted to follow? Should she just enjoy this unique, new, passionate relationship with Jack, whilst on holiday, and screw what the others thought of her? Then return home and end things with Robert. Perhaps start afresh with Jack. But there was so much to consider? Where would they live? Would he stay in the UK or would she have to move to the US? What about her business?

It was far too early to contemplate decisions like this, but how would it work with a vast ocean between them? Should they take things one day at a time? What about his stubborn, futile views on raising a family? She wanted children. He didn't. These were all things that needed discussing, but it was far too early in "not even a relationship" to do so. Or should she just forget all about Jack Bloody Vincent, once and for all? The questions circled round and round in her head. All. Night. Long. She would just make a choice, and then would change her mind thereafter.

Thank God they were returning to Mombasa later that morning. She wanted to get out of this place, this place that held so many fond, and terrible, memories. This place that made her want to fling open her door, run along the corridor and into his arms. But she couldn't do it.

After having had little or no sleep, she wearily rose out of the crumpled sheets, showered and changed, and then finally packed her bag, ready to leave. She whispered a silent goodbye to the room where they had spent so much time wrapped in each other's arms.

Waiting for their bus to arrive, she wandered down to reception to check out and meet the others. She merely glanced at Madison. She mumbled vague apologies to no one in particular, then went over and stood with Harry, who at least looked pleased to see her, his bad mood having vanished.

"You okay?" he asked. She just shrugged her shoulders in response.

Jack looked furious. To her relief, the bus arrived before he could come over and talk to her. She handed the driver her small piece of luggage and boarded speedily. She sat down next to Ingrid, with Harry and David behind them.

Jack walked past her, looking extremely hurt, incensed, and exceedingly hungover. His hair was a mess, he was still unshaven, and he was wearing the same clothes he had on the previous night. He didn't even so much as glance in her direction, but merely stormed to the back of the bus and threw his bag on the seat, appalled that she hadn't even the courtesy to come over and talk to him, to give him any kind of explanation or reassurance whatsoever. He reached into his bag and pulled out a half empty bottle of Jack Daniels and lit up.

"Bit early isn't it, Jack?" enquired Harry, "and the sign says no smoking?"

"What are you? My fucking father?" he growled in response.

"I'm just saying …"

"Fuck. Off. Harry."

"There's no need to act like a prick, Jack."

"Harry. I'm warning you. One more word," he snarled malevolently and finished the rest of his alcohol in one large mouthful. He sat there for the entire journey, leaning against the window, fast asleep.

Ingrid and Isabella spent the long, uncomfortable journey locked in inaudible conversation, initially avoiding the topic of what had occurred over the past few days, in case of being overheard by the others, but then eventually they talked about it quietly, between themselves.

"Ingy, what have I done?" whispered Isabella, wiping tears from her eyes.

"I don't know. But you both look bloody miserable," commented Ingrid.

"It's such a mess. Don't you see? What do I say to Robert? I've never cheated on anyone in my life. How do I get myself out of his mess?"

"Well, it's bloody obvious if you ask me," said Ingrid. "Go home. Dump him and marry that gorgeous, tortured, but pissed, comatose man behind you. Simple."

"It's not that simple, Ingrid."

"Izzy, the guy's in love with you."

"So he says. I hardly know him. I've been with Robert for years. What will he say? I can't just go home, unpack, and casually mention, oh, by the way, I've been seeing the most attractive guy on the planet. Do you mind leaving?"

"Izzy, Robert's a prat. He's never deserved you. The guy behind you? He absolutely adores you. He'd never hurt you. Unlike Robert."

"What are you saying Ingy, spit it out?"

"Well, are you sure you want to hear this?"

"What?"

"Well, you remember last year at Ladies' Day?"

"Yes."

"He tried it on with me."

"Robert?"

"Yes. Robert."

"Really," she gasped, shocked, "Why didn't you tell me before now?"

"Oh, wake up and smell the coffee, Izzy. The guy treats you like shit. You're the only one who can't, or won't, see that. If he tried it on with me, someone he doesn't even really like, how many others have there been? He's probably hit on every one of your female friends. I've heard through the grapevine it's happened before. I hate doing this to you and I wouldn't have told you in other circumstances, but the guy is an arsehole. Every party he's been to. If it hasn't been me, it's been someone else he's drooling all over. And what about all the time he spends away? What do you think he's getting up to?"

"Don't be ridiculous. Don't turn all this around on Rob. It's me that has been unfaithful here, not him. It's me."

"Come on Izzy. There's nothing to think about. It's over with Robert. As for Jack, that's your decision, but Robert, a simple decision."

And she thought about it. She thought about nothing else for the rest of the journey, digesting all this new information.

"Oh, Izzy, by the way?" said Ingrid.

"Yes?"

"Fucking great shot with the wine."

"Don't," groaned Isabella, turning red as the heat rose in her cheeks. She turned around to glance at Jack, in a sound sleep, despite the side of his head jolting back and forth against the window as the bus lurched along. She could practically smell the alcohol fumes from here.

***

CHAPTER FIFTEEN

When they finally arrived back at their hotel in Mombasa, it was dark and there was a slight chill in the air. They all returned solemnly to their rooms, Isabella and Jack not even so much as acknowledging each other. He was still infuriated with her and was very hungover.

Within a few minutes of returning to her room, before she even had time to unpack her bag, she heard someone knocking determinedly at her door.

"Yes?" she breathed, knowing instinctively who it was.

"It's me. Let me in. We need to talk," he said with more than a faint hint of menace in his voice.

"Can't you leave me alone for two minutes?" she replied, trying to sound annoyed, but sounding unconvincing.

"Let me in now, Bella, or I'll break the goddamned door down."

Not wanting to cause a further scene and not doubting he meant it, she unlocked the door and let him in. He looked appalling. He followed her through to the bedroom and took hold of her shoulders and pleaded with her, "What the hell's happened? Why have you been ignoring me? I'm going insane here. Is it because of what Madison said to you?"

"Jack please, I just need a little time."

"For God's sake, what for?" he implored. "I've given you all the time you need. And who gives a fuck what she said to you?"

"Look. Now's not a good time," she whispered, trying to keep her cool.

"Not a good time," he bellowed, "Are you fucking

serious."

"You're still drunk."

"I've never known a woman to play as many games as you. You're driving me mad."

"I'm not playing games," she stated rationally.

"So, what the hell's going on?"

"She's right. They're right. I've got a boyfriend back home. Before we can go any further, I have to sort things out with him. And also, the others are all treating me as if I'm some kind of slut. I feel like I'm on a roller coaster, which is totally out of control. I need time to think. Sort things out."

"Don't start all this crap again. There's nothing to think about, okay?" he said, cupping her face with his hands. She shrugged him away from her. "Not that it's any of their fucking business anyway," he continued, "But if you want, we can explain to the others that we've fallen in love and then we carry on with what's left of our vacation. We go home. You sort your shit out. It's easy."

"Jack, you really do not know, do you? It's easy for you to say, it's not your life that has been turned upside down. Please, I'm begging you. I need to get my head around all of this. I need to think about what I want and what I'm going to do. Please, just give me some space. It's all just so complicated."

"Shit man. What kind of space do you need? I love you and I'm sure you feel the same. Do those few days mean nothing to you?"

She remained silent.

"Bella?"

She still said nothing.

"I leave you alone for a few hours and you come up with all these ridiculous thoughts and excuses. I should never have left your side. You felt something for me, right?"

"Look, I don't know how I feel," she lied. "Just back off. I need some time, that's all. I'll talk to you later."

"Right. Your call. I'm going. I'm obviously not getting anywhere here and I'm sick of your fucking mind games. You know where I am if you need me. I plan on enjoying the rest of my vacation," and he stormed out, slamming the door behind him, looking pained and furious.

She spent that evening, and the best part of the following day, holed up in her room. Although she didn't have an appetite, she persisted in ordering bottles of cold water until she ran out. She texted Ingrid to make feeble excuses and to say she was unwell (again).

She wouldn't answer the door to Jack either when he knocked and called her name twice.

She still hadn't heard from Robert, despite leaving several brief messages and texts. Although she'd been away from Jack now for nearly a couple of days, she still felt confused about the situation. It was him and him alone that occupied all of her waking thoughts and even when she fell into a light, disturbed sleep, she dreamed about him constantly. She had missed him desperately, but knew she had to decide before she saw him again. God, it would be so easy to just run along to his room and pick up where they had left off, but even that seemed like years ago and she didn't want to confuse matters further.

Why had she put herself in this situation? Especially with a man she had disliked until recently. They had only spent a few hours together. Was it worth giving up everything she knew, just for that? A man she fought and loved with equal intensity. She knew nothing about him. Could she even trust him?

Later that evening, no further forward with her thinking, she dressed casually and made her way down to the quieter bar beside the pool and order herself a rum and coke. She had eventually calmed down a lot and had reached the conclusion that she should talk this through with him, at least. She owed him that. Perhaps a little reassurance from him would make the world of difference. It couldn't make things any worse. She only hoped he had simmered down a bit.

As she sat there fidgeting with her fingernails, perched

on a stool, sipping her drink, she groaned inwardly as she saw Madison approaching. She was the last person on earth she wanted to see. She was now regretting leaving the confines of her room. Oh God, spare me the pleasure of her company.

"Ahh, the ubiquitous Isabella," Madison nodded scornfully, "Feeling better, I hope?"

"Can I get you a drink?" asked Isabella. Let's try to not make things any worse, she thought to herself.

"A dry martini," she asked the barman and sat down on the empty stool next to Isabella. "Nothing too wrong, I hope?"

"I'm fine now thanks and Maddy, I'm sorry about the other night. I should never have done that."

"Apology accepted."

Isabella waited for the same from her, but it didn't come. They sat in uncomfortable silence for a few minutes before Madison said, "You've missed a fun few days. Volleyball. Swimming. Dancing. Such fun."

"Sounds good."

"We did karaoke again last night, and we had a blast. I cajoled Jack into singing a duet with me."

"Oh, yes?" she groaned.

"He has got a marvellous voice, hasn't he? Talking of Jack, you haven't been trying to avoid him, have you?"

She tried to think of something to say in response, something that didn't sound ridiculous and futile. But it had upset her that Jack could carry on singing, dancing *enjoying the rest of his vacation* as he'd said, whilst she had been thoroughly miserable and lying dejectedly in her room.

"Of course, I haven't been trying to avoid him." She lied.

"Okay, I believe you. But do you mind if I give you a brief word of advice?" her tone brimming with malice.

"Well, it depends on what or whom you're going to advise me about?"

"Look, just don't get yourself too worked up about Jack. That's all I'm saying. He isn't worth the heartache."

"Oh. You would know I suppose?" she snapped, feeling

quite sick suddenly, sick of Madison, sick of her absurd innuendoes.

"Of course I'd know. I wonder how many times he has done it to me. How many times have I just had to accept, that Jack just isn't boyfriend material? How do you think I felt, knowing he'd moved on to you in Nairobi? I guess that makes you sloppy seconds?" she said maliciously with her intrusive, accusing eyes.

"What? What are you saying?" she gasped. Surely not.

"Izzy darling, who do you think he was sleeping with at the beginning of the holiday? In London before that too. He doesn't enjoy being alone, you know? A man that looks like that, Isabella, can have his pick of the ladies."

"You can't be serious?" she gulped.

"Isabella, wake up, darling. The delectable Mr Vincent has quite a reputation with the ladies. Surely you knew that? All the girls in the office are certainly aware," she said hysterically. "What did you think? He was celibate until you? Come on, you're surely not that naïve?"

"No." Isabella inhaled.

"So, as I say, don't be upset about him. He's not worth it. Yes, he's marvellous in bed and that body ... his hands. Well, we both know now, don't we? He knows exactly the right buttons to press, but ..."

"I don't want to hear any more." She said, absolutely sick to her stomach, a tightness in her chest. She was trying to stop herself from crying, from screaming, from punching Madison hard in the face.

"Isabella darling. You haven't fallen for him, have you? Just last night, when we were having a little chat, I was saying to him ... Isabella? Are you alright? Where are you going? You haven't finished your drink?" she shouted after her, as Isabella ran off sobbing, stumbling blindly towards her room, her legs weak, where she opened the door and vomited into the toilet.

What a bastard. How could he? What had she done? Jack and Madison? Ugh. The thought made her sick again.

Two women in the space of a few days. No wonder Madison had been so pissed off with her. How could she have been so gullible? Of course, she'd even seen it with her own two eyes, Madison and Jack sneaking into his room. Revolting. What an absolute idiot she'd been.

She kicked off her shoes and flopped onto her bed, sobs racking her whole body for hours and hours as she stared up at the ceiling, still not truly believing that everything that had happened was real. When her phone rang and rang, she ignored it and eventually, in the early hours, the tears stopped and a deep, vengeful loathing of Jack Bloody Vincent consumed her. Deep down, she'd known all along it had been too good to be true. Thank God she had found out now, before things had gone any further, before any further damage could occur. She knew what she had to do. She took out her phone and booked herself the next flight to Heathrow. She would have to hurry as there wasn't long to pack, get a taxi there and check in.

She made it in time. She texted Ingrid whilst at the boarding gate. *"Something urgent came up at home. Have had to return immediately. Sorry, no time to explain. Izzy."* She was on her way home.

***

CHAPTER SIXTEEN

After a long, torturous flight, she arrived safely home the following day, grateful to find the house empty. She had been dreading Rob being home.

As she wandered through the house, she couldn't help but notice how impeccably clean and organised everything was. It was a relief to know that someone had taken care of it while she was away.

She emptied her luggage, sorted out her dirty washing and a pile for dry cleaning, and stored her suitcase in the spare room.

She went back downstairs and began leafing through her pile of mail left on the kitchen bench. She binned the enormous pile of junk mail; the rest was pretty mundane stuff. She wondered if Bibi had done that, as well as cleaned and tidied the house? It didn't look like Robert had been home in the last couple of weeks at all.

She put the kettle on and made herself a cup of black coffee, trudged back upstairs to her bedroom, and then fell onto the bed, feeling as if her heart had shattered. Her guilt and embarrassment were off the scale.

Several hours later, her phone rang and woke her up, with a call from an unrecognised number. They left a message, which she played back,

"Bella? Bella? Are you there, baby? Pick up. For God's sake, call me back. What's happened? Please talk to me, baby. Reply to my texts, okay? Let me know you're ok?"

When she looked, there were dozens of texts from him as well.

"Screw you, you bastard!" she screamed into the air and threw her phone across the room, sending it crashing to the floor. Shit, she thought to herself, I hope I haven't broken it. Making her way to it, she bent down and retrieved it. She turned it over to check it was okay and then blocked his number. She never wanted to hear from, or lay eyes on him again.

Bibi turned up the following morning to collect the mail and water the plants. She walked through into the kitchen and screamed when she saw Isabella sitting there, looking absolutely ravaged. She had never seen her friend looking so frail and wretched, "Isabella. You're home."

"Surprise." Isabella said dryly, before bursting into tears.

"Darling, whatever's the matter?" she asked, concern etched on her face, coming over to give her friend a big hug. "Let me make us a cup of tea and you can tell me what's going on."

Whilst waiting for Isabella's hiccups to stop and whilst enjoying a lovely cup of a tea, Isabella gave her friend some context. She was relieved to get it all off her chest. Relieved to have her best friend to talk to. Relieved to find some comfort– someone she could confide in completely and someone who would not judge her, no matter what had happened.

"Phew, Izzy, what a mess." Bibi exhaled strongly through her lips, "What a player."

"Tell me about it."

"What does this Jack say about it?" asked Bibi, frowning.

"Nothing. I haven't spoken to him," she said.

"Izzy. Talk to him, get his side of the story. Get an explanation from him about why he treated you so badly."

"I don't want to talk to him. Ever. Again."

"This Madison sounds like a nasty piece of work. Maybe you shouldn't believe everything she says, though?"

"Bibi, I saw them with my own two eyes." She thought of them walking along the corridor, like a couple of children, giggling, disappearing into his room, and felt sick again.

"What are you going to do about Rob?"

"I don't know yet. I don't know what I'm going to say."

"Well, I can't make that decision for you, but does he need to know? Maybe you shouldn't say anything - just act as if nothing has happened. Go back to normal."

"No. That chapter's definitely over. Where is he, anyway?"

"No idea. Haven't seen him at all."

Bibi stayed all day, and they talked, and with the comfort of her friend, Isabella felt much better. Bibi only left when Isabella reassured her she would be fine and was going to take a long hot bath.

"Promise you'll call me if you need anything?" Bibi asked.

"I promise. Now go. Thanks for everything, Bibi. I don't know what I'd do without you, really."

Robert did eventually return home later that evening and gave her a less than tepid welcome. He feigned curiosity about her holiday, but wasn't interested. He didn't explain where he had been for the past two weeks, and neither did he explain why he hadn't called or texted. The time difference didn't cut it, in her opinion.

She heated him up the casserole she'd made earlier, and sat watching TV whilst he remained on his phone.

"So," he said eventually, setting down his phone, "You had fun then? You've a great tan."

"Yeah, it was great, thanks. The safari was brilliant. You would have loved it."

"I didn't think you were home for a couple of days?"

"Really. Oh."

The house phone rang, interrupting them.

"I'll get it," she said, jumping from her seat.

"No, stay still, it's here, I'll get it. Hello? Hello?"

"Who was it?"

"No one, wrong number. Sales call?"

"Anyway, back to your holiday. I'm sure they were all great fun," he mocked. "Any sex?"

"What do you mean?" she gasped, gulping in a deep breath, her face draining of all colour.

"Ingrid? That other tosser, Harry?"

"No, not as far as I know. The young couple, Fiona and Ewan, paired off, I suppose. You don't know them, though. Ingrid mentioned something about her and David, but I don't know if anything will come of it. Right, I'm turning in."

"It's good to have you home. Place was empty without you, that's why I stayed up in the company flat most of the time."

"It's good to be home. Robert."

"Yes?"

"Nothing. It can wait." Now wasn't the time to have a deep and meaningful.

It was the same all weekend. Polite conversation. He did not talk to her, really, or touch her. They were civil, but that was it.

Throughout the weekend, she received countless texts from Jack, from Ingrid's phone, from Harry's. She deleted them all.

They both returned to work on Monday. He left early for Birmingham, before she'd even woken up, in fact. He merely left her a note on the kitchen worktop, letting her know he'd be away all week.

She showered, made herself a light breakfast, drank several cups of black coffee, and headed into work. Pleased to be getting back to normality. Pleased to have a distraction from the events of the preceding weeks.

As she got in her car, the sun was shining, the radio blaring, so she pressed a button and the roof of her Mercedes elegantly folded away into the boot. She drove through the village and headed towards the M25 and the M3. The traffic was exceptionally light for a Monday morning, but as she left the main road and turned right, near Earl's Court, she found herself in a queue, bumper to bumper, all the way to her showroom, which she eventually reached just after 8.15. This was a relatively late start for her. If she was project managing a job on-site, she liked to be much earlier.

Having parked in her designated space, she walked across the road. She put her key in the door, but it was already unlocked. She loved entering her own elegant and inviting design studio and showroom, where customers wandered through each section, artfully arranged, to inspire and captivate; perhaps perusing the latest in fabrics and wallcoverings from top design houses, Osborne & Little, Zoffany, Christian Lacroix and Mulberry. She loved all the different accessories on offer, from sumptuous velvet sofas, handcrafted statement lighting, glassware and wall hangings to small, exquisite decorative pieces and ceramics, sourced from renowned artisans and luxury brands around the globe. Every piece exuding an air of refinement and sophistication.

"Isabella, welcome back," said Elizabeth, her store manager, already looking busy behind her desk, reading through her emails.

"Hi Elizabeth. It's good to be back. I've missed you all and this place. Ok, can we have a staff meeting when everyone arrives and you can all fill me in?"

"Perfect. I scheduled nothing in your diary today or anyone else's, so we could do just that. A couple of exciting prospects to go through, including a boutique hotel in Mayfair, just up our street."

"Sounds good. Oh, before I forget, this is for you," she said, handing her ever-faithful assistant a box of her favourite perfume.

"Isabella, wow, thank you. You shouldn't have."

"Yes, I should. You deserve it. I don't know what I'd do without you."

Isabella trusted Elizabeth Llewellyn, her "right-hand woman" of the past 2 years, to handle her business competently and with the same dedication as Isabella herself. She was 8 years older than Isabella and the two women got on well, both in a professional and a personal capacity. Although what had happened over the past two weeks was far too personal to divulge. Oh, the humiliation.

Isabella recruited Elizabeth when she opened her studio a couple of years ago. Effortlessly, she slipped right into the role and was truly delightful. She lived in Clapham, so the location was ideal for her daily travel to work. She not only managed the day to day running of the showroom and store, liaising with suppliers and buyers, as well as the accounts, but managed the designers' diaries to perfection.

As MD and principal designer, Isabella ran a fairly small, but successful, business. Her company could facilitate any design project from advice on a single room to an entire remodel and full-scale renovation. The newly enlisted and well qualified designers were also a great asset to her business and, on hand, to provide expert advice and personalised recommendations. They frequently organised workshops, design seminars, and special events at the store.

A typical workday for Isabella could include meeting with the client, usually visiting the property initially to provide a free consultation and providing examples of recent projects from both her own and her team's portfolio. They discussed colours, furniture, artwork and exchanged ideas of how best to achieve the required results, all within the required budget. Then, Isabella produced a visualisation on their in-house software, ready for presentation to the client. She had a keen eye for interpreting the client's ideas and could provide a pretty accurate analysis of their requirements and could visualise and convey her ideas, making adaptations as required. Finally, if the job was a go, she would produce a finished plan, providing full details as regards furniture, lighting, flooring, soft furnishings, all meticulously and selected to achieve the perfect look. She loved wandering round art galleries, stately homes, museums and exhibitions to glean ideas and inspiration. Her team now offered a small, but highly skilled, professional and dedicated team of specialists. They all had great flair and could see each project through the various states of the design process, ensuring they followed the concept through to completion and detail. The finished results rarely left her clients disappointed.

After chatting with Elizabeth for several minutes, she walked upstairs and opened the door to her large office, which was as beautifully decorated as her own home and she loved working on her designs from here. The atmosphere was understated luxury and impeccable taste. Soft instrumental music usually filled the air, creating a tranquil backdrop and the expansive windows adorned with chic displays offered a tantalising glimpse into the world of luxury interior design.

She dropped her bag next to her large Queen Anne desk and removed her jacket and hung it on the coat hanger in the far corner. She sat down in her black leather Eames armchair and started sifting through her emails and leafing through the many files and messages left on her desk. As usual, Elizabeth had sorted them so the most important were at the top, and after an initial glance, she could see there was nobody who needed contacting. Everything had continued smoothly in her absence. Thank God. The last thing she needed was a catastrophe here as well.

She buzzed Elizabeth and asked her to gather the troops for a catch up, which ended up taking up most of the morning. They went through some proposals, scheduled appointments, booked appointments for two of their designers to attend a training course, confirmed a booking for a stand at the Chelsea Crafts Fair and they proof read an article on herself and the business to appear in an upcoming interiors magazine.

"Thanks everyone, that was great. Well done for keeping everything going whilst I was away. Now let's get back to work."

Everyone returned to their stations, and Elizabeth left

her with a fresh mug of coffee.

A short time later Elizabeth buzzed her, "I've a Jack Vincent on the phone. Says it's urgent?"

"Tell him I'm busy. If he calls again, I'm out," she stated.

"Shall I ask one of the other designers to deal with it?"

"No. It's personal. Elizabeth, I do not want to speak to him. At all okay?"

"No problem."

Shit. He was calling her office now.

She tried to forget about him and threw herself back whole-heartedly into work. The end of the day swiftly approached and Isabella felt shattered by 6pm.

"I'm heading home, Elizabeth. You nearly finished for the day?"

"Yep, just a couple of emails left. I also want to finish this proposal, then I'm done."

"Thanks, you're a star. Now don't stay too long, okay?"

"By the way, he called you over a dozen times."

"Who?" she said sharply, knowing damn well who.

"Mr Vincent. American."

"I see. Well, don't worry about it. Night Elizabeth."

"Night Isabella. Good to have you back."

Over the course of the following week, she threw herself into work. However, her heartache was taking its time to recede, especially whenever she thought of Jack. Being back at work gave her something else to concentrate on though, but it didn't help that he called multiple times a day by the time the first week was through. Her anxiety was off the charts. Luckily, Elizabeth fended them all, so Isabella didn't have to respond to them and thankfully Elizabeth didn't push her about who he was or what he wanted. However, she wasn't naïve and must have grasped some idea of what was going on. She'd also missed, and not replied to, lots of texts and calls from Ingrid.

On the Friday night, she was still in the office about 7pm. Elizabeth was just leaving when Isabella heard her talking in hushed but firm tones to someone downstairs. She heard raised voices, then two pairs of footsteps running up the stairs.

"Isabella? You in here?"

Shit.

"Mr Vincent. Look, I've told you already, you can't come in here." Elizabeth stressed, compounded now by anxiety.

Isabella's door burst open.

Jack stood in front of her, glaring at her. Anguished.

"Isabella, I'm sorry. I tried to stop him," implored Elizabeth.

"Isabella. I need to see you," he begged.

"It's okay Elizabeth, you go," said Isabella.

"I'm not leaving you. With *him*."

"Really, Elizabeth. It's fine. Go home. I'll see you on Monday."

"Well, if you're sure," she looked blatantly hostile towards Jack.

"I'll be fine," said Isabella, rubbing her forehead.

Neither of them uttered a word until Elizabeth left the building and they heard the main door close. They merely glowered at each other furiously, smouldering like a volcano about to erupt.

"What the hell are you playing at?" she snapped after what seemed like an age.

"What am I playing at? What the hell are you playing at?"

He looked so tanned, so ruggedly handsome. Stop it Isabella. "How dare you?" she shouted.

"You wouldn't return any of my calls. You're not speaking to Ingrid. Anyone. What was I meant to do? I had no choice."

"So, you just turn up and make a scene? I'm sorry, I didn't realise the world revolved around you. My mistake."

"Quit it with the attitude, Bella."

"What if the rest of my staff were here? Customers?"

"At seven o'clock at night?"

"Don't be funny Jack. What do you want?"

"What do I want? Are you fucking serious?" he roared, half hysterical.

"I've never been more serious," she deadpanned.

"Bella. What the hell's going on? What are you playing at? My God. How many times have I asked these same darned questions?"

"What are you talking about, Jack? What do you want from me?" she asked in her most icy tone of voice.

"You know damned well what I'm talking about. No explanation. Just run the fuck away."

"A death in the family," she said.

"Yeah? Who?"

"None of your bloody business."

"I've been worried sick. We all have."

"Madison included?"

"Madison? What's she got to do with this? Look, we need to talk. I'm out of my mind. I'm only in London for a few more days. We have to sort this mess out before I leave."

"What mess?"

"Isabella. Stop playing with me," he howled, "Have you sorted things out your end?"

"Sorted things out, my end. Like what?"

"You know exactly what I'm talking about. Have you finished things with the jerk?"

"The only jerk here, Jack, is you?"

"Bella, baby, please? I don't wanna keep dancing round the issue, do you? I've missed you," he added.

"Before you continue, I only have this to say. You are nothing to me. Nothing. You never were. It was a holiday fling, fuelled by way too much alcohol. Nothing more," she stressed.

"What the actual fuck?" His face revealed the look of someone who had experienced a punch in the guts.

"You tried too hard to impress me and it's backfired. Unfortunately, I've seen through your pretence and have seen your true colours."

"What the hell are you talking about?"

"I mean it. I've told Robert everything and thankfully, he forgives me. He's giving me a second chance. In fact, we're getting married," she lied. "I never want to hear from you or see you again. Do you understand?"

"Isabella." He bellowed, half laughing at her.

"Do you understand?" she roared.

"Baby, we'll never find something like this again."

"Thank fuck for that."

"You can't be serious."

"I've never been more serious about anything in my life. Now leave me alone. Get out of my office. Get out of my life. You were a mistake. The huge, gigantic, fucking Godzilla of all mistakes." She hissed.

"You don't mean this, Isabella ..." he whispered, pale suddenly.

"And if I'm honest, you never did it for me, anyway."

"What are you talking about?"

"You heard me. If truth be told, I would have preferred Harry. But I ended up with you — sloppy seconds, isn't it? Now get the fuck out of my space."

"Do you hear yourself? Are you genuinely convinced of what you're saying? Do you mean we just forget everything and go our own ways? I don't believe you. You're lying. After everything we had, we said."

She could almost feel his anguish, his physical pain. She could hear the heartbreak in his voice. It nearly tore her apart, but that's what had to be done. She had to protect herself.

"Do I make myself clear?" she added finally.

He didn't respond.

"Do I make myself clear?" she said even louder.

"If you're sure that's what you want," he whispered hoarsely, as if someone had extinguished a flicker of light within him, causing his eyes to lack their usual spark. Despite all attempts to hide his emotions, his facial expression betrayed his inner turmoil, revealing a profound sense of loss and longing.

"Goodbye Jack."

She waited until he too left, his movements slow and listless, lacking the energy and vitality he once possessed, then sobbed uncontrollably into her hands.

***

CHAPTER SEVENTEEN

After life had settled back to normal over the forthcoming weeks and the pain subsided, she had two things left to do. The first was to call Ingrid. She was dreading it. What must she think of her, blanking her for weeks? The second was to have *the chat* with Robert.

"Ingrid, it's me."

"Isabella. Thank God. Are you okay? You know we've all been trying to reach you? Why have you been ignoring us, me?"

"My apologies. Apologies for not getting back to you earlier and for not explaining my sudden departure, but an unexpected situation arose here. Unfortunately, there was no time for goodbyes when I had to return to the UK."

"Everyone's okay though? God, I thought someone had died? I'm sure you said that someone died?"

"No. It's fine. Just an old family friend, thankfully nothing too serious," she felt horrendous for spinning such a web of lies, but it was easier.

"Oh, thank goodness. Oh, I didn't mean it like that, sorry. I hope they're okay? I just mean, I thought it was the whole Madison thing. The Jack thing. It was pretty dramatic and awkward."

"No, it's fine."

Ingrid let it go. She didn't push it.

"You know Jack has been going out of his mind? Frantic. He's been calling me all the time, wanting to know what's happened. He even threatened to ambush you at home, but I wouldn't give him your address."

"He ambushed me at work."

"Oh, God."

"Yep. That's all over now, thankfully. I told him I made a terrible mistake."

"Did you though?"

"Absolutely. It was a blip. A moment of madness. A brief holiday romance," she said coldly, "If he calls you, you must stress this. Tell him I'm utterly ashamed and appalled at what I've done. You must stress I never want to see him again as long as I live and Ingrid. Tell him I'm back and more in love with Rob than ever."

"Is that the truth?"

"It's the truth," she fibbed, yet again. "I don't want him turning up anywhere else. I want no more of this nonsense, okay?"

"Okay Izzy, but I hope you've thought about this?"

"Of course, I've bloody thought about this. Look, I never want his name mentioned again. Is that clear?"

"All right, all right, calm down. I just hope you know what you're doing, that's all? He seemed pretty smitten Iz."

"I know what I'm doing. Now enough of this crap, how about you?" and they began chatting about anything and everything except Jack Bloody Vincent. Task one completed.

Task two happened a few weeks later. She arrived home, hung up her jacket, and took off her shoes. Robert was on the Mac, flicking through her photos.

"Hey you. You never showed me these?" he said as she walked over to him, feeling sick. The last thing she wanted to do was go through photos and see *his* smiling, handsome face and then remember the anguish in his voice during that last fateful heart-wrenching night in her office. She had been doing well at blanking the whole thing. Memories, both good and bad, came flooding back.

"Really? Well, I suppose you're never here, Rob? Bit difficult, if you're not here?"

"Who's this then? Harry?" he asked, ignoring her barbed comment.

"Yep."

"Didn't recognise him. Wow, he's aging well," he said, looking at Harry, gorgeous and tanned, "Great photos."

"This one?" he asked, pointing to David. She went through them all, showing him who was whom.

"Good looking bunch."

"Hmmm," she mumbled. She didn't want to do this.

"Look at him here?" he said, before adding "Harry? You're on his knee. Bet you wish you were single, eh?"

"Don't be silly. He's a friend."

"But there's history there?"

"Ancient history."

"God, looking at him and the American, I better get myself down to the gym," he said.

"There's nothing wrong with you, Rob."

"Good job I'm not the jealous type. Most guys wouldn't be overly keen on seeing photos of their girlfriend with a bunch of good-looking dudes like these - bodies like gladiators."

"Good job you're not most guys then, hey," she smiled. If only he knew. "Robert? There is actually something important I need to talk to you about ..." she said, fiddling with the edge of her seat. And that was it, really. After several hours, she had finished task two.

Bibi came over that weekend and she told her everything that had happened, whilst they enjoyed a Chinese takeaway and a bottle of wine.

"I'm so glad you spoke to him and it's over and done with," said Bibi.

"Me too. I'm so glad he's gone. We were roommates, basically. There wasn't anything left at all. He took it pretty well, really. It was all very civil, very grown up. I told him I was unhappy, felt as if we were no longer living together as a couple, strangers almost."

"And he's moved into the company flat?"

"For now, until I can buy him out. He wanted nothing, apart from his clothes and a few personal effects, *too artsy fartsy* here for him, apparently. Doesn't like my taste, can you believe?"

"I can't believe he went so easily."

"Neither can I. No tears or tantrums. No recriminations. Just. Well, just ... civil."

"Do you think there's anyone else?"

"I don't know, and to be honest, I don't care."

"And the entire conversation started whilst he was looking at your holiday photos?"

"Yep. I just thought, right now or never?"

"Did you tell him?"

"About *him*?"

"Yep,"

"Nope. No point. However, he asked if something had happened in Kenya. If there was anyone else and I said no."

"Talking of photos, I want to see them," exclaimed Bibi.

"No. I don't want to see them again." She wailed.

"Izzy, please. I want to see everyone I've heard about."

"Oh God, ok. Bring your wine over here and sit at the desk. They're bigger on the computer. You're lucky I haven't deleted them yet. Okay, so this is Ingrid, Fiona, HER and me, stepping off the plane in Mombasa."

"I see what you mean about her being OTT and what is she wearing? She looks like she's about to chair a meeting. No one would believe she's just spent hours on a plane. Ingrid looks the same as I remember."

"This is *him*," she grimaced, pointing to Jack smiling casually at the lens, smoking away on a cigarette, dark shades covering his beautiful eyes.

"Jesus Christ. Italian Stallion. No wonder you had an affair. Hell, I'd have had an affair."

"No, you wouldn't. You love Darysus too much. He's not

that good looking, is he, though?"

"You are joking, right? You can tell he's American - British guys don't look like this."

"And this is Harry."

"Holy shit. He's yummy too. They would have had to fight me off with a bat. I would have been like a bitch in heat."

"You're gross."

"You're lucky. I'd have given my eyeteeth to have gone on holiday with these guys."

"Yeah, and look where it got me."

"Well, it's done now. History. Blimey, how would I have chosen between Harry and Jack? How did you choose?"

"I didn't choose. It just kind of happened. There was nothing I could do to stop it. Believe me, I tried."

"Oh, Izzy, I hope you haven't made a big mistake by letting him go. He looks gorgeous."

"He was a fuck boy, Bibi. A fuck man."

"Fuck man," Ingrid laughed, "Anyway, are there any Singapore Noodles left?"

"Scrummy aren't they." And they both continued looking through the rest of the photos, whilst polishing off their Chinese food.

***

CHAPTER EIGHTEEN

Life without Robert was fine, easy. There was no transition period. After he had removed all his belongings, you would never have known he had been there.

Firmly closing that chapter of her life, she put it all behind her. She threw herself into work as normal and didn't miss him at all. She felt quite low in herself and tired and guessed that everything that had happened was catching up with her.

Elizabeth was worried about her. One day in the showroom, she had nearly fainted, but Isabella assured her she was fine. All she had been doing was not eating. She also resigned from the tennis club-she just didn't have the time or the inclination any more.

Unfortunately, although Robert rarely entered her thoughts, she still occasionally thought of Jack. The regret and guilt from her past actions and decisions consumed her. She wondered where he was. She wondered what he was doing. He crept into her thoughts while she was lying alone in her bed at night, staring up at the ceiling. She wondered about a different outcome, longing to undo past choices and considering missed opportunities. Then feelings of remorse and self-blame filled her, burdening and overwhelming her. She also wondered how she could have been a fool, to have been completely and utterly taken in by him. There'd be no way she'd be as gullible next time, if there was ever to be a next time.

As time passed, she decided enough was enough. Feeling tearful and unlike herself, she realised that moping around was doing her no good and decided enough was enough. So, she accepted an invitation from one of her clients who was going out for a drink with a group of friends. There was a mixed group of fifteen going that Friday night. Unfortunately, none of the rest of her team were going, but she thought what the hell, she wanted to go anyway.

Charlie, the client in question, was handsome. She didn't know precisely how old he was, but had an idea that he may be a year or two younger than her. He was very rich and successful, with a wicked sense of humour. She enjoyed his company, and she also knew he had a massive crush on her.

They first met when she received a request to take on the formidable task of renovating his family home, where he had lived since he was a small child. His parents had died years before, leaving him with this large, imposing house that direly needed attention. She had done a wonderful job, modernising both the interior and exterior. He'd pestered her incessantly for months afterwards to go on a date with him and she'd always said no, but they'd become friends.

He lived not too far from where she lived, so he offered to pick her up on the Friday morning in question and drive her to work, so that she could have a drink that evening without worrying about her car.

After a busy day's work, he picked her up at 6pm and they drove to an Irish themed bar, where they were apparently to meet all the others. It started well. They were having a good time, and she was enjoying herself for the first time in what felt like ages. They were a fun bunch, laughing and joking and making her feel human again.

However, after she'd finished a couple of glasses of wine, she felt quite queasy, but tried to put it to the back of her mind. It was impossible to ignore, though; she felt violently sick. She sat down to see if that would help, but it didn't.

"Isabella, are you okay?" asked Charlie.

"No Charles, I'm not. I'm afraid I feel sick."

"You look awful."

"Look, I'm sorry to spoil your evening, but would you

mind if I went home? I've obviously eaten something that hasn't agreed with me."

"Sure. You look pretty green. Let me get you an Uber."

"Thanks Charles, I am sorry about this. I'm sure it's nothing serious, probably cheap wine or a mild case of food poisoning."

"Are you saying I was a cheap date?" he said.

"No silly. I'm sorry, that didn't come out right, did it?"

"Don't worry, I know what you mean. I hope you're okay, that's all. Great ... our first date and you're ill."

"I'm sorry Charlie."

When she arrived home later, she just crawled into bed and lay there by herself on her side, feeling revolting.
The following day, she felt perfectly normal again, if not tired, but definitely more like her usual self.

On Sunday, she spent a quiet morning reading the papers, having a cup of tea and some toast. She had offered to cook a Sunday roast for Bibi and Darysus later, and they were all looking forward to it.

She prepared a large roast lamb, with all the trimmings, accompanied by fresh, steamed vegetables, and for dessert, she made a mouth-watering sticky toffee pudding.

Her friends arrived at two o'clock. They had a catch up and she served their dinner shortly afterwards.

"This is delicious Izzy. I wish Bibi could cook like this," said Darysus.

"Charming. Who the hell makes all your meals?" answered Bibi indignantly.

"Well, you open the box darling and put it in the oven."

"Darysus that's not fair," said Isabella, "I've had some delightful meals at your place."

"Yes, all courtesy of Messrs Marks and Spencer."

"You dick!" shrieked Bibi. "Don't give away all my secrets. Isabella, whatever's the matter? You've gone green."

"I think I've got a bug, Bibi. I haven't been feeling too hot for a couple of days. I thought I was over it, but obviously not. Excuse me, will you?" and she ran to the downstairs loo, reaching it just in time before she was sick.

"Nice," said Bibi, as she re-joined them, "You see Darysus? Her cooking isn't that great after all."

"I'm sure it's nothing and I'm sorry if I've put you off your dinner," Isabella wailed, "And if it is a bug, I hope you don't get it."

"Don't worry Aziz am, we've finished, haven't we Bibi? And it was lovely," said Darysus.

Bibi and Darysus helped her with the tidying up, helped her to clear the table and load the dishwasher.

"Can I get you a coffee?" asked Isabella.

"No, we'll get going and leave you in peace. Try to get some rest," said Bibi. "Get yourself to the doctors Izzy. You never know, you might have picked something up on holiday. It's not that long ago, you know, and these things can last for ages."

The reason for her nausea became blindingly obvious whilst she was lying in bed that night. She didn't have to book a doctor's appointment to know what was wrong with her. She instinctively knew.

After spending a seemingly never-ending and apprehensive day at work on Monday, she simply went to the local chemist after work and bought herself three pregnancy tests.

She got home and followed the first one's instructions to the letter and waited a few agonising minutes for the results. As she had guessed, positive. Oh, my good God. What on earth had she done? She sat there shaking, in a state of shock.

Both tests she took had the same result. She hadn't slept with Robert since long, long before she went on holiday, so he was definitely out of the picture and the only plausible conclusion was that it was Jack's baby. She was pregnant with Jack's baby.

She estimated it was approximately twelve weeks since her last period–twelve weeks. The realisation hit her and made her feel sicker than ever. She walked around the house for hours in a daze. Panic engulfed her, her thoughts racing about the implications and responsibilities that she faced.

She made a doctor's appointment the following day and was a nervous wreck by the time she arrived at the surgery. She sat in the waiting room anxiously, her legs bouncing up and down whilst she flicked through old, dog-eared magazines. Why was it that every article seemed to be connected to children and babies and also, why did everyone in the waiting room either have children or seem to be heavily pregnant? There seemed to be no getting away from the fact. Was it her imagination or had she just not noticed these things before?

"Miss Michaels," she heard the muffled voice of her doctor say over the intercom, so she leapt up and headed towards his office.

He had a very kind and reassuring manner, and she had known him for years. He confirmed, if her dates were correct, she was indeed about twelve weeks pregnant.

He asked her if it was a planned pregnancy, to which she simply shrugged her shoulders. What could she say? Err no, I slept with some guy on holiday and got knocked up and haven't seen him since? She was still in a state of shock and did not know what to say to him. She was also completely and utterly terrified. And also, she felt alone. He advised her what would happen next and also gave her alternatives. Should she not want to go ahead with the pregnancy, he could also point her toward whom to contact should she need more advice.

She left his office in a daze, assuring him she'd let him know her plans shortly, and went home and called in sick for the rest of the day.

She spent the next few days roaming around the house, appalled at herself for her lack of responsibility. Why had she got herself into this mess in the first place? She wasn't a teenager. She knew all about birth control. Why hadn't she taken more care? Jesus, with his background, she could have caught anything. She felt desperately isolated, but then finally decided the only person she could speak to, naturally, was Bibi.

She called her friend at work and asked her to come over that evening, as she had something she needed to talk to her about.

Bibi arrived at 7pm, and they sat in the lounge.

"What's up Izzy? Nothing wrong, is there?" Bibi asked, concern etched on her face.

"You could say that. I'm pregnant."

"Shit."

"I knew you'd say that."

"Shit. How did that happen?"

"How do you think it happened?"

"You know what I mean. Are you going to tell Robert?"

"Robert? What does he have to do with this?"

"Well, you can't keep it from him. He has a right to know."

"Oh, shit Bibi. Don't you see? It's not Rob's baby. What the hell am I going to do?"

"What do you mean it's not Robert's baby?" she looked perplexed. "Oh shit. You don't mean?"

"That's exactly what I mean."

"This Jack guy?"

"Yep. It's Jack's baby. The person I had a fling with on holiday, the *few nights* stand, the mistake."

"Izzy, why were you so bloody careless? Are you sure it couldn't be Robert's?"

"Of course, I'm bloody sure. We haven't slept together in God knows how long. It's 100% Jack's."

"Oh."

"Yes, oh."

"Are you going to speak to him? Tell him?"

"You are joking?"

"Aren't you self-sabotaging a bit here?"

"Do you not listen to a word I say? He's the last person

on the planet I want to talk to. He's a complete shit. I want nothing to do with him. And now this," she cried.

"Okay. Okay. I'm sorry. It was only a suggestion. Look Izzy, you only have two options."

"Thank you," she said sarcastically.

"You either have an abortion or you have this baby. Do you think you could manage a baby on your own? Do you know how difficult that would be? What about your work?"

"Thanks for the empathy, Bibi. Just cut straight to the chase. Look, would you like a cup of tea?"

"Yes, but you sit there. I'll go make it."

Bibi returned a short time later with a freshly brewed pot of tea. She noticed Isabella had been crying.

"I suppose this explains the sickness," she said, handing Isabella a tissue.

"Yep. But what am I going to do? I've thought of nothing else since I found myself in this ludicrous mess. What do I do?"

"No-one can make that decision for you. Only you know what's right."

"But I don't know what's right. That's the problem." She wailed, before bursting into tears again.

They sat for hours and hours, talking about *what ifs* and *whys* and how she would cope, and what options were open to her. Bibi confided in her she'd helped a friend go through a termination several years earlier and it was a terribly hard decision for her to reach, emotionally as well as morally. Could Isabella go through something as traumatic as that, when all she'd dreamt about her whole life was having a baby? Okay, maybe she had presumed that she would have been in a relationship or married, before having a family, but things never worked out, did they? However, if she decided she didn't want this baby, Bibi would help and support her the best she could. Bibi promised her that whatever decision she reached, she would remain there for her, by her side, helping her face whatever needed facing.

After Bibi had gone, Isabella sat alone for hours in front of the fire, pondering her future. She tried to watch television to distract her thoughts, but again, every advert seemed for nappies or babies and every time she flicked through channels, there was some reference or another to them.

She finally decided on her own a few days later and knew there was no going back. She was going to have this baby. Her baby. She had plenty of money in her savings, her business was doing well and it could manage without her for a while and with a little help from Bibi, she'd manage on her own. People had babies all the time. She could take a few months' maternity leave and then return to work, initially part time. All she had to do was find a suitable nanny for the baby. Lots, if not most, of mothers returned to work nowadays. Okay, it wasn't ideal, being a single parent, but she had no choice. She would love this baby with all of her heart and soul and would do the very best she could for him, or her.

She phoned Bibi the following morning and told her. Her friend was beyond delighted and stressed again that she would be there, by her side, all the way.

"Thank you, Bibi. I don't know what I'd do without you."

"I'm glad we're having a baby. It'll be hard work, but won't it be fun?"

"I hope I'm doing the right thing?"

"I'm sure you are. I've already thought of a couple of names."

"Bibi."

"Well ... you know, I got so excited about the baby, I started thinking of names."

"Talk about jumping the gun."

She waited another four weeks, then called her parents individually and told them she was expecting. Initially, they both felt astounded and overwhelmed, but it soon became apparent they were overjoyed with the news.

"Oh, and there's more." She mumbled. Unfortunately, she hadn't been in contact with them for at least a few months, so had to explain to them she and Robert had broken up some time earlier.

They both obviously presumed it was Robert's baby anyway, and she didn't want to go into any more details than was absolutely necessary, so let them believe that was the case. She didn't want to complicate the situation further.

However, they urged her to get in touch with him and maybe start afresh now there was a baby to consider? Perhaps things would be better?

After much discussion and wrangling, she convinced them that this wasn't an option. She would have to manage on her own, with Bibi's support. She told them she had received a letter from Robert to tell her he was living in Birmingham. His life had taken a new direction. He had signed the house over to her. He wanted no more from her and wished her well for the future.

Her mother offered to come and stay nearer the time the baby was due, but Isabella firmly declined. She had never been close to her mother since her parent's divorce a long while ago and she certainly didn't relish the thought of her putting in a sudden appearance in her life.

Her mother had always been distant, so preoccupied with her own life, she rarely spared a thought for her one and only daughter, only caring about her latest interests and flings. Her priorities remained centred on herself, leaving little time or attention for her daughter.

When she had split from her father, she had had hardly any contact with her mother whatsoever. She followed her own life path. Isabella had only seen her at brief intervals over Christmas and perhaps once or twice, at most, throughout the rest of the year. She had always been too worried about her latest boyfriend or too engrossed in her delightful new circle of friends in Cheshire to worry about Isabella.

Over the years, she had forgotten birthday cards and

presents and had also turned down many invitations from Isabella's father to join them occasionally, which led Isabella to feel that they were now just casual acquaintances. She had almost little or no interest in Isabella's life. She didn't know the names of her friends, what she liked to do in her spare time, what her job entailed. They were only strangers, really, and neither of them had any intention of changing the situation.

Isabella was on fairly close terms with her father and her stepmother, but they now lived several hours away in Cumbria and she didn't see them as often as she would have liked. Robert and she used to travel up to see them three or four times a year, but even that had become less regular, what with one thing and another. Perhaps the baby might bring them closer together. Although she doubted it, really. They had their lives, and she had hers.

***

CHAPTER NINETEEN

Over the next few weeks, she sometimes regretted her life-changing decision. Especially when she was feeling the 'what was supposed to be' morning sickness at various times of the day. She found it a struggle to get into work some mornings.

However, when she did eventually make it in, Elizabeth would appear seconds later with a mug of warm, sweet tea and some dry ginger biscuits for her. She would stare miserably at the mountain of correspondence to go through that day, the endless list of emails that needed responding to, the decisions to be made and would wonder, in despair, how she would ever get through it all.

As advised by her midwife, Iris, she tried drinking ginger ale and eating ginger biscuits to combat the sickness, but this didn't work. Nothing did. There were lots of different theories about morning sickness and what cures it, put forward by her friends, all with good intentions, but nothing seemed to work.

She also felt low first thing in the mornings when she was alone and feeling vulnerable. She had no one to share her thoughts and fears with, no one just to sit and have a chat with. Someone who could reassure her and make her feel better.

She went for her very late first ultrasound at the start of December. She was both excited and agitated, tapping her fingers incessantly on her legs impatiently, but felt even more sorry for herself, when she realised she was the only one alone in the waiting room. There were countless couples sitting together, whispering between themselves, holding hands, but she kept on her brave face and she sat drinking obligatory plastic cups of water to fill her bladder. She looked around at all the other expectant mothers with their partners and other relatives, and felt sad and lonely and a little bitter.

She loathed hospitals at the best of times, and by the time it came for her appointment, which was nearly an hour late, she was impertinent and uncooperative with the doctors and midwives, complaining about everything from the lengthy wait, to the uncomfortable facilities and shabby surroundings.

However, when she eventually lay down on the bed and she turned her head to look at the screen and saw the little foetus wiggling about in her tummy, she burst into tears. For the first time, she realised what was going on with her body. This was the reason she was feeling so grotesque. She felt an overwhelming surge of love for this tiny little creature cocooned safely inside her body.

Feeling astonished, she couldn't comprehend, and it seemed incredible that what she was seeing on the screen was in her stomach. As the technician moved the wand over her belly, she pointed out *its* remarkably developed little arms and legs, waving furiously and confirmed, thankfully, that all was well with the pregnancy considering she was at 21 weeks already. And thankfully and most importantly, there were no obvious anomalies with the baby's organs and everything was looking healthy.

She was so proud later on showing everyone the photo of *her* baby–the little hands waving in the air and kicking legs, tiny toes, and of course, the most important thing, the little tiny heartbeat. It was real, after all. It was surreal for her to witness the tangible evidence of her growing child deepening her emotional connection to the pregnancy.

She hired some of her reliable contractors to carry out some alterations and to turn the spare room into a nursery. It was an enchanting, airy room with a picture window overlooking the back garden and another smaller window on the side–plenty of natural light. She spent hours with Bibi pouring over paint and wallpaper swatches and fabric samples from the best design houses.

They also spent hours at weekends hunting in little craft and antique shops for furniture for her to upcycle. They found an old pine chest, which she lovingly sanded, painted and waxed. Bibi bought her a unique hand-stitched patchwork quilt and some new cotton bedding to go into the beautiful crib. Isabella also found a pretty Victorian nursing chair in wonderful condition and she placed it in the little bay window.

The rest of the furniture, including rocking chair, wardrobe, tallboy, changing unit, they picked up in specialist shops, auctions and even an old blanket chest in a salvage yard, which she eventually planned on using as a toy box.

The finished result was delightful, and she loved sitting in the room, late into the night, whilst her stomach grew, trying to imagine what it would be like with a little person, her little person, lying in the crib beside her.

By now she had a quite a bulge showing from beneath her clothes, although it was only those who knew she was pregnant who could tell. She still looked in exceptional shape, carrying no extra weight. It was difficult to tell she was expecting at all.

She spent a quiet Christmas and New Year, mostly at Bibi and Darysus's, grateful for the rest and the mollycoddling and also had a couple more, successful dates with Charles. He had taken the news that she was pregnant fairly well, but she could tell he didn't see their relationship headed in quite the same direction any more. He thought of her now as a good friend, rather than as a potential partner. However, he still asked her out to dinner on Valentine's Day, but she kindly declined. She spent the evening at home in front of the television.

She returned home after another busy day at work, cooked herself some pasta, changed into her jarmies, then switched on the TV. After half an hour, there was a knock on the door.

Wondering who on earth this could be, she pulled the front door open and gasped to see who was standing on her doorstep.

"Robert."

"Hi Izzy."

"What are you doing here?"

"Are you going to ask me in, or are you going to leave me here freezing?" he smiled.

"Sorry. Come in. Come in," and she opened the door wide for him to pass.

They walked through to the lounge.

"Nothing's changed," he noted, looking around.

"Nope. Everything's more or less how you left it. How are you? Please, sit down."

"Thanks, I'm good. You?"

"Well. You know. Just the same."

"Really?"

"Really. And you?"

"Work is going well." I earned a promotion through my hard work.

"Well done," she commented.

"Even more travelling involved. I'm overseas a lot more now, too."

"You must never be home."

"Nothing's changed, eh?"

"Sorry Rob. I haven't offered you a drink. Can I get you anything?"

"A beer would be good?"

"No beer I'm afraid. No call for it now you've gone." She smiled.

"You haven't met someone else then?"

"No," she stated simply.

"I'll just have a glass of water then, please."

She went to the kitchen to fetch them both a glass of water. What did he want, showing up here out of the blue?

All became abundantly clear as she returned with the drinks.

"So, Isabella. When were you going to tell me?" he asked.

"Tell you?" she asked.

"Yeah. About the baby?" he stated.

She was unsettled. How had he found out? She didn't know what to say. She was totally unprepared.

"You ought to have told me straight away."

"Why?" she asked.

"Why? For goodness' sake, don't you think I have a right to know? A say in things?"

"Like what? What on earth do you want a say in?"

"Well, if I'm honest, now's not a good time for me," he said, itching the side of his temple.

"What are you talking about?" she asked, stunned.

"With my promotion. I think I should have at least been consulted. I've met someone else, you see. This will make things ... well, err, complicated."

"Really?"

"Yes. Tina. We live together."

"Go on," she sat for a few seconds to absorb this latest bit of information.

"She'll be less than thrilled to find out I'm going to be a father."

"Robert. There's absolutely no need to worry. You aren't going to be a father." She said.

"Don't deny it. I can see it with my own two eyes. You haven't put on weight, Izzy. That's a bump."

"I know it's a bloody bump, Rob. What I mean is, you aren't having a baby. I am. And second, you're not the father."

"I don't understand?"

"You're not the father. Simple as that."

"You mean?"

"Yes. What did you think? I was going to have the baby then turn up on your doorstep? Beg you to come home? Stump you for child support? Plead for you to come back to me," she laughed again.

"Something like that, I s'pose," he grumbled.

"You're so bloody self-centred."

"Now hang on a minute. That's not fair. I came to you, remember?"

"Yeah ... to tell me you didn't want to be a daddy. To see if it was too late to get rid of it?"

"You lied to me," he stated.

"What do you mean, I lied to you?" she asked.

"I asked you if you were seeing anyone else and you said no."

"And I'm not." She explained.

"So, what happened? You had a one-night stand. That's not your style?"

"Something like that. I don't want to go into it. It's none of your business."

"You cheated on me," he blurted. His face was a picture.

She remained silent.

"Of course. No wonder you didn't want to tell me. What? He dumped you?"

"Shut up Rob. It's none of your business. All you need to know is that it's not yours, okay? Now I think you should go." She began to cry. She couldn't stop herself.

He came over to comfort her. "Shh," he whispered as he wrapped his arms around her.

"I'm sorry." She gulped.

"Me too. I shouldn't have got you in such a state, in your condition and all."

When she calmed herself down, she said, "Rob? I'm sorry. I had a fling, but I don't want to go over old ground. It's over. But surely it must be a relief to know it's not your baby? You can go back to Tina, or whatever she's called, and carry on with the rest of your life."

"I suppose," he whispered, releasing her from his arms.

"What's wrong?" she asked.

"Well ... I don't feel like I thought I would feel."

"What do you mean?"

"When I got here tonight."

"Yes?"

"Everything seems so familiar. I miss it. I miss you."

"I miss you too," she said, was that honest?

"I kind of now wish it was my baby. Maybe we could have made another go of it?"

She just smiled. "Maybe." She knew it was more relief that he was feeling now, nothing more.

They chatted affably for a couple more hours. He didn't push her for any more information about the father of the baby. They remained in neutral territory and talked about old friends, their careers and when he left just before midnight, she was sorry to see him go.

"By the way," he said as he was walking out the door, and turned to give her a quick kiss on the cheek.

"Yes?" she asked coyly.

"Happy Valentines."

In early March, Bibi decided Isabella needed a break, as she was looking so exhausted. So, they booked a long weekend break together in the West Country, Bibi assuring her the fresh air would do her good.

When the time came, they were both looking forward to their mini-break. They took turns on the long drive, through the ancient landscapes and rich farmland of South West England, through secluded villages, country towns and historic sites. En route they made a brief stop at Stonehenge, on the Salisbury Plans, the prehistoric ritual monument or whatever it was, built in the late stone and early bronze ages. They took some photos of the stones and sat afterwards in the car enjoying a picnic, before commencing their journey.

After driving for another couple of hours, they finally arrived at their wonderful hotel, originally built in the 16th century. Acres of National Trust countryside surrounded the hotel, originally built in the 16th century, and nestled amongst charming beech woods, providing them with magnificent views from the windows of their adjoining rooms.

The hotel itself had low-beamed ceilings, an excellent restaurant and reputedly its own ghost. The lounge bar had welcoming log fires, antique furniture and oak-panelled walls, snug corners and a flag slate floor.

As soon as they arrived, they fell in love with the place. The weather gods were smiling down on them and they were close by to small fishing villages, bustling ports and superb coves nestling in the rugged coastline. They spent a glorious weekend walking in the sunny but chilly air along the beaches, paddling in rock pools and walking around the many little gift and antique shops, where they bought lots of delightful things for the baby.

They had hoped the sea air and break would do Isabella some good, but unfortunately, she still felt lousy the whole time. She couldn't believe that something so small, growing in her tummy, could make her feel so off-colour. Why was she one of the unlucky ones, for whom the sickness didn't subside after the first 3 months?

As they made their way home after a pleasant, relaxing weekend, they stopped off at a small thatched pub overlooking a river for lunch. An abundance of bric-à-brac, old photographs, and plenty of brass and copperware adorned the bar. They sat by an enormous log fire and Isabella ordered trout fillets in Pernod and cream and Bibi opted for chicken breast cooked in cider. Their food arrived a short while later, freshly prepared, served with perfectly cooked vegetables, and they both enjoyed their dishes immensely.

"Isabella, have you heard from Ingrid lately?" Bibi asked.

"I wrote her a long email and explained that Robert and I had broken up. I also told her I had found out subsequently that I was expecting, but asked if she could keep this little piece of information to herself, for obvious reasons. She then phoned and congratulated me a few days later and I explained that I'd be raising the baby alone. She obviously thought I was mad, but also thought I was very brave. Since then, we haven't spoken. I don't think she has any interest in pregnant women or babies."

"What about Jack Vincent?" she dared, not having mentioned him since the two previous conversations about him. Once upon Isabella's return from Kenya and thereafter, when Isabella announced she was pregnant. She noticed Isabella visibly wince at the mere mention of his name.

"What about him? Do you mean have I heard from him?"

"Yes."

"No. Thank God. Thankfully, that's all behind me now."

"Tell me. Apart from obviously went on between you two, what was he like?"

"Truthfully? He was the most handsome, attractive and sexy man alive," she giggled, "He literally swept me off my feet. He blew me away, as they say. When he walked into a room, literally every woman turned to stare at him. Such magnetism."

"The photos I saw, he looked gorgeous–dark, brooding. And the bad points?"

"Facetious. Swears all the time, you'd hate that. Moody, arrogant, derisive, surly and unpredictable."

"Sounds charming."

"Doesn't he just." She added with an ounce of irony, "Oh, and he smokes constantly."

"Yuck."

"Yet our similarities were astounding. I believe that's ultimately where the problem lies. We were too alike. Unfortunately, his charm and good looks masked the real person underneath. I guess he was what you'd expect of a real player–relies on his looks to get what he wants, which unfortunately, because of how he looks, women fall easily for him. Clearly multiple people, me included. With no sincere intentions and, at his age, obviously no commitment."

"Really? Was he never married then?"

"No. Well, that's what he told me, anyway. But then again, he could have been feeding me another line. He's clearly very smooth, flattering, but underneath, selfish and opportunistic."

"Are you sure he betrayed you? What if he was telling the truth and that other woman was lying? How do you know she didn't make the whole thing up?"

"Don't be ridiculous. Why would she do that? It was just him. He's a massive player. There are loads of men around like him. They can't ever be with one woman. Look how old he was, and he'd never been married. Never even been in a long term committed relationship. That says it all. Remember when I first met him? I couldn't stand him. I wish I'd listened to my gut. Then somehow, he worked his magic on me and I, like everyone else, bowed to the inevitable. He must have thought I was such a fool. But forget him, the only important person now, is the little one here," she said, rubbing her tummy.

"Isabella, don't you think you should tell him?"

"Bibi please." She begged.

"Sorry, but he should know."

"I've told you. This is my baby. Mine. He'll never know."

"Don't you have a legal right to tell him?"

"Don't push it Bibi."

"I think you're making a big mistake."

"Will you stop? You don't even know the guy."

"That's not the point."

"Look. It took me bloody ages to get over Jack Vincent. That chapter is closed. I don't want to talk about him again, okay?"

"Okay."

"But don't you think the baby will want to know who its father is?"

"I'll deal with that when the time comes. Now enough."

They followed their lunch with some coffee and sat enjoying the impressive views from the windows.

"So, have you decided on a name for this baby yet?"

enquired Bibi.

"Still nothing definite. I like Freddie, if it's a boy, after my grandad. I quite like Frank."

"Yuck. That's gross."

"After Frank Sinatra. What's wrong with that?"

"I don't like it. What about Herbie?"

"Goes to Monte Carlo?"

"It's a nice name?"

"For a dog."

"George?"

"No. I've a client called George. He's horrible."

"Alistair?"

"No, I've an ex-boyfriend called Alistair."

"Henry?"

"Not bad."

"What about girls' names? I like Megan?"

"Yeah, that's nice. I like Daisy. Sophie. I also like Alexandra."

"Harriet's nice."

"I used to go to school with a tall girl with red rosy cheeks called Harriet."

"It's going to be so hard to choose." wailed Bibi, taking a last sip of her coffee. "Blimey, look, we'd better get going Izzy." They started getting their things together and settled the bill.

As they walked outside, they had to wait until a large, modern coach pulled into the tiny car park and manoeuvred into a ridiculously small space. They both watched as a crowd of burly men dismounted, one by one, heading for the bar.

Bibi watched as a startlingly handsome man walked towards them. "Isabella?" he asked, beaming down at her friend and enveloping her in an enormous bear hug.

"Harry. My God. What on earth are you doing here? Bibi, this is Harry Jacobs. Harry, Bibi Javid."

They both shook hands and greeted each other warmly, Bibi not taking her eyes off him. "Delighted to meet you." She gushed, giving Isabella one of her "why did you let this one get away" looks.

"We played against Plymouth yesterday in a cup match and the lads and I have just stopped here on the way home for a bite to eat. What a coincidence. How are you?"

"Good. Good. You?"

"Fine Isabella, just fine. It's just great to see you again. I've missed you."

"Me too," she answered.

"So, what's been going on? What are you doing here?" he enquired, and then looked down at her stomach for the first time. "Wow. Are you …?"

"Yes, Harry I am. Due in just under a couple of months."

"Wow. Who would have thought it? Robert's one lucky fella. Are you okay? I mean, do you feel okay?"

"I'm good. Thanks for asking. Looking forward to him or her being born now," she shot Bibi a look as if to plead, say nothing you shouldn't. Her fear was overwhelming. She didn't know what to say to him. She wanted to get away, quickly.

"Harry, we were just on our way home, I'm afraid. I don't mean to be rude, but if you'll excuse us?"

"Of course. But give me your new number. I'll call you?"

"Great. I'll look forward to hearing from you. Goodbye Harry," and she gave him a quick peck on the cheek.

"Goodbye Izzy. Bibi, nice to have met you, if only briefly."

As they walked back towards their car, Bibi playfully slapped her arm and said, "Now why didn't you ever mention how insanely gorgeous *he* was?"

"I did. I showed you the photos."

"He's luscious. And the way he looked at you. Wow! He's in love."

"Bibi please. Don't be ridiculous. Yes, he's luscious, but he's a wicked devil."

"But you still gave him your number?"

"I guess I would love to keep in touch with him. Don't

look like that. As a friend. He knows we can be nothing more than friends?"

"Why? Is he gay?"

"No." she shrieked with laughter, "Harry's the last person on earth to be gay. He's a typical male. Red-blooded and has never, ever had a serious relationship in his life. I didn't or don't want to be another notch in his belt, that's all. There again, maybe I would have fared better having a quick fling with him. No emotional attachment. Anyway. He's great fun and maybe down the road I could do with some cheering up."

"God, you know how to pick 'em don't you?" groaned Bibi, "Well he can cheer me up any time." she then added. "When are you going to tell him it's not Robert's baby?"

"I'm not."

"What do you mean?"

"I won't say anything. Like everyone else, he will just have to reach his own assumptions."

"I don't like this game you're playing, Izzy. It's dangerous."

"You don't have to."

***

CHAPTER TWENTY

To Isabella's delight, Harry 'phoned her out of the blue one Saturday afternoon in late March.

"Isabella. Harry. How are you?"

"Fine, Harry and you?"

"Great, thanks."

"Lovely to hear from you," she said.

"Lovely to speak to you, too. It was wonderful to see you, fat tummy and all."

"Hey. Don't be mean. We've got lots to catch up on, haven't we?"

"We sure do. Look, I hope you don't mind, but I will pass near you tomorrow on the way back from some friends and I thought maybe you could use some company? Maybe we can catch up then?"

"Harry, that'd be fabulous. I can't wait."

She gave him her address, and he told her to expect him the following afternoon.

He arrived the next day just after two o'clock, carrying an enormous bunch of calla lilies.

"Isabella, you look wonderful," he said, giving her a big bear hug. "Being pregnant suits you. You look even more gorgeous than usual, if that's at all possible."

"You old charmer. You don't look too bad yourself." and she and led him through to the lounge. "Thanks for the beautiful flowers you shouldn't have. I'll just get a vase. Can I get you a drink?"

"A soft drink would be great, thanks. Lovely place," he said, taking in the impressive surroundings.

"Sit down, please. Make yourself comfy."

"Coke okay?"

"Perfect."

"Fat or diet?"

"Either. Don't mind."

She returned shortly thereafter, carrying their drinks.

"Thanks, Iz. Robert, around?" he asked innocently.

"No."

"Expected?"

"No. Harry, we've split up," she explained.

Before she could continue, he said "Oh Isabella, that's dreadful. What a bastard to leave you in this state."

"No, really Harry. It's not like that. It was a mutual decision, before I found out I was expecting, in fact. He didn't leave me in the lurch. If that's what you're thinking and I'm okay. Ingrid knows, but apart from her, I prefer to keep it quiet. About us breaking up, I mean? I don't want people feeling sorry for me or anything like that. Promise you won't tell anyone?"

"Okay, if that's what you want, I swear," he said, crossing his heart playfully, "You know people will know, eventually." He wondered what the big secret was, why she didn't want anyone to know.

"Does this mean I'm in with a chance?" he added, teasing her.

"What do you think?" she smiled.

"Shit. Worth a try, though. Let me know if you change your mind?"

"Will do Harry."

"So, how've you been, really?" he asked, noticing how cosy and warm her home was. She certainly had a wonderful place.

"Apart from feeling like a sick dog, wonderful." She then told him in graphic detail the many revolting side effects of being pregnant.

"Enough. Enough," he cried, "I'm not one for gory details." He laughed, "what are you trying to make me sick too?" They continued to laugh and fool around for hours. He eventually felt plucky enough to bring up Kenya.

"Izzy, why did you run out on us all like that without speaking to any of us, to Jack?"

"Harry, it's forgotten history. Let it go."

"But what happened?" he pushed once more.

"Nothing. As I told Ingrid, something came up back home. I had to fly home a little earlier, that's all."

"But what about you and Jack?"

"There was no me and Jack," she stated.

"But I thought?" he left the question hanging in the air.

"Look Harry. It was nothing, a fling, a mistake, an affair. Call it whatever you like. But it's over. I don't want to talk about it."

"Well, whatever it was, it destroyed Jack." He couldn't believe her cold heartedness. He wouldn't have believed it if he hadn't seen it for himself.

"What?" she gasped.

"It's true. He was a broken man for months. He wouldn't talk to any of us. Whatever happened, or should I say didn't happen, completely devastated him. We've only seen him once or twice since, when he's been over visiting from the States. He asks about you every time. Have any of us seen you? That kind of thing?"

"Really? What a shame." She said in her most sardonic tone, "He's devastated." She asked in amazement, "What the hell's he got to be devastated about? He's the one that took my world, shook it upside down and then left me there, trying to rebuild my life."

"What are you talking about, Izzy? From what I can gather, the guy was, or is, totally in love with you and you ran out on him, back to Robert, with no kind of explanation whatsoever."

"Oh, please Harry," she cried indignantly "I've told you, I don't want to talk about it, it's finished."

"Okay, whatever you want," he said, not understanding.

He felt sure there was more to it than she was letting on.

"Sorry to be so invasive, but what about Robert? Is he to be part of the baby's life?"

"No, he's not" she wasn't giving anything away.

"You have told him, haven't you?"

"Of course, I have."

"And?"

"And nothing. It's all sorted. Look Harry, this is my life. I have my reasons and you can't come in here, not having seen me for months, telling me what I should and shouldn't do. This is my baby. I've made my decision and have come to terms with the fact that I'm going to be a lone parent. It's not the middle ages, you know. Women can do this on their own.

After a few seconds of uncomfortable silence, the doorbell rang. She rose to answer it. It was Bibi.

"Bibi. Hi come in. You remember Harry?" she said, pleased with the intervention.

"Of course." She smiled, "Not a face I'd forget that easily."

"Bibi? Looking as gorgeous as I remember."

The three of them sat down and spent the rest of the evening chatting, talking about light subjects. To her relief, no one mentioned Jack, Robert, and the baby again. She was sorry she'd been so short with him. He brought her back to life and was great company. She hoped she hadn't upset him too much.

Tears welled up in her eyes as he walked away, leaving her feeling a deep sense of sorrow. However, his promise to stay in touch more regularly provided some solace.

"Wow," said Bibi after he left, "I can't believe you don't want to shag him. He's so hot. If I was single, I'd literally throw myself at him."

"Bibi. Is that all you bloody think about? You're shameless."

Over the next few weeks, Harry kept his word, and they spent many hours chatting on the phone, messaging and Face-

Timing. Recurrently, she would phone him in floods of tears if she was feeling vulnerable, and he was proving to be a very loyal and wonderful friend and she was enjoying male company for a change.

She met him several times for lunch in town and they met up for a drink after work one evening. It was nice to meet up with someone who made her feel sexy for a change, rather than just a big fat lump.

Other than the odd lunch and evening out with Harry or Bibi, she socialised little, if at all, during her pregnancy and she gave up alcohol. She felt too tired most of the time and after a hard day at work, the last thing she felt like doing was going out again, so she would just flop on the sofa, sometimes after stopping on the way home for a take-away.

Occasionally, she went out with some friends that still played at the tennis club and once she even allowed herself to have a glass of wine, something she regretted the next day, as she felt so ill. Obviously, the wine didn't agree with the baby or the baby didn't agree with the wine.

She tried going to the cinema a couple of times with Bibi and Darysus, but just felt uncomfortable and claustrophobic and fidgeted the entire way through. She preferred to just watch a movie at home instead. Harry came over a few times and they sat glued to the small screen, munching on popcorn and junk food.

However, the most disastrous and unforgettable evening and one of the few times she ventured out during her last trimester, was for a friend's leaving do at a trendy wine bar in the centre of London.

She'd known Sally Thomas for several years, having worked together briefly in the past. Sally was moving to Paris because a major French design house had offered her a prestigious position. An opportunity she couldn't refuse. Isabella felt it was appropriate to put in an appearance, as she probably wouldn't see Sally again for a while.

She found, despite her reservations, she was having

quite an enjoyable time, standing with a group of Sally's friends, laughing and joking. They were a sociable bunch and were clucking over Isabella like a bunch of mother hens.

They were busy taking it in turns to relay the gory details of their own particular experiences of labour and the graphic details of the births of their own children.

"Don't. No more. You're frightening me to death," wailed Isabella, who then just glanced over at the main door, which had just opened for the umpteenth time that evening, blasting in the cold air from outside and she nearly fainted.

"My God Isabella. It's not that bad, sweetheart. Have we said too much?" laughed one petite blonde girl.

"Isabella, what's wrong? You look like you've seen a ghost," said Jane, one of Sally's closest friends.

"I'm okay, really," she stammered, looking pale.

"God. Your contractions haven't started, have they? It's probably Braxton Hicks?" said another girl.

"No really, I'm fine."

"Your waters haven't broken?" another.

"No, honestly."

"You don't look ok."

"I've got to go," she mumbled to no one in particular.

"Look, sit back down. You look all overcome," said another kind girl.

She was in a complete and utter state of panic. On one of the only evenings she had been out in months. In a tiny bar, in the middle of one of the largest cities in the world, why on earth did Jack Bloody Vincent choose this one to walk into with a stunning girl by his side?

She rapidly finished the water. Grabbed her coat from the back of a chair, made her apologies and said her farewells all the while, and tried to leave before he noticed her, too.

Just as she thought she'd made it and just as she was about to open the main door, she heard his gruff voice resonating behind her.

"Bella."

She tried to ignore him and carried on, regardless. She was nearly there. Just two more steps.

"Wait. Isabella."

Fuck.

She felt him tug on her arm and she turned around to face him.

"What?" she snapped venomously. She was staring directly into his gorgeous face. He looked staggeringly handsome, more so than she had dared to remember. Just seeing him like that, so unexpectedly, so close, rendered her nearly speechless. His dark, brooding, frowning, yet concerned eyes looked at her with such tenderness, such longing. She felt weak and her heart nearly melted. And then, when he smiled ever so tenderly at her, his complete face lit up. His eyes. She felt as if she was drowning in his eyes. But her voice didn't betray any of this. They stared at each other for what seemed like an age.

"Oh, it's you. How nice," she managed sarcastically.

"I thought it was you," he stammered, his eyes drinking her in.

"How are you?" she said coldly. He looked amazing. He looked the same. Still tanned. Still unshaven, rugged, and gorgeous. He was wearing a black open-necked shirt (as usual) and black trousers. He looked exactly like he did when she first laid eyes on him at Ingrid's party, all those millions of years ago. That same electricity. That same spark.

"Good. Good. And you? How are you? You look radiant."

"Yes" was all she could manage.

"What are you doing here?"

"I could ask you the same thing."

"We've come for a quick drink."

"So, I see. She's pretty," she whispered, nodding toward his date.

"I've missed you."

"Huh."

"You broke my heart, you know?" he smiled. He was

drinking her in, "My God. I've just noticed. Are you? I mean, are you?"

"Fat?"

"No, of course I didn't mean," he said, "You are, aren't you?"

"Yes," she whispered.

"Congratulations. You must be thrilled?"

"Thank you. I am. I mean … we are. We're delighted," she looked to her right and noticed Sally's group of friends looking at her strangely, wondering what was going on, wondering who this man was. Please God, don't let them come over or say anything to prolong the agony.

"I'm pleased for you, Bella, really. When are you due?"

"Soon," she said vaguely.

"Boy or girl?"

"I don't know."

"What are you hoping for?"

"I don't know."

"Look, don't let's just stand here by the door. Come join us? I'm just buying Helene a quick drink. She won't be stopping long. Maybe we can talk?" he looked at her beseechingly.

"No," she whispered. Join them for a drink. How dare he. "I've got to go."

"Please? I need to talk to you. I must talk to you. Don't just go. Please," he begged, "There's so much we need to talk about."

"We have said everything that needed to be said, Jack." She glanced then at the attractive, immaculate woman stood behind him, who was looking at them both curiously. Wondering whom this large, fat, frumpy woman was chatting to her date, no doubt. She smiled at Isabella, her eyes empathetic. Great. She was nice, too. Or was it pity?

"I can't. I must be going. Robert's waiting for me."

"I see," he said sadly.

"It was nice to see you. Have a great evening, both of you," she looked back in the other woman's direction and then back at him, "Goodbye Jack" and before he could say anymore, she turned and ran as fast as she could in her delicate condition, out of the door, slamming it firmly behind her. Leaving him staring unhappily into thin air after her.

She stumbled along the pavement, tears blinding her way, until she reached her car. She fumbled with her keys, opened the door and sat there, hunched over the steering wheel, sobbing for ages and ages, pain etched into every fibre of her being, until she finally pulled herself together enough to drive home.

She lay awake for hours, Jack occupying all of her thoughts. She could close her eyes and conjure his face like a photograph. Once again, he opted for a short haircut, but this time there were additional specks of grey, which made him look even more attractive. His square, chiselled jaw, his piercing dark eyes and soft, sensuous lips. His face etched with concern as he looked at her. He had looked so healthy, so safe and welcoming. He had looked for one split second as if he was going to reach out to her, like he wanted to tell her something. She had wanted to fall into his arms. She wanted to feel safe again. She was sick of feeling so alone and only he could have made things better.

"Why?" she screamed out loud, punching her pillow. Why had she seen him now? Why had he seen her looking enormously pregnant and fat? Why was she feeling so alone and vulnerable? Why was he with some young, gorgeous woman, with full pink lips called Helene? Why had she told him Robert was waiting? Why? Why?

Ridiculous thoughts whirled round and round in her head. She couldn't believe he could have this effect on her still, after all this time. She thought she had put it all behind her.

At about three in the morning, she could stand it no longer and picked up the phone.

"Yep," mumbled a gruff, sleepy voice.

"Harry, it's me," she sobbed.

"Izzy? Is that you? What's wrong? Is it the baby?" he

gasped, suddenly wide awake.

"No, we're okay. Well, the baby is. I'm not" and he listened to her sobbing, breaking her heart, but he could barely understand what she was saying.

"Isabella. Slow down. Tell me what's happened please," he begged, deeply worried about her. Then he heard her more clearly.

"I saw him."

"Who?"

"Him. With some amazing bloody French woman called Helene."

"Who Isabella? For God's sake, you're not making any sense. What French woman?" he asked groggily.

She calmed herself down a bit more, and he eventually got the complete story out of her.

"But why did you let him think you were still with Robert?" he asked in amazement.

"It doesn't make any difference whether I'm with Robert." She screamed.

"Of course it does, you little fool. Why would you lie to him?"

But he couldn't make any more sense out of her as he listened to her crying for the best part of an hour. He had heard no one so wretched. So bereft. Her anguished sobbing made his own heart ache for her. He wished he could help her. Be near her.

"I'm coming over," he said finally.

"No, don't. You've got work in a few hours."

"Screw that. I cannot listen to you like this over the phone. I'll be there in 45 minutes," and he hung up on her.

Picking up her glass of water from the bedside table, she took a little drink before unhooking her dressing gown from the back of the door. She glanced at herself in the mirror. She looked appalling. Her face was all red and blotchy, and her stomach looked huge. Her hair was a mess. Great.

She waited downstairs until eventually at about 5.30am she heard his car pull up outside. She opened the front door and he couldn't believe it when he saw her standing there, still crying.

"Isabella, sweetheart. Come here," and he pulled her into his arms and gave her an enormous hug, holding her like a small child. He cooed and shushed until she calmed down again.

They walked into the lounge, and he told her to sit down. He went outside and came back with a big basket full of logs and some kindling, and lit a fire. He then went into the kitchen and made them both a mug of steaming milky hot chocolate. Finally, he grabbed an old cashmere blanket from the back of the sofa and wrapped it around her shoulders and over her, then sat down next to her.

"Isabella. I still don't understand what happened?" he asked, cupping her hands in his own.

"Jack. Jack" she hiccupped.

"What did he say?"

"N.n. nothing, exactly."

"So, let me get this right. You saw Jack with another woman."

"Helene."

"Helene. Right. He sees you're pregnant. You tell him Robert is waiting for you. What else? Is it because he was with another woman?"

"No. Not really."

"If he hurt you so terribly and you say you no longer have any feelings for him, why does he have this effect on you? You dumped him, remember? Do you still have feelings for him? Is that it?"

"No." She sobbed.

"This is more than just your bloody hormones. You still love him."

"I don't love him. I hate him."

"Izzy please? Don't take me for such an idiot. There's

more going on here than you're letting on. Now I didn't come here at silly o'clock in the morning to be fed a load of crap. Are you going to tell me what's going on?"

She mumbled some more ridiculous and feeble excuses, not making much sense at all. He still didn't understand. But then, after a couple of minutes of her incessant rambling, it eventually dawned on him. It hit him like a ton of bricks.

"It's his baby. Of course. Why didn't I see? Why didn't you tell me?" he yelled.

"No. No. Please." She shrieked, as sobs once more racked her body.

"Please tell me Isabella. The truth. Am I right?" he asked more gently now.

Then she broke down and confessed the whole story. It was Jack's baby. Robert didn't even enter the picture. Harry obviously knew most of what had gone on in Kenya, so she didn't have to go into too much detail. She told him everything, except the true reason for the breakup. She glossed over what Madison had told her about that hellish, shocking evening in Mombasa and the true reason for her swift return to England.

"But Isabella, it's his baby. He has every right to know. You must tell him." He said firmly, angry at her for keeping such a tremendous secret. "Who else knows?"

"Bibi."

They talked and talked for ages, and she eventually brought him round to her side. It was over with Jack; he need never know. He didn't want children. Ever. And certainly not with some woman he'd had a brief, casual affair with. He lived on the other side of the world. She would manage quite well on her own. She made him swear he would never tell a single soul, and he foolishly promised.

Only after she'd considerably calmed down later that morning did he leave her. He made sure she would be okay and said he would call her later.

He left feeling guilty and in a horrible position. Jack was a good friend. He had known him for years. Surely, he was where his loyalty should lie? He ought to tell him the truth. At least Isabella should. But she was adamant. It was her life.

***

CHAPTER TWENTY-ONE

A few weeks before her due date, she finished work, and it was definitely not too soon. She was feeling round and tired all the time. She was relieved to no longer have to travel to London each day, to visit client premises, to deal with suppliers and speak to a multitude of people all day long.

By now, she felt as if she was waddling all the time, rather than walking, so it was nice to have finished work and be able to spend some time resting during the day. She was suffering with insomnia and was consequently reading dozens of books and watching the latest movies late into the night. Thank God for Netflix, so it helped to have a nap in the afternoon. She was also experiencing increased discomfort because of the baby's size and position, suffering from severe backache, pelvic pressure and swollen ankles. Subsequently, she felt constantly tired.

She read many books on parenthood, including frightening chapters on pain relief and what to expect in labour, which all just seemed to terrify her more.

She packed her bag of essentials for both herself and the baby and made sure she was ready for her trip to the hospital. Bibi was to be her birthing partner and was on call.

Overdue and after a week having an untold amount of Braxton Hicks, she finally awoke at about 7am on Tuesday 23rd May, with quite severe contractions, but initially put it down to 'tummy ache'.

She tried to ignore the discomfort and, just as she was

drifting back off to sleep, she felt a popping sensation down below. She screamed out loud, "Shit, something's happening," and leapt up from the bed and saw what she had been dreading. Her waters had broken. They were pouring down her legs and she couldn't believe how much there was – an egg-cupful my arse.

She picked up the phone to call Bibi, "Bibi, I think the baby's coming. Can you come and get me now?" she wailed.

"Now? Oh God. Stay there. I'm on my way."

Isabella then phoned the Central Delivery Suite and informed a kind, patient sounding midwife her waters had broken. She was told to stay calm, have some breakfast, have a bath, and come down to the hospital a bit later on. Keep calm. She thought to herself. She had never been so scared in her life.

She made herself a cup of tea and tried to eat a crumpet she had toasted, but felt too anxious to eat, so ended up throwing it away.

She ran a bath, jumped in, then out, not pausing for a seat, in too much of a panic to do anything too constructive, and then she changed into some comfortable clothes. She had an urge to go to the toilet, but didn't need to. Then went back and tried again, same result.

Bibi arrived about 30 minutes later and they grabbed her bags and set off for the hospital.

Halfway there, Isabella became hysterical when she remembered she had left behind her flask full of chipped ice.

"Never mind," said Bibi, "We'll make do without."

"That's easy for you to say. It's not you having this bloody baby." Isabella snapped irately.

"I know, I know. I'm sorry."

"Me too," said Isabella apologetically and took hold of her friend's hand. "I'm terrified, that's all."

When they eventually arrived at the hospital, just a few miles away, Bibi stopped the car outside the main entrance and told Isabella to wait inside whilst she went to park the car.

As Isabella sat alone in the empty foyer, she was trying

to calm herself down a bit by taking some deep breaths. What the hell had she done? She had never felt so terrified in her life.

After a short while Bibi appeared, smiling encouragingly at her and they walked up to the Central Delivery Suite and a member of staff buzzed them in.

They sat silently in the waiting room, just looking around at the walls decorated in old-fashioned, seventies-style wallpaper and occasionally smiling at each other. The television was on in the background, but neither paid any attention to it. A young couple kept coming in and out of the room and to Isabella, it sounded like they had been back and forth to the hospital all week, with many false alarms.

"Perhaps mine's a false alarm too," Isabella whispered eagerly and hopefully to Bibi.

"I don't think so. This is the real shebang."

Eventually, to her great relief, her midwife, Iris, arrived about nine o'clock and escorted her to a little room opposite for examination.

They hooked her up to a Doppler so they could listen to the baby's heart and all sounded well. By now she was having mild, irregular contractions and Iris fitted her TENS machine. They transferred her to the maternity ward and informed her it could be a long wait yet, as nothing much was happening at the moment.

She tried to lie on the bed on the ward, whilst Bibi sat chatting to her, but as she couldn't lie still, they went along to the snack bar to get something to eat and drink.

A couple of hours later, her contractions got a lot closer and a lot more severe. She was increasing the TENS machine to full capacity, but it wasn't making any difference. She was panicking and told Bibi she must fetch someone. The pain was getting much worse, and she was losing it.

Iris returned about ten minutes later, with Bibi in tow, and Isabella told her she was having contractions every 4-5 minutes and was desperate for some pain relief.

They took her back to the Central Delivery Suite, and she

stopped en route to lean back against the corridor walls when the contractions ripped through her body.

Upon arrival, the doctors examined her and found that she was 5cm dilated, which meant she was halfway there. They couldn't believe how fast she'd progressed in the space of a couple of hours. She was contracting every 4 minutes, and they were lasting about 40 seconds.

At about two thirty that afternoon, she was told to have a bath and try to relax herself, and all the while, the contractions were becoming more and more severe. Bibi came into the bathroom and sat with her, looking just as nervous as Isabella.

"What if I can't do it?" whispered Isabella.

"You will. But don't worry, everything will be okay, you'll see. It'll all be over soon," her friend offered.

"But I don't know what to do?" she snivelled.

"Please Izzy. You must stay calm and focussed. Everyone has babies all the time."

"Not me though and anyway, what makes you such an authority on giving birth? You don't know what you're talking about."

"I know, I know."

After only a couple of minutes, they went back into a little room set aside for Isabella. As the contractions worsened, someone guided Isabella on how to use the gas and air. She soon began to enjoy and utilise it fully, even though it didn't relieve the pain.

Isabella, therefore, told Iris she wanted an epidural. Iris went to locate the Sister, who told her in no uncertain terms that there wasn't long to go and Isabella didn't need an epidural.

"But I want an epidural." Replied Isabella sternly.

"But you're so close now," the Sister replied.

"Look. I said I want an epidural." She snapped through gritted teeth.

"Keep yourself calm, dear," she replied.

"I was bloody calm until you started on me," she hissed. "Now get the bloody thing."

"Okay, okay, I'll see what I can do."

After the sister had left the room, Bibi whispered in her ear, "You know The Exorcist? Well, you just reminded me of the girl in it. I expected your head to spin round any minute."

"Oh heck. Was I that bad?" grimaced Isabella.

"Worse."

Anyway, it did the trick as the Sister soon returned with the Anaesthetist. By now Isabella had had her fair share of gas and air and as the Doctor sat on the bed next to her, trying to explain what was about the happen with the epidural, she began to giggle and laugh hysterically, because of the effects of the Entonox. Of course, this started Bibi off and they both sat laughing at the ridiculous situation they found themselves in. They kept apologising and saying, "I'm sorry, I'm so sorry." Whilst falling about each other. The anaesthetist, unfortunately, did not seem to see the funny side of it and regarded her sternly. He sprayed a local anaesthetic onto her lower back and instructed her to stay still while he inserted the needle. This proved difficult, as she was having very rapid and painful contractions. However, she kept still long enough to insert the needle. All she felt was a cold, whooshing sensation in her back.

The epidural differed from what she thought it would be. She could still feel everything. It just didn't hurt so much. To her dismay, she could still feel the contractions.

While various machines, including the baby heart monitor, connected to her, she lay and listened to the loud noise of the baby's heartbeat.

At around four o'clock, the midwife announced Isabella was fully dilated and ready to push. She found it so difficult and so painful, and she wasn't even sure if she was doing it right.

Bibi started shouting, "I can see the head! I can see the head. It's got dark brown hair."

However, after what seemed like hours, the midwife decided that she'd pushed enough and needed help. The baby's chin was pushed upwards and had got itself stuck.

One of the worst parts of the entire experience was hearing the agonising screams from the adjacent rooms. She could hear the most ear splitting, overwhelming screams from the other women in labour and kept saying to Bibi, "I can't do this. I want to go home."

"It's a bit late now, Izzy." Said Bibi.

About nine o'clock, after hours of pushing and hard labour, the Doctors arrived and gave her a top-up epidural. They then hoisted her legs up into stirrups, which was not the most pleasant situation she had ever found herself in. Bibi was constantly there, helping her with the gas and air and reassuring her.

She was tired by now and hazily remembered them telling her she was going to have an assisted delivery. This required an episiotomy and a Ventouse delivery. Whilst they kept fiddling with various parts of her anatomy, she was told to wait and then do one more huge push.

She could feel everything and kept screaming, "I can't breathe. I can't breathe." The baby was kicking with all of his or her might on her ribs and she literally could not breathe.

From somewhere within, she managed the biggest push of all and then she felt a funny, indescribable feeling and shouted, "Bibi? What is it? I don't like it."

"It's the baby's head. Oh, I can see its head." Bibi cried in return.

"Oh, bloody hell it hurts." She screamed.

"Come on Isabella. One more push."

"I hate you, Jack Bloody Vincent." She sobbed at the top of her voice.

She felt her stomach deflate next, as if someone had sucked all the air out of it. She remembered looking down and amongst the haze of doctors and activity, seeing a tiny baby, her tiny baby, being held up in the air.

She heard Bibi shouting, "It's a boy. It's a beautiful little boy."

Half crying, half asleep, she kept asking repeatedly, "Is he alright? Is he alright?" and she thankfully heard them all reassuring her that the baby was fine, he was perfect.

There followed a hive of activity. They handed the little bundle straight to the paediatrician for cleaning up and checking. Then the midwife was measuring and weighing him.

And finally, someone placed her little baby in her arms so she could give him his first cuddle. The nurse placed the little baby, whom she had carried for over nine months, in her arms, leaving her so overwhelmed that she didn't know what to say. She finally said, through tears, "Hello, little baby. Hello. I'm your Mummy."

Her next thoughts, as she looked at her new precious, tiny son, were that he looked exactly like Jack. A crunched up, wrinkled, but exquisite Jack.

He was 45cm long and weighed 8lbs 7oz. He was born at 10 o'clock on the 23rd of May and had a mass of dark curls.

Iris glanced over and said, "What's his name?"

And Isabella replied "Theodore. Theodore Michaels. Teddy for short,"

"He's beautiful, absolutely beautiful. And so tiny and perfect," said Bibi with tears in her eyes, huddled over the sleeping child, in his mother's arms.

"Isn't he just? He's just adorable. I am filled with happiness. I love him-I just love him. Even though I should be tired, it feels like I'll never be able to sleep again. I never want to take my eyes off him," said Isabella, looking every inch the proud parent, she now was.

"He looks a little like you."

"He looks a lot like his daddy," she said.

They whispered to each other for a while until Isabella eventually said, "Look, Bibi. It's terribly late. Go home and get some sleep. I'll see you in the morning, okay?"

"I don't want to leave you."

"Please? We'll be fine. We all need our rest. Now go okay, before I call the nurse."

Once back on the ward, Isabella spent hours and hours just thankfully gazing at her new baby in wonderment. She felt an overwhelming rush of emotions as she gazed at his tiny features, his delicate little fingers, and his peaceful expression as he slept. She felt a profound sense of love and awe. Every detail seemed perfect, and an indescribable feeling of joy and wonder filled her. For hours on end, she lay there, soaking in the sight of this precious new life she had brought into the world. She had done this. She found herself unable to look away, captivated by the miracle of existence and a deep bond formed as she began to imagine the adventures and experiences that lay ahead together. Just the two of them. Only once in the early hours of the morning did she think about someone else. Someone who looked exactly like the little bundle lying peacefully swaddled in a blanket and she felt a pang of regret that he would never know this feeling of ineffable love and devotion, he would never know this captivating little child, watch him grow, wonder what he'd do with his life. But it still hurt to think of him, so she tried to banish all thoughts of him from her mind. She just looked forward to taking her baby home, to starting afresh and build a new life with her little boy.

The following morning Bibi returned with Harry closely behind. He was carrying an enormous basket of beautiful fresh flowers, complete with blue balloon exclaiming, "It's a boy."

They both took turns to hug Isabella and then looked down at the little sleeping bundle and both shed a few tears.

"I'm so proud of you, you know. Going through all that alone," said Harry, taking her hand in his own, "But we're both here for you now and will look after you, won't we, Bibi?" he winked.

"We sure will Izzy."

"Was it really awful?" he asked gently.

"It was ... it was bloody terrible. Worse than you could ever imagine."

"But worth it?"

"Abso-bloody-lutely. Just look at him."

***

CHAPTER TWENTY-TWO

Her friends were true to their word. Over the next few weeks, they both took turns looking after Isabella and baby Teddy. Anyone who didn't know any better would have assumed Harry was the doting father, as he fawned and cooed over the new baby, he had even taken a couple of weeks off work so he could be on hand to help her.

They took it in turns to help with the household chores; Harry helped prepare the feeds when Isabella struggled to breastfeed herself any longer and it made him feel important. Bibi helped make meals, and they both took it in turns to look after the little one whilst his exhausted mother had a well-deserved rest in the afternoons.

She had many visitors over the next few weeks, including her parents, separately of course; friends and work colleagues and she received an array of pretty, predominantly blue coloured cards through the post. She also received a beautifully wrapped parcel, full of delightful gifts for the baby, from Ingrid.

It was hard work, and she felt as if she was in a daze most of the time through lack of sleep, but she was enjoying motherhood immensely. Teddy was an engaging baby and, by eight weeks old, was sleeping for about 6 hours a night.

Over the coming months she watched in amazement as he gave his first smile, started holding things in his hands, began laughing and chuckling and squealing aloud and sat unsupported for the first time. Everything was new and exciting for them, and they enjoyed him immensely.

When Teddy was six months old, Isabella returned to work on a part-time basis, working a maximum of three and a half days per week, sometimes from home, other times she had to go in. She tried to ensure she spent as little time away as possible from her beloved son. But as she was a lone parent, she had no option but to return to work, if they were both to survive. She counselled extreme caution in choosing her projects. Nothing that might overrun, or was too far away from home.

Luckily, another good friend of Bibi's had recommended an excellent nanny who had left a family when her two charges had started school. At 58 years old, Bernadette (Bernie) Phillips was happily married to Christopher for the past 34 years and had two grown-up children of her own. She provided an Enhanced DBS check and excellent references, all thoroughly checked out by Isabella and a wealth of experience working with and looking after children. She fortunately lived only a 5-minute drive away from Isabella's and was incredibly generous and flexible with her time.

Within weeks, the two were firm friends and Isabella, at last, felt she could relax and entrust Teddy in Bernie's more than capable hands. Most importantly, the little boy warmed to Bernie immediately and Isabella had no qualms about leaving him in her care.

Bernie was often around when Harry was visiting Isabella and, like Bibi, thought he was wonderful. He more than likely visited them so often so he could see little Teddy. He loved him like he was part of his own family and spoiled him rotten. When he'd go to leave, Bernie would tease and pester Isabella constantly about him.

"He's so handsome and kind," she'd say. "Why don't you marry him? He adores you and dotes on the little mite."

"Bernie, Harry's a marvellous friend, nothing more."

Once when Isabella was out at work for the day, Bernie subtly tried to question Bibi as to the identity of Teddy's father, but Bibi was a loyal friend and would never give too much away, only to admit that it had been a brief, casual affair, that's all.

"So, they split up before little Ted was born?"

"Not even that long, I'm afraid. It was literally a few days, a brief liaison. Call it what you will, but he never knew or will never know that Teddy exists, unfortunately. It all ended in tears and I don't know what Izzy will tell Teddy about his father. She hasn't decided yet."

"How sad, he'll never know his daddy. I'm sure he looks on Harry as a father figure, you know?"

"Possibly, but as he gets older, Isabella will explain."

"There's no chance of this other fella putting in an unexpected appearance then?"

"No, it's definitely finished. As far as we're aware, he lives overseas, so there's no chance of her bumping into him."

"Sad I'd say."

Me too, thought Bibi, but she would never voice this out loud.

Isabella was enjoying being back at work, out in the 'real world' again, but looked forward to coming home and spending a quiet evening alone with her little boy.

She was back to her magnificent self and her figure had returned more or less to how it had been before she'd given birth. Luckily, she hadn't suffered from stretch marks and hadn't had a weight problem. One of the lucky few.

From time to time, nice, eligible, attractive men asked her out on a date, but she politely turned them down, not wanting to waste any precious time away from her son.

"You can't hide yourself away forever, Izzy." Bibi would complain constantly, "You must go out." But Isabella always had an excuse. She just didn't want to go out.

Teddy was an enchanting child, with his father's dark brown hair and his mother's stunning blue eyes. He had warm olive skin and was exceptionally tall for his age, often being mistaken for much older than he was.

Isabella was ecstatic at his first word "Mama" and, like all mothers, believed her child was the most beautiful in the world.

On her days off and at weekends, she would take him to days out in the park, feeding the ducks, farms, the zoo, enjoying picnics. They visited her store, where everyone swarmed around him, clucking affectionately.

To Isabella's relief, Teddy loved Bernie; he had no problem being left in her company. Equally, Bernie loved him as if he were her own grandson. He also enjoyed spending time with Bibi and was a terrible flirt. Teddy loved being around Uncle Harry, who continued to spoil him immensely. He doted on him as if he were his own, and what was even more delightful was that Teddy reciprocated this affection so unconditionally. In fact, it was Harry that got his first ever smile.

Isabella took little Teddy to stay at Harry's a few of times over a long weekend. When Isabella first visited his large Edwardian house, she felt enchanted and insisted on having a guided tour before they settled down. Isabella found the décor very impressive. The kitchen was bright and modern, which was complemented by Harry's abstract art and furniture. The room she loved most was the impressive orangery, with expensive rattan furniture, amongst an array of plants–jasmine, ferns, grapevines and lots of other leafy green plants.

They wandered back along the dark, imposing hallway; through to the elegant, bright living room, central to which was an enormous handcrafted fireplace. Bold furnishings filled the room, along with a beautiful display cabinet that showcased a stunning piece of flawless craftsmanship by Rene Lalique. Fabulous Osborne Little wallpaper covered the dining room opposite, from ceiling to wood floor. A large sold mahogany English 18th century dining table dominated the room, complete with many works of art, including an original

Picasso and Corot.

Harry led them upstairs to the main bedroom where a four-poster bed, in an art nouveau design, with its curving and undulating lines, stood in the middle of the vast room. Cream silk decorated the entire bedroom, from the walls to the furnishings, creating a calm, but opulent atmosphere. Another charming feature of the room was a later, art déco chaise longue, with sleek streamlined forms, sited underneath an enormous bay window, where the light could penetrate and spread around the whole room. There was an atmosphere of extreme elegance and sophistication.

The startling bathroom featured black and white handcrafted marble tiles that covered the walls and ceiling, along with a massive oval marble bath at the centre, resembling a swimming pool in size.

"Definitely a man's bathroom," said Isabella. "Although you have good taste, Harry. This house is amazing."

"Just like you," he'd teased.

"I'll be on my toes the whole weekend. What if Teddy breaks something? All your lovely treasures."

"Don't worry Izzy, they're only things. I don't care one bit." But she couldn't fully relax.

During this time, Harry continued to have many brief, enjoyable affairs, but he introduced no one. None lasted over four or five weeks. She felt honoured, though, that he felt close enough to her to tell her about his 'girlfriends'. However, same old story, as soon as they became too close to him, put just a little pressure on, he ended it.

"You'll end up a sad, lonely old bachelor." Isabella would warn him, "With no-one to care for you?"

"I've got you."

"For God's sake Harry. I mean it. There are plenty of girls out there who, for who knows what reason, would settle down with you."

"That's the problem Izzy. I don't think I could devote

myself to one person, unless it's you, of course," he'd joke.

"But don't you want your own children?"

"I'm more than happy with my life as it is Isabella. Anyway, I don't tell you how to run your life–you've never been out on a date forever."

They remained the best of friends, but that was all. He teased her constantly about being celibate and said she was turning into an old maid.

To her irritation, both he and Bibi conspired to get her fixed up and out on one- or two-blind dates, but they were a disaster. The men seemed to only want one thing and whey they found out about the little boy at home, that was the end.

But she didn't care about going out on dates. Life was blissfully uncomplicated. She was happy. She had a beautiful little son. Good friends. A pleasant home. A thriving business. What more could she want?

One evening, not long after Ted had just celebrated his second birthday, Harry came over wildly excited.

"You'll never guess what?" he exclaimed.

"What?" she said in amusement.

"Ingrid and David are getting married."

"What. You mean David, her boss David?" she felt so incredibly guilty that she did not know what her friend had been up to over the past few years.

"It's true. They announced their engagement today."

"I don't believe it. I knew they were dating on and off a while back, but I did not know it was so serious."

"Neither did any of us. They broke the news today during a staff management meeting of all places. They're apparently getting married in September and we're both invited."

"My God, it's so soon. Are they sure? How can things have happened so quickly and with no one knowing?"

"Of course, they're sure, silly. They're in love."

She phoned Ingrid later than evening. "Why didn't you tell me?" she cried. "I know we have spoken as little since Teddy was born, but wow, that's one hell of a secret."

"It wasn't a secret Iz, we just haven't spoken as much as we used to."

"I'm sorry."

"It's not your fault. We both have just had different things going on. I hardly knew what was happening myself. You sort of knew we'd been dating for a few months, having a ball, just enjoying ourselves. Then things started getting a little more serious. For the first time in my life, I didn't want to be without him-I wanted to see him every night. I missed him like crazy when he was away. I don't want to go out any more. Can you believe that? All I want is him."

"I get that. I'm like that with Teddy. Why would I want anything else when I have everything I need right here?"

"I'd rather spent a cosy night in with David. Just the two of us, cuddled up with a bottle of wine and a movie."

"Who is this talking and what have you done with my friend Ingrid?" she laughed.

"I know. I know. It's crazy. But he's the kindest, most generous person I've ever met."

"And very rich."

"There is that. But that doesn't matter. I love him - I've never been in love before. I may have thought I was, but this is different. Oh Izzy, he's wonderful."

"I'm so happy for you. So, what happened? When did he propose?"

"Last week. Wednesday, at a charity event. He just pulled out a little red box, from Cartier obviously, and popped the question."

"Wow."

"We're marvellous together. He's the most wonderful man I've ever met. I'm a changed woman. I can't think of anything more fabulous than spending my life with him and, who knows, we may have a little toddler like yours."

"You're not ...?"

"No, silly."

"Well, I'm surprised, but so happy for you both. It's about time someone made a decent woman of you. Although I'm peeved that it's taken you this long to even tell me you're more than just dating." And they continued to laugh and joke for ages, like old times.

"You will come to the wedding, won't you, Isabella?"

"Of course, I will. Just let me know when and where?"

"Well, the when is definitely September, as I'm sure Harry has told you and wait for it–the where is, umm, Las Vegas?"

"My God Ingrid. But I can't go to Las Vegas?"

"Of course you can. You must. You're going to be my one and only bridesmaid."

"What about Teddy? I can't take him to America. He's too little. He wouldn't sit through the flight."

"Don't look for excuses."

"I'm not. But I don't think I can?"

"Leave him with your nanny? He won't miss you for one week, surely?"

"I'm his mother, for God's sake. Of course, he'd miss me. You know nothing about children, do you?"

"Please Izzy. I need you. One week. That's all. Think about it?"

"Okay, I'll think about it."

***

CHAPTER TWENTY-THREE

Harry and Bibi argued with her and cajoled her over the forthcoming months. They convinced her that Bernie would take good care of Teddy for just over a week, with Bibi available if needed. Harry assured her they would have a wonderful time together in Las Vegas and perhaps they would have a brief break first in LA or San Francisco.

"But what if he's poorly?" She whined, contemplating every awful possibility.

"He won't be. And if he is, Bernie can look after him and if, God forbid, it's worse, which it won't be, we can fly home."

"But I feel so awful about leaving him. He's so little."

"Isabella, he'll be positively fine."

They all eventually persuaded her to go. It was all arranged for the third week in September.

They'd fly to Los Angeles, where they would spend a few days, before moving on to Vegas. She felt terribly guilty for leaving Teddy, but they all agreed he would be in expert hands and the break would do Isabella the world of good. She hadn't had a proper holiday for ages.

"Mama go howday" Teddy would exclaim, not knowing what holiday was or meant. Not knowing that his mummy was about to leave him behind for more than one entire week.

Many times, she nearly changed her mind, felt like cancelling, but Harry was there to reassure her that everything would go off smoothly.

The morning she was leaving for Los Angeles was

awful. She cried as Teddy clung to her screaming "Mummy. Mummy." And felt undeniably guilty all the way to the airport.

As soon as she got to Heathrow, she phoned Bernie to see how her beloved son was and, of course; he was perfectly fine.

"He's fine," She exclaimed happily, as she ran back to Harry to tell him the good news. "He's playing with his Brio. He stopped crying as soon as we'd pulled away in the car."

"You see? He will be perfectly looked after. Don't worry," he said.

They wandered around the Duty-Free lounge and she bought herself some more perfume and stocked up on her Elemis.

They then sat down for a quick bite to eat and a coffee. Anyone would have thought they were a happily married couple, the way they were so comfortable with each other. They both looked smart and were a stunning couple.

The flight left on time and they were soon on their way to LAX. To her delight and absolute surprise, Harry had purchased First-Class seats. In fact, he had booked and planned the complete trip, so everything was to be first class, the flights, the hotel, the transport. She was a little embarrassed that he wouldn't let her pay her own way. He insisted. It was his treat.

"You won't expect anything in return, will you?" she said.

"By now, Isabella, I know I will get nowhere with you. You won't even relent after a few drinks. You're a closed book."

They enjoyed a surprisingly nice in-flight meal and then settled back to watch the latest Will Smith movie. After it finished, Isabella asked, "So do we know anyone else going to this wedding in Vegas?"

She had asked Ingrid on a couple of occasions, but she had been vague and assured her it was just close friends and family. No work colleagues. So that allayed any fears about bumping into anyone from Kenya.

"Besides us, I believe there'll be another 60 or 70."

"60 or 70. I thought it was close friends and family," she wailed.

"That is. Parents. Grandparents. Brothers and sisters. Aunties and uncles. He apparently has a big family, dozens of cousins, that kind of thing, and a dozen of their closest friends."

"Gosh. Aren't we privileged?" she said.

"Yes, I believe so," he said, avoiding any further discussion. "So where do you fancy going to in LA?"

"Everywhere. I want to go shopping on Rodeo Drive. I want to go where all the tourists go, I suppose," she said eagerly. "Oh, and of course I must get something to wear for the wedding, seeing as I am a bridesmaid."

"Talk about leaving it till the last minute. Could you not have got something before we left? There are shops in London, you know?"

"I know silly. But when do I get the chance to go shopping in peace anymore? I've discussed it with Ingrid, asked her what I should wear, but she's left it totally to my discretion, as long as it's not white to clash with her dress and the flowers are pink."

"Ingrid wearing white. Have you ever heard of such nonsense?"

"Don't be mean Harry ..."

They both also had a nice nap during the flight and arrived in LA feeling fairly relaxed.

They arrived at the Beverly Hills Hotel on Sunset Boulevard in their chauffeur-driven limo, and Isabella couldn't believe that he had reserved one of their expensive bungalow suites.

A porter led them outside, along the winding paths to their private bungalow, beautifully situated amongst lush hibiscus, blooming bougainvillea and tropical palms.

Isabella ran around their luxurious residence like a little child in a sweetie shop. It was the ultimate indulgence, beautifully furnished, with a wood-burning fireplace, two bedrooms, a modern kitchen, a dining room, a private patio, its own pool and jacuzzi.

"We'll unpack first and then how do you fancy going out for a drink and something to eat, Isabella?" Harry called from his bedroom.

"Sounds great. I'm famished. Just give me 5 minutes to have a shower and change out of these clothes, okay?"

"Harry, this is marvellous," she exclaimed a short time later.

"You're marvellous. You deserve to be spoiled."

After they'd both freshened up and changed and she had texted home to check on Teddy, they headed to the world-famous Polo Lounge. They ordered a couple of drinks from the Martini Menu, whilst they perused the wide selection of cuisine available on the menu and looked around at the refreshed, elegant surroundings.

Isabella was both astounded and excited to see Nicholas Cage dining with a couple of friends and Harry had to reprimand her several times for staring.

"Will you stop being so ill-mannered and stop gawking?"

"I can't help it. I mean, Nicholas Cage. Will you get his autograph for me?"

"Don't even think about it."

"You're so mean."

"You're so star-struck."

"But he's even more gorgeous in real life. Please, Harry."

"Isabella enough. If you think I'm going up to Nicholas Cage, you've got another thing coming."

"Spoilsport."

After being shown to their delightfully situated table on the patio, set amongst palm trees and vividly coloured flowers, Harry ordered a bottle of vintage champagne and then ordered their meals.

A soothing warmth enveloped the surroundings,

beckoning them to savour the outdoors in the early evening.

Isabella settled on the most delicious sounding Chicken Tortilla soup with spring onion, avocado and cheddar cheese, followed by a tomato and buffalo mozzarella salad.

Harry opted for assorted seasonal mushroom polenta with mascarpone, followed by country style meatloaf with roasted garlic mashed potato and roasted corn sauce.

They both couldn't refuse the desserts and ordered the chocolate Chambord souffle cake with white chocolate truffle ice cream.

"So, what do you fancy doing tomorrow?" he asked, wiping his mouth with his pristine white napkin.

"I must get my outfit for the wedding."

"Rodeo it is then."

"Precisely. You know, I haven't felt this pampered and spoiled for ages. I could get used to this."

"How many times have I told you I could give you this and more?" he said with a sweeping gesture of his hand.

"Yes, but then you'd get bored with me and I'd no longer have your friendship," she stated.

"I know, you're right. We don't want to spoil what we have," he said, cupping her small hands in his large hands. "But don't you ever wonder, though, what it would be like?"

"What? To sleep with you." She laughed raucously.

"Yes. It's not that funny, you know."

"Not really, no."

"Liar."

"No, really. Of course I haven't."

"Wow. You know how to make a guy feel wanted."

"I'm sorry. But you know I'm right." There was a pregnant pause. "Why have you?"

"What?"

"Wondered what it would be like to sleep with me?"

"All the time."

"God, you pervert," and she playfully slapped his hands away.

They spent the rest of the gratifying, quiet evening just chatting and people watching. It was a glorious night, warm, without being uncomfortable.

They eventually went to bed about midnight and she fell asleep within minutes. To her dismay though, woke at about 5am-she lay there in the dark for about an hour, but then she heard Harry cough from the room next door. Rising to her feet, she poked her head around the corner of his door.

"Harry? Are you awake?" she whispered.

"Sure am. I've been awake for the past half hour."

"Me too. We've both been lying there wide awake and not said anything," she said, "It must be jet lag. I'm starving, are you?"

"You're always starving. But yes, I'm famished. Do you fancy room service?"

"Sounds wonderful." She said and bounced onto his huge queen bed, whilst he ordered a relative banquet from room service.

They sat together on his bed; Isabella in a pale pink silk slip and he in his boxers, eating freshly baked croissants and eggs benedict, followed by a round of crispy, warm toast and marmalade. They washed all this down with freshly squeezed orange juice and strong percolated coffee and they were giggling like a couple of naughty school children enjoying a midnight feast.

"Don't you think this is disgusting, considering the size of the meal we had last night?" he said.

"Definitely."

"You know" he said, looking at her quizzically.

"What?"

"You look incredible."

"I look like shit."

"No, seriously Izzy." He reached over and stroked her arm.

"Harry." she pleaded. He was making her feel uncomfortable now. "Stop kidding around."

"I'm not kidding-I think I love you."

"I love you too."

"But not in that way?"

"No Harry. I love you as my friend. One of my best friends. We can't ruin what we have."

"Why would we ruin anything? It might make things better?" he leant over and suddenly kissed her on the mouth, then sensing her astonishment, he pulled back and asked "Don't you fancy me?"

"Harry, I can't believe you. You know where we stand. I've never led you to believe otherwise."

"I'm sorry," he said, his eyes sparkling, "It's just ... you're driving me crazy in that thing." And he grabbed her arms and threw her on her back and sat astride her, looking down at her.

"Harry. What are you doing?" she screamed, "I'm warning you."

"Yeah?"

"Try kissing me again and you're dead."

He started tickling her and biting her neck. Then he kissed her again on the mouth. At first, she responded. Wow! This was totally unexpected, and it felt fantastic. It had been so long since a man had even held her, but reality hit her — it was Harry, for God's sake. What were they doing? He was one of her best friends.

"Harry stop."

"Isabella, please?" he whispered huskily.

"We'll regret this."

"No, we won't. Trust me."

"Please."

"Didn't you think that felt good?"

"That's not the point."

"Of course, that's the point. I'm a man, you're a woman."

"You're my best friend."

"Even better. What's the problem? We're both single. We've no ties. What can hurt?"

"We can Harry. It's not right, you know it's not. Ew I feel

sick suddenly. It's like kissing your own brother."

"Wow, thanks for that. Isabella, you know you want me." He said then, sensing things were going no further, he tried to bite her neck again to lighten the intense mood.

"Harry," she screamed, laughing her head off by now, "Get off me, you plonker."

"Right. That's your last chance." He smiled, before jumping off the bed.

"Last chance?"

"Yeah. I'm not making a play for you ever again. You're obviously passionless, if you can't even fancy me."

"Oh my God. You egotistical bastard." And she threw a pillow at him.

"I'm going for a cold shower," he pretended to sulk, before adding, "You know, you're the first woman ever to reject me."

"Really?"

"Really"

"You don't hate me?"

"I told you. I love you," and he left her.

Later that day, after a lazy couple of hours, they stepped out of their hotel and Isabella announced she wanted to walk. Harry insisted no one walked in LA and anyway, did she have any idea how long Rodeo Drive was?

"But it's only down the road?"

"Isabella, we have a perfectly good limo at our disposal and anyway, I'm not carrying all your bloody bags. Perhaps if you'd been more ... co-operative earlier?" he joked.

"I knew you'd hold it against me. I hope my turning you down hasn't made things difficult? Have I hurt your feelings?" she said, nudging him with her shoulder.

"I'm only joking. I want nothing from you. Come on, we're not walking and that's that."

So, feeling a little over the top, but enjoying herself all the same, their driver waited patiently whilst they perused the meticulously curated window displays and trailed in and out of the various immaculate designer stores along Rodeo Drive.

She bought a new handbag and overnight bag at Louis Vuitton. Harry bought himself an exquisite new briefcase.

They stopped at an outdoor cafe and enjoyed a freshly brewed coffee and pastry.

She had a glorious time at Chanel and then at Gucci, trying on some gorgeous outfits.

"You look like a model." Said Harry as he watched her admiringly, exuding confidence and poise, coming in and out of the changing rooms to parade the outfits in front of him.

"I feel like one in these clothes." She said, settling finally for a long black dress, with small drop sleeves and a high draped effect front neckline, which hugged her figure to perfection.

They found a wonderful little children's boutique, and she bought Teddy some enchanting little outfits, some with matching socks and hats, and Harry insisted on buying him a new winter coat and a wonderful outfit in Dolce and Gabanna.

Harry purchased a new suit, shirt, and tie at Ralph Lauren for the wedding and Isabella admitted, to his delight, that she had never seen him look more handsome.

"The thing is, you'll look far too classy for Vegas." she said, "Are you sure you don't want something with a few more studs and tassels?"

"Hey. That's not a bad idea."

"Don't," she groaned.

She found exactly what she wanted for the wedding from Harry Winston's. It had a plain, yet graceful quality. A pale pink strappy ankle-length dress. It hugged her body perfectly and looked amazing. Just in case it should turn cooler in the evening, she bought a baby-pink cashmere cardigan to wear over the top.

She then purchased a pair of Kate pink iridescent pumps from Louboutin and searched for a bag to finish the look, settling on the Loubi54 clutch, crafted in pink suede, adorned with strass, perfect.

Just as they were calling it quits for the day, she spied a black long column dress with a back split and double satin straps over the shoulders and a black, cowl back, bias cut, satin dress by Prada, which she swiftly added to her purchases. "I think that about does it, don't you?" she said.

"No wait. We must go to Cartier," he added.

"Okay, if you insist," she said.

However, she felt mortified when they arrived at the store and discovered he wanted to buy her a present.

"Harry you can't."

"I can."

"But what for?"

"Because I want to. Now no arguing."

"You're feeling guilty for trying to seduce me, aren't you?" she whispered, giggling.

"No, I'm just hoping I can buy my way into your panties."

"I knew it."

They spent ages poring over the grandiose jewellery; Isabella wouldn't say which pieces she liked, as she felt so abashed that he was paying for them. Eventually, though, he found an exquisite set of earrings, necklace and bracelet, made in white gold, set entirely with pure and generously shaped diamonds which were on sale for thousands and thousands of dollars.

"Try them on." He offered eagerly.

"Harry. I can't. They're far too extravagant."

"Please. They'll look stunning on you" and he was right. She tried them on and admired herself in the mirror.

"Wow," she said simply.

"We'll have these," Harry said to the assistant.

"No," she gasped, "Harry please."

But no matter what she said and despite her trying to dissuade him, nothing would deter him from purchasing them for her.

"Harry, they're amazing and beautiful," she exclaimed

afterwards, whilst they reclined in the limo on the drive back along Rodeo Drive to their hotel, "They're the most heavenly things I've ever seen. I'll be terrified wearing them."

"Nonsense. You'll outshine even the bride."

"I hope not. She'd love that. Thank you so much. You're too generous. I don't know what to say?" and she leant over and kissed him on the cheek.

That afternoon, she called home to check on Teddy, who was absolutely fine, and afterwards they relaxed and caught up with some sunbathing whilst lying by their own private swimming pool.

She turned to him and said, "Harry, you realise how much money we spent today? You especially," she winced.

"I know. Isn't it great? You should indulge yourself. You've become too overwhelmed with motherhood. It's time for you to go out and enjoy yourself more."

"Don't start this crap again, Harry."

"I'm not. But this is the first time you've done something for yourself since little Teddy was born."

"That's being a Mummy. I've a little boy now, he takes priority. My life is his life."

"Well, I think you're too young and beautiful to be stashed away like a hermit."

"That's excessive. I date. I go out."

"Date? You've been out, what, twice, to dinner?"

"Do you think I should sleep around? That's not my scene and you know it."

"I'm just saying ..."

"Well, don't."

The following morning, they drove down Hollywood Boulevard to Mann's Chinese Theatre, where they marvelled at the grandeur of the architecture and immersed themselves in Hollywood history. They compared hand and footprints with the iconic movie legends and Isabella took many photographs of all her favourites; Walter Matthau, Jack Lemmon, Dean Martin, Frank Sinatra and Clark Gable. She compared her own prints with Ava Gardner, Jane Russel and Marilyn Monroe, whose prints seemed tiny. Walking along the Boulevard, the glitz and glamour and energy of Tinseltown surrounded them. They watched street performers and browsed the souvenir shops before, to Harry's disgust, Isabella insisted on getting a map of the star's homes. They asked their driver to proceed around the palatial estates of Beverly Hills, Bel Air and the Hollywood Hills, peering in through the landscaped security gates of the homes of the rich and famous.

"This is so revolting," he complained. "I feel like a peeping tom. A stalker."

That evening they went to the movies and saw what Harry described as a 'chick-flick' followed by a superb dinner at Chasen's.

The following day they fancied a trip to the beach and their driver dropped them off so they could walk along the wide boardwalk of Venice Beach, an outdoor circus, teaming with rollerbladers, jugglers, fire-eaters and other wacky characters. It was an overload of sights, sounds and experiences as they strolled along, greeted with street vendors selling artworks, the performers showcasing their talents and the scent of the salty sea air filling their lungs. Colourful murals adorned the buildings, while the rhythmic sound of waves crashing against the shore created a calming backdrop. People from all walks of life mingled along the path, giving it a diverse and eclectic feel.

They walked south to Muscle Beach, site of the legendary weight-lifting centre, where Harry couldn't help but compare himself with the hunks of muscle pumping iron.

"I could take him," he stated.

"I'm sure you could," she said.

Before heading north to Santa Monica, they stopped at a chic little cafe on the beach for a bite to eat. Along Ocean Boulevard, they enjoyed a leisurely stroll, savouring the serene experience that offered breathtaking views and a sense of tranquility. Greeted by the cheerful hustle and bustle of visitors enjoying the amusements and panoramic ocean vistas, they walked around Santa Monica Pier. They continued along the boulevard, the sound of rolling waves accompanying their journey, creating a soothing soundtrack to their walk. They passed by upscale restaurants and quaint cafes, catching glimpses of surfers riding the waves and families building sandcastles on the beach.

As they approached Palisades Park, the atmosphere shifted to one of quiet contemplation. Lush greenery lined the pathways, and they paused for a break underneath the shade of a cypress, offering them respite from the sun.

He watched her lying there. She looked like a young girl, with her hair tied back in a ponytail, skimpy T-shirt and shorts and trainers. He didn't think it was fair. Even though he loved Teddy too, she deserved so much more. Being beautiful and intelligent. She was a young woman, for goodness' sake. She was hidden away like a nun. But boy, was she stubborn.

She noticed him staring at her.

"What are you thinking?" she asked, smiling at him.

"Nothing," he replied, feeling himself redden.

"You don't give up, do you?" she said.

"I'm just enjoying being with you."

"Me too. I've had a wonderful couple of days. I just feel so guilty, as Teddy would have loved it here."

"He would. We'll have to come back with him," he said.

"I can't wait to go to Vegas. I hope I love it as much as I love LA."

He remained completely silent. She didn't notice.

***

CHAPTER TWENTY-FOUR

The following day, they caught their internal flight to McCarran International Airport, arriving a short time later at the global capital of gambling, gaming and entertainment, Las Vegas. They arrived at the phenomenal resort in the middle of the Nevada Desert just before dark, so didn't get the same impact as those arriving at night. Isabella's jaw dropped as she laid eyes on rows upon rows of slot machines. At the airport.

Exiting the airport, the desert heat and the glimmering skyline of Las Vegas greeted them in the distance. Their cab driver merged onto the freeway, the iconic architecture of the city's resorts and hotels gradually coming into view, each one vying for attention with its extravagant displays and towering structures.

Their drive took them past famous landmarks such as the Luxor, with its pyramid-shaped silhouette and the iconic Welcome to Fabulous Las Vegas sign.

As they continued on, the scenery transitioned from the opulence of the strip to the vibrant energy of downtown.

As they approached their hotel, The Golden Nugget, they encountered the historic charm of Fremont Street, where classic casinos and neon signs lined the road, reminiscent of the city's golden age. Harry had chosen this location instead of The Strip, as it was the original core of the city and he wanted to experience the authentic Vegas.

They stepped out of their cab and their gaze went upwards, as they witnessed thousands of lights displaying animated scenes overhead. Their hotel was directly below the Fremont Street experience, a 1500 ft long, 100ft high canopy of covered pedestrian mall where neon lights and music shows, all choreographed in dazzling displays of colour, were playing above. Seeing this for the first time evoked a sense of excitement and awe.

"Look. There's the Four Horseshoes and look down there. The Kicking Cowboy," she exclaimed excitedly, "It's just like the movies." Isabella span around, looking in amazement at the dazzling array of neon signs and bustling crowds creating a spectacle unlike any other.

Eventually, Harry dragged her into the hotel reception.

"I can't believe I'm here." She cried, "I'm so excited."

"Glad you came?"

"Definitely."

A spacious and grand atrium greeted them and they walked through the cool and opulent lobby, adorned with sparkling chandeliers, polished white marble and gleaming brass, to the reception.

Whilst Harry checked them in at the priority desk and a porter looked after their bags, Isabella drawn to the sound of slot machines and the hum of conversation. It filled her with a sense of excitement and anticipation for the adventures that awaited in the casino–occupying meters of floor space, packed with million-dollar slots, video poker, blackjack, craps, roulette wheels and much, much more and the noise was incredible. There were scores of holiday makers; many in Hawaiian shirts and shorts, all stood in front of the slots with their buckets of quarters. Others stood around the table placing their bets eagerly and all spending their hard-earned cash, hoping their luck would finally come in. It was like entering another world. She found it exhilarating and fell in love with this dynamic, spectacular city.

Harry eventually caught up with her, and they headed up to their suite.

"Look at that," cried Isabella, as she pointed out the

largest golden nugget in the world housed in a glass case.

They sauntered past the Olympic-sized swimming pool, surrounded by palm trees and a cooling mist, amongst which dozens of men, women and children lay about in the warmth.

They both declared they couldn't wait to dive in. The weather outside was a withering 92 degrees still, but inside the air-conditioning was a glorious welcome.

Harry had reserved a luxury 2-bedroom apartment suite in the Spa Tower and again Isabella marvelled at the luxurious and indulgent retreat. The spaciousness and elegant design, modern furnishings and beautifully appointed rooms struck her. The living area had a thoughtful layout with plush seating arrangements and tasteful décor that exuded style and comfort. Large windows offered them a panoramic view of the Las Vegas skyline, providing a sense of tranquillity amidst the excitement of the city. She wandered through to her bedroom, a sanctuary of relaxation, featuring a sumptuous king-sized bed adorned with premium linens and pillows–she couldn't wait for a restful night's sleep. She peered into the sleek en-suite bathroom, complete with spacious walk-in shower, luxurious bathtub, marble countertops, offering her a spa like experience right in the comfort of their suite.

The suite offered them a welcome retreat from the non-stop activity surrounding them. The calm serenity and excellent taste amazed Isabella. Not what she had been expecting of Las Vegas. She just remembered seeing dozens of movies with seedy motels, a parking lot out front, a flickering neon sign and a general air of neglect. Drug deals and the FBI listening through the walls of a bedroom with outdated décor and worn stained carpets. Oh, and a poorly maintained bathroom, with leaky taps and a lingering smell of mildew. What a contradiction it was.

The plan was to meet with Ingrid and David later that evening at Caesar's Palace. After they had unpacked, had a little rest and washed and changed, they went outside to catch a cab to The Strip. It was only then, now it was dark, that Isabella could truly experience the glamour and glitter of Las Vegas.

As they stepped outside, she gazed in wonderment at the lights of the 4Queens and Sam Boyd's Fremont and the other luminous casinos surrounding them.

"Look at the lights." She exclaimed as they climbed into the back of the air-conditioned cab.

"Amazing, huh? Caesar's Palace please," said Harry to the driver. She watched in wonderment as they passed the Stratosphere, Circus Circus, Stardust and Treasure Island.

As they pulled up to the lavish Caesar's Palace on the heart of The Strip, they looked to their right and could see the Mirage with its immense lake and erupting volcanoes in full flow. Opposite, they could see the Imperial Palace, the Flamingo Hilton, Harrah's and further down Bally's. "It's wonderful." She cried, "Everything I thought it would be and more."

It was 10pm at night and the place was swarming with people. It was still about 80 degrees and humid. They entered The Forum, to do a quick bit of window-shopping, the inside of which resembled an ancient roman streetscape with immense columns and arches, ornate fountains and statues. They stared in wonderment as the robotic statues of Baccus, Plutus, Venus and Apollo in the Festival Fountain came alive before their eyes.

They meandered past the storefronts and looked up at the barrel-vaulted ceiling, upon which was painted blue sky with white fluffy clouds, emulating a sunny Mediterranean day.

They stopped for a cocktail in the bar of Planet Hollywood, before retracing their steps and joining the seemingly never-ending, moving walkway into the incredible world of opulence and palatial grandeur that is Caesar's Palace. The grand hotel was the last word in pseudo-Roman splendour, with colonnades, pillars and statues all surrounded by hand-painted murals. They made their way through the vast, noisy casino to a lounge bar where Harry had previously agreed to meet the others.

"Izzy. Harry. Over here," they heard Ingrid call, waving them over.

The old friends reunited at the bar, their faces lighting up with excitement as they embraced each other.

"Ingrid, you look amazing." Isabella cried as she hugged her friend tightly, delighted to see her. She then turned to hug David. "You are obviously having a wonderful effect on her, David."

"May I say the same for you, Isabella? You are looking as gorgeous and sexy as ever," he said.

"Watch it, buddy. You're marrying me tomorrow." Ingrid laughed as she playfully hit him on the arm.

They settled into some comfortable leather stools, surrounded by the buzz of conversation and clinking glasses.

"I can't believe we're finally here. It's been way too long," said Ingrid.

"I know, right? Isn't it wonderful?" exclaimed Isabella. "When did you arrive?"

"Yesterday. We're so excited," replied Ingrid.

"Are you staying here?" asked Isabella.

"No, we're next door at the Bellagio. It's amazing. Wait until you see it. Our suite's incredible, isn't it, honey?"

"Very opulent." David smiled.

"Ours is too, isn't it, Harry? We're at the Golden Nugget, downtown."

They ordered a round of drinks from the server.

"Isn't this exciting?" cried Isabella.

"Aren't you glad you came?" replied Ingrid.

"Oh yes. I wouldn't have missed this for the world," said Isabella.

"What Las Vegas or our wedding?" said David.

"Both, silly," said Isabella.

"So, what have you been up to? How's Teddy?" Ingrid asked.

"Oh, you know the usual: work, family. Teddy's fine. Great."

"She's only 'phoned home about 20 times since we've been in the States," quipped Harry.

"Nonsense," said Isabella. "Anyway, enough about me. What about you? How's life treating you?"

"Life's been good. We've been travelling a bit, trying new things. Honestly, it's so great catching up with you."

They all chatted happily together, conversation flowed, filled with laughter, reminiscing about old times and excitement about the upcoming nuptials. As they raised their glasses in a toast to the friendship and the bride and groom to be, the bar in Caesar's Palace became a backdrop for a cherished reunion between old friends.

Drinks were flowing and Isabella felt thrilled to see Ingrid and David so happy. They made an adorable couple. David seemed so much more relaxed and fun than when she'd last seen him.

Isabella looked around at the hundreds of gaming tables and the rows upon rows of slot machines, surrounded by people all hoping to beat the system and win the big one.

"It's astounding here," she said, a bit later on, "I love it."

"It's true," said David. "You either love it or hate it. I don't think there's a middle line."

"Well, I think it's wonderful," Isabella stated. "I can see why you wanted to get married here. I never want to go home. Tell me, why did you decide on Las Vegas?"

"Well, as you know, it's my second marriage ..." David began.

"Thanks for reminding me," grumbled Ingrid.

"Not just that, though. We're too old to have a big white wedding," he added.

"Speak for yourself. You're not old darling, you're just a classic," said Ingrid.

"I think it's an excellent idea. Although, I've been in Las Vegas all of a few hours and have yet to chance my luck. Harry? Will you come with me?" she asked, dragging him to his feet, giving him no say in the matter.

They tried their luck on the slot machines, which chimed relentlessly, their colourful displays enticing them to try their luck. They then walked over to the roulette wheel and placed their bets, their hearts racing at every turn. The card tables buzzed with energy, the shuffling of decks and clinking of chips adding to the excitement.

Amidst the throng, they watched the high rollers mingle amongst them, and cheers erupted as someone hit the jackpot. The cocktails continued to flow and time seemed to stretch and contract, each moment filled with the promise of triumph, but in reality, the sting of defeat.

They returned to Ingrid and David a short while later, Isabella having lost hundreds of dollars within what seemed like the space of a few minutes.

"It's not like the tiny little casino in Mombasa now, is it?" said David.

"No, no, I suppose not," Isabella whispered.

Ingrid was still astonished the mere mention of the place could send her friend hurtling back to that uncomfortable place locked away in her mind and heart. Harry noticed and changed the subject. "So, what are the plans for tomorrow?"

"Well, we're spending the day in bed or by the pool," Ingrid said, "I know which one, if David has his way," looking at him and smiling seductively, "Then, our wedding ceremony will take place at the Chapel at 7pm tomorrow night."

"How strange and brilliant, getting married at night. And very Las Vegas," said Isabella, laughing, "Is Elvis going to be there?"

"No, unfortunately," said Ingrid, "I wanted to get married by Elvis, but David insisted, if we were getting married here, it was to be as un-tacky as possible."

"If that's possible," he said.

"So, when are the others arriving?" Isabella asked. She had had so much to drink by then and was tired, so she was totally oblivious to the nervous glances exchanged by the other three.

"My parents are already here. They came with us," said

Ingrid. "They can't wait to see you again. And David's parents and brother, Michael, are arriving first thing in the morning and meeting us, hopefully, for breakfast. The rest of the gang are arriving tonight and throughout tomorrow, I believe. We'll probably only catch up with them all at the ceremony and the reception afterwards. Everyone's made their own arrangements. We've been truly lucky."

"Great," said Isabella. "I can't wait to meet them all. I'm looking forward to this."

Isabella and Ingrid then continued to chatter and at great length about dresses, make-up, flowers and everything else to do with the wedding the following day. The anticipation of the big day, adding to the giddy energy between them.

Ingrid squealed with excitement. "Can you believe it's finally here? Tomorrow is the big day."

"I know. I can hardly contain myself. You're going to be the most stunning bride ever."

"Stop it, you're making me blush. But seriously, I couldn't have asked for a better bridesmaid than you. I'm so glad you're here."

"Aw, thank you. It's such an honour to be part of the day. I can't wait to stand by your side tomorrow."

"I'm just so grateful to have you here with me, sharing in this special moment."

"Me too. Now let's toast to love, laughter and happily ever after ..."

They clinked their glasses together, the excitement and anticipation of the wedding, filling the room with warmth and joy and they stayed that way until the early hours of the morning when they eventually called it a night.

"Have you noticed there're no clocks or windows in the casinos, Isabella?" Harry said on the way back to their hotel in the cab.

"No? Why?"

"So you never know what time of day or night it is. They want you to forget time and spend as much time and money as possible."

"That'd be easy," mumbled Isabella.

They awoke late the following morning and, after an eagerly awaited and rapidly devoured brunch, they spent the rest of the morning and early afternoon lazily relaxing in a plush lounger outside their cabana and by the crystalline pool. The sound of cascading fountains mingled with the gentle hum of conversation. Isabella still had a healthy tan gained over the summer, and Harry regarded her approvingly as she lay in the sweltering heat and took the occasional refreshing dip in the pool to escape the desert heat. Attentive staff members catered to their every need, keeping them topped up with refreshing beverages and delectable snacks to keep them fuelled throughout the day.

Palm trees swayed gently in the breeze and Isabella read her book while Harry snored next to her.
Eventually, Isabella went back to the suite before him and she phoned Bernie to see how things were going. She spoke briefly to Teddy, who was having a wonderful time without her and didn't seem to miss her at all. He was more interested in telling her about the latest episode of Paw Patrol.

After a short while, she took the elevator to the fourth floor of the Hotel Spa. She had booked a wonderful late afternoon of sheer pampering, starting with a refreshing massage. She then stepped into the whirlpool bath, where she simply relaxed for 15 minutes, followed by the eucalyptus steam room and finally a stimulating Swedish shower.

After changing out of her robe and slippers, she walked next door to the salon, where she enjoyed a mini-facial, followed by a manicure and pedicure. Then, a professional applied her make-up and shampooed and blow-dried her hair. She looked like a million dollars and felt thoroughly relaxed and ready for the long evening ahead.

She returned to her room and changed into her new pink dress and accessories from Beverly Hills and as she walked into the sitting room, Harry wolf-whistled.

"You look sensational," he said. "Your afternoon of self-indulgence has obviously done you the world of good." Her hair was gleaming, her skin glowing with health, her make-up perfect and she looked breath-taking in her new dress.

"You don't look bad either." He was also looking tanned and healthy.

"You nearly forgot these." He smiled, opening the red box full of exquisite jewels.

"Never. Oh my God. I'd forgotten how stunning they were. I can't believe you bought these for me. It's the most generous gift I've ever had in my life."

As he helped her put on the jewellery, they admired the gleaming gems in the mirror.

"Wow." Harry stated.

"Wow," said Isabella, "You know, I think they may have cost more than my house."

"If only it was you and me getting married tonight. What with my money and your looks ..." he sighed sadly.

"Oh, shut up you loser. You'd run half a mile if I even mentioned the word marriage."

"Not with you, I wouldn't. We're practically a man and wife anyway, the time we spend with each other. The only thing missing is the sex. As Nietzsche said, *it is not a lack of love, but a lack of friendship that makes unhappy marriages.* We have both–love and friendship."

"Yes, but after 3 weeks of being married to me, you'd be off screwing some other bimbo."

"Never."

"Anyway, I don't find you attractive," she teased.

"Now I *know* that's a lie. Who could resist me?"

They continued laughing and teasing each other to the bar, where they enjoyed the best part of a bottle of champagne, before catching a cab to the Bellagio.

"I feel quite tiddly." She giggled. "Perhaps I shouldn't have drunk so much champagne on an empty stomach. We've a long evening ahead of us."

"Tiddly. That's such a funny word. Anyway, how can you say you've an empty stomach - you've been eating on and off all day? You'll be fine." I hope, he thought to himself.

When they pulled up under the porte-cochere, valets opened their doors and assisted their exit. They both gaped in wonderment at the beauty and elegance of their surroundings. The large man-made lake with its cascading fountains shooting water to various heights and directions and the impressive façade of the hotel.

They walked inside the beautifully designed lobby and asked a staff member for directions to the South Chapel.

Upon arrival, an officiant greeted them and gave Isabella her hand-held bouquet of roses and fragrant stephanotis, as well as a triple rose hairpiece, both of which perfectly harmonised with her dress. Thank God she'd gone for pink.

Someone handed Harry his boutonniere, and he pinned it to his lapel.

They stood to the side to wait their further instructions and watched as groups of other guests arrived and then headed into the chapel itself, where the harmonious sound of a live harpist would greet them.

Ingrid and David were evidently in a side room talking to the Minister, whilst the rest of the congregation were already in their seats.

Minutes later, Isabella recognised Ingrid's parents, Rose and Daniel walking towards them and went over to say hello, before bringing them over to introduce Harry.

Ingrid and David returned and hugged Isabella and Harry, just as David's parents and his brother entered. They all exchanged affectionate greetings and introduced the ones who hadn't met before. Everyone was chatting nervously and all the men were complementing the bride and the bridesmaid on their stunning outfits. Ingrid looked sensational in an elegant creation from Isabella Christiansen, her hair piled up high with a baby's breath halo and a glorious cascading bouquet of fresh roses in her arms.

They also all paid a lot of attention to Isabella and were looking in astonishment at her jewellery.

"They're not real," gasped Ingrid.

"'Fraid so," giggled Isabella. "Harry bought them for me in LA."

"They're soooo beautiful. Hey wait, it's my wedding. Where are my baubles?" said Ingrid.

"Ummm, the 10ct diamond on your finger's not a bauble?" sighed David. "Jeez, not bad for just good friends, Harry."

"He's trying to buy my love," joked Isabella.

"He's doing a damned good job," said Ingrid.

"Yeah, but she says she doesn't fancy me," moaned Harry.

"He finds it hard to believe that anyone couldn't possibly fancy him," said Isabella.

"Okay. Is everyone ready? We all here? Can we take our places?" the Minister asked in his Southern drawl, walking over to join them, interrupting their friendly, edgy banter.

"Not quite," stated David. "There's one more I'm afraid. Can we wait a couple of more minutes? I'm sure he'll be here soon. My best man."

"You're not the best man?" Isabella asked Harry sharply.

She noticed the look on Harry's face and said abruptly, "Who'll be here soon? Who's the best man? Who are we waiting for?"

Everyone heard her, but no one answered.

"Harry? Harry talk to me? Why aren't you answering me?" she said shrilly. But she knew. In the back of her mind, she had thought there was something they weren't telling her. She knew something funny was going on. She had thought the worst-case scenario, Madison. But it was worse. Much, much worse.

And then she saw him, almost physically felt him,

walk through the door towards them. He was more gorgeous than she could have remembered. His commanding presence drawing attention from all around him. His sun-kissed skin, bronzed to perfection. A healthy glow radiating from his complexion, accentuating his rugged features and adding an irresistible allure to his appearance. She wanted to fall on her hands and knees and crawl right through the door. She felt as if she were about to faint. From her keen eye, she could tell that he wore black Dolce and Gabbana from head to toe and had a ridiculous grin on his face as he spied her. Dark, tousled hair framed his chiselled jawline and intense gaze, lending an air of mystery and intrigue to his ruggedly handsome face. He obviously had no more idea that she would be here than she had about him.

"You stupid bastard." She said aloud. No one knew if she aimed this insult at Harry, Jack, or even at herself.

She then turned around and hissed at Harry, "How could you? You bloody knew, didn't you?"

"Isabella please." Harry begged her, "I'm sorry. So sorry. I knew if you had any idea Jack was coming, you wouldn't have come."

"Bloody damn right I wouldn't have come. How could you?" she had to fight herself from bursting into tears.

"Hi everyone," said Jack brusquely, "Wow man, what a welcome. What did I do?"

"Isabella please," said Ingrid calmly, grabbing hold of her forearms, "It's my wedding. As Harry said, we knew if we told you Jack was coming, you wouldn't have come. I wanted you to be my bridesmaid."

Isabella looked crestfallen by now and Jack was looking exceedingly uncomfortable, as were both sets of parents; they did not know what was going on and wondered why she was making such a commotion and whispered amongst themselves.

"I think we should take our seats, don't you?" said Ingrid's mother to no one in particular.

"Good idea," said someone else. And both sets of parents, David's brother and a couple of other guests, made a rapid escape to join the others waiting patiently in the chapel. The minister followed them shortly afterwards.

"Isabella please, darling?" begged Harry, putting his arm around her. "It's Ingrid and David's special day, their big moment. Please don't spoil it."

"Yes, please come on, sweetheart, for us?" pleaded David.

"I can't believe you'd be so cruel," she snapped at Harry, "I want to go."

"Isabella. You're my bridesmaid," begged Ingrid.

"Look, I'm sorry," offered Jack, his piercing eyes, deep and soulful, held a hint of mischief and confidence, hinting at the depth of character hidden beneath his exterior. "I shouldn't have come. I didn't know you'd be here."

"No, you shouldn't have come." Isabella hissed venomously.

"Isabella," whispered Harry, "Stop being childish. Please try to be an adult about this. We're talking years ago here. Jack is one of David's closest friends."

"And I'm supposed to be one of Ingrid's. And don't tell me I'm being childish, you, you absolute shit," she replied stubbornly.

Somehow, after much cajoling, they persuaded her to stay and promised that everything would be okay.

Isabella was livid. Seething. But, there was no getting out of it. There was nothing she could do. She couldn't, in all honesty, let down one of her oldest friends. She would simply ignore him. Pretend he didn't exist. But hell, it would be hard.

After a few embarrassing minutes, the men were all directed into and asked to take their places in the hushed, soothing little chapel.

"I'm so sorry Izzy," whispered Ingrid.

"I forgive you. Just. I'm truly sorry for acting like such an arse. I was in shock," said Isabella remorsefully.

"Please try to behave? For me?"

"I'll do my best. I promise," she grimaced.

The harpist began playing Mendelssohn's Wedding March. Isabella followed Ingrid slowly down the aisle, which was already scattered with fresh white and pink petals, as the congregation turned to watch their approach. Was it Isabella's imagination, or was everyone looking at her and whispering about her and her earlier spectacle? Oh God, how mortifying. Hopefully, it was just her imagination, and they were regarding the bride.

Ingrid took her place next to her future husband and Isabella took a seat next to Harry at the front. Thankfully, she was on the opposite side of Jack and didn't even so much as glance in his general direction as the minister began the service.

Isabella took in the stunning venue; the architectural details, stained-glass windows, and intricate woodwork. It was a romantic and intimate setting for the ceremony.

David and Ingrid were holding hands and looked very much in love. Isabella felt a little guilty for tainting their happy day. She would have to be on her best behaviour from now on. Why was she so easily triggered? Why wasn't she one of these people with a poker face? She would have to keep her emotions in check from now on. If she could.

She noticed the minister nodding at her expectantly. Shit, she should have been paying attention. He wanted her, as a witness, to join them. Then, to her absolute horror, he motioned Jack, as best man and second witness, to take his place alongside the bride and groom. Fuck. Shit, is this a church? Should she be swearing, albeit in her head? Oh bollocks. How could she have been so naïve? She hadn't thought about him in a long time and it just hadn't entered her head he might be a guest, let alone the best man. He could have at least shaved. God, she could be so stupid sometimes.

"Go on then. Get up there," hissed Harry, nudging her.

"Oh my God," she groaned to herself as she stood up and then purposefully stepped on Harry's foot.

"Ouch, watch it," he gasped as she pushed roughly past him.

Isabella remembered very little of the wedding vows. Being in such proximity to Jack again made it difficult for her to concentrate. She felt his dark, piercing eyes on her throughout the ceremony, but she couldn't return his gaze. She snuck a glance every now and again at his strong build, his broad shoulders and muscular physique exuding strength and vitality. Every movement he made, fluid and graceful, was a testament to his athleticism and natural poise.

Her anger towards Ingrid was desperate, but it was Harry who incensed her the most. It was unbelievable to her they could do this to her, especially given her opinion of him. She turned to glimpse Harry just once, who was nodding encouragingly at her. She just gave her most evil eyes in return.

After the immortal words "I now pronounce you husband and wife," there followed the obligatory handshaking and backslapping and the cries of congratulations.

They followed someone outside into the wilting heat for photos in front of Lake Como.

Isabella heard Jack call behind her, "Isabella. Please. Can I to talk to you?"

"Just bugger off and leave me the hell alone, will you?" she hissed in return.

He simply shrugged his shoulders and lit a cigarette. He didn't want to cause a further commotion in front of the other guests.

The photographer took countless snaps of the wedding party, first in front of the mesmerising display of the fountains, before they moved on to the botanical conservatory and gardens. Amongst the floral displays, Jack closely observed Isabella. Her flowing dark hair cascading down her back in tousled waves, reflecting a lustrous shine in the light. Those eyes, that mesmerising shade of violet, deep and captivating that he remembered so well. Her delicate, yet striking features, with high cheekbones and soft sculpted jawline and full expressive lips. Her smooth and radiant skin, with a natural glow that enhanced her beauty even further. He still felt that sense of allure and magnetism surrounding her. Her timeless beauty that still captivated him and had left such a lasting impression on him.

As the group moved towards the awaiting restaurant for a champagne reception in the bar. Isabella pulled Harry to the side and let the rest of the party pass them by. "Harry you bastard. You devious, lying bastard. You knew he was going to be here. Why didn't you warn me?" she hissed, trying hard to control her tears, but not succeeding. He thought she was going to hit him.

"Izzy please. You're being totally irrational."

"Irrational. You complete shit. Don't you remember what he did to me?" she wailed.

"This isn't about you, it's about David and Ingrid-their day. It's what they wanted. Now please try to act like a grownup for once. Put this tedious dalliance behind you and stop acting like a spoiled brat."

And with that, she slapped his face fiercely hard, leaving a stinging red handprint on his cheek.

"You absolute bastard. I hate you." She screamed.

And all he did was take her in his arms and held her tightly, smoothing her hair with his hands, rocking her gently, kissing her cheeks, "Izzy darling. I'm sorry. I'm so sorry. Ingrid made me promise. She wanted so much for you to be at her wedding. We knew you wouldn't come if you knew Jack was going to be here. I didn't mean to sound so callous. But this, this *thing*, whatever it is, has gone on too long. For Christ's sake, it was years ago. You had a brief fling with the guy. Please put it behind you. Walk in there like the lady you are, dazzling, dignified and don't let Jack know he bothers you, okay? Do it for me Izzy, I beg you?"

"Okay, I'll try," she hiccupped, "But I can't promise. He's the father of the person I love most in this world, for God's sake. He hurt me more than anyone ever has in my life."

"Oh Isabella, I'm sorry, I'm so sorry," he soothed. "It'll be okay. I promise. You must try, for all our sakes. I don't know all the ins and outs of you and Jack, but it's ancient history. You've both moved on."

"Is he alone?" she whispered.

"What do you mean?"

"Harry? You know damn well what I mean."

"As far as I know, yes."

"Still playing the field, you mean?"

"Isabella," he groaned.

"Okay. Okay. God. I'll do my best."

"Please? Show him a little respect. You know what I think."

"Oh, enlighten me with your infinite wisdom. I could use a good laugh."

"He is the father of your child."

"Be quiet. You think I don't know that?"

***

CHAPTER TWENTY-FIVE

Harry returned to Le Cirque to join the others, but first Isabella headed directly to the ladies' room. She checked and reapplied a little makeup and ran her fingers through her hair. Despite her previous outburst, she still looked phenomenal. She glanced in the mirror for one last check and then reached up and ran her fingers along the diamond necklace glittering around her neck. Poor Harry. What had she done to him? She was sure the reaction had been so profound because she had had too much champagne earlier. She was over Jack and felt guilty for taking her fury out on Harry.

She re-emerged several minutes later, looking just as beautiful as before, and no one would have noticed she had just been crying her heart out. At least she hoped not.

As she walked confidently towards the wedding reception, heads turned to look at her. A member of staff opened the door to the bar. She took a deep breath. Here goes, she thought to herself and entered the room assuredly. David and Ingrid greeted her, whilst everyone else stood around chatting.

"Isabella. Champagne?" enquired David.

"I'd love some thank you" and she downed the whole glass there in front of them. "I'm sorry about before." She whispered to Ingrid.

"Me too. Forgive me?"

"Never." Smiled Isabella.

"Right, now everyone is here. Let's get this show on the

road," called David after an hour.

A staff member led them through into the main colourful restaurant with its sumptuous silk-tented ceiling and murals, which overlooked the lake. Isabella walked around the tables and discovered that she was thankfully sitting on the opposite side of the room to Jack. At least they'd thought of that. She sat between Harry and David's brother, Michael.

For the appetiser they enjoyed pan seared black truffle potato gnocchi with crispy baby artichokes and rock shrimp. Followed by an entrée of filet mignon with foie gras, shallot marmalade crouton and vegetable gratin, which Isabella enjoyed immensely. She also, rather foolishly, drank glass after glass of excellent vintage champagne and wine during the sensational meal.

"Slow down a bit, sweetheart," whispered Harry.

"Don't tell me what to do. You bastard." She hissed.

"I see your mood hasn't changed then."

"No thanks to you, you shithead. If I wanted to hear from an idiot, I'd watch the news."

"Such a lady."

Despite the circumstances, she enjoyed herself, no doubt helped by the myriad flutes of champagne eagerly consumed. There was an excellent atmosphere in the colourfully decorated room, with a quartet playing in the background and people were chatting and laughing and all seemed to be thoroughly relishing in the surroundings.

Whilst devouring her Peche Melba, Michael was busy regaling her with his recent travels to the Far East. She particularly loved his insight into Malaysia. She had travelled fairly frequently, but had never been East and found his stories very entertaining and amusing.

"Isabella?" Harry tapped her on the shoulder.

"What?" she snapped. "Please don't interrupt me when I'm ignoring you."

"Nothing" he grumbled.

She felt guilty then. She'd been giving him the cold

shoulder and enough was enough. Poor Harry. She decided she was being more than a little rough on him and eventually tried to include him in their conversation.

"You've forgiven me, then?" he whispered into her ear.

"No. But I think I understand."

She only glanced once in Jack's direction. He was engrossed in deep conversation with a girl sat next to him; one of David's nieces, who looked all of twenty-five. To his other side was the girl's mother, and he looked as though he was enjoying himself. He had removed his jacket and loosened his tie and was fake-smoking a cigarette. She could almost pick out his heated rumble from across the room, amongst the scores of other people. He was commanding attention with his effortless sense of style and confidence. She could tell his undeniable magnetism was captivating all those around him, drawing them in with his charm and charisma. He was the epitome of rugged masculinity, a vision of beauty and strength that left a lasting impression of all who encountered him. Unfortunately, that included her.

Interrupting her thoughts, she heard David cry above the din, whilst jingling his spoon against his flute of champagne, "Before we enjoy our coffee, may I make a toast?" and he rose from his seat beside his new bride.

"I'd first like to say thank you all for coming such a long way, Michael, especially–Singapore I think? Well, anyway, it's great to see you all. I won't go on for too long ..." he paused, as people cheered and shouted hooray, "... and we won't have the usual speeches, as you've probably realised, this isn't the usual wedding ..." more cheering and whistling, "Anyway, thanks again for coming and I hope you enjoyed the service back at the chapel," more applause and cheering, "Keep drinking, there's a lot more where that came from, although from what I can see a few of you have had quite a lot already. On that note ... Isabella, thank you for being the bridesmaid. You look delightful." There was a chorus of approval and a smattering of applause. "And thank you, Jack, for being my best man. But most of all, I'd like to thank the beautiful Mrs Matthews," more whoops, "For taking the plunge and making me the proudest and happiest man alive and becoming my wife. Ingrid, I love you with all of my heart — even though you made me get married in Las Vegas." There followed lots of laughter and ahh's and a few tears shed by the women. "Now, I hope you all enjoyed your meal and after you've finished your coffee, please join us in the Monet room for some dancing." David added finally.

After a while, the organisers directed them to their allotted function room where a six-piece band played everyone's favourite all-time artists, such as Nat King Cole and Tony Bennett.

Isabella was sitting around a table with Harry, Michael, David and Ingrid and both sets of parents.

David stood up after a short time and led his new bride to the makeshift dance floor and they swayed, gazing lovingly into each other's eyes to *Let There be Love*.

"Doesn't she look super?" said Ingrid's mother as she watched her daughter tenderly.

"You must be very proud," replied Isabella.

"I am. Are you okay, dear? You seemed a little upset earlier?"

"I'm fine now, thank you. Sorry for making a scene."

"Don't worry. Man problems?"

"'Fraid so," said Isabella, cringing.

Just then Ingrid's father joined them and led his wife to the dance floor and joined Ingrid and David, followed thereafter by many other couples.

"As I'm best man, I believe I have the pleasure of dancing with the most beautiful bridesmaid?" she heard Jack growl behind her. He leaned inwards and held out his hand.

She was just about to refuse and create another squabble, but then remembered what Harry had said earlier and threw caution to the wind.

"I'd be delighted," she answered acerbically, and placed her hand in his own. The touch was electric. He must have felt it, too. It was impossible to disregard. He led her to the dance floor, placed one arm on her hip and clasped her other hand, pulled her towards him and they moved gracefully around the floor to an Andy Williams' number. With each movement, their breath mingled in the space between them, creating a sense of shared intimacy and desire.

Their eyes locked for a second in a passionate gaze, conveying unspoken longing. As they moved in sync, their movements became fluid and effortless, guided by an invisible force that drew them closer with each step.

His hands caressed her skin, tracing the contours of each curve with tantalising precision, igniting sparks of desire that smouldered beneath the surface.

The music wrapped around them like a warm embrace, cocooning them in a world of their own creation. Their bodies moved in perfect harmony, a dance of desire and familiarity that spoke volumes without a single word being spoken. With each slow, deliberate movement, they explored the depths of their connection, losing themselves in the intoxicating rhythm of the music and the passion that coursed through their veins.

"I did not know you would be here, honestly," he said eventually, looking into her eyes. He looked so handsome. She had forgotten what it felt like to be so close to him. He smelled delicious, exactly as she remembered.

"Really?"

"Cross my heart," he smiled.

"I wish I'd have known."

"Wouldn't you have come?"

"Definitely not."

"Well then. It's a good job you didn't know. For Ingrid's sake. And mine," he whispered.

She ignored him.

"You know, you took my breath away earlier, when I walked into the chapel and saw you. You looked like a vision. I couldn't believe my eyes. It's so good to see you. You don't know how much I've missed you. How often I've thought about you. Longed for you ..."

"Please," she hissed. She didn't want to hear this.

"No really. I mean it. How've you been?"

"I've been okay, you know, life goes on, and you?"

"The same. But honestly, it's been a journey. Took some time to heal and move on, but I'm doing okay."

"I'm glad to hear that. I've had my ups and downs, but hey we're both still standing."

"Look, I know things ended messy between us, but I just want you to know I don't harbour any ill feelings."

"I appreciate that, Jack. And I want you to know the same goes for me. Water under the bridge, right?"

"Right, so maybe we can catch up some time, grab a coffee or something?"

"Look. This isn't such a good idea," and she returned to her seat, leaving him there standing alone.

However, he wasn't to be deterred. He collected his drink from his own table on the other side of the room and made his way over to her. She groaned as he sat down next to her. She could see Ingrid and David were dancing, so she concentrated on Harry at the other side of the table and pleaded with him with her eyes to save her. He just merely nodded encouragingly. The bastard.

"Are you here alone?" he asked, removing a cigarette from his pocket and putting it behind his ear.

"What do you mean am I alone?" she snapped, but before he could answer, she slurred, "I know. You mean are you in with another chance? Can you feed me a load of bullshit and then sleep with me before we go our separate ways again? Jack, you are so bloody obvious."

"Isabella. What the hell are you talking about? I only meant, are you here with Robert or are you travelling alone? It wasn't a come on if that's what you think. We're way past that, don't you think?"

"I came with Harry, okay. Not that it's any of your damned

business, but Robert and I are no longer an item. We finished a long time ago."

"Really?" he asked incredulously. "What about the marriage?"

"What marriage?"

"Well, weren't you having a baby?" he asked.

"Yes, but this isn't the 1800s, Jack. People don't have to get married just because they're having a baby."

"So, what about the baby?"

"What about the baby?" more sarcasm.

"Well, I only ask because last time I saw you, you were pregnant and I do not know if you have a little boy or a girl. Well?"

She felt surprised, but pleased that Ingrid or Harry hadn't informed him. "I have a little boy, Teddy. He's the light of my life. My joy, my entire world, and I miss him terribly. I wish I'd never left him."

"And his Dad?"

"What about his dad?" she inhaled sharply.

"Does he see him?"

"No."

"No? Why not?"

"He's had nothing to do with him since he was born, and it will remain that way."

"The bastard. Did he leave you? I always knew he was an asshole."

"Look Jack. Your attempt at conversation is very nice and all, but I have nothing to say to you. Now please go away and leave me alone. You and I are little more than acquaintances now, and I'm finding your questions a little too personal."

"Isabella ..." she heard him call, before she stood up and staggered around the table to sit next to Harry.

"I will never, ever, ever, understand this darned woman as long as I live. She's the most exasperating ..." Isabella heard Jack bark through gritted teeth as she left. She didn't hear the end, but heard him kick the chair next to him. Although she didn't hear what he said, everyone around them couldn't help but hear him and witness his rage, his temper flaring. He lit his cigarette and finished his Jack Daniels. "Another double," he called to a passing waiter and handed him his glass.

"Sir, you can't ..."

"Don't even." He roared. Then turned to look at Harry, who simply raised his eyes to the ceiling and shrugged his shoulders, as if apologising for her behaviour. Jack merely shook his head as if in defeat and ignored the looks of horror around him as he continued to smoke indoors. He saw security walking towards him and dropped his cigarette into a half empty glass of wine.

"Alright, alright," he growled.

"Was that so bad?" asked Harry, as she plonked herself down next to him.

"Don't even start. He was asking far too many questions."

"Do you think he knows anything?"

"Of course not. Come on, let's dance." And before he could resist, she pulled him to the dance floor sexily and in the dimly lit room, a slow seductive melody filled the air, setting the mood for an intimate encounter.

"Izzy, are you sure you can manage this? Don't you think you've had a bit too much to drink?"

"What are you? My Dad? I've never felt better," and she proceeded to gyrate and swirl, and rub herself sexily against Harry as they stood close together, their bodies pressed against one another as they swayed gently to the rhythm of the music. All the while, she could feel Jack's burning eyes on her, watching her every move.

"Calm down Izzy. There's people watching and I know this isn't for my benefit," he grumbled.

"Who gives a shit?" and she continued to drape herself all over him. She put her arms around his neck and then ran her hands through his hair. "I feel like kissing you?"

"Really?" he stated. He knew exactly what she was up to.

"Harry, you really are handsome, you know?"

"Isabella. You're drunk."

"Nonsense. I really think you're right?"

"About what?"

"About us silly."

"Izzy, please don't do this," he pleaded.

"I want to." And she grabbed his head and pulled him towards her and kissed him long and hard on the mouth. He waited until she pulled away.

"Well, don't look at me like that," she snapped.

He grabbed her hands and said, "Let's sit down. You're making a fool of yourself. Don't make me look like a fool, too."

"I thought that's what you wanted?"

"Rubbish. This is for Jack. You're trying to make him jealous. And using me to do it."

"This has nothing to do with Jack."

"I'm going to the bar. Do you want a tea? A coffee maybe?"

"Champagne," she slurred.

He returned with her drink a short while later. "I'm going to mingle. I suggest you do the same," and he left her sitting there, staring into the enraged eyes of Jack Vincent. However, after several minutes, he got up and went to chat with someone over by the bar.

Michael came over to chat to Isabella and they talked and enjoyed a few dances, then he introduced her to some more of his family.

After a couple more hours dancing and chatting with their guests, David and Ingrid made their excuses and wandered back up to their room to bed. The management informed everyone that they could stay as long as they wanted, and the evening would only end when the last person left.

By then, Harry and Michael were at the bar in a heated conversation about the state of the economy and Isabella was again sat drowning her woes.

"I feel kinda futile, stood over there on my own," Jack said, smiling at her gently as he wandered over and sat down next to her. She didn't respond.

"You know, I'd like it if we could at least be friends?" he said.

"I don't want to be your friend, Jack. Don't you get it?" she replied.

"Not really, no? I'll never understand you Bella?" Again, she didn't respond.

"One moment, we had the world in our hands. I could see our whole lives mapped out in front of us. We could have been so happy, made a life together. And the next minute you'd gone. Just ran away. No explanation. Why? What did I do that was so terribly wrong? Don't you think I deserved some kind of explanation?"

"No. You obviously read a lot more into the situation than there was. It was a brief affair. There was no life together, not in this life, not in any life. To me, it was a mistake. It should never have happened. I returned home to England, and that was that as far as I was concerned. People make mistakes all the time."

"But the time we spent together? It was bliss."

"It was nothing."

He looked hurt and distressed, not believing that he'd misjudged her so completely. That she could be so cruel. There again, did he believe her? He felt there was more to it than she was letting on. There was definitely something unspoken. He just couldn't get through to her.

"It's funny," he said, trying to lighten the mood between them. "Do you remember I told you I wanted to take you to Las Vegas one day? And here we are."

"Mmmm," she mumbled, trying to ignore him.

"You look even better than I remember, and that dress is sensational. You look stunning, Bella," he whispered, leaning further towards her. "Do you know how difficult this has been for me, too?"

"For you? What the hell has been difficult for you?"

"You dumped me, remember? I was in love with you. The things you said to me. You called me sloppy seconds, do you remember that?"

"Did I?"

"Do you know how much you hurt me? Are still hurting me?"

"Look, just leave it for Christ's sake. I'm sick of going over and over this. With you. With everyone. It's ancient history, and it's dragged up all the time."

"It's not ancient history. I have to watch you and Harry all over each other, playing happy families."

"Look, can you just change the bloody subject? I'm getting bored with this now."

"Sure," he smiled, "Nice diamonds."

"Harry."

"You serious?"

"Generous isn't he."

"Are they real?"

"He took me shopping at Cartier in Beverly Hills."

"Extravagant."

"You know Harry."

"Wow, it must be serious. So, how've you been? How's your design business?"

"Good thanks. And you?"

He told her about what he'd been doing over the past couple of years, the increase in business ventures, his travel to different parts of the globe. He knew she wasn't paying particular attention. She'd had far too much to drink, but he just wanted to be near her.

In fact, from her point of view she was having to more or less squint one eye to even focus, "You still smoke like a chimney" she commented as he lit up his hundredth Marlborough, "How do you get away with smoking inside?"

"I just do. My only vice, apart from Jack Daniels."

"Your dress has changed, though. You look smart."

"Ya think? Good, huh? I thought I'd better try. Tonight, anyway."

"You look nice. Smart suits you," she breathed.

"Thank you, Bella," it was the first kind words she'd spoken.

"So how often do you visit the UK?" she asked, feigning interest.

"At least once a month at the moment. We're opening a second office in the North and I just wanted to get that off the ground before leaving them to it. I think it's time I quit all this travelling and learn to take a bit more of a back seat, but it's difficult. Unfortunately, I still feel every project is my baby and forget I have more than competent staff, able and willing to handle all these affairs. I should enjoy myself more, relax a bit. But you know ..." he paused, "It's not the same, not having someone to enjoy a vacation with."

"No Helene?" she asked sarcastically.

"Helene?"

"The woman I saw you with in London?"

"Oh her. Man, you've an excellent memory. She was a corporate lawyer, a business associate. We went out for dinner and a drink. Once, that's all. And there's been no one in my life ... since you," he added quickly.

"Oh," she didn't believe him for one second, but didn't want to be drawn further into discussion.

"What about you and Harry? Are you ...?"

"No."

"So, what was that before?"

"What?" she asked, confused.

"On the dancefloor? Was that an act?"

Oh shit, she'd already forgotten about her early display. "I don't want to talk about it," she offered stubbornly.

"So, there's no one either?"

"No. Not at the moment." She tried her best to focus and meet him directly in the eyes. The pain she saw there dumbfounded her. They were like huge, dark, muddy pools of despair. He was obviously still very hurt. He carried an air of sadness and heaviness that was palpable even from a distance. His eyes, once bright and lively, now seemed dull and empty, conveying a deep sense of sorrow and pain. Lines etched his forehead and his shoulders slumped forward as if weighed down by an invisible burden.

He continued talking about his company, but she wasn't really listening. She was too busy regarding him closely. Noticing he looked older, but even more charismatic. He was still the most striking man she'd ever laid eyes on. She was in a trance listening intently to him talk, her head tilted, playing with hear ear lobe, as she watched him. Despite his strong, gruff New York twang, it was surprisingly soothing and familiar. His solid defined jaw. His huge, chunky neck, his solid build. The way his Adam's apple bobbed up and down as he talked. The way his eyes lit up his face as he smiled. However, in his gaze was a haunting emptiness, as if lost in memories of happier times or consumed by thoughts of what could have been. Has his face ever seen a razor …?

"… Bella?"

"Sorry?"

"You were miles away. Are you tired?"

"Choo much to drink," she slurred.

"Listen?"

"What?"

"It's our song," and yes, the band had begun a fairly good rendition of *All the Way*, although the vocalist was no Frank Sinatra, or even Jack Vincent come to that.

"Oh, no," she groaned. She had had far, far too much to drink and was feeling quite emotional. She didn't want to hear this. Not now. Not sat here with him.

"Come on, let's dance?"

"I don't think I can? Anyway, where did you get *'it's our song'* from? We never had a song?"

"It doesn't matter," he muttered. He longed to hold her in his arms again, but he didn't want to push her.

"Do you have a song for everyone you've slept with?"

"Just leave it Bella." He sighed, exuding an aura of profound sadness and anguish, pain etched into every fibre of his being.

"Suits me," she snapped.

However, despite her initial reaction at seeing him again and putting aside all her earlier feelings of resentment and hatred towards him, she found being in his company this evening less of a chore than she'd imagined, perhaps because of his melancholy. Perhaps she was more resilient. She felt more than a little sorry for being so openly aggressive towards him and, therefore, tried to make amends. These persistent feelings of bitterness only prolonged her ongoing anger and were of no use to anyone, least of all her. Although she still found him exceptionally attractive, she no longer felt any remorse or upset in his presence and she honestly believed that she was in a better place now. She had moved on with her life and he was definitely in her past. She was kidding herself.

"Are you missing your little boy?" he asked.

"Desperately. It's the first time I've been away from him."

"Must be tough."

"It is." She then opened up to him a little more and told him all about her adorable little boy back home, whom she was missing so much. She forgot to whom she was talking to. What he had meant to her. She just enjoyed his company, and they chatted for what seemed like ages.

"Am I boring you?" she asked once, when she noticed him trying to stifle a yawn.

"Baby, I could never find you boring. I love hearing about your life. I guess I'm just tired."

"Me too. I think it's about time we called it a night?" she offered.

"Have you seen the time?"

"Have you seen Harry?"

Harry was fast asleep, snoring on a couch nearby.

"I'm sorry about before, Jack," she said, meaning it this time. Now she was over the initial shock.

"Forget about it," he answered, gazing directly into her eyes. "You know, we seem to have finally gotten on well this evening, or is it just my imagination?"

"No. I've enjoyed it too," she said. Had she? Really?

"Perhaps we can be friends after all?"

"Perhaps," she said, "Come on Harry" she called, attempting to shake him awake.

"Hmmmmm?" he grumbled.

"Time to go, buddy," said Jack, lifting him to a sitting position.

"Jack? Izzy? Shit. I must have fallen asleep."

"No shit, Sherlock," said Isabella.

"Where are you staying? I'll get you a cab?" asked Jack.

They walked outside and he nodded to a cab driver, "The Golden Nugget," and he helped them both into the car, "Listen, there's a bunch of us meeting for lunch tomorrow. Can you come? I'd like to see you? See both of you, before you go?" he said.

"I'll see what Harry says, but I guess so."

"Try?"

"I will. Goodnight Jack."

"Goodnight Bella." He leant in and grazed her cheek with his lips, then banged on top of the car to let the driver know they were ready. "I've missed you baby," he added as they drove away.

***

CHAPTER TWENTY-SIX

Isabella woke about 11.30am to the sound of her phone ringing next to her bed. "Hullo?" she said sleepily.

"Morning Bella."

"Jack." Oh shit. It all came flooding back. Well, the parts that she remembered, anyway.

"Did I wake you?"

"Mmmm. What do you want? How did you get my number?"

"Brunch, remember?"

Shit.

"We're meeting in just over an hour?"

"Oh. I don't know if we can make it. Harry's still fast asleep."

"Wake him."

"I don't know ..."

"Come on Bella. Come see David and Ingrid before they go off on honeymoon?"

"How come you're so chirpy?" she moaned, emerging from her slumber.

The prospect of seeing you again, he thought, but what he said was, "I've been up for ages, I've been for a run and a swim, now are you coming?"

"I'll see." She could picture him in his swimming shorts.

"Bella?"

"Okay, okay. I'll wake him. Oh God, my head."

"Take an Advil and drink plenty of water. I'll text you

the address. Meet us outside the main entrance on Convention Center Drive. Tell the cab driver. He'll bring you. 1pm."

Oh God, she groaned. What had she done? What had she said last night? Oh God, it was all coming back to her. She got up, grabbed a bottle of water and walked through to Harry's room. "Wake up. Time to go."

"What?" he grumbled.

"We're meeting the others in just over an hour."

"What others?"

"Ingrid. David. Michael. Some others I don't know. Oh, and Jack."

"Did you say Jack? What the actual ..."

"I did indeed."

"Holy crap." What was going on now? He pondered.

"I know. Tell me about it. Oh, and Harry, I'm so very sorry about last night. For kissing you and for acting like a complete prat and for making you feel like a dick."

"Forgiven. So, are things okay between you guys?"

"Things are okay," she smiled.

"Thank God for that. I don't think I could take much more."

They met as arranged, outside the restaurant on Convention Center Drive. As their cab pulled up, Ingrid, David, Michael, Jack, and some others were waiting for them.

"Hi everyone." Isabella said, more cheerily than she felt and hugged Ingrid and David, "How are the newlyweds this afternoon?"

"Great. Tired, but great," said Ingrid, "You?" she added to Isabella.

"I'm good. A little hungover and more than a little mortified. I'm so sorry."

"No problem Izzy. As long as everything's okay."

"Bella. How are you?" asked Jack, and he leant towards her and kissed her lightly on both cheeks, then turned, "Harry? You good?" Jack's face was dark. He was obviously the worse for wear too. He had sounded a lot brighter on the phone than he looked in person.

"Good, mate, thanks," replied Harry, returning his bear hug.

"Okay, let's go inside. This heat's exhausting," said David.

"I'm surprised you came?" said Ingrid to Isabella, as they all made themselves inside.

"It's fine. We're good. I'm sorry for nearly ruining your day and making a complete arse of myself. I think Jack and I are good. We kind of came to an agreement."

"That's good Izzy" Ingrid said.

"I'm surprised you wanted to meet up with us all, first day of being Mrs Matthews?" Isabella replied.

"We're great. We wanted to see you guys before we go off to the Turks and Caicos."

"Oh, that'll be amazing. You'll have a wonderful time. I'm so jealous. Although after this, I'll be ready to head home. I'm missing Teddy."

"What'll be amazing?" asked Jack.

"Our honeymoon," answered Ingrid.

They ordered drinks and perused the menu. No one fancied alcohol, so they all selected something refreshing, and after their waiter advised them of the daily specials, he left them alone.

"Thanks for a wonderful wedding, you guys," said Isabella. "We had a great time, didn't we, Harry?"

"I think so," he said.

"Really?" replied Ingrid, searching her friend's face.

"Truly. It was fab" said Isabella.

The others also extended their agreement and chatted animatedly about the occurrences of the previous day's wedding, their spirits still buoyed by the joyous celebration the night before.

The newlyweds, glowing with happiness, sat together hand in hand, savouring the moment of togetherness after the whirlwind of the night before.

They all shared stories and laughter as they reminisced

about magical moments from the previous evening, an air of contentment and satisfaction in the room, as everyone reflected on the love and happiness surrounding the couple.

Isabella sat comfortably between Jack and Harry and felt at ease in their presence. They all enjoyed an array of delicious treats; freshly baked pastries and seasonal fruits, fluffy pancakes and crispy bacon. The aroma of coffee filled the air, and they were all in fabulous form, despite nursing their hangovers and as they exchanged fond memories and heartfelt congratulations with the newlyweds, showering them with love and well wishes for the journey ahead. Each bite savoured, each sip of coffee cherished, as they basked in the warmth of love and camaraderie that surrounded them.

"I'm proud of you," whispered Harry, "You're putting on quite a friendly act ..."

"It's not an act," she whispered back. "I'm fine. It's all good."

"That's good," Jack interrupted their conversation.

Isabella was embarrassed when she realised he had heard them and asked, "Why's that?"

"Well, I thought we could all meet up later on tonight?" he said, finishing a mouthful of pancake smothered in syrup.

"Sounds good. That okay with you, honey?" said David.

"Great," said Ingrid. "What did you have in mind, Jack?"

"A show?" he said.

"Superb," said Michael, "Which one?"

"I don't know. What about Cirque du Soleil?" he offered.

"No, thanks," said Harry.

"Wayne Newton?" offered Michael.

Jack groaned.

"So?" said Isabella, "Any more ideas?"

"Legends in Concert?" Michael offered.

"Legends?" said Ingrid.

"Yeah. It's a copycat thing. You know, singers taking off big-name acts. Elvis. Neil Diamond ..."

"Sounds fun," said Harry, "You up for it, Izzy?"

"I suppose ... I was hoping for an early night."

"Come on. It'll be fun," pleaded Jack. "I'll sort the tickets?"

"Well, if everyone's all going ... I will not be the party pooper and stay in on my own all night."

"That's my girl," said Harry.

After they'd finished a pleasant brunch, they all returned to their respective hotels. Harry and Isabella returned to their beds to sleep off their hangovers, as did David and Ingrid–for different reasons. Jack went to check out some of the other hotels and casinos and eventually returned to his own, where he booked the tickets to Legends in Concert, before making some 'phone calls to the office. He also left messages for the others, informing them where and when to meet.

As soon as Isabella woke up, she phoned home. Everything, to her immense relief, was still fine. Bernie and Teddy were managing admirably without her.

She woke Harry and told him the plans and they both went into their own bathrooms to get ready. She enjoyed a long soak before changing into the dress she'd purchased from Gucci in LA.

"Too-wit, too-woo," whistled Harry when he saw her.

"Thank you. Not too dressy?"

"Not at all. You look perfect."

"You don't look too bad yourself," she commented on his dinner attire.

Jack had booked their seats for the 10 o'clock show, so Harry and Isabella headed downstairs into the hotel's casino and settled themselves at the bar for a couple of gin and tonics before they caught a cab to the Imperial Palace on the Strip.

"You're okay about this?" Harry asked her, as they sipped their drinks.

"You mean Jack?"

"Yeah? You two seem to run hot and cold?"

"It's not that. I think we've both come to the realisation that we can be friends. I guess he's fun to be around. But this no strings thing seems to work."

"Same old story," he mumbled.

"What do you mean?" she asked.

"The no strings thing? That's the line you fed me. Now Jack. What is it with you?"

"Don't start Harry, I'm not getting into this again."

"Okay, okay, I'm sorry."

"Come on. It's nine thirty, let's go," she said.

Upon arrival at the Imperial Palace, they stepped out of their cab into the still exceptionally warm evening and entered the hotel.

They met up with the others in the foyer and made a remarkable group. The men had all tried with their outfits too and were in DJs, and the women looked fantastic in their evening dresses.

"You look stunning." Whispered Jack, as he came and greeted her, then stood at her side, his hands clasped behind his back. He smelled gorgeous.

"You look good too. Jack Vincent in a suit again, twice in two days. I'm astounded."

"I do smart, you know …?"

"You should do it more often. It suits you."

"Nah, not my thing. I feel too uncomfortable."

"You look it. Now stop fidgeting."

"Yes, ma'am."

They navigated their way into the theatre and a staff member escorted them to their table in the middle.

"Hey. This is great," said Harry.

"Good seats," commented Michael.

Harry purchased some red roses for the ladies and then Jack ordered bottles of champagne.

"Not again. I don't think I can," wailed Isabella.

"Would you like something else?" asked Jack.

"No, it's fine, I've just done nothing but drink and eat."

The show begun shortly thereafter, and they had a wonderful, fun time singing along with Elvis, Judy Garland,

Nat King Cole, Michael Jackson and Neil Diamond, plus several more *stars*.

When the show finished, they made their way to a quiet little bar to have a catch up.

"That was sensational," said Ingrid, "Such fun."

"Great wasn't it," said Harry. "They should have had you up there, Jack. You could have done ole blue eyes. Trouble is, they'd never have got you off."

"Hey. I'm not that bad, am I?" said Jack.

"Once you start, you never stop," chuckled Ingrid.

"Right, what does everyone want to drink?" asked David.

"No more, please," sighed Isabella, "just a coffee for me, please?"

"Me too" said Harry.

"Me three," said Jack.

"Coffees all round then," said David.

Amid the bustling ambiance of the venue, the friends huddled together, their faces alive with excitement and enthusiasm. They eagerly shared their thoughts and impressions of the performances they'd just witnessed.

"Wow, wasn't that incredible?" said Ingrid. "Elvis had me convinced I was watching the real deal."

"I know, right? And did you see the energy during Michael Jackson? I swear, I felt like I was at one of his concerts from the 80s," said Harry.

"Absolutely. And Whitney Houston? She had me in tears with her powerful vocals."

"I couldn't agree more. Each performer brought their A game," added Jack.

"And the medley they did, with all the legends coming together for a grand finale. It was great," said Isabella.

"Definitely. And the best part is sharing it with great friends like you all. Thanks for coming along for the ride," said Jack. "By the way, I've got something to ask you all?"

"You have?" Ingrid perked up.

"I'd like to invite you all on vacation on my new yacht

next May? I'll be sailing around the Greek Islands and I'd love it if you could all come?"

"You have a yacht?" said David. "Since when?"

"You could have told us earlier," remarked Ingrid, "When we were looking for a honeymoon destination?"

"You're going to the Turks tomorrow," said Jack.

"That's not the point," shrugged Ingrid.

"We'd love to, thank you, Jack. Sorry about my wife," said David.

"Speaking on my behalf already, I see, husband."

"Come on. Let's not be witness to your first fight." said Harry, "Well, count me in. I fancy a bit of sailing. Thanks Jack. The Greek Islands sound great."

"Terrific. Well, we'll definitely be there, won't we, darling?" said Ingrid.

"If you say so," said David.

"Thanks for the invite, Jack, but I'll be in Hong Kong, a busy time for me," said Michael.

Isabella had remained silent throughout. Okay, they were friends now, just, but she hardly wanted to go on holiday with the guy.

"Isabella?" Jack ventured carefully.

"Out of the question, I'm afraid," she said.

"Why?" said Harry and Jack together.

"For one there's Teddy."

"And?" enquired Harry.

"Well, that's enough, for starters. He's far too young to go on a boat."

"Nonsense," said Jack. "I went sailing from as young as two."

"Yes, but he's not you, is he, Jack?" and then Isabella clamped her mouth shut when she realised what she had just said and glanced anxiously at Harry. What had she said? Harry just grimaced.

Jack wondered what the strange look was that he had just witnessed between Harry and Isabella, but ignored it.

"Bella, please? Just think about. If Harry, David and Ingrid are coming, we'll have a wonderful time. No strings, I promise. I swear. If that's what you're worried about?" Jack asked.

"It's not that," she said.

"Please Izzy. It'll be such fun. We can all take turns looking after Teddy?" said Ingrid.

She kept saying no and meant it. She didn't want to go, so they didn't push her.

As they all stood up to leave, Jack kept her behind.

"Bella, I'd love for you to come? Just as friends, of course, I realise now that's what you want. But think about it, okay? The trip, that is?" he said.

"I've already told you I can't. What about Teddy? I can't keep going off on endless holidays, leaving my little boy behind. He's not a pet dog. I can't just put him in kennels."

"Of course not, silly. Bring him? I'd love to meet him? There's plenty of room and crew on board to help out. He'd love the boat, the sunshine. We will all have a fantastic time? We'll all take care of him. Please think about it? Maybe I can call you?"

"Well ... I don't know Jack."

He sensed her hesitation. "Please Bella, just think about it?"

"Okay, I will, but I'm not promising anything. Look, we should be going."

They caught up with the others, and everyone wished Ingrid and David a happy honeymoon, and they all hugged and kissed each other fondly.

"Goodbye Jack," she whispered as she leant towards him and froze as he put his arms around her tightly and held her close. His touch literally swept away her. She could remember his smell so vividly. She remembered how good he felt. And then, she wasn't sure, but as he pulled away from her, she could swear she heard him breathe I love you. But he'd turned away, and she merely put it down to her imagination.

On their last day in Vegas, Isabella woke to hear Harry on the phone. "Sure, no problem. We'll see you there about three then?" and he put the phone down.

"Who was that?" she enquired.

"Jack."

"Jack? What did he want?"

"He wanted to know if he could come with us to the Grand Canyon today."

"And ...?"

"I told him it was fine."

"Did you now. And that's okay with me, is it?"

"Don't be an asshole, Isabella. He's on his own and merely wanted some company."

"I bet he did. I thought we'd all said our goodbyes yesterday," she mumbled.

"What's the problem?"

"No problem," she snipped.

They met him later that afternoon at the airstrip, and the three of them greeted each other fondly.

"You didn't mind me tagging along with you guys?" enquired Jack.

"No, it's fine," she answered guiltily.

"Great." He said eagerly.

They followed the guide to their state-of-the-art helicopter and then boarded the glass-bottomed, climate-controlled cabin. As the helicopter prepared for take-off, the highly experienced and knowledgeable pilot instructed them to strap themselves in and put on their headsets for personalised narration.

"This is fun," said Harry as the blades whirred.

"I'm terrified," squealed Isabella as excitement pulsed through her as she rubbed her hands together nervously.

"You'll be fine," said Jack, and stroked her leg energetically.

The whirring of the rotors filled the air as the helicopter

lifted off the ground and they experienced a smooth ascent into the vast Nevada sky. They enjoyed spectacular views of the iconic Vegas Strip sprawling below, gradually revealing the rugged beauty of the Mojave Desert. The vast expanse of desert unfolded beneath, its ochre hues punctuated by clusters of Joshua Trees and winding roads. They flew over the Hoover Dam, the imposing Lake Mead and the mighty, swirling Colorado River, before flying over the spectacularly panoramic and breath-taking Grand Canyon West. The weather couldn't have been more perfect. The views of this awesome land from the helicopter's windows and floor were crystal clear. They witnessed some of the most colourful and geological formations in the world and they truly appreciated one of nature's grandest masterpieces.

The pilot then descended about 4000 feet onto the floor of the canyon, at the Hualapai Indian Reservation. They stepped out of the cool aircraft and the heat was incredible. With a glass of champagne in hand, they enjoyed some hors d'oeuvres while marvelling at and drinking in the sheer magnitude of their surroundings, the unique perspective of its geological wonders. They marvelled at the rock formations sculpted by forces of nature over the millennia.

"Quite a sight, huh?" commented Jack.

"Have you been here before?" asked Isabella.

"Yeah, a few times, always at the top, though."

"I'm going to chat to the pilot," said Harry and walked back towards the helicopter.

"I've enjoyed seeing you Bella," said Jack.

"Me too. It's been fun."

"I've missed you, you know?"

"Yes," she said, "It's been nice seeing you too."

"I think Harry's in love with you?"

"No Jack," she said, "We're just close friends." She fiddled with her hair self-consciously as he stared at her.

"For now. I think he wants more."

"I know he'd like more, but I see him more like a brother.

Honestly, there's nothing romantic there at all. I love him, but as a family."

"You don't want a relationship?"

"Not with Harry. But maybe one day. Maybe I'll meet someone in the future, but for now, I'm not looking. I don't need the hassle."

"Shame Bella. You're young, you're beautiful. Any guy would be lucky to have you."

"Even with my temper and moods?" she giggled.

"I guess you are hard work."

"Hey," she feigned annoyance.

"You need a man who can handle you."

"I'm not sure anyone could handle me, Jack?"

"Bella ..."

"Time to go guys," called Harry, sauntering back over, "Ready?"

"All good" said Isabella. Thank God. Good timing, Harry. Who knew what Jack was about to say?

They climbed back on board and the pilot flew towards the Grand Canyon National Park, with its exceptionally deep, steep-walled canyon. The aerial excursion took them deep into the sharply eroded canyon. With its characteristic forms, the colours coming alive in the sun cast ever changing shadows and hues across the landscape.

Their return journey was just before nightfall and took them back over downtown Las Vegas, before finally coming back down to earth. The natural beauty they had just witnessed left them with a sense of wonder and awe. The memory of their helicopter flight would linger in their minds for years to come, a testament to the power and majesty of the natural world.

"Wow," exclaimed Jack, as he helped Isabella down from the helicopter. "Did you enjoy that?"

"Sensational. I wouldn't have missed that for anything. I feel queasy though."

"Me too," quipped Harry, "Worth it, though."

They all agreed it was an unforgettable experience, one that had left them literally speechless.

"Well, I guess this is goodbye for sure," Jack said. "Harry, thanks man, it was great." He reached out to shake his friend's hand firmly and patted his back.

"Glad you enjoyed it. Glad you came today," he said, returning Jack's handshake and giving him a bear hug.

"Me too. Goodbye Harry. See you soon and take care of this one, okay?" he said, pulling Isabella in for a tight embrace, expressing his love and affection physically.

There was a gentle sway as they held each other, their bodies pressed close, finding solace and comfort in the familiar embrace. As they leant in to each other, a sense of peace washed over them, melting away the stresses and worries of the day. They exchanged whispered words of farewell and affection, and in that moment, time seemed to stand still as they basked in the warmth of their friendship.

As they finally released their embrace, a soft smile graced both of their lips, their hearts filled with gratitude for this moment.

"Safe trip home Bella. It was good seeing you. And think of Greece, okay?"

"I will Jack."

"I'll be in touch okay?"

"Okay. Goodbye Jack."

"Ciao Bella. I'll miss you."

"Don't," was all she said, as she turned to catch up with Harry and their waiting car.

Longingly, he gazed after her. He felt as if his heart were being torn in two again. He couldn't bear the thought of her leaving again. Their embrace had spoken volumes, conveying a depth of emotion between them that words alone could not express. A gesture of love.

***

CHAPTER TWENTY-SEVEN

On the flight home the following day, both still feeling exhausted from the events of the preceding days, Harry brought up Jack's invitation. "Why don't we go? What's there to lose?" he said.

"Look Harry, I thought I was over him. I was enjoying his company. But it's just too weird?"

"What's weird? That's crap. I'll be there. Ingrid and David. And think about Teddy. You've never taken him on a proper holiday. He'd love it."

"Don't you think it will be awkward? What if he asks questions about Teddy? Puts dates and times together?"

"No chance. As far as he and everyone else are concerned, he's Robert's baby. Only you and I, oh yes, and Bibi, know the truth. He need never know. Although you know my feelings about that."

"Harry."

"Isabella. You admitted yourself last night. He's a great guy. He would make a wonderful father."

"Harry. I've put Jack and what happened behind me. I don't want him in my life anymore. Anyway, he made himself perfectly clear about what he feels about being a father."

"I know. I know. But he's not asking you that. All he wants is for a few good friends to go on holiday together."

"You don't think, … well …, I mean, now that he knows there's no Robert and I, … well … you don't think he'll expect anything of me?"

"Like what?"

"Do I have to spell it out?" she said.

"Would that be so terrible?"

"Absolutely. I could never go back with him," she said. "That door's closed."

"Well, that's okay then. We'll all go together as friends. Teddy and I will be your chaperones. I'm sure Jack sees your future as purely platonic."

She spent the rest of the flight wondering whether she could deal with Jack being back in her life again. If she was honest, she had thoroughly enjoyed being in his company again. Being around him was a breath of fresh air. He made her laugh and his spirits had been upbeat the whole time they had been together. He had made no attempt whatsoever to push her into anything other than friendship, and he seemed to have put the past behind him. But was there too much water under the bridge? The only time she felt a tug at her heartstrings was when he was laughing and his eyes sparkled and it reminded her so much of her son. A surge of astonishment overwhelmed her as she observed the striking resemblance he shared with her son, his eyes wide with wonder as he took in the breathtaking scenery from the helicopter. He had certain mannerisms, which she had clearly seen in her own child and it startled her. A couple of times, she turned away from him, in case her eyes betrayed her. Did she want to risk getting close to him again? Would anybody notice that Teddy's smile was exactly the same as Jack's? Would they notice the way their brows furrowed in concentration, making them look identical? She had closed that door once, she had put a lock on her heart. Did she want to risk opening it again?

They arrived home early the following morning, all smiles, eager to see little Teddy again, carrying their luggage filled with gifts for him. Predictably, the weather was grey and wet and there was a chill in the air.

Isabella opened the door and walked into the lounge,

where Teddy and Bernie were playing jigsaws on the floor. The little boy saw his Mummy and shrieked, then ran over and threw himself into her arms and hugged her tightly and Isabella knew she was home.

Over the next couple of hours, Bernie relayed, with Teddy's stilted help, the events and 'traumas' of their time together. Teddy hadn't eaten for two days, as he'd had a slight temperature. There was an outbreak of head-lice at playgroup, although so far, Teddy had escaped being contaminated. "I wouldn't mind anyway Mummy. It would be like having little pets in my hair," he said with all seriousness, which made the adults roar with laughter. Isabella smiled and felt her heart warm, to hear the wonderful every day, pleasing stories. Life was back to normal.

Isabella returned to work the following week, and soon she was back in her old routine. There were a hundred and one things to sort out in the office. The rent review was due. There were two or three projects in the pipeline that only Isabella could manage, where the clients insisted she dealt with them personally. Two of her staff's annual performance and salary review were due. But she relished in it all.

It was Isabella's birthday a few months after she returned home from the USA. To her part relief, part disappointment, she hadn't heard any more from Jack.

To her dismay, Bibi called round one evening and told her she had arranged a dinner party, a kind of blind date/single friends affair for the evening of her birthday and there was no getting out of it.

"Didn't you think to check with me I might have made plans already?" Isabella moaned.

"Like what? With whom?"

"You never know."

"Look, it'll be fun. There will be three eligible bachelors for you to choose from," she said.

"Please Bibi. No more of your single guys. They're all either boring, newly divorced and/or feeling sorry for themselves. I can't bear another evening of polite and strained conversation with complete prats."

"You cow. Most of these guys are friends of Darysus's, or people I know through work. You're so judgemental."

"Great way to spend my birthday." She mumbled sarcastically, "I'd rather be sitting in front of the TV with a bottle of wine."

"Well, aren't you just a ray of sarcastic sunshine today? Stop moaning and acting like an old woman. You're coming whether you like it."

On the day itself, Harry arrived first thing with a bundle of beautifully gift-wrapped parcels. A pair of gold earrings from Tiffany & Co. A new purse from Celine. A new tennis shirt. A silk scarf from Fendi. Some Belgian truffles.

She chastised him for his generosity and indulgence. However, his gifts were so thoughtful, he had even thought of little Teddy, so he wouldn't feel too left out. He had brought a little present for him as well. His first rugby ball.

"That's so thoughtful of you, Harry. You shouldn't have spoiled us like this," she said and gave him an enormous hug. "Thank you so much."

"Oh, I nearly forgot ..." and he rummaged around in his large Polo holdall, "Ingrid and David asked me to give you these."

She opened the smallest one first, reading the card, "To Isabella, with lots of love from Mr & Mrs Matthews" and gasped when she saw a dainty and exceptionally pretty cameo brooch, which she loved.

"Surely, they can't have bought me something else," she exclaimed, beginning to tear at the final parcel.

But as she opened it, she knew it wasn't from Ingrid. She had only ever told one other person about these things.

First out of the parcel was an impeccable, signed, first edition of The Sinking of the Titanic and Other Great Sea Disasters by L T Myers; second, came a funny little plastic snow globe of a prehistoric-looking creature, swimming in a lake–obviously a trinket from Loch Ness and finally a superb watercolour of Bermuda, by a well-regarded local artist.

"What strange presents. Who are they from?" asked Harry.

"He remembered." Isabella gasped.

"What? Who?"

"Do you remember our flight to Mombasa?" she asked.

"Of course."

"Well, whilst Jack and I were talking to each other …"

"Okay …"

"Well, I told about the three things that fascinated me most whilst growing up. The Titanic. The Loch Ness monster and the Bermuda Triangle. Don't you see? He remembered it all, all that time ago. Look at these gifts. Why?"

"He remembered because he's in love with you. You don't have to be an idiot to see that. Don't look at me like that."

"Don't be ridiculous Harry and don't step on that piece of Lego."

"Ouch. Of course he is. Don't you see? You and Jack are the only two people on this planet that cannot see that you are clearly and obviously meant to be together. When you we were in Vegas, it's obvious you're still besotted with each other."

"We're not. I know, and he knows it." She said defiantly, "We got on well in Las Vegas, yes, but that's because we both know where we stand with each other. And that it was only a couple of days. Friends. Nothing more."

"Well, that's that then. All you have to do is write a nice thank you note, short, to the point, thanking him for his marvellous choice of gifts. You can also tell him you're considering Greece."

"I am? Do you think that's wise, considering the circumstances?"

"Isabella, it's a holiday, not a marriage proposal. You are being silly. If you and Jack can be friends, then everything will be okay. I'm going. Ingrid and David are going. It would be a shame for you and Teddy to miss out. At least think about it some more. Hey …" he added, "That painting's lovely. It'll look great in your bedroom."

"Mmmm" was all she mumbled, and she drifted back to Jack and their conversation on the flight to Mombasa.

She remembered they'd been talking comfortably about their favourite music, movies, books, actors and actresses and, conversely, those they didn't like.

"I'm not interested in anything, Harry Potter. Awful, diluted derivative stuff," she said.

"I concur," he said.

"But my favourite song in the world …" she thought about it.

"Go on" Jack had urged.

"Andrea Bocelli and Sarah Brightman."

"Con Te Partiro?" he offered.

"Time to Say Goodbye? If so, yep."

"Good song. I love BB King. I played electric guitar in a blues band when I was at college," he had said.

"Really? Are you any good?" she'd asked.

"Well, not BB King good," he'd said.

"Naturally."

"Not bad, I s'pose."

"You sing. You can play the guitar. Is there anything you don't do?"

He'd merely smiled at her and uttered, "Now. That would be telling."

They had continued to talk and found out they both loved the theatre, although he regretted not having ever visited the West End, as he had never had the time. He had seen many shows on and off Broadway, but would still love to see a production in the West End.

"Les Mis is my favourite. I just love the music." She sighed.

"Movie wasn't bad either," he had replied.

"Hugh Jackman. I just love him."

"Do you now?" he said.

They both loved old movies and talked about their favourites. His Brief Encounter, hers An Affair to Remember.

"You love the old love stories too, then?" she had smiled at him.

"Yeah, but don't tell anyone." He'd smiled wryly. "I often fill my face with a tub of Ben and Jerry's in front of the TV."

"Isn't that a girl's thing, sitting in front of the telly, crying into a tub of ice-cream?"

"Hey. You don't get the monopoly on ice-cream. Guys like it too, you know."

Isabella had then told him about the three things that had captivated her most since childhood.

He'd teased, "Let me guess? Harassing innocent men like me; taking over the world and Emeline Pankhurst?"

"No. I'm being serious." She'd said, fiddling with her hair self-consciously, "Ever since I was a little girl, three things have fascinated me. The Titanic, The Loch Ness Monster and the Bermuda Triangle," and they'd continued to discuss all three at length.

"Don't you think it's strange that so many ships and planes mysteriously disappeared? I mean, usually the weather's good. It happened in daylight and after a sudden break in radio contact, whoosh–they disappear without a trace." She'd exclaimed.

"Haven't they put that down to mechanical problems, inadequate equipment or inexperienced personnel?"

"Oh, you're such a realist."

"Really? I've flown several times to Bermuda and I'm still here?"

"What about the Loch Ness Monster? I expect you have a theory about that too?" she'd asked.

"Sure. Pure crap."

"What about all the sightings?"

"What sightings? All baloney. A good marketing ploy to bring in American tourists and other suckers all around the world, like me. We would never have heard of Loch Ness if it wasn't for the Monster."

"Rubbish. I think it exists. You wouldn't catch me swimming or sailing on Loch Ness. It would terrify me."

"Bella honey. Are you serious? Don't tell me you believe in the Yeti, too?"

"Well ..."

"Man. For such a rational woman."

"What about the Titanic? That was real."

"Now that I know."

"You know, if I'd been on the Titanic, I would never have left my husband behind."

"If you were my wife, I'd have forced you into a lifeboat."

"I'd jump out."

"I'm guessing you would have let Jack on your door?"

"Of course I would. There was plenty of room. Selfish cow."

"Anyway, time for another drink," he had stated.

Isabella had regarded him closely through her lashes, twisting her hair between her fingers. Not only was he extremely handsome, he was witty, clever, charming and caring. Had she mis-read him? "I'd like to think we could be friends, Jack?" she'd smiled.

"I'd like to think we could be a great deal more than that." He'd said, almost in a whisper.

She'd ignored him.

"Just one thing?" he'd smiled at her.

"Yes?"

"Would you make room for me in a lifeboat?"

She'd raised her eyes in protest and sighed, "You're incorrigible ..."

Harry took Isabella and Teddy, together with Bernie and her husband, out to lunch to a local pub to celebrate Isabella's birthday and over their delicious freshly prepared meal, Harry had yet another surprise for Isabella.

"Isabella, there's something I need to tell you, and I don't know what you're going to say."

"Oh God Harry, what now?"

"I think I've met someone."

"What," she exclaimed, nearly choking on her pudding.

"A girl, well, a woman."

"No. When?"

Bernie smiled at Isabella's reaction.

"About a week after we got back from Vegas."

"What? And you said nothing."

"There was nothing to say."

"And there is now?"

"Well, I think there is. Her name's Eva and I've been seeing her for quite a while now."

"Why haven't you mentioned her before?" she asked, looking hurt.

"You know me. I wasn't sure at first, but…" he left the sentence hanging in the air.

"Serious?"

"I think it could be. She's the only woman I've met; present company excluded," he smiled, "who hasn't wanted something from me. She has her own career, her own friends, is terribly independent. In fact, she reminds me a little of you," he said. "She's attractive, but not one of my usual Barbie types."

"God Harry. I don't believe it. When can we meet her?"

"Well, if it's okay with you, I was going to suggest she come to Greece with us?" he saw her face darken. "That's if we can persuade you to come, of course. What do you think?"

"Shit. It must be serious if you're inviting her on a holiday. But what about me?"

"What do you mean, what about you? You're not jealous, are you?"

"No, you fool. What I mean is, if there's Ingrid and David, you and what's her face, then that only leaves me and Jack."

"No Izzy. You and Teddy. There is no you and Jack, remember? Anyway, how do you know Jack isn't taking someone?"

"Is he?" she gasped.

"I've no idea," he said, "Anyway, stop looking for excuses. We'll all get on like a house on fire."

"You think?"

"I know."

That afternoon, she spent the rest of her time playing with Teddy, then whilst her baby boy had an afternoon nap, she thought about Harry's confession. How did she feel about him having a "girlfriend?" It wasn't as if they were in a relationship, but she felt a little weird knowing there was someone else, possibly a special someone else, in his life. Why hadn't he told her earlier? Would it change their friendship?

She then felt compelled to write a thank-you note to Ingrid and David and more importantly, Jack. She sat down at her bureau and pulled out some pretty cards.

Ingrid's was easy. She soon had a quick note jotted down, then sealed the envelope. Jack's wasn't so simple. She made several attempts, but ended up tearing each card up and throwing them in the bin.

She eventually settled on, *Jack. I can't thank you enough for the very special gifts. I can't believe you remembered after all this time. I shall treasure them always. It was great seeing you at the wedding and I apologise for my initial reaction. My behaviour at the beginning was phenomenally bad. I don't know what came over me - the champagne, probably. Thankfully, we could mend bridges and make a fresh start. I hope you are well and I send you my best regards. Isabella.*

Was it too formal? Too brief? She did not know, but decided it would have to suffice. Unfortunately, he had left no return address, so she addressed it to him, c/o Ingrid.

Bernie arrived a short time later, so she could get ready for the soiree at Bibi's. She had a long, relaxing bubble bath (thanks Bernie), then decided on an elegant, beautifully cut, black trouser suit, with a silk camisole.

She arrived for the dinner party in excellent spirits after having spent a pleasant birthday so far. She rarely liked this kind of affair, but found herself sandwiched between a self-assured Neuro-Surgeon called Jonathan Hayes and Sebastian something or other, a University Lecturer. Both were attractive, and both spent a hilarious evening vying for her attention.

As she helped Bibi carry out some of the dirty dishes, she confessed she was enjoying the male attention and competition. "All this flattery is doing me the world of good," she chorused.

"See. Now you know what you've been missing," said Bibi.

At the end of the evening, she finally agreed to have dinner with Jonathan the following week.

The evening soon arrived for her date with Jonathan. He turned up in a taxi and left the meter ticking whilst he came to the door to collect her. She asked him in whilst she collected her bag and briefly and awkwardly introduced him to Teddy and Bernie.

"We shouldn't be late, Bernie. Oh, and I nearly forgot, Harry may stop by to drop off a new backup drive for my computer."

"No problem Isabella. I hope he doesn't come after nine. There's a documentary I want to watch on the BBC."

"He promised me he won't be late Bernie, but you know Harry."

"Well, don't you worry. Take your time now and have a nice evening. Nice to meet you Jonathan," she added, giving Isabella a less than conspicuous conspiratorial wink. Isabella groaned and, as Jonathan turned his back, she gave Bernie a faux-stern glare.

Bernie shrugged her shoulders as if to say, "What?"

"I'll see *you* later," said Isabella as she closed the door and stuck out her tongue at Bernie.

They headed towards Old Windsor and stopped at a charming little restaurant. She found Jonathan quite distant and hard work at first, but as the evening wore on, she realised he wasn't shy, but simply lacking in interesting conversational skills. He had been okay at Bibi's? Okay, he could talk about himself and his work non-stop, but simply wasn't interested in anything she had to say. She couldn't deny his attractiveness, but his conceited nature made her feel small and insignificant. Nothing she could put her finger on, but he had made quite a few snide and inappropriate comments about her business and some other things he'd said ... just didn't feel right.

His favourite subject was definitely himself, "... navigating through the labyrinth of the brain. My every movement is calculated, every incision purposeful ..."

In the end, she just shut up and pretended to listen. Her mind wandered to Jack and she couldn't help but compare them. He wasn't as tall as Jack. He wasn't as muscular as Jack. Wasn't as good-looking. He didn't have the same sense of humour. Come to that, he didn't have any sense of humour. Had her note to Jack been too impersonal? Would he reply? Should she have made her letter longer? Would Ingrid remember to give him the note? Should she go to Greece with the others? How would she get on with Harry's new "girlfriend?"

"That's like my patient with a ruptured intracranial aneurysm ... Isabella? Did you hear what I said?" she heard Jonathan ask her sharply.

"I'm sorry, you were saying?"

"It doesn't matter. You obviously weren't interested," he said haughtily.

"I seem to have drifted into a world of my own. You must excuse me, I'm so tired, what with working all week and looking after a two-year-old."

"Yes, it must be tough," he mumbled derisively. "Lots of brain surgery involved there."

"There's no need to be facetious, Jonathan. I think it's time we called it a night, don't you?"

He settled the bill, and they waited impatiently for the

taxi to pick them up. Why the hell had she agreed to go on a date with this arsehole?

They pulled up to her house, and she briefly thanked him for the evening and leapt out of the car. Before she knew it, he'd paid off the taxi driver and was walking after her.

"I'll walk you to your door?" he called.

"There's no need." She turned around, stunned to see his taxi driving away.

"No, a gentleman doesn't let a lady walk home alone."

Which gentleman, she felt like asking, but offered "Thank you for tonight," with as much enthusiasm as she could muster, "But how do you plan on getting home now you've let the taxi go?" She wasn't paying attention to his reply and was rummaging around in her bag to find her keys. Where the hell were they?

"It doesn't have to end here," he said smarmily, moving towards her.

"I have an early start."

"Come on Isabella? The night's young."

"I'm sorry Jonathan. I've had a nice evening, but …"

"Just one coffee?"

"No. I'm afraid not. My sitter will be waiting to go home."

Without warning, he lunged towards her and stuck his tongue down her throat.

"Jonathan. What the hell are you doing?" she gasped, taking a stepping back, completely taken by surprise, wiping his drool from her lips.

"Come on, we had a great time. Stop being a tease."

"Will you get off me?" she yelled, but then he pushed her hard against the wall. She banged her head, hard, against the bricks.

"Ouch. You're hurting me. What the hell do you think you're doing?"

"I only want one kiss," he leered. He was disgustingly drunk and turning fairly aggressive with his posturing, making himself appear larger and more threatening than he was. He grabbed hold of the back of her head and pulled her towards him.

"Get off me!" she yelled, raising her voice, trying to assert her displeasure and assert some dominance. "Bernie," she shrieked, her bag falling to the floor, its contents spilling all over the ground.

At that moment, the outside light came on and her front door burst open. Isabella and Jonathan froze, like a couple of small animals trapped in a car's headlights.

"What the hell are you doing?" roared Jack. Jack? What the hell was he doing here? His savage eyes darting first at Isabella, then in abhorrence at the drunken man stepping away from Isabella.

And before she knew what was going on, Jack leapt out of the doorway, grabbed hold of Jonathan and shoved him backwards forcefully with the palm of his hand.

"Who the hell are you?" slurred Jonathan.

"None of your darned business. Now get out of here before I call the cops." The tone of his voice told Jonathan he was not to be messed with.

"What's going on?" It was Harry, towel in hand, running from the downstairs bathroom to see what all the commotion was about.

"I'm going. I'm going," muttered Jonathan, not liking the odds, before zigzagging back down the driveway.

"Harry. Jack." She gasped and bent down to pick up her belongings, trying to take a few seconds to pull herself together.

"Get in." Commanded Jack after she'd finished.

"What the hell's going on?" asked Harry, bundling her inside and shutting the door behind them.

They walked into the lounge and all sat down and looked at each other, silent for what seemed like an eternity.

"Where's Bernie? What's going on?" she asked anxiously. "Teddy?"

"Teddy is fine," said Harry.

"What are you doing here?" she asked Jack. She literally couldn't believe her eyes.

"I was with Harry. He dropped off your Seagate thing."

"Harry?" she asked, looking for an explanation.

"What he said."

"What the fuck was going on? And who the hell was that prick?" asked Jack.

"Jonathan. Bibi set us up on a date. It was horrible," she snivelled.

"Good job we were here," said Jack brusquely. "What the hell were you playing at?"

She pinched the bridge of her nose, began to cry and fumbled in her pocket for a tissue. She endeavoured to explain what they had just witnessed as best she could... "And then you burst through the door. Just why are you here?" she asked Jack again.

"I was with Harry. I'm staying with Harry."

"Harry?" she asked.

"We got caught up in a meeting. We literally just got here about half an hour ago."

"Where's Bernie?"

"I dropped her home," stated Harry.

"And who stayed with the baby?" she asked incredulously, knowing full well what the answer was going to be.

"I did" said Jack.

Isabella gasped out loud and glared at Harry, "Alone? You left him here with Teddy alone?"

"What's wrong with that?" asked Jack. "Hell, I save you from the rapist ..."

"He wasn't a rapist." She snapped indignantly.

"Yeah, yeah, whatever. Nice date there Bella." Jack said sarcastically, ever the smooth talker, a remark that set her blood boiling.

"Don't you speak to me like that? You're acting like my father. I didn't realise I needed your approval. You shouldn't even be here."

"Isabella. Really. Teddy is fine. We were simply waiting for you to come home, then we were going," said Harry.

"Thank God we *were* here," mumbled Jack.

"I can manage fine without you." She hissed.

"Looks like it." Jack added tersely.

"Will you two stop?" snapped Harry.

"I'm sorry. I'm shaken up, that's all. Thank you, Jack. Harry. I'll be fine now. You two get going. It's late."

"We're not leaving you," said Jack.

"I'm fine, really," she pleaded, rubbing the back of her head.

"What if he comes back?" he asked.

"He won't."

"How do you know?"

"I agree," said Harry, "He wouldn't dare come back. He saw the two of us. He doesn't know that we're leaving."

"I'd rather stay," stated Jack.

"I'd rather you leave," responded Isabella.

"I'll get our coats," said Harry and left the room.

Jack came over and knelt before her. "Are you okay Bella?" he asked, concern etched on his face, as he stroked her arm, then tucked a stray hair from her face, displaying tenderness and intimacy.

"I'm fine, really. Just an over-zealous date, I'm afraid." She was so humiliated.

"Man, when I heard you shout for Bernie and saw what was going on ..."

"I'm mortified."

"I'm sorry for shouting, for being shitty with you. The thought that the guy could have hurt you was something I couldn't handle. I don't know what I'd do if anyone hurt you."

"I'm fine Jack."

"Do you usually go on dates with guys like that?"

"It's the first date I've had in ages and the last, hopefully."

"What a sleaze ball. I'm glad you're okay."

"You frightened him half to death. Me as well, come to think of it."

"I was ready to kick ten tonnes of shit out of him."

"I'm glad you were there. Thank you, Jack."

"Me too. It's good to see you. Although the timing isn't perfect."

"It never is. I still can't believe you're here, though. In my home."

"It's real nice."

"Come on Jack, you ready?" It was Harry, interrupting them.

"Bella, I don't want to leave you alone," sighed Jack.

"Jack please. I'm fine. How many times do I have to say?"

"You're still shaking."

"Honestly, I'll make myself a mug of hot chocolate, then I'll go straight to bed."

"Any strange noises, you call us okay? Call the cops."

"Okay."

"Well, goodbye Isabella. You've a beautiful home, by the way, from what I've seen. Don't worry …" he saw the look on her face, "I've only been downstairs. And I got your note. Thank you."

"Goodbye Jack. Goodnight Harry" she hugged them both briefly. "Harry, I'll talk to you tomorrow," she said through gritted teeth and gave him one of her stares.

"Oh, oh. Looks like I'm in trouble. Come on, Jack, let's get out of here."

The following morning, she woke early and phoned Bibi, "Bibi, it's me."

"Hello me. Jesus, it's early. How did the date go?"

"It was bad. Don't you ever set me up with anyone again? Do you understand? The guy's a complete dick. To cut a long story short, he came on to me, big time." And she continue to relay the antics of the previous night.

"Oh my God. He's a bloody doctor."

"I don't care what he is, he was disgusting. It was obvious I found him repulsive."

"I'm so sorry Izzy. So, after he grabbed you, what happened then? How did you get him off you? How'd you get him to stop? Were you scared?"

"Jack stopped him. And yes, I suppose I was scared."

"Jack. What the hell was Jack doing there?"

"Well, he came with Harry whilst I was out."

"What did he do?"

"Well, he just burst out the front door and shoved him halfway across my drive."

"Was he on a white horse?" Bibi said.

"I guess he was pretty marvellous. Jonathan scuttled down the road with his tail between his legs."

"So, then, what happened?"

"Nothing."

"Nothing?"

"Well, Jack and Harry came in, made sure I was okay, then said goodbye, that's it really."

"Did he kiss you?"

"Of course he didn't kiss me."

"I still don't understand what he was doing there?"

"Neither do I really? Listen, I've got to go. I'll explain more later after I've spoken to Harry."

"Did he look the same?"

"Who Harry?"

"No, you fool, Jack."

"Exactly the same."

"Nice. Wow, I'm stunned."

"He looked upset, too. Angry, but upset."

"Do you think he still has a thing for you?"

"I do not know. Look Bibi, I've got to go. Teddy needs his breakfast. I'll talk to you later."

She hung up, then dialled Harry's number.

"Yes," he grumbled into the phone.

"It's me," she stated.

"Isabella. Do you know what time it is?"

"Of course I do. What the hell were you thinking bringing Jack to my house? Leaving him alone with Teddy."

"Good morning to you, too."

"I'm not kidding Harry. I can't believe you did that."

"It's not a big deal. I had to drop your back-up drive in – you told me you needed it for Monday. Poor Bernie looked tired, so I took her home. That's it."

"That's it. You left him here, alone. In my house. He could have been doing anything? Been looking at anything?"

"What. You think he was going through your underwear drawer?"

"You know that's not what I'm angry about."

"Jeez, we save you from Merv the Perv and you're angry with me?"

"That's beside the point."

"No harm done. You'll be seeing him soon anyway, when we go to Greece. You've got to face him and spend time with him, eventually."

"I haven't decided if I'm going yet."

"Oh, for God's sake. It's true what Jack says. You should come with a warning label."

"Did he say that?"

"Not in so many words."

"Harry?"

"I can see his point, though. Whenever you see him, you change. You become a crazy woman."

"I wonder why," she huffed.

"Get over it, Izzy."

"Drop dead, Harry." And she slammed the phone down.

***

CHAPTER TWENTY-EIGHT

A couple of weeks later, Isabella woke early and, after checking to see if Teddy was still sleeping, crept downstairs to check the post. There were a few bills, a couple of mailshots, and a postcard depicting an aerial shot of Central Park, New York. She knew whom it was from and turned it over at once, and saw his handwritten scrawl. Her heart was pounding. *Ciao Bella. I hope you're good. Just to say I'm thinking of you and looking forward to seeing you again (hopefully in Greece). I hope Harry can work his magic on you. Take care (and no more dates). My fondest wishes. Your friend, Jack.* He also gave his cell number.

She read and re-read his card, time and time again over the next few days and after finally being bullied and blackmailed into a decision by Harry, Isabella finally agreed to go to Greece with them all.

"You'll have to let him know," said Harry.

"Can't you? Please?" she whined.

"Isabella, don't be ridiculous. Phone him. Politely accept his invitation. He already knows Eva and I are going."

"You could call him at work?"

"Isabella," he roared, "You have to speak to him some time, for God's sake," he roared, "We'll all be cooped up on a boat soon."

"Okay, okay. I'll text him?"

"You won't. Call him."

She finally plucked up courage one evening once she'd

worked out the time difference. With Teddy safely tucked up in bed, she knew there would be no interruptions. She gulped down a glass of red wine, then dialled his number. She ended the call after a couple of rings. Shit.

"Come on Isabella, you can do this," she said to herself and with trembling hands she re-dialled his number, her heart pounding with a mixture of excitement and trepidation. As the phone rang, each ring felt like an eternity, until finally, he picked up and his voice echoed through the line, sending a shiver down his spine.

"Jack Vincent."

She paused, her heart pounding more than ever. Could he hear it?

"Hullo? Hullo? Anyone there?" he asked.

"Jack."

"Isabella. Bella, is that you? I don't believe it," he recognised her voice immediately. "How are you? It's great to hear from you. My God, I don't believe it." He sounded ecstatic.

"I'm good. Fine thanks." She didn't know what else to say.

There was a pregnant pause.

"And Teddy?" he asked carefully.

"He's great. Thanks for asking. You? How are you? I'm not disturbing you?"

"Of course not. I'm good. Busy. So, been on any more dates recently?"

"Funny." She said witheringly.

"You sure know how to pick 'em."

"Don't I just. I seem to have a penchant for arseholes."

"Ouch. Present company excluded, I hope."

"Touché. So, how's life in the Big Apple?"

"I'm in Philly at the moment."

They exchanged polite pleasantries, but underneath lay an ocean of unspoken emotions, a chasm too vast to bridge. He was hanging on her every word, drinking in the sound of her voice like a parched wanderer stumbling upon an oasis.

"Mm," she said in reply to one of his questions.

"Are you biting your bottom lip?"

"What? How did you know?"

"When you're nervous, you bite your bottom lip."

"I do?"

"You do. It's sexy."

"Jack," she groaned, "Stop."

"Well …? Did you call for any reason or just to hear my voice?" he teased. She could picture his expression. She could imagine him smiling down the phone at her. Ruffling his hands through his hair, perhaps rubbing the stubble on his jaw. She wondered what he was wearing. She could hear him inhale deeply on his cigarette, then exhale.

"Ummm. It's just I called to let you know …" she realised she was biting her bottom lip. Who knew?

"Yes?" he growled.

"We'll be coming to Greece. Both of us."

"You are?" he breathed in disbelief. He couldn't hide the amazement in his voice.

"Yes, if that's still okay? If there's still room?"

"Oh my God, yes. Bella, I can't believe it. I can't wait to meet your son."

"He will be safe?"

"I swear. I saw him, you know?"

"You did," she gasped.

"Yeah. That night Harry and I came to yours. I sneaked upstairs and watched him sleeping."

"You didn't? You … you … did? But you said you only stayed downstairs?" Bloody Harry, she was going to kill him.

"You don't mind, do you?"

"It's a bit late now."

"He's a beautiful boy."

"I know."

"Just like his Mommy."

"Do you think so?"

"He looked so perfect. So peaceful. He was breathing so

quietly, I had to bend down and check on him. I put my ear to his lips."

"Jesus Harry. I can't believe he just let you wander up there."

"Not his fault. I wanted to see this little boy Harry talks about all the time."

She knew what he meant though about the breathing and added, "When he was a tiny baby, I used to go check on him all the time to make sure he was still breathing. I used to pick him up and prod him, just to make sure he was okay and, of course, thankfully, he always was. I'd feel stupid afterwards."

"He's amazing. You're amazing. I can't believe that bastard left you and you've had to do this all on your own."

She changed the subject. "So Greece?"

"Yep? We'll have so much fun. I'll teach him to swim, to fish."

"Jack. He's only two."

"Never too early. I still can't believe you're coming." He sounded like an excited little boy, still tethered to memories of their past.

"Jack, just one thing?"

"Anything."

"No strings?"

"No strings, baby, I promise."

As they bid each other farewell, his heart ached with the weight of unrequited love, the distance between them magnified by the silence that lingered long after the call ended.

May approached swiftly and as the day to leave for Athens grew nearer, Isabella felt more and more disconcerted. She kept searching for excuses to back out. What if it was like Kenya? Teddy would be hell during the flight. What if he fell overboard? What if she and Jack spent the weeks arguing? She was building herself up into such a state, she convinced herself she was unwell and couldn't go after all.

On the morning of the flight, she was so tense she was

even snapping at Teddy and reduced him to tears several times. She packed and repacked their suitcase, then started all over again.

"Ted. What have you done with Mummy's keys?" she shouted at her little boy.

Harry and Eva were arriving shortly to collect them and take them to the airport, where they would meet Ingrid and David. Isabella had yet to meet the new lady in Harry's life and was obviously a little apprehensive. Would they get on? Would Isabella's presence threaten her in his life and vice versa?

Harry arrived on time and she was flustered as she opened the door.

"Hi," said Isabella, "Come on in, please."

Harry introduced Eva to "my two-favourite people." Eva had pale-blond, almost white, long hair, tied back in a ponytail. Standing at around five foot six, she was incredibly slender. She had a few freckles on her nose, warm friendly eyes, and appeared very approachable. She was casual, but elegantly dressed.

"And you must be Teddy." Eva said warmly, kneeling down to talk to her child at eye level and asked him, "I understand you're Harry's best friend? Harry was right, you are a handsome little boy and so grown up."

Teddy smiled shyly and hid behind his mummy's legs.

"And Isabella. It's lovely to meet you at last." And rather than taking Isabella's outstretched arm for a handshake, she pulled her into a warm hug.

"You too, Eva. I've heard so much about you. It's a delight to finally meet you in person."

"You have? Oh goodness, what's Harry being saying?"

"All good, I assure you." She said. She liked Eva straight away.

"Are you guys ready?" asked Harry, smiling at her affectionately.

"As ready as we'll ever be, I guess," Isabella groaned and rolled her eyes upwards.

"What's the matter?" he asked, "We're going on holiday."

"I'm not feeling too good," she sighed.

"Isabella, there's nothing wrong with you."

"I wish I'd never agreed to go," she moaned.

"Nonsense. We'll have a whale of a time," he bawled and swept Teddy off his feet into his arms, "Uncle Harry's going to teach you how to swim."

"Oh God." Isabella groaned.

"What can we help with?" asked Eva.

"Car seat. Pushchair. Suitcase. Bags?" grumbled Isabella, looking at all the surrounding paraphernalia.

"No problem. We can help. You have a beautiful home, by the way. Harry tells me you're a designer. You can tell you've fantastic taste."

"Thank you," Isabella smiled.

With her enchanting presence, Eva effortlessly won over Teddy, leaving him utterly charmed, even more so when she produced a gift bag for the flight, full of fun age-related activities.

"She's gorgeous." Whispered Isabella to Harry, whilst Eva squatted down talking to Teddy.

"I hope you get on," said Harry warily. "I don't know what I'd do if you two didn't get on."

"I'm sure we'll be fine. From what I've seen so far and from what you've told me, I think we'll get on fabulously."

After they had gathered all their belongings, locked up and put everything in the car, they were soon on their way to the airport.

Isabella and Eva continued to hit it off and were soon laughing and joking and taking it in turns to tease Harry. Eva was considerate with Teddy, considering she hadn't been in contact with many small children before and kept him occupied and chatting away in the back, throughout their brief trip.

Despite the little Harry had told her about Eva, Isabella could see that they were very much in love. Eva would frequently gaze at him adoringly and he'd return her smile in the rear-view mirror. She didn't seem a pushover and Isabella knew they would become firm friends.

"So, tell me about your job Eva, Harry tells me you're an Occupational Therapist?"

"Yep. It's very rewarding. I love it."

"So, what does it involve? I'm not sure what an OT does?"

"I help people of all ages overcome their challenges and regain their independence in their daily activities."

"What challenges?"

"Could be an injury, illness, developmental issues. The main thing is to empower people to live their life to the fullest. Every day brings new opportunities and challenges to make a difference in someone's life."

"Must be rewarding. Very different from what I do, which seems meaningless in comparison."

"Don't be silly. Not at all. What you do is wonderful. Still important. Harry's shown me pictures. A person's home is their sanctuary."

Heading towards departures, they dropped the car off with a valet service. They then checked in seamlessly and met up with Ingrid and David in the lounge–both looked well and marriage obviously suited them. They were all looking forward to their holiday and were pleased to see each other again. Everyone introduced themselves to each other and made a lot of fuss over Teddy. They were all animated, and laughter and chatter surrounded them as they discussed their plans and visions for the upcoming adventure in Greece. They swapped past travels; a sense of adventure and camaraderie binding them. Teddy sat on his mummy's knee and remained quiet, but listened wide eyed to the adults' chatter, soaking in every word.

The flight to Athens was uneventful. The five of them took it in turns to have Teddy on their knee, who was lapping up all the attention he received from them. Teddy, who had never flown before and had never met Ingrid, David, or Eva before, behaved well. But thankfully, they all took immediately to each other.

"Are you okay, Izzy?" asked Ingrid as they stood in the galley to stretch their legs. "You seem a little tense?"

"The prospect of seeing Jack," she stated.

"I'm sure it'll be fine. Have you spoken to him recently?"

"A couple of times. Once to say we were coming and then he rang me a few days ago to check everything was okay. We've shared a few texts as well, just friendly catch ups. You?"

"Same. He was over briefly recently and David and I met up with him for a drink."

"Really? Was he okay?"

"Just the same–gorgeous. Abrasive. Jack."

"Hmmm" was all she could say in response. That was what she was dreading, if she was honest.

"Eva seems nice?" said Ingrid, changing the subject.

"Doesn't she? I think we'll all get along great. Harry adores her."

"I know. Can you imagine? I didn't see that one coming." said Ingrid.

"Neither. She seems lovely, though."

"Really lovely. Have you been to Greece before?"

"No, you?"

"No, I don't think any of us have apart from Harry. I wonder what Jack has planned for us?"

"Not sure, but I'm sure it'll be good fun."

"I just hope there's plenty of room on the boat. I don't want to be cramped and we find we're all on top of each other."

"I'm sure not. We're all adults, apart from Teddy, and will need our own space. We might kill each other otherwise."

***

CHAPTER TWENTY-NINE

They arrived safely at Athens International to see glorious sunshine. They retrieved their luggage from the carousel, then navigated the maze of corridors and signage and they finally reached the arrivals hall. Isabella spied Jack patiently waiting for them, a huge grin on his face.

None of them had any idea that he had been there for hours, pacing up and down, bubbling with excitement, awaiting their arrival. He too spotted them and was waving eagerly. He was already tanned and looked fit and healthy in his frayed, worn shorts and white t-shirt. She couldn't see his eyes because he was wearing dark shades and a New York Yankees cap.

Harry hugged him first and then introduced him to Eva, before he greeted the rest of them, exchanging high-fives and hugs, saving the biggest hug of all for Isabella, "I'm so glad you came," he whispered, as he held her close to him, before swiftly pulling away and saying, "And who is this young guy?" and he knelt down next to Teddy, snuggled in his buggy, clutching his blankie.

Teddy smiled bashfully and clutched his blankie even tighter.

"This is Teddy," said Isabella proudly and nervously, "He's exhausted I'm afraid and didn't sleep at all during the flight."

"Well, Teddy, it's lovely to meet you. You're beautiful just like your Mom. I'm Jack and I can't wait to show you my boat and I hope you will be my co-captain and drive it for me sometime?"

Ted regarded him wide eyed and then looked at his Mummy.

"We'll see Teddy," she said. "Be a good boy, okay?"

"Ok." He said and jumped out of his pushchair. Isabella just managed to just grab hold of it before it toppled backwards. She watched as her son took hold of Jack's hand as they all made their way outside to the car and Isabella didn't take her eyes off the sight before her: Jack holding onto Teddy's, sweaty, chubby little hand and she watched as he bent down every now and again to say something to her son. She felt nauseous.

Harry glanced at her and smiled, as if to reassure her.

"Wow, feel that heat," gasped Ingrid, as they stepped outside where the warm Mediterranean sun beckoned.

"Good, huh?" replied Jack.

"Amazing," cried Ingrid.

"He seems nice," she heard Eva whisper to Harry.

God, what had she let herself in for? Isabella groaned inwardly.

The heat was searing as they made their way to their luxury van in the parking lot, ready to ultimately whisk them away to their Greek adventure.

Harry, David and Jack loaded the luggage into the trunk and they all piled into the van, the excitement of their journey ahead filling the air with an infectious energy.

"Oh, please Jack. Can you put the air-con on? I'm roasting," wailed Ingrid, fanning her face with a magazine.

"No problem Ma'am. Right, Harry, I need you to help navigate. I've got on board sat nav, but the roads are the stuff of nightmares," said Jack as he turned on the ignition.

"Now he tells us," groaned Harry.

They made their way through the vast landscape, unfolding like a tapestry before them, towards the ancient port of

Piraeus. Through the windows, they caught glimpses of the vibrant, sprawling metropolis before them. All but the two front passengers watched eagerly out the windows, whilst chatting amongst themselves about their forthcoming holiday.

"Will there be room for all of us, Jack?" asked Ingrid.

"Yeah, will we won't have to share and bunk up with each other?" asked Harry.

"I know you're all friends, but that's a little too close for me," said Eva.

"Just wait and see. You'll be fine," said Jack.

Twice, Isabella caught him staring at her through the rear-view mirror, smile and then glance back at the road before him.

They manoeuvred through the noisy traffic and frequently got stuck in jams, where impatient drivers honked their horns at each other and shouted obscenities. Goats and horse-drawn carts ambled along the roadside, where towering palm trees lined the streets, their fronds gently swaying in the breeze. Amongst the perpetual concrete apartment buildings and hustle of this energetic city, was the juxtaposition of colourful bougainvillea cascading from balconies, adding splashes of vivid pink and purple to the urban scene.

As they passed through neighbourhoods and districts, the bustle of everyday life unfolded around them. Street vendors selling fresh produce from roadside stalls, while locals lingered at pavement cafes, savouring espresso and engaging in animated conversation. In the distance, the shimmering waters of the Aegean beckoned, their azure depths mirroring the cloudless sky above. Finally, the port of Piraeus came into view; a bustling hub of activity as boats bobbed up and down and ferries came and went ready to their next destination–the idyllic Greek islands beyond.

As their van pulled up to the harbour, a team of impeccably dressed crew members awaited their arrival and, with practiced efficiency, sprang into action, greeting them all with warm smiles and attentive gestures. Some assisted and whisked away their luggage and bags, while others extended a helping hand to escort them along the gangway to Jack's gleaming, luxurious and unexpectedly enormous yacht. The crew introduced themselves, then assisted them with boarding, ensuring a seamless transition from land to sea, welcoming them with glasses of champagne and iced water.

"Some boat." whistled David.

"Boat?" said Ingrid. "It looks like a floating palace."

"You never said it was this big," said Harry.

"I had no idea" gasped Isabella. She guessed correctly that there would be room for them all after all.

"I've never seen anything so opulent," said Eva, "What's it called, the QE2?"

"You'd give Abramovich a run for his money, that's for sure," said David.

"She's over 250 feet, capable of sleeping twelve guests and up to fourteen crew," answered Jack proudly.

"Wowzers," exclaimed Harry.

"Is it fast?" enquired Ingrid.

"Top speed of about 25 to 30 knots," replied Jack.

"Doesn't mean a lot, I'm afraid. I take it that's a yes?" said Ingrid, sipping her champagne.

"Yes, she's fast, and she's a beauty," said David admiringly.

"What's her name?" enquired Eva.

"All the Way" said Jack.

"Weird?" she replied.

Isabella remained silent. Fuck.

Jack led them up some steps to the veranda deck, where they all gazed in amazement at the unequalled surroundings adorned with marble floors and intricate woodwork, setting the tone for the lavish experience that awaited them in the days ahead. They chatted enthusiastically and pointed out the opulence surrounding them, whilst oohing and aaahing at their plush environs. With her large sun-drenched decks and open spaces, it looked the ideal place for a comfortable and relaxing time on the sea. It was obvious there was plenty of space to sunbathe comfortably and rest and recline on the sumptuous loungers, perhaps step into the large bubbling jacuzzi, perfect for soaking up the Mediterranean sunshine before enjoying refreshments in the cool of the bar lounge.

Jack directed them into the wide laid team cockpit and, after introducing them properly to the captain, Jack (no seriously), pointed out the navigation instrumentation, the satellite communications and chart table. It was truly awe-inspiring. Classic styling and craftsmanship, combined with state-of-the-art performance, the boat was a technical masterpiece of grace, power and, most of all, comfort and extravagance. This was a 5* resort that would offer them changing views of the islands every day and provide the ultimate luxury.

The dedicated crew were there to meet their every need, whose unwavering commitment to service would ensure the guest experience would be nothing short of extraordinary. From the captain and deckhands to the chefs and stewards, each member of the crew Jack had selected was a consummate professional, dedicated to exceeding the expectations of his and his esteemed guests.

Jack introduced the professional chef, Joe, who would prepare gourmet dining options. His team were on hand to create culinary masterpieces and local specialities, using the finest ingredients sourced locally; whatever they wanted, in the practical and spacious galley.

Jack then led them up another flight of beautifully moulded, polished mahogany and aluminium steps, which led onto the main deck. He showed them around the vast main salon, where mahogany, marble, and leather contributed to the ultimate elegance and sophistication. They could look both to aft and to port, through the vast windows and doors leading onto the decks. Large comfy sofas, lavish fabrics, sumptuous furnishings, and bespoke finishes filled the room, lavishly illuminated by well-placed lighting. There was even a full-size grand piano and on one wall, rows of polished glasses gleamed from the light of a ship's lamp on the opposite wall.

"Look at all the boats and ferries," said Harry, lifting Teddy up to look out of the windows.

"Fish. Fish," said Ted.

"Yep, there'll be fish in there," said Eva.

Thereafter followed the dining saloon where the wood panelling was used to great effect, central to which was a large dining table, where they could spend many a convivial supper. Each room showcased original works by renowned artists from various periods and styles, using the finest materials and the best wood for decoration. Treasured family photos and an array of decorative items sourced from around the world provided a glimpse into Jack's discerning (and surprising) taste and appreciation of fine craftsmanship. Isabella spied a couple of black and white framed photos from Kenya; of the captivating landscapes, the animals they'd spotted on safari, and one of the group. Ouch. Overall, the yacht reflected a sophisticated blend of luxury, culture, and personal taste, creating an immersive and refined experience that none of them had expected.

Apparently, the top deck offered its own helipad. There was also a hydraulically operated swimming platform on the stern and water toys garage housing an impressive array of watersports equipment; jet-skis, paddleboards, kayaks, inflatable towable toys and windsurfing gear. They were certainly in for a fabulous trip.

Integrated into the yacht's exterior was a designated area for storing a RIB and a speedboat ready to transport them to and from shore, whisk them away on excursions or to explore coves and beaches.

Finally, he showed them to their accommodation. His master suite and owner's cabin looked to starboard and was a sanctuary of luxury, featuring a kingsize bed, private lounge area, study and en suite bathroom, complete with a jacuzzi tub and steam shower. It had antique charts, brass lamps, ship models, leather-bound books, and plenty of dark wood decorating it, and Isabella thought it suited him to perfection.

The entrance to the guest staterooms was via a private hall and they were equally impressive, offering plush bedding, ample storage and panoramic views of the sea beyond. You could operate everything, including the blinds and curtains, with your phone. Each room had their own hidden state-of-the art entertainment system, offering them a range of options to unwind and enjoy their favourite movies or music. Each room had a comfortable seating area, perfect for relaxing with a book, and each room had its own en suite bath or shower room.

"I think I could get used to this," said Eva, as Jack showed her and Harry to their suite.

"Okay for you guys?" asked Jack.

"Wonderful," giggled Eva, holding onto Harry's hand and beaming.

The others followed Jack along the corridor to the next door.

"And you, Isabella and little Teddy, are in here," he opened the door with a flourish, "Ta da. I hope you'll both be comfortable in here? Sharing a bed, I mean? I didn't know if he was still in a crib or not."

"This is perfect, thank you, Jack, it's wonderful" said Isabella politely as she led her son into their suite, where their luggage was already waiting for them.

"Will you be okay?" he asked. "Can I get you anything?"

"We will be fine, Jack, thanks. Better than fine, this is marvellous."

"I aim to please. Settle yourselves in, then meet us on deck when you're ready, okay?"

"Great, see you shortly."

After Jack closed the door and had left to show Ingrid and David their suite, Isabella noticed the lavish king-sized bed, adorned with fine, white, pristine linens and an array of plump pillows, promising them a restful night's sleep after a day of adventure on the open sea. She groaned to herself, "That won't stay clean for long, will it, Teddy?"

The suite was a sanctuary of luxury and indulgence; the bed positioned strategically to fully appreciate the panoramic views through the large windows. Everything from the walls to the furniture in the room was solid mahogany, plush carpets beneath their feet and soft ambient lighting, creating a sense of warmth and intimacy. There were some delightful old oil paintings in lavish gold frames on the walls. She didn't recognise any of the artists, bar one. She wasn't positive, but one glorious masterpiece definitely looked like an original Henry Moore.

There were a couple of brass bedside lamps on either side of the bed and Teddy headed for one and began flicking it on and off.

The fully fitted bathroom, featuring luxurious marble finishes, a spacious walk-in shower and a deep soaking tub, offered views of the sea and beyond. High end amenities and plush robes, even a Teddy sized one, and toiletries from Hermes, added that extra touch of comfort and sophistication, ensuring they would feel pampered and rejuvenated throughout their stay. He had thought of everything.

Isabella was busy unpacking their belongings when she heard a knock at the door. It was Harry.

"We're all getting changed into our swimsuits and meeting on the boat deck, okay?" he asked, then added, noticing her unpacking her bag. "Hey. One of the crew unpacked ours?"

"Yep, they offered, but I would rather do it myself. I'll see you in a few minutes. I'll just finish unpacking, then I'll meet you up there. If I can find my around, that is."

"I know, right? We may need a map to navigate this baby. Incredible, isn't she?"

"I had no idea." She giggled, "See you soon."

"Her name?" he said.

"I know." She winced.

She finished putting their things away, then changed Teddy. She put him in a pair of blue and white checked swimming trunks and then had a fight with him over a little sunhat and a life preserver that Jack had left for him.

"Look Ted, for the last time. If you want to go upstairs, you must wear this, okay?" she snapped.

After a further struggle, her son finally relented and Isabella could change into her own one-piece swimsuit and matching sarong. Putting on her sunglasses, she took hold of Teddy's hand.

"Come on sweetheart, let's go find Uncle Harry and others."

"I like it here Mummy."

"Me too darling, but you must be a good boy for Mummy, okay?"

"Okay."

As Jack sat waiting on the sun-bathed deck, he spied Isabella and Teddy emerging from their suite below. Her flowing sarong billowed gently in the sea breeze. She radiated elegance with every step. Her swimsuit, adorned with intricate patterns and shimmering accents, hugged her curves in all the right places, accentuating her natural allure. Clasping her child, providing comfort and protection, she guided them on deck towards them with a tender smile, her eyes sparkling with warmth and love. Teddy beamed with excitement and looked up at her with adoration, their bond palpable in the air.

They made their way towards the sun-drenched lounge chairs where the others were waiting for them.

Ingrid and Eva were applying copious amounts of sun cream as she settled into a chair alongside them and lifted Teddy onto the seat next to her. Her gaze drifted out over the vast backdrop, a tranquil smile played on her lips. In this moment, she embodied a timeless elegance and maternal love.

"Drink, madam?" asked one of the crew.

"Please. Can I have an orange juice?"

"No problem."

"Isabella. Teddy," exclaimed Jack. "Come and see what I've got." He opened the lid of a strategically placed hidden storage compartment, within which was stowed an assortment of brand-new children's toys amongst the snorkelling equipment, balls and frisbees.

"Mama," shrieked Ted.

"Wow," said Isabella, "Jack, you shouldn't have."

"Yes, I should. These should keep him occupied for a while," he said, whilst Teddy began rifling through the cars, dinosaurs and other treats on offer.

"It's very thoughtful of you, thank you." He had thought of everything.

Jack took her orange juice from the crew member, Jess, and handed it to her. "Teddy, would you like some orange juice too?" he asked.

"Yes," said the little boy eagerly.

"Yes, what Ted?" Isabella frowned.

"Peas."

"There's a good boy," she said.

"We thought we would remain here in the harbour tonight and then maybe have a stroll around the city tomorrow. That sound okay?" asked Jack.

"Wonderful. I've always wanted to explore Athens. Mm, this juice is delicious, freshly squeezed too."

"You and Teddy need sun cream, Bella," Jack ordered.

"Yep, thanks. Got it."

They spent a glorious afternoon sipping cold drinks, lying in the sun, savouring the moment, as the waves lapped gently against the hull. Seated in the plush lounge chairs, they took full advantage of the sublime view; they clinked glasses, enjoyed conversation and shared laughter. The atmosphere was relaxed. They relished in the special character of their setting, the hub of activity, the small fishing boats and larger sailing boats, the ferries, all coming and going in and out of the busy harbour, the largest in the Balkans. They all took turns watching and playing with Teddy, as did several crew members. Isabella was grateful for the help and rest.

"So, what are you reading Bella?" asked Jack, noticing she had had her head in her well-read book most of the day. It bore the marks of its journey through her hands and mind, its cover worn and creased, its spine cracked and well-loved, its dog-eared pages evidence of her deep engagement with the text.

"Maya Angelou's *And Still I Rise*."

"Powerful stuff, hey."

"You've read her poetry?"

"Yep. Hasn't everyone? *You may trod me in the very dirt / But still, like dust, I'll rise.*"

And still he continued to surprise her.

That evening, they did, in fact, remain on board amidst the backdrop of twinkling city lights and majestic yachts bobbing in the harbour. The conversation flowed, lively anecdotes and contemplative reflections. They talked about travel adventures, business ventures, personal passions and philosophical musings. Eva fit in seamlessly with the group and they all liked her.

They enjoyed a quiet, and palatable informal dinner prepared by Joe. To start, he had prepared a local fish soup, followed by the tastiest kleftiko and Greek salad Isabella had ever tasted, served with warm, soft pitta bread, all guzzled with bottles of local wine. For pudding, they enjoyed galaktoboureko, a traditional Greek dessert made with a custard in a crispy filo pastry shell. Thankfully, he offered hotdogs and fries to Teddy, much to his and Isabella's relief.

"I could get used to this relaxing lifestyle, and it is only day one. You're a sly one, Vincent, keeping this beauty to yourself," said Harry, puffing on a Cuban cigar and enjoying a brandy.

"Well, man, you know," said Jack, shrugging his

shoulders.

They all had a wonderful time engaged in spirited discussion and friendly banter, laughing and joking and they soon felt relaxed and at home in their lavish surroundings and Jack and the crew fawned all over them, making sure that everything was perfect for the beginning of their holiday. He told them just to ask one of the crew, or himself, if there was anything at all they needed, anything. Thankfully, he didn't particularly pay Isabella any more attention than the others. He was polite and mindful, but once or twice she caught him regarding her intensely, and she wondered what was going on in that gorgeous head of his.

He was fantastic with Teddy and if he noticed he was playing up a little, or was acting grumpy, he would distract him and pick him and show him the twinkling lights of the city, pointing out various things on the boat, anything to make him laugh and smile again.

Harry and Eva couldn't keep their hands off each other and it made Isabella a little uncomfortable to see them all over each other. She had never seen Harry so openly tactile.
Isabella eventually took her little boy to bed, when he fell asleep on Ingrid's knee, exhausted and set up the video monitor Jack had so thoughtfully provided, so she could watch him carefully.

"I love you sweetheart," she whispered as she tucked him into their luxurious bed with his blankie placed carefully near him, should he want to reach out for it in the night.

He stirred and whispered, "I love you Mummy."

"You go straight back to sleep, darling, okay?"

"Ok Mummy. I like Jack and I like his boat even better."

"He likes you too, sweetheart," her heart fluttered. "Now sleep tight. Don't let the bedbugs bite."

She re-joined the others, where they were enjoying the balmy evening. Their discussions were light and humorous and at no stage did anyone refer to Jack and Isabella's past.

"Shall we go in?" said Harry. It was getting chilly now.

"Sure. Follow me," said Jack, "Ladies …" and he held out his hand with a flourish to let them through to the main salon.

In the dimly lit lounge, the soft glow of the vintage lamps and the gentle haze of smoke that hung in the air from Jack's cigarette set the ambiance.

"I love it in here. The atmosphere is sooooo relaxing," sighed Ingrid, as they all chose a comfortable seat.

"Glad you like it," said Jack, grinning.

"What's not to like?" said David.

One of the crew, Stefan, took their drink orders and walked over to the bar and fixed them all another round of drinks.

They chatted and laughed as their friendships deepened and bonds strengthened, all of them contributing to the conversation. They exchanged jokes, and laughter filled the air. While they consumed vast amounts of alcohol and settled into a moment of quiet contemplation. Eva broke the silence, "Do you play Jack?" she asked, nodding towards the piano, its polished surface gleaming under the warm light.

"A little."

"A little? Don't be modest," said Harry.

"Modest? He's as modest as this boat," said Ingrid.

"Care to give us a tune?" smiled Eva.

"No, it's late," he grumbled.

"Come on Jack, don't be a spoilsport," said Harry.

"I didn't know you could play?" said Isabella, smiling at him.

"Pretty please?" begged Ingrid.

"Come on Jack. Anything we want, remember?" said David.

Jack got up and sauntered over to the piano, a cigarette dangling from the corner of his lips, its tendrils of smoke curling upwards in lazy spirals as he played, the smell of whiskey lingering in the air.

He played a few notes and said, "I haven't tuned it."

"Don't make excuses Jackie, play us a tune," moaned Harry.

"Any requests?" he asked them, as he played a few notes from *Live and Let Die.*

"Hey. Not bad Jackie boy," said Harry.

"Where the hell did Jackie boy come from?" said Jack. He was enjoying himself now. He'd changed the tune to *Let There Be Love.*

"Dunno." Harry slurred, "It suits you."

Jack played beautifully. With his dark, tousled hair, he exuded charm and allure. His chiselled features illuminated by the soft glow of the piano keys, casting shadows across his angular jawline and captivating eyes. Dressed casually in a linen shirt that stressed his muscular physique, his sleeves rolled up to reveal strong, agile hands that glided effortlessly across the keys, coaxing melodies from the instrument with practiced ease.

"Do you know the theme from *An Affair to Remember*?" asked Eva. "I love that film."

"Me too," said Isabella, "It's my favourite film ever."

"Who doesn't love Cary Grant?" sighed Eva.

"The film title's pretty ironic, don't cha think?" whispered Ingrid to Isabella, as Jack played.

"Shut up," hissed Isabella, playfully slapping her friend on the hand.

"Oh. My. God. I think I'm going to cry," wailed Eva. "That's it. It's perfect."

"Come on, ladies … join in." called Jack, "*La laaaaa la laaaaaa … da daaaaaa da daaaaa da daaaaa … la la laaaaa la la la la remember.* Anyone know the darned words?" He looked perplexed as he played, his fingers dancing across the keys with fluid grace, infusing each note with emotion.

"I think it has more effect without the singing," said David.

Jack changed the tune once more, and he began singing properly this time, as he continued to play "*For what is a man, what has he got, if not himself, then he has naught"* and the others joined in raucously *"to say the things, he truly feels; And not the words of one who kneels ..."* His eyes, half lidded as he lost himself in the music, a faint smile playing at the corners of his lips.

And thereafter followed Sinatra, after Sinatra, followed by some more modern classics and soulful ballads, followed by more Sinatra. They were all singing to their hearts' content and enjoyed themselves thoroughly as they sang long into the night. He finally ended with *As Time Goes By* and as the final chords of the song echoed through the room, he took a slow sip of whiskey, the amber liquid glinting in the light and with a quiet nod of appreciation, he acknowledged his friends' applause.

"Another one of my favourites," sighed Isabella.

"Here's looking at you, kid," smiled Jack, winking at her.

"Listen to ol' Jackie boy," said Harry.

"Will you quit it with the Jackie boy?"

"Play it again Jack," said Harry.

They all retired to bed in the early hours of the morning and Isabella felt a little lonely as she climbed into bed next to her son, as she heard Ingrid and David tiptoe past her door, giggling in the corridor. She wished she had someone to share this wonderful holiday with, like Harry and Eva or Ingrid or David. She kissed Teddy gently on his forehead, turned on her side and wrapped her arms round her fluffy pillows and presently fell asleep.

***

CHAPTER THIRTY

They all surfaced one by one, in various moods, at a fairly reasonable hour the following morning. Teddy had spent an excellent first night in his new surroundings and, thankfully, had let Isabella have several hours of sleep.

"Mornin'," called Jack, as Isabella and Teddy arrived on deck. The scent of freshly brewed coffee filled the air, beckoning them to the breakfast table.

As they took their seats around the table, the friendly smiles of the attentive crew greeted them, ready to cater to their every need.

"How are we feeling this morning?" asked Harry, "Sore head?"

"Surprisingly no. I'm tired though."

"Hungry," said Teddy.

"Here, both of you help yourself to something to eat," offered Jack.

"I just fancy a black coffee, thanks Jack," as she poured herself a steaming mug full and then began assisting Ted with some fruit and toast, "I enjoyed myself last night, it was fun" she said.

"Me too," said Jack, "Although I'm a little hoarse this morning."

"Jack's a little horse?" asked Teddy, and they all laughed as Isabella tried to explain.

"You gave it your all Jackie boy," said Harry.

"We all did, I think. We must have been very loud. God knows what the crew must be thinking," said Eva. "You're very talented, Jack. I'm very impressed."

"They don't care. We'll do it again, plenty of time," said Jack.

"Sounds good Jackie boy," said Harry.

"Enough already," said Jack, punching his friend in the arm.

Ingrid and David joined them shortly afterwards, and they all enjoyed the lavish breakfast spread before them, meticulously arranged on a gleaming table adorned with crisp linen and fresh flowers; flaky croissants and buttery pastries to colourful fruit platters and artisanal cheeses. The crew regularly topping up their freshly squeezed orange juice or steaming cups of tea or coffee.

The atmosphere was relaxed elegance, with them all exchanging casual conversation as they sipped their drinks and sampled the delicious fare before them.

As the morning sun, in shades of pink and orange, changed from a soft golden glow over the calm waters, the morning unfolded and the sun climbed higher in the sky. The tone created an atmosphere for a day filled with adventure, relaxation, and the joys of life aboard a luxury yacht.

They all agreed they couldn't come to Athens without visiting the Acropolis, so after they had all washed and dressed in cool, comfortable clothes, Jack drove them once more into the city.

Harry was again helping with navigation and got them lost several times. He had them wrongly driving down pedestrian-only lanes and struggled with trying to avoid the plenty of one-way streets, before they amazingly found somewhere to park their large van.

As they stepped out into the sun-drenched streets of Athens, the Acropolis rose majestically in the distance, its ancient ruins beckoning like a beacon against the bright blue sky. The air was warm and fragrant with the scent of olive trees and Mediterranean herbs as they walked around the warren of bustling, crooked little streets lined with beautiful cafes and terraced tavernas; lively street markets and shops selling souvenirs and local crafts. Occasionally, the sound of

Greek music drifted through the air and they couldn't help but gaze in wonder at the city's long and rich history alive in front of them, modern combined with the ancient. They all admitted they could conjure up images of the temples of old and racing chariots.

"You know, like the Olympians?" said Eva.

"You mean like Usain Bolt?" said Harry, doing his signature lightning bolt. They all groaned.

As they drew closer to the Acropolis, the towering columns of the Parthenon came into view, standing sentinel atop the rocky hill. After climbing the ramps and pathways to the site of the Acropolis, the centre of the ancient world, Harry helping Isabella with Teddy's buggy, they arrived at the ticket office, where they joined the stream of tourists and visitors making their way to the grand entrance and the amazing archaeological site, surrounded by the timeless beauty of marble temples and crumbling ruins.

They hiked on a journey through history for about 20 minutes up to the theatre of Dionysus and then to the Propylaea. The sound of their footsteps mingling with the murmur of conversation, occasionally stopping to take photos, capturing the iconic sights and admiring the views of Athens spread out below them.

As they reached the final ascent, they caught their breath and, having previously seen many photos before, nothing prepared Isabella for the immensity of the awesome Parthenon. It was still the principal attraction, despite it being systematically restored, meaning there was building works and scaffolding on parts of the structure.

Exploring the greatest of all archaeological sites, they walked around and marvelled. Then, they perused the superb theatres, ancient temples, and statues. They all felt very humbled walking in the middle of these temples, still standing after over 2,000 years, a testament to the enduring legacy of ancient Greece. They found a few shady spots where they could rest and have a drink of water.

At the far end, after climbing even higher, taking the rocky, slippery paths and slopes, they gazed at the phenomenal vistas right across the vast city in all directions and all agreed it was worth the uphill walk.

They could see what seemed like the whole of Athens stretched out endlessly below them; a panorama of white-washed buildings and red-tiled roofs; the Old Town Plaka, the Olympic Stadium, and other startling views of the area down to the sea.

Jack showed them the location of their harbour on the shore of Attica and also pointed out the deep blue sea beyond.

Thankfully, despite the searing heat, Teddy was pretty good throughout, initially enjoying running about for a time, finding bits of "treasure" and then eventually falling asleep in his pushchair.

After a brief respite, they continued back around the Acropolis and down the hill into the ancient Agora below.

They stopped at a little outdoor kafenio, the pulse of Greek life, for a late lunch and enjoyed many glasses of ice-cold, freshly squeezed, frothy lemonade and mountain tea.

Afterwards, they walked around the bustling and colourful, charming old Turkish quarter of Athens, Plaka, on the north-eastern slopes of the rock of Acropolis, the historic part of the city.

They wandered with swarms of other visitors and Athenians, through the labyrinth of narrow, winding lanes, houses, pretty squares, columns, churches, old-fashioned tavernas, market stalls, open-air cafes and icon and antique shops.

After a while, the intense heat was getting to them all and Teddy was getting weary and a little grizzly, so they headed back to their van. They were boiling and tired, but stopped at a little market on their way back to collect some fresh produce to take back to the boat for Joe.

"Are you okay Bella?" asked Jack, noticing she was lagging behind.

She removed her earbuds, cutting off Bono's soaring vocals. "Fine, thank you Jack. Just a little worn out, I'm afraid."

"We've certainly walked a fair way, today haven't we, in this heat too? Shame we didn't get longer to explore the museums and galleries."

"That's okay. I think I've pushed my luck with Teddy, anyway. I don't think he would let us walk silently around a gallery."

"Oh hell. I'm so sorry," he exclaimed.

"Why?"

"You've had to push that stroller for most of the day in this heat. Here, let me take him for you," and he gently nudged her out of the way and took hold of the handles.

"Thanks. You don't realise how heavy he is until he's in this thing."

"The hills and heat haven't helped," he smiled.

"No, I guess not," she replied wearily, looking down at her son, fast asleep, with rosy red cheeks and hair wet with perspiration.

"He's beautiful," sighed Jack.

"Thank you."

"He looks like you."

"You think so?"

"Definitely. You're a wonderful mother."

"I try to be, but it's tough."

"I bet. Does he ever ask about his father?"

"Not really, no. He's known no difference," she stammered. Dangerous ground.

"He's a cute little guy, funny too. I like him."

"He likes you, too. And your boat even more." She said.

"I'm glad you're here. Are you glad you came?"

"Definitely. I've enjoyed it so far."

"What, even pushing this thing?" he said.

"I'm used to it, although not in heat like this."

They eventually located the little back street where they had parked their van and swiftly loaded themselves and their belongings back into it. They turned on the air conditioning before heading back to the yacht, feeling exhausted.

By now it was half-past six. Isabella gave Teddy his tea – a generous plate of fruit, meat and vegetables, all chopped up in bite sizes pieces by Joe, followed by a bath and then he was ready for bed. The poor little mite was completely worn out and unable to move. Isabella was worried about putting him down to sleep so early, he might wake after a few hours, but risked it anyway. She joined the others on deck, all looking red in the face from where they had had too much sun. She put her end of the monitor down next to her so she could see and hear Teddy, just in case he did wake.

"Man. What a day." Jack sighed.

"I'm pooped" said Ingrid.

"I shouldn't have worn wedges," wailed Eva, "My feet are killing me! I've got blisters on my blisters."

"You're lucky you didn't break your ankle," said Ingrid.

"Yep, trainers next time Eva," said Isabella.

"What's next?" asked Harry, as they reclined in various states of fatigue as the crew members served their cold drinks.

"We don't have an itinerary as such," replied Jack, "but here, let's have a look at this map," and the men huddled around eagerly.

"I thought we'd head southwest to the nearby Saronic Gulf Islands, perhaps mooring at Aegina, which is only an hour away or maybe Hydra? Then sail past the Cyclades, perhaps stopping at one or two, before making our way to the Dodecanese Islands, around Crete, before heading back to Athens."

"Sounds great," said David.

"The good thing is, we can drop anchor whenever or wherever we feel like it, can rest up for as long as we like, or go ashore and visit. There are some idyllic little inlets and bays around the islands."

"This is heaven," said Ingrid. "How long can we stay?"

"As long as you like," Jack chuckled.

The skipper gently manoeuvred their yacht away from the dock, where people watched at the sheer majesty, with great ease from the harbour, its engines thrumming as it began its graceful departure and they made their way southwest. With precision and expertise, the skilled crew members stood at the helm, guiding the vessel through the bustling harbour waters. The views were a feast for the senses. To the port side, the vibrant colours of fishing boats and pleasure craft dotted the water, their sails billowing in the gentle breeze. To the starboard side, the majestic silhouette of cargo ships and ferries looming against the horizon, their towering masts and smokestacks adding to the spectacle.

Ahead, the open sea beckoned, a vast expanse of sparkling blue stretching to the horizon. The sun cast a golden hue over the water, illuminating the waves with a dazzling brilliance as seabirds swooped and lunged in search of their next meal.

As the yacht gained momentum, it glided past the breakwater and out into the open sea, leaving the hustle and bustle of the harbour behind. To the southwest, the coastline stretched out in a sweeping arc, dotted with picturesque villages, sandy beaches, and rugged cliffs.

They all watched as, with each passing moment, the views became more breath-taking, the beauty of the Greek coastline unfolding before their eyes. With the wind in their hair and the fading sun on their faces, they settled in for a journey filled with unforgettable moments and impressive scenery.

The sun was setting over the skyline as they spent a quiet evening on deck, peering out at the turquoise sea as they sailed towards Aegina. Teddy remained in bed, leaving the women to relax and the men to talk about their forthcoming holiday.

As the aroma of grilled meat and fish wafted through

the air, the group of friends gathered around the table laden with an array of delectable mezedhes fresh from the grill. As they sampled the delights, a symphony of flavours and textures treated their taste buds–creamy tzatziki, tangy feta cheese, crispy calamari, and tender lamb kebabs, all bursting with flavour. Glasses of boutari nauoussa wine, its rich red hue inviting sips of indulgence and its velvety smoothness complementing the bold flavours of the food. Laughter and chatter filled the air as they settled in for another leisurely feast all prepared by Joe and his team, their spirits buoyed by the warmth of friendship and the promise of culinary delights under the canopy of stars above.

Amidst bites of savoury grilled meats and succulent fish, the conversation flowed, amidst playful banter and lively debates, each story more colourful than the last, accompanied by bursts of laughter, nods of agreement and heads shaking in despair.

"Isn't this glorious," said Ingrid. "While it was raining back home, we are sitting outside at night and it's still warm."

"I could stay here forever," sighed Isabella.

They all noticed Jack give her a look, which spoke a thousand words.

He had been keeping a respectable distance from her. He was friendly, but not overly so. He was terrified of scaring her away. Isabella appreciated his consideration and felt relaxed in his company. Although that unmistakable pull was still there. That electricity, which she tried so hard to deny.

As the air got cooler, they made their way back indoors and sat around in the comfy chairs, chatting and enjoying coffee and tea, before watching a movie and then finally making their way one by one to bed.

The following morning, Teddy woke Isabella early, so they read some books and played around in bed for a while, but he soon got antsy, so they headed up to the deck for breakfast, which was already bathed in sunlight, the sky painted in shades of pink and orange.

"Morning," said Jack cheerily, as they arrived. He was sitting alone, enjoying a cup of coffee and rifling through his phone.

"Hiya Jack" returned Isabella. She felt unnerved as this was the first time they had been alone since they had arrived.

"Did you sleep okay?" he asked generously.

"Like a log. I enjoyed the movie last night."

"The oldies are the best," he said.

"I couldn't agree more. Where are we?" she asked, regarding the shoreline not far off.

"That's Aegina. I think we'll probably go ashore later."

"It looks beautiful," she said as she stared out across the bay at the lush and varied landscape. Rugged cliffs, white sandy beaches, and quaint villages characterised the coastline, with whitewashed houses nestled amongst the verdant hills. The water below them was crystal clear and as the yacht gently swayed with the rhythm of the waves, the panoramic view unfolded before them.

"Help yourself to some coffee and whatever you fancy to eat," he said.

"Should we not wait for the others?"

"No, it's fine. Help yourself."

So she did. She poured herself some coffee and selected a freshly made Danish pastry. She filled a small bowl with some cereal for Teddy, who was crouched down sifting through toys in "his" box, and poured him some apple juice.

After settling her little boy in the shade with his breakfast, she sat opposite Jack. "This is wonderful. You certainly don't do things by half around here, do you?" she smiled, pointing at her surroundings with a piece of pastry before popping it in her mouth and then wiping away at the crumbs on her lap.

"I like to enjoy myself on holiday," he smiled, setting down his phone.

"I can tell. This yacht is amazing. When you invited us, I

had no idea? I certainly didn't expect this splendour."

"Exceptional isn't she."

"Thank you for having us."

"It's my pleasure. It's wonderful seeing you all again, you know. I've enjoyed meeting and spending time with Teddy, too. Are you both having a good time?"

"Wonderful. You're spoiling us rotten."

"I aim to please. He's very well behaved," he nodded in Teddy's direction.

"He has his moments. You didn't see him last night in the bath." She said.

"Oh, so he has his mummy's temper then?" he said.

"Me," she smiled. "I don't know what you mean."

"Eva seems nice? Harry's smitten."

"She's great. I don't know her that well, but she's just my cup of tea," she smiled.

She relaxed then, at his laid-back, easygoing manner and they chatted like a couple of old friends, enjoying their breakfast in the remarkable location, where they soaked in the beauty of Aegina, enjoying the peace and solitude of being surrounded by the expanse of the Aegean Sea.

She remembered something. "Thanks again for my birthday presents."

"You're welcome."

"You shouldn't have, you know?"

"Why?" he enquired.

"Well ... it's just ..."

"Didn't you like them?"

"Of course, I did. It's just they were so generous, the book, the painting especially. I googled the artist."

"Nonsense. I knew you'd like them, that's all. A bit of fun."

"Well, all the same, it was very kind. I love my painting."

"It was my mother's," he whispered.

"What?" she gasped.

"My mother's. It was her favourite painting. My father

bought it for her for their ruby wedding anniversary when they visited Bermuda."

"Why on earth did you give it to me, then? Won't she notice it's gone? I'm sure she'll be thrilled when she knows you've given her favourite painting to me."

He was silent and looked forlorn suddenly. "She's gone," he said, almost in a whisper, and he looked so sad.

"What." she gasped.

He looked heartbroken, and she felt like reaching out to him, as he tried futilely to hide his emotions.

"Last year."

"Oh Jack. I'm so terribly sorry, I know how close you were. I didn't know," she whispered.

"It's okay. I'm just about coming to terms with it. I can just about talk about it now."

"What happened?"

"Cancer."

"Jack, that's terrible. I'm so, so sorry."

"It was awful. It was all quick, but not, if you know what I mean. My father will never recover. He misses her dreadfully. We all do."

He was silent then, trying to compose himself. Losing his mother had a profound and deeply emotional effect on him and left him shattered and adrift on a sea of grief. Waves of sadness, anger, and disbelief still crashed over him, threatening to engulf him in an overwhelming sense of loss. Memories of shared moments and cherished conversations at the end flooded his mind and mingled with the pain of knowing that she was no longer there to offer guidance, support, and unconditional love. In the wake of her passing, he grappled with a profound sense of emptiness, as if someone had taken away a piece of his very being. He had only ever felt like this once before.

"I'm sorry. I don't know what to say," and she reached out to touch his hand.

"Anyway, let's not talk about this now," he said,

changing the subject, trying to avoid any further heartache or discussion about his beloved mother. And he pulled his hand away and lit up a cigarette.

Sadness engulfed Isabella. She knew how close he had been to both his parents. She also felt terrible about the painting. Why had he given it to her? It should have remained with Jack in the family.

"Jack, can I just ask you one more thing?"

"Shoot."

"The painting. Why me?"

"Honestly? I don't know. It just felt right. I wanted you to have it, especially with your Bermuda triangle fascination."

"Oh. Well, thank you. I love it. I'll treasure it - even more so now," was all she could say.

How could he tell her he had discussed the picture with his mother before she'd gone? She had asked him to give it to the woman he truly loved with all of his heart, like his father loved her. He had simply obeyed her wishes.

The others arrived a short time later for breakfast, a couple noticing the weighty atmosphere, but not saying anything. They greeted each other and were all soon tucking into the spread before them.

They discussed going ashore in the tender in an hour. Isabella noticed that all the time Jack seemed concerned with everyone's welfare, constantly in command. She noticed he was both firm and direct with his crew and they carried out his instructions to the letter. He possessed an innate dignity that his rough persona couldn't wholly conceal. He consulted all his guests about how they wanted to spend their time - he didn't want anyone to do what they didn't feel like doing, and he was keen to make sure they were all enjoying themselves. How could they not be in these surroundings? She also noticed he wasn't swearing nearly so much and guessed, correctly, it was because Teddy was around.

When they were all showered and ready, he gave

instructions to the crew to ensure a smooth and safe journey when heading to the shore. The crew then gave them all a safety briefing before seating them securely in the sleek and stylish tender, ensuring Teddy was securely fastened into his life jacket.

As the tender glided away from the yacht, it navigated the calm cerulean waters towards the pretty bay. Despite the early hour of the day, they already had to avoid the many windsurfers, pedalos, and speedboats.

At a long sandy beach surrounded by lush vegetation, the crew aided them all in stepping ashore. They headed straight to the beach bar to grab a cool ice cream before gathering at the water's edge, eager for a quick dip in the pure waters and relaxing for a brief spell before continuing their exploration. They waded into the shallow waters, the cool embrace of the sea refreshing against their skin. Laughter filled the air as they splashed and played, revelling in the moment's joy. The girls floated lazily on their backs, their bodies buoyed by the gentle waves, whilst the boys engaged in playful games of tag and chase. Isabella took hold of Teddy's hand, his eyes wide with wonder, hesitating at first, before taking his first tentative steps into the sea. His laughter started ringing out like music as he splashed and giggled amongst the others.

After drying off and changing back into their clothes, they decided first to visit the classical fifth century Temple of Aphais. Stephan was to remain behind to look after their launch. As the taxi pulled away from the sandy shores of the beach, the salty sea breeze gradually gave way to the scent of pine trees and wildflowers that lined the winding coastal road. As they wound their way inland, the landscape transformed into crops of pistachios, almonds, grapes, citrus orchards and olive groves. Along the route, they passed through charming villages and quaint hamlets, where whitewashed houses with colourful shutters dotted the landscape. After half an hour, they arrived at the incredible hillside setting in the centre of the island, surrounded by pine trees.

Stepping out of the taxi, the imposing façade of the Temple greeted them, its columns standing tall against the backdrop of the sky. They perused at leisure the ancient ruins and relics of the temple and took in the views of the spectacular views of Aegina island and across the Saronic Gulf to the mainland, before taking a taxi to the other side of the island, again along the beautiful coastline to the seaside village of Marathonas.

Arriving in the coastal town, its idyllic setting struck them. They walked along the waterfront, enjoying stunning views of the sea and distant islands on the horizon. They settled on a traditional cafe sited right on the beach, where they enjoyed a very late lunch, the gentle sea breeze caressing their faces as the sound of waves crashed against the shore, providing a soothing backdrop. They all agreed the views were like something out of a picture postcard. The sun was shining, and the town was buzzing with people enjoying the day in the cafes, restaurants and ouzerias. Athenians apparently came here to escape the city, drink ouzo, eat seafood and watch the fishing boats. The crystalline sea, the powder blue cloudless sky, the surroundings were truly exceptional. The sun was still at its most fierce and they happily sat down in the shade, escaping its brutal glare. Again, the atmosphere was carefree, their laughter and chatter filling the air.

They all took it in turns to walk about with Teddy during the meal, as he was getting bored with just having to sit. Isabella found it particularly touching as watched Jack walk her son, hand in hand, down a few steps to a stretch of sand and showed him how to build sandcastles. He ran up and down the beach with him and picked him up and threw him up and down in the air, making him shriek with laughter.

She watched as they walked along the beach and with each step; they scanned the glistening sand, Teddy's eyes alight with excitement as they searched for treasures hidden amongst the grains. Bent low, they eagerly scoured the shoreline for shells, their fingers sifting through the sand in search of hidden gems. Jack kneeled beside Teddy, his weathered hands deftly plucking shells from the sand and presenting them to his young companion with a smile. Together they marvelled at the intricate patterns and vibrant colours of each shell, turning them over in their hands as if examining precious jewels. Their laughter mingled with the sound of the surf, Teddy racing ahead and then stopping, eager to uncover the next treasure waiting to be discovered.

Isabella watched in silence as her beloved little boy sat together with Jack on the sand, their pockets full of shells and their hearts full of memories. In this moment, surrounded by the beauty of the beach and the boundless expanse of the sea, she saw the bond forged by the simple pleasures of exploration, discovery and the timeless magic of the beach and she felt as if her heart were going to split in two.

Between bites of food and sips of wine, the conversation took on a more introspective tone.

"He'll make a natural father one day," commented Ingrid.

Isabella looked at Harry sharply.

"Does he have a girlfriend?" asked Eva innocently.

"No. He's never been married either," Ingrid pointed out.

"Goodness," asked Eva, "Straight men, of that age, are not usually that looking"

"He just hasn't found the right person, that's all" said David, looking at Isabella, who looked down and pretended to be studying her feet intently. Harry obviously hadn't told Eva about their brief but passionate affair and Isabella was thankful for his discretion.

"But he's sooo handsome," drooled Eva.

"Hey. Your boyfriend is sitting here?" complained Harry.

"My husband is sitting here," said Ingrid, "And I completely agree, the guy's gorgeous."

"Isabella, get in there, girl. What's stopping you?" said

Eva.

"I, I, don't think so. We're just friends, that's all," stuttered Isabella.

"Why ever not? There's nothing stopping you?"

Isabella looked uncomfortable. Out of the corner of her eye, she witnessed Harry shaking his head strongly at Eva, as if to warn her, leave it.

Jack and Teddy returned seconds later and the little boy launched himself straight at his mummy to show her the collection of shells that they had found on the beach.

"Hey. What's with the long faces?" said Jack, taking long gulps of cold lager, "That was fun."

"Look mama." Teddy exclaimed, uncurling his little white, chubby fingers to reveal a pretty pink shell, "Shell mama, shell."

"Yes darling, a shell. That's so pretty. Did you find it on the sand?"

"Yes."

"It's a present from both of us," said Jack.

"Thank you, darling," she said, giving Teddy a hug. "It's wonderful."

"Do I get one of those too?" said Jack. "I found it?"

"'Fraid not." She smiled coyly.

"I like Jack, mama," said Ted.

"That's nice darling."

"I don't know about you guys, but I think it's time we headed back," said Harry, getting up from his seat.

"Good idea," said David. "We've wandered about enough for today. I don't know about you guys, but I'm knackered. I just want to get back to our floating palace and relax."

"Just give me a couple of minutes to reapply Teddy's sun cream, okay?" whispered Isabella. She was so embarrassed and so uncomfortable.

Harry huddled next to her and whispered, "Are you okay?"

"What do you think?"

"Difficult, huh?"

"You could say that."

"Tell him Izzy," he pleaded.

"Be quiet." She hissed.

"It's not fair. Stop procrastinating. I love you, but you're doing a terrible thing. Tell him Izzy. If you don't, I will."

"Don't you dare. I'd never speak to you again."

"Tell him Izzy."

The plan was to have another night back on board and then set sail early the next morning, further south, past Poros to the jet setter haven of Hydra. However, when they returned to the yacht, the men decided they were all going to have some fun and aquatic adventures. Laughter and excitement filled the air as they donned wetsuits and lifejackets, preparing to make a splash in the waters, clear as glass, below. First, they climbed into kayaks, paddleboards and inflatable towables, exchanging playful banter and friendly competition, the men particularly eager to showcase their skills and athleticism on the water. Cheers and applause rang out as Harry and Eva navigated a challenging obstacle course on a jet ski.

Jess watched Teddy on the platform, where he was more than happy merely filling his bucket with seawater, as he splashed and squealed with delight, and watched his Mummy and friends, their voices carrying across the water.

Between exhilarating rides, thrilling jumps and swimming, they took breaks to cool off with refreshing drinks and lounged on the sun-drenched deck and basking in the sun.

Someone then had the great idea of jumping off the side of the yacht into the sea. With the warm sun kissing their skin and the gentle breeze tousling their hair, they all gathered on deck, excitement pulsing through their veins as they prepared to take the plunge into the refreshing embrace of the sea below.

Isabella watched as one by one they approached and then jumped off the edge of the yacht. Her anticipation was building with each step closer to the precipice, her heart pounding and adrenaline coursing through her veins. She paused.

"Come on, Bella, jump," cried Jack, as he watched Isabella hesitate on the side of the boat.

"I'm scared." She yelled, breaking into a cold sweat, her palms clammy, a fight-or-flight response, as she looked far down below at the others treading water, waiting in the sea for her.

"Come on Izzy, you can do it." called Harry, who had just gone beforehand, entirely fearless as he'd made the leap.

She squished her nose together, took a deep breath and leapt off the side of the vessel, screaming with terror all the way before plunging into the warm inviting waters, where her friends were all waiting for her, congratulating her.

As she resurfaced, laughter erupted from her lips amid the joyous shouts.

"Oh my God. That was terrifying but exhilarating," she cried, as she waved back up at Teddy, who was watching her from the arms of Jess. "Mummy's fine." She called to reassure him.

"Well done Bella. Fun huh?" said Jack.

"Petrifying," she cried.

The silky water was invigorating, and as she swam about, she felt a sense of pure exhilaration and relaxation before they all headed back in.

Back on deck, they exchanged high fives and cheers, their faces flushed with excitement and their spirits soaring after a fabulous time in the sea.

As the afternoon stretched into evening and the sun dipped lower on the horizon, casting a fiery glow across the sky, they gathered on deck, their skin salty from the sea, and watched the spectacular sunset. They shared stories of triumphs and challenges, offering words of encouragement and support to each other as the sun dipped below the horizon, casting a warm glow over them. The cares and worries of the world melted away as they lost themselves in the simple joy of just being together, sharing in a moment of pure happiness. Amidst the beauty and luxury of the yacht, they continued to forge their friendships while discussing plans, swapping recommendations for must-visit destinations and bucket list experiences. They reminisced about their favourite moments of the day, recounting tales of daring feats and hilarious mishaps with infectious enthusiasm. They were creating memories that will last a lifetime, celebrating the joy of adventure and the pleasures of being together on the open sea.

The following day, they awoke to find themselves on the other side of the island in yet another delightful location; the skipper having continued their journey whilst they slept.

Today, however, no one fancied going ashore, as they were all worn out from the last couple of days, so the captain just continued to sail around the island at a leisurely pace.

They lay on deck sunbathing, whilst enjoying the unforgettable views the wind-tormented, rocky island offered; the magnificent villages, with their small churches and monasteries and the restaurants and cafes on the waterfront. They sailed past small inlets and harbours before dropping anchor just off land at a busy resort town.

The views held no draw for Jack. His eyes were drawn constantly to Isabella's radiant presence. Dressed in another stunning bikini, her long hair piled high on her head, each step she took was with a mesmerising grace. Her captivating smile lighting up her face when playing with her little boy, revealing a hint of mischief and charm that drew him in like a moth to a flame. As she lounged on the sunbed, she was a vision of beauty against the backdrop of the endless sea, captivating him. He had his thoughts interrupted.

"Well, I don't know about everyone else, but I fancy going out tonight. Anyone fancy a club?" suggested Harry. "We could go to dinner, then on to throw some shapes?"

"Wonderful," said Ingrid, "I'm in."

"Me too. I love a good boogie," chipped Eva.

"But what about Isabella?" said David, noticing her reticence. "She can't go without little Teddy?"

"Perhaps one of the crew could babysit?" suggested Ingrid.

"Oh, don't worry about us," said Isabella, "We're tired aren't we little one, we'll stay on board and have an early night. You all go ahead. I could do with an early night."

"Me go," said Teddy to his mother.

"No darling. It's nearly your bedtime."

"Well, if you sure you don't mind Izzy?" said Ingrid.

"Not at all. You all enjoy yourselves. I'll ask the crew to prepare me a salad or something."

They all showered and change, whilst Isabella gave Teddy a bath and read him a story, before tucking him in and humming a soothing lullaby. Again, because of all the fresh sea air, he fell straight asleep. She lay down beside him as he peacefully slept, his chest rising and falling in a gentle rhythm. His innocent little face, softened by the tranquillity of slumber, a picture of angelic beauty. With each breath, he seemed to exhale the cares of the day away, his tiny fingers curling as he drifted deeper into dreams. The soft glow of moonlight filtered through the curtains, casting a gentle halo around him, illuminating the innocence and purity that radiated from within.

As she watched over him, a swell of love and tenderness filled her heart, overwhelming her with a sense of gratitude and awe. In that moment, though, all the worries and stresses of the world didn't fade away, as a profound sense of guilt and anxiety overshadowed these feelings. His innocence and vulnerability reminded her of the preciousness of life and the beauty of simple moments like this, moments she treasured. Moments she was keeping all to herself.

Breaking the quiet contemplation, she received a text from Bibi and replied straightaway,

How's your trip?

Brilliant. Thanks. How's you?

All good. Everyone getting on ok?

Great. No issues. Eva's lovely.

Great and Teddy's ok and enjoying himself?

He's having the time of his life–all the attention in the world from everyone.

And Jack?

Fine. We're getting on great. All's well.

Not shagged him yet then?

Bibi. No, and I don't intend to.

Fool.

Don't go there Bibi. I'm not.

Nothing to lose and you could do with some.

I'm going now. Nice relaxing evening planned, reading my book–the others are going clubbing.

Well enjoy. I'm jealous. Love you.

Love you too.

Isabella showered and changed into a comfortable pair of linen trousers and a skimpy, cool vest-top, which perfectly showed off her sun-tanned shoulders, before she returned bare-foot to the salon where the others were enjoying an apéritif. She was glowing with health and even with no make-up on looked classically beautiful. Her hair was still damp and hung loosely around her shoulders.

"Hey Izzy," called Ingrid.

"Wow, look at you guys all dressed up, you look fab," remarked Isabella.

"We're just about ready to go. Are you sure you don't mind? We can stay here if you'd prefer," offered Ingrid.

"Really. Go enjoy yourselves. I'm worn out. I might just watch a movie and read my book before turning in early."

"What about something to eat?" asked Eva.

"Don't worry, it's all sorted," said Jack, who had just wandered into the salon, looking tanned himself and very handsome in an old t-shirt and khaki knee-length shorts. Typical Jack, obviously not feeling the need to dress up like the others.

"Okay, if you're sure, we'll be off then," said Harry, kissing her on the cheek.

"You all look great, have a good time," said Isabella as they bade their farewells.

As they all left, Jack remained where he was.

"Aren't you going?" she asked, her stomach sinking, as she knew instinctively his reply.

"No. I can't leave you here alone. You're my guest."

"Jack, please. Don't be absurd. I'll be totally fine here."

"It's too late anyway," he said. "The chef's prepared dinner for two."

"Jack," she groaned. She was pissed off. This was a situation she could do without, and she really had been looking forward to some alone time and an early night. Snuggling up in bed with her little boy.

"Anyway, you're not the only one who's exhausted and, if I'm honest, I don't fancy playing gooseberry with those two love-struck couples."

"I know what you mean," she said nervously. "Sickening, hey?"

"Can I pour you a glass of something?"

"I'd love a glass of wine, if that's okay?"

"Sure. Or champagne? They've some on ice?"

"Sounds good. God, we've all drank so much on this trip."

"Good, though."

He poured them both a flute of pink champagne and sat opposite her on one of the large comfy leather sofas and they sat silently, but not uncomfortably, for a few minutes.
Jess arrived a moment later and announced that dinner was ready to be served on deck.

"Do you always live like this?"

"What do you mean?"

"Well, like Elon Musk?" she said.

"No, but I could definitely get used to it. Beats my customary peanut butter sandwiches and a bottle of Bud in front of the big screen."

They walked outside into the cool night air.

"Warm enough out here for you?" he enquired.

"Perfect. This looks wonderful. You shouldn't have gone to all the trouble. I was just happy with a salad on my lap."

White linen, silver cutlery, and crystal glasses adorned the set table. The champagne Jack had opened earlier was cooling in a bucket of ice on the table. Fresh flowers and candles adorned the table and the twinkly lights were already on.

Joe had prepared a beef tomato salad with buffalo mozzarella in a dressing of olive oil, garnished with pine kernels. There was a bowl of fresh lemon drizzled olives, crusty bread, fresh, crunchy vegetables and selection of dips; tzatziki, humus and taramasalata.

"I hope this is enough for you?" Jack stated, as they took their seats opposite each other.

"It's perfect, thank you," she acknowledged, tugging a blanket from the back of her chair and placing it around her shoulders.

She gazed out at the dark night skies that had enveloped them, broken by the lights twinkling on the shore. It was a perfect evening.

The conversation flowed easily. She told him about a recent project she'd undertaken for a wealthy Arab Sheik in Wentworth. He seemed genuinely interested in her talent and enjoyed hearing about her ideas and from where she gleaned inspiration.

"Harry referred him," she advised.

"Sounds amazing. Talking of Harry, I wonder how they're getting on?"

"I dread to think. I'm sure they'll have a fab time, though."

"Didn't fancy it?"

"No. Especially when Teddy will be up at the crack of dawn." She then talked about Teddy and waffled on and on about her beloved son.

"I'm boring you, aren't I?" she smiled, trying to read the bemused expression on his face.

"No. Not at all. I love hearing about you and your life … I think … I think you're extraordinary."

"Please. My mundane life?"

"Hardly mundane. Anyway, you know how I feel about you," he mumbled, not meeting her eyes.

"Jack, please, let's not spoil things," she implored.

They had finished their supper by now and Jess had just opened a second bottle of champagne and poured them each a glass.

"This 'just friends' thing working for you, huh? Anyway, I'm not spoiling things, but there is something we need to talk about," he said.

"There is?" she asked, dreading what he was going to say.

"I still need an explanation."

"What kind of explanation? I thought we had already done all of this," she gulped. Everything had been going so well and now he wanted to bloody spoil things. She knew they shouldn't have been left alone. She'd kill bloody Harry when she next saw him.

"I want to know exactly where we went wrong? Why you still hold me at arm's length? Why you are so happy to be my friend, but won't talk about anything that's important? Please, Isabella. You owe me that, at least?"

"Jack. I don't owe you anything," she stared at him, returning his tormented expression. "You told me there'd be no strings on this trip and here you are pressurising me again."

"Pressurising you?" he snapped, with a ferocity that had more than the usual edge, "All I want is a goddamned explanation. I can't move on unless you tell me what happened in Kenya?"

"So here it comes. The real Jack. Have you been playing *Mr Nice Guy* these past few days?"

"What are you talking about?"

"Well, you've been fun, attentive, generous and now the old Jack appears. You know what happened in Kenya? It was a fling."

"Come on," he sneered. "It was more than that and you know it."

"That may be. You can elect whatever narrative you choose, but it's over."

"Is it? That's easy for you to say. You've moved on. You've got your life, your son. My life is empty. Barren. There's nothing. I was so in love with you." His face had darkened, and he was obviously still furious, his muscles tensed with emotion. He boiled over so easily. One minute he was calm and chilled, the next …

"What are you talking about?" she snapped.

"Okay, I've got my friends, my company …"

"This boat," she smiled, trying to ease the tension that had once again surfaced. She didn't want to rise to the bait on this occasion. She couldn't face one of their monumental fights now.

"Yes, this boat," he smiled, "But it's just stuff."

"Wonderful stuff," she grinned.

"Okay, okay, I'm sorry. You're right. It's ancient history," he lied, "But …"

"No buts Jack."

"Hell, you're one tough broad."

"Broad? Does anyone use that word anymore?"

"What's wrong with broad?"

"It's very archaic and not very politically correct."

"Since when have I been politically correct, doll-face?" he was teasing her now, "Come on, let's go back inside, you're shivering."

They walked back indoors, and he closed the doors

behind them.

"Can I fill your glass?" he asked.

"You're trying to get me drunk."

"You're already drunk."

"Ouch," she said as she fell back onto one of the sofas.

"Movie?" he asked, as he handed her a fresh glass and sat down next to her.

"Sounds good. What do you have in mind?"

"You choose? Romcom? Thriller? What do you fancy?"

"*Black Panther*? I haven't seen it yet."

"So, you're a Marvel fan?"

"I guess. Not as much as Tarantino and M Night Shyamalan, my absolute favourite movies ever."

"*Glass*? Fab movie."

He grabbed a Hermes blanket from the back of the sofa and placed it over them both as they watched the movie. Within half an hour, they were both fast asleep, snuggled next to each other.

The film score woke them both up and she got to her feet.

"Well, I guess I still haven't seen Black Panther. I'm going to bed. Thanks for tonight."

"You're welcome. Bella?"

"Yes?"

"I'm sorry about before."

"No problem. All good?"

"All good. Oh, and you know I'm still in love with you," he said and ran his hands through his hair.

"Oh, for God's sake, don't you ever give up." And she spun on her heels and left him, as he called after her, "Never."

She didn't sleep that night. She tossed and turned and dreamt of Jack.

***

CHAPTER THIRTY-ONE

The others returned safely in the early hours of the morning and they headed straight to bed, just before the boat set sail and turned east, heading unhurriedly towards the Cyclades Islands.

Isabella and Teddy rose first and after breakfast, played together and lay in the sun on deck. Jack joined them late morning.

"Hello you two," he called.

"Hi Jack" said Isabella, as Teddy ran over to greet him.

"I could get used to this," he said as he returned the little boy's hug.

"I'm sorry about last night," he whispered humbly over the top of Ted's head.

"Forgotten" she smiled.

They sat together comfortably playing with Teddy and some Lego, periodically glancing out at the clear turquoise scintillating water that surrounded them and the breathtaking scenery slipping by.

"This is the most relaxing time I've had in ages," said Isabella, twiddling with her hair.

"Me too," he replied.

"I could stay on here forever."

"I wish you would," he breathed, staring at her intensely.

"Jack."

"You know what I mean, though."

"The wonderful part about it all is, we've no set routine. Every day we get to see a new island with its own character and charm. There's always something lovely to see, to do. The weather's glorious."

"You're glorious," he stated.

"Jack."

"Especially in that red bikini," he drooled.

"Perv."

"Do you fancy a swim again this afternoon? You haven't tried snorkelling yet?"

"Sure, if everyone's up for it, when they eventually get up, that is."

And they were up for it. They all relaxed on deck, four of them nursing catastrophic hangovers, and when the boat came to a standstill, the same four jumped overboard, loaded with masks, flippers and snorkels into the deep indigo waters of the Aegean Sea.

"Can I bring Teddy in?" asked Jack.

"I guess so. Not jumping off the side, though."

"No problem. I'll take him down the steps, rather than the platform."

"That would be great. Teddy, do you want to go swimming with Jack?"

"Yes peas."

Isabella regarded him closely as he carried Teddy conscientiously down the steps into the waters below, where Harry and Eva and Ingrid and David were swimming about freely.

The little boy was a little reticent at first and Isabella was mildly anxious, but as soon as he got used to the temperature, he had a wonderful time splashing and playing with the others in the sea.

They all took turns diving beneath the surface of the coastal waters, where they gazed at the myriad shoals of fish and wondrous plant life. It was an unforgettable experience, offering a glimpse into the vibrant marine life and underground water landscapes.

Isabella soon joined them, whilst Jack looked after her son. Isabella also slipped beneath the crystal-clear water and was greeted by a kaleidoscope of colours and textures. The sunlight filtered through the water, casting shimmering rays of light that illuminated the sandy seabed below. Schools of colourful fish darted in and out of the coral reefs, their scales glinting in the sunlight as they navigated their underwater realm. Gentle currents swayed the seagrass and seaweed, creating an otherworldly ballet of movement and motion, both intriguing and terrifying Isabella at the same time. As she glided effortlessly through the water, the silence of the underwater world enveloped her, broken only by the soft sound of her own breath, the gentle waves and the squeals of laughter from the others. It was a moment of perfect serenity that soothed her soul and invigorated her spirit. As she resurfaced, her heart was brimming with wonder and awe. "That was incredible," she simply breathed.

After they had climbed back on board, dog-tired, the crew upped anchor and they set sail for the most northerly island in the Cyclades, the second largest and most green and fertile in the group, Andros.

The girls and Teddy plunged into the cascading jacuzzi, whilst the men lay on deck in varying states of relaxation.

"Teddy darling, don't drink the water." Isabella pleaded. She glanced over and noticed Jack engrossed in his laptop.

"Good looking, isn't he?" said Eva, noticing Isabella staring at Jack.

"Mmmmm. I suppose so?" she replied.

"I'm sure he fancies you, you know. The way he's always staring at you. Wouldn't you agree Ingrid?"

"Yep," said Ingrid, giving Isabella a beseeching look, as if to say 'Well, what can I say?'.

"He's great with Teddy," commented Eva.

"He doesn't want kids," stated Isabella.

"Fine, but why doesn't he have a girlfriend?"

"I wouldn't know," said Isabella, feigning lack of interest.

"He just seems so … so eligible, you know? Judging by this boat, it's clear that he's obviously loaded. He's wickedly handsome. Fantastic body. Good, if not dry, sense of humour. He's very sexy. He swears and smokes too much, but that aside, what's the catch?"

"You sound as if you've got a crush on him yourself," snapped Isabella.

"No. No. Not at all. Too in love with Harry. I just wondered what his story was? Why he's single? You'd make a stunning couple."

"No story, not that I know of," said Isabella.

"Jack is Jack. As you see him. No airs or graces. There is no hidden story," said Ingrid.

"I'm intrigued," said Eva.

"Teddy please darling. Don't drink the water," begged Isabella, putting an end to the discussion.

It wasn't long before they could make out the diverse outlines of the beautiful island of Andros, protruding from the blue waters of the Aegean, bathed in the red light of the lowering sun.

They headed towards the capital and harbour of Andros Town, standing on a rocky out-crop on the east coast and, after showering and dressing for the evening, made for town on the launch.

It was soon noticeable that it was another beautiful town, however, with its own unique beauty, with many little churches and small white houses set amongst steep and narrow alleys. As they walked, the salty breeze carried the odour of salt and wildflowers.

By now, Teddy was fast asleep in his buggy, wrapped in a fluffy blanket and clutching one of his new favourite toys from his new best friend, Jack. Harry had offered to push him and they all ambled along, trying to find somewhere nice to eat. They meandered through the elegant town, with magnificent buildings, through the pedestrianised main street, paved with marble slabs and lined with old mansions, now converted into shops and offices. The sound of church bells filled the air, mingled with the chatter of locals going about their daily routines.

Having wandered through the labyrinth of small lanes, they eventually settled on a taverna behind the main square, offering a range of traditional fayre to suit all of them, which also gave them pleasant sea views.

They ordered stuffed vine leaves and mezes to start, followed by moussaka and octopus with greens.

"I think it's about time we tried some ouzo," said Harry.

"I've never tried it, but it sounds dangerous," said Isabella.

"Me neither" said Ingrid.

"It's a little like Pernod," said Jack.

"Oh, no," said Isabella, "I feel the headache coming on already."

The waiter served the ouzo in 2 glasses, one with ouzo and one with water.

"What do we do?" asked Isabella.

"Tip the water into the ouzo," instructed Harry.

It turned milky white before Isabella tried it.

"Yummy." She said, gulping it down in one go and smacking her lips.

"Oh God," laughed Harry, "Somebody stop her."

They had a fantastic evening, enjoying both the food and the company. They drank copious amounts of ouzo and were all feeling a little worse for wear. Most, if not all, of them were slurring their words.

The conversation turned to Ingrid and David's wedding in Las Vegas.

"It sounds such fun," enthused Eva, "I wish I could have been there."

"I wish you could have been," said Harry, pulling her closer towards him.

"So, you all went?" asked Eva.

"Yep" said Jack.

"Even you Isabella?"

"Even me Eva," said Isabella.

"Have you ever been married? Harry never tells me anything." She asked Isabella pointedly.

"No."

"Never close?" she continued.

"Not really."

"Why not? You've been in love, though? What about Teddy's father?"

"I don't think now's the time, do you? Let's not spoil the atmosphere," she said a little too harshly, and she noticed Harry give her a little frown.

"Sorry Izzy, I didn't mean to pry. What about you, Jack?" she pushed.

"Nope."

"Never anyone special?" she carried on.

"Oh yes. There was someone *really* special," he said earnestly and gave Isabella a penetrating glare.

"What is this? Twenty bloody questions." said Isabella, getting aggravated with Eva.

"So, what happened, Jack?" continued Eva, ignoring her. She was genuinely intrigued and paid no attention to the uneasy fidgeting of the others.

"Eva, please," said Isabella shortly, "Who cares? Let's stop this nonsense?"

"Nonsense? No, wait. Eva asked us, so … so … what *did* happen?" said Jack and he turned to stare directly at Isabella once more. "Tell us? What *did* happen Bella?"

Eva looked perplexed and turned to ask Harry. Harry shook his head beseechingly at Eva. Ingrid groaned and put her head against David's shoulder. "Here we go again." She grumbled.

Jack continued, "Well?"

"Well, nothing," retorted Isabella angrily, crossing her arms across her chest stubbornly, signalling her resistance to any further questions. She could murder Eva at this precise moment. "I don't think now's the time."

"Now's never the time with you, is it Bella?" Jack thundered.

"You're making a scene, guys," groaned Ingrid.

"Tell me something new," grumbled Harry.

"What I'm trying to damn well say here, Eva," said Jack, his face thunderous by now, "Is I have absolutely no idea what happened. You'll have to ask *her*. *You* don't know? I don't even know. She says I was a fling. A mistake. Her words ... a huge fucking mistake. But why? I have absolutely no fucking idea." He hadn't taken his ferocious gaze from Isabella.

Tension crackled in the air as the two ex-lovers found themselves locked in a heated argument, their voices rising in anger and frustration at the obstacles in their paths. Their friends watched uncomfortably as the exchange unfolded before them.

They hurled words like daggers, each one laced with resentment and hurt from past wounds. Accusations flew back and forth, echoing in the space between them, as they dredged up old grievances and unresolved conflicts.

The friends shifted, unsure of what to do or say as the argument escalated. Harry tried to intervene, attempting to calm the situation and diffuse the tension, whilst the others look on in shocked silence, unable to tear their eyes away from the unfolding drama.

"Oh, for fuck's sake," yelled Isabella, pushing back her chair, knocking over her glass.

"Harry. Look after Ted for a minute will you" and she stormed off into the night in a fit of anger, leaving the others staring after her in disbelief.

She didn't know where she was going, she just needed to get away. Why was it, whenever they were enjoying a few drinks, Jack turned the pressure on? Why couldn't he just leave her alone, for God's sake?

She had just reached the end of the street and was wondering where the hell to turn to next, when she felt someone grab her arm and turn her roughly around.

She was staring directly into the raging, antagonistic face of Jack.

He looked straight into her eyes and before she could say anything, pulled her head ferociously toward him and kissed her with such desire, it shocked her.

She pulled back and slapped him hard across the cheek. "How dare you?" she screamed.

"Enough of this crap," he spat into her face, "Why don't you tell me what the fuck I did that was so terrible? I've reached my limit, I can't bear it any longer. I can no longer hold myself responsible for my actions. Pussyfooting around you all the time. I'm god dammed sick of it. I'm in love with you, for God's sake. Completely and totally in love with you. Crazy about you."

"Don't be so ridiculous. Get a hold of yourself, you fuck-wit."

Tempers flared, emotions ran high, and the air crackled with the raw intensity of their exchange. It was a clash of wills, a battle of egos, as each of them fought to be heard and understood, unwilling to back down or concede defeat.

Amid the chaos, they screamed hurtful words, crossed lines, and pushed boundaries to a breaking point. The argument raged on, leaving them both feeling shaken and unsettled by the ferocity of their exchange.

It was only then that she realised a bustling restaurant, filled with patrons enjoying their meals to their immediate right, was watching them. They must have heard everything, their fragile peace shattered by the ferocity of their exchange.

"Isabella, please, I'm going out of my mind," he yelled, grasping hold of her shoulders.

"Jack, you're making a scene." She yelled, anger

radiating from her as she stood, trembling with emotion, her fists clenched at her sides.

"I'm making a scene? Ha. That's rich. Remind me, am I supposed to care? Let them stare."

"No strings, remember." She laughed hysterically. "What happened to the *just good friends* crap you promised, you arsehole?"

They continued to exchange words, sharp and cutting, as unresolved tensions boiled to the surface.   Jack's expression hardened with each accusation, further fuelling her fury. Unable to contain her emotions any longer, she took a few steps and her hand darted out, seizing a nearly full carafe of red wine from the nearby table. With a primal scream of frustration, she hurled the carafe towards him; the liquid exploding in a crimson arc directly over him.

"Now, just go back and leave me the fuck alone." She screamed at him.

The restaurant fell silent, the clatter of cutlery and the murmur of conversation coming to an abrupt halt as all eyes turned towards the scene unfolding.

He gaped at her in astonishment, while she stood staring back at him for several seconds, before her rage subsided and she realised what she had done. Oh my God. Poor Jack. She felt mortified. Then she burst into nervous laughter. Dark, red stains covered his hair, head, face, and shirt. Drips of red wine cascading down his forehead and she just doubled up with laughter.

"Hey. that's my wine," called a young Greek guy in stilted English, standing up to face them.

Everyone in the restaurant was staring at them with a mixture of astonishment and horror at the scene that had just enfolded in front of their very eyes.

"Sorry. I'm so sorry," answered Isabella. She couldn't believe what had just happened herself. Now the red mist had waned. She placed the now empty carafe back in its original position and backed away gingerly.

"Here buddy," said Jack, reaching into his pocket and pulling out a wad of soggy notes. "Here's about a hundred Euros. This'll cover it. Sygnómi. Gynaíkes."

At that moment, the entire restaurant broke into fits of laughter and began clapping with glee at the spectacle they had just witnessed.

"Americans," shrieked someone.

"British," said the guy with the wine, as if that explained everything.

"Let's get out of here before we get arrested," said Jack and he gripped Isabella's hand tightly and yanked her away from the restaurant back towards the others.

And then, as quickly as it began, the patrons chattered, the memory of the violent outburst lingering in the air long after they'd gone.

"I'm sorry, Jack. Truly."

"Me too," he grinned, before they both burst out laughing again.

"I don't know what came over me," she howled.

"Well, I know what came over me. I stink. What is it with you and red wine?" he bellowed.

They arrived back at their restaurant, where the others were waiting patiently, wondering what on earth was going on.

"What the hell happened to you?" gasped Eva as they all stared in bewilderment, taking in the wine-soaked Jack.

"Isabella. Isabella happened to me," said Jack scathingly.

No-one dared question them any further, but they could sense the frenetic atmosphere that enveloped them.

"We've all had a lot to drink," said Harry diplomatically. "I think we'd better get going."

"I think that's a good idea," said Jack, wishing at this moment, he'd never laid eyes on this darned woman.

Neither of them so much as glanced at each other all the way back to the yacht.

"What the hell happened?" enquired Harry.

"We got in a row," stated Isabella.

"Did you tell him? About Teddy I mean?"

"Of course, I didn't bloody tell him."

"God, you're an immature pain in the neck, Izzy. You leave a hell of a trail of a mess behind you wherever you go and you make my life a living hell at times."

"Fuck off Harry. Leave me alone."

"Thank God your son was fast asleep and didn't witness your ridiculous behaviour."

When they eventually arrived back at their vessel, Eva and Harry headed straight to bed, so she could question him in private about the incredible turn of events that had taken place earlier. She did not know what everyone was hiding from her. Why had no one told her about Jack and Isabella? What was the big secret and why were they both still so mad at each other?

"We're calling it a night too," said Ingrid. "Will you two be okay?"

"I'm going to change," said Jack sullenly.

"Yes" snapped Isabella, "I'm taking Ted straight to bed" and she picked up the sleeping babe from his pushchair and carried him along to their stateroom. Thank God, as Harry said, he hadn't been an eyewitness to her atrocious behaviour, fuelled by way too much alcohol.

Isabella was still fuming, habitually at her own behaviour, but also with Jack. She was too wired to sleep, so thought she'd sit up on deck alone and get some fresh air, try to clear her mind.

She poured herself a coffee, then went outside and leant against the handrail and stared out at the twinkling lights of the shore. It was a glorious evening. There was a full moon and a sky full of silver, sparkling stars. Peace and tranquillity at last.

"Isabella."

"Oh no, not again," she groaned, hearing Jack call her name. "Look, I've apologised. I'm mortified, okay. But please, I beg you, can you just leave me in peace?"

"Another pleasant welcome," he said.

He had showered and changed out of his wet clothes.

"I'm sorry about your clothes," she whispered.

"Screw my clothes," he snapped, he clearly was still fuming. "Look Isabella. This is my boat. You're my guest. But I swear, unless you tell me what I did wrong …"

"You'll what? Throw me overboard?" she hissed.

"Why are you doing this to me?" he thundered, then turned back inside and poured himself a large Jack Daniels over ice and lit a cigarette.

She stormed after him with all the grace of a hurricane, her eyes shooting daggers at him. Enough was enough. "Okay, you bastard," she yelled as she stood facing him with her hands on her hips. "You won't let this go. You wanna know? I'll tell you." She was seething by now. He could see the rage etched on her face. He had never, ever seen her so angry. "Do you remember Kenya?" she spat, running her hands through her hair out of exasperation.

"Of course I remember Kenya. That's where all this crap started."

"Are you going to let me finish?"

"Be my guest." And with a flick of the wrist, he made a flourish, inviting her to pass by him. His gesture was fluid, if not a tad ironic.

"Okay, you supercilious prick. After the game park, we returned to Mombasa, right?"

"After the game park? That's all you can call it?"

"We returned to Mombasa, right?"

"Right? For fuck's sake."

"I spent a couple of days holed up in my room alone, wondering what to do. Feeling guilty. Ashamed. Mortified."

"More so than tonight's childish dramatics?" he asked sarcastically.

"Don't," she snapped.

He remained silent then, whilst she paced back and forth

around the room in a state of agitation and anxiety.

"We had just spent the most amazing, wonderful days together, the best days I'd ever spent in my life, come to that. It was pure heaven. I foolishly thought we had something. You told me you loved me," she laughed hysterically, "I finally decided after much soul searching, that I no longer wanted to be with Robert, I had fallen completely and utterly in love with you … no wait, say nothing, you promised. Just back off." She said, holding out her hand to ward him back from her. He looked stunned.

"Where was I? Oh yeah, I was going to finish it with Rob, not a simple decision to make. I was prepared to follow you to the end of the earth if need be, just so I could be with you. I came down later to tell you …" her voice broke now.

"Yes?" he croaked. He was astounded, overwhelmed. He hadn't known what to expect, but he certainly hadn't expected this.

"Only to be accosted by Madison."

"Madison? What the fuck's she got to do with this?" he snapped.

"What did you think? I wouldn't find out? You'd play me for a pushover. Stop … just wait, okay? Don't say anything, you piece of shit. Anyway, she told me all about the same wonderful couple of nights you two had spent together and how …" She broke down into floods of tears then "… you and she had, well, you know. You'd fed her the same bullshit. She told me how great you were in bed, for God's sake. Do I need to say anymore? Get the picture? I was sick to my stomach. I still am." And with that she lunged the frame with the photo of them all in Kenya across the room towards him. Luckily, it missed and sailed silently past his head, before crashing noisily to the floor. Shards of glass cascading everywhere.

Isabella sobbed resoundingly and fell bodily onto the sofa and held her head in her hands, before hugging herself tightly, seeking solace and reassurance.

"Isabella," he thundered.

"You treated me like such a fool. Made me a part of your silly game. Made me believe you were in love with me, too. How could you do that? How could you sleep with two women within days of each other? It still makes me feel sick. What kind of man are you? I'm lucky I didn't catch something horrible." And she looked up at him then, her face awash with tears.

She watched the colour drain from his face as he fell back onto the sofa opposite her. He set his glass on the table between them. She watched him bury his face in his large hands and rub his face.

Then, after what seemed like an age, he lit another cigarette, looked up at her and said simply, "You fool. You dumb fool. You're not the dumbest person I've ever met, but you'd better hope they don't die," he suggested.

"What?" she yelled, "How dare you."

"I thought you were an intelligent woman, for God's sake."

"You pig," she gasped.

"Don't you see? Don't you see what she did? It's not true. None of it." He was shouting at her, at the top of his voice. So loud, she thought he might wake the others. The crew could obviously hear them.

"I was nowhere near that fucking woman. It was all in her head. I no more fucked Madison ... than I fucked David," he screamed, "How could you fall for such crap? Why didn't you confront me? Look at what she's done. Why didn't you talk to me?"

"Don't lie and squirm your way out of it. I saw you." She screamed back at him.

"Saw me? What are you talking about?"

"I saw her sneak into your room. Both of you. Are you telling me nothing happened?"

"Of course, nothing happened!" he yelled.

"So, what were you doing?"

"I don't know ... we had a couple of drinks. I can't

remember."

"Convenient," she said. She didn't believe him.

"I swear to you. We had a couple of drinks and that was it. I may not remember what we did, but I know what we didn't do. For God's sake, she lied to you, Bella. Hell, do you think I'd sleep with a woman like that? I haven't been with another woman since you. How could you have been so fucking dense? How could you jump to conclusions without asking me?" he was bellowing at her.

It took a while for it to sink in.

"You mean?" she said lamely.

"Of course, I mean," he groaned, "It was all lies. Complete fabrication. I loved you and only you. I loved you wholeheartedly. I wanted to spend the rest of my life with you."

"Oh no," she whispered, "But why? Why would she do that? She more or less told me you shagged anything that moved."

"Because she's an asinine, jealous, twisted bitch of a woman. She was jealous of you. As soon as she set eyes on you, you could see it. We all could. You have everything she hasn't, beauty, warmth, tenderness. I thought, intelligence. And you let her ruin everything."

"I let her ruin everything?"

"Yes," he wailed. "All this time, I thought ..."

"Oh Jack, what have I done?" she cried, hugging her knees.

"All this wasted time. Why didn't you say anything? You didn't even tell Harry?"

"No." She whispered, taking in the gravity of what he was telling her.

He walked over and sat down beside her. "You've been incredibly naïve and gullible. I'm so pissed with you. I could have sorted and explained all of this years ago."

"I need a stiff drink" said Isabella, walking over to the bar and pouring herself a brandy, "Can I have one of those too?" she asked, nodding towards his cigarettes.

"Help yourself," he said, after reading the look on her face, as if to say, don't you dare try to stop me.

She took a cigarette from the packet and he lit it for her. She sat back on the sofa to face him and knocked back the rest of her liquor.

"I screwed up, huh?" she said.

"Big time."

"I'm sorry about your photo frame."

"Don't worry about it. I want nothing to remind me of that woman, anyway."

"Now what happens?" she asked gingerly.

"I don't know. I don't know how I feel at the moment."

"I'm going to bed Jack."

"Me too."

"Goodnight."

"Night."

And they both went their separate ways, both hurt, angry and brimming with many mixed emotions and trying to get their heads around what they'd both learned that night.

***

CHAPTER THIRTY-TWO

The night stretched on endlessly for Isabella, a restless abyss of tossing and turning as the weight of regret hung in the air. The remnants of the heated argument lingered like a bitter aftertaste, haunting every corner of her mind with its echoes of anger and frustration. It had been brutal.

With each passing hour, sleep eluded her as she replayed the events of the evening in her mind. The memory of harsh words spoken in haste and the sting of wounded pride weighed heavily on her conscience, casting a shadow over the darkness of the night.

As the minutes ticked by, a sense of unease settled over her, fuelled by the gnawing realisation that she was wrong. The weight of the mistake was heavy on her chest, suffocating her with its crushing burden of guilt and remorse. What had she done?

She tossed and turned, unable to find solace in the darkness as the truth of her error gnawed at her conscience like a relentless predator. The silence of the night, deafening, broken only by the rhythmic beat of her heart and the gentle waves lapping against the hull.

The following morning, Isabella was the last to join them at the breakfast table. The tension was still discernible between the two of them. No one dared comment on the previous night's antics, and not one of them dared to comment on the unpleasant atmosphere. This usually contented group, for once, was essentially silent. Even the crew picked up on it and were tiptoeing around them. Teddy was enjoying a lie in, so he wasn't even around to ease the unease.

"So, what's happening today?" Harry asked as brightly as he could.

"Do you mind if we stay on board?" said Eva to Harry, "I'm bushed."

"Me too. I could do with another day just lying on deck, taking in the scenery," agreed Ingrid.

"Harry, Eva, could you look after Teddy?" asked Jack, glaring at them.

"What?" gasped Isabella in utter stupefaction.

"Of course, …" started Harry, unsure of what the right answer should be.

"Don't," said Isabella, staring at Harry.

"You heard." Jack snapped. "Harry, can you take care of Teddy for Bella?"

"Why? What are you doing? I'm not going anywhere?" shrieked Isabella.

"You are. We are going ashore. You and I," he stated simply.

"Oh no, we're bloody not." She snapped.

"Look, Harry, for the last time, I'm taking Isabella ashore. We have some things to discuss and hopefully resolve. Can you take care of Teddy or not?" he said firmly, tossing his napkin onto his finished plate.

"Of course we can," said Harry and Eva together. "Yep, no problem." Oh my God, this was so awkward.

Isabella shot Harry another filthy glance. "I'm not leaving this bloody ship."

"Isabella. Be quiet," hissed Jack.

"Look Izzy, I think Jack's right. You obviously have things to discuss," said Harry to her.

"We have nothing to say to each other. I'm not going and that's that. You can't make me go anywhere." She challenged Jack.

"Isabella. You're coming," Jack stressed.

"Look," shouted Ingrid, jumping from her seat, "I'm sick to death of you two. Isabella, you're one of my best friends, but I swear, you're beginning to piss me off. Go with him. See what he wants?"

"I'm not interested in what he wants," she grumbled stubbornly.

"Talk to him. We're all sick of this bullshit," snapped Ingrid.

"I don't want to talk to him," Isabella sulked childishly.

"Isabella. You're impossible," bellowed Jack, tossing his hand in the air.

She ignored him.

Eva and David were shuffling uncomfortably in their seats, and the crew had disappeared.

Ingrid continued, "There's no harm in it. What have you got to lose? If I'm honest, it'll be good to get rid of the pair of you. This crap has gone on for far too long. Can't you just put the past in the past and get on with it?"

"Ingrid, stay out of this," warned David.

"I will not." She snapped, "You'd better see what the hell he wants, otherwise ... whatever he has to say, I'll say the same, but worse," she shouted at Isabella. Never had she known two people so constantly at each other's throats, "All we hear is never ending bickering and banter, both of you trying to outdo the other–it's bloody ludicrous."

Isabella began to cry. This was mortifying.

Harry reached over and took hold of her arm. "Please? For all our sakes? See what he has to say?"

"Okay, okay. You win. But he can do the talking. I've said all I'm going to say, I'm done. Now, I'm going to get changed and grab my stuff. Harry, Eva, please take care of my son."

A short time later, after showering and getting ready, and settling Teddy with Harry and Eva, she found herself alone with Jack in the launch, speeding and bouncing across the turquoise water, heading towards shore. She did not know who had roped her into this and felt sick to her stomach.

They reached the shore, and he jumped out first into the shallow warm water and moored the launch. "Here, take my hand," he instructed, turning to help her, the first words he'd uttered since they'd left the boat.

"I can manage," she snapped and jumped easily overboard, catching her foot on the side and nearly stumbling.

"Suit yourself."

They walked in complete silence, him ahead of her, briskly and with purpose until they found a waiting taxi.

"Get in," he ordered, opening the back door for her. She obeyed.

"Menites," Jack said to the driver as he got in and sat next to her.

They travelled in complete silence still, the air electric between them. She stared out of the dusty window, lost in thought, as they travelled through the lunar landscape, the fertile valleys and over hills, past steep slopes filled with olive trees, fig trees and orange and lemon groves. They arrived at the mountain spa village and Jack asked the driver to stop. He paid the driver for their trip.

"Well?" she snapped, squinting her eyes from the glare of the sun.

"Well, what?"

"What are we doing here?"

"Oh, you are talking then? Seeing the sights," he stated.

"Sightseeing," she gasped.

"Precisely. We're on vacation. It's what we Americans do. We see the sights."

"What? What are you talking about? You brought me here to see the sights?"

"Yup. Now follow me."

She followed him, but she was fuming. She was stuck in the middle of bloody nowhere and wasn't in a co-operative mood. What was he playing at? Sightseeing.

However, the impressive, leafy village, a bustling hub of activity where locals gathered to socialise and relax in the shade of ancient plane trees, soon softened her mood. They enjoyed a diverting, if not again silent and awkward, walk around the village, surrounded by verdant hillsides, where crystal clear water and natural underground springs flowed through marble fountains and troughs, creating a refreshing oasis in the village's heart.

He led her along a cobblestone path to The Church of Agia Marina, with its striking bell tower and ornate frescoes. A heavy silence hung between them. Each lost in their own thoughts as they walked side by side, but worlds apart. The weight of unspoken words pressing down on them. The whitewashed walls of the church stood sentinel. Their timeless beauty, a stark contrast to the tension that simmered beneath the surface.

Occasionally, a fleeting glance or a hesitant touch would betray the longing in their hearts, but still neither dared to break the silence that had settled between them. And so they continued their wordless journey around the church, Jack lighting a candle for his dear, departed mother; the echoes of their footsteps mingling with the quiet rustle of the wind in the olive trees. A poignant reminder of the distance that separated them despite their physical proximity. If she was honest, she was enjoying the brief respite from the searing, eternal heat, but was dreading what lay ahead; surely, he hadn't just planned a day of seeing the sights? But if that's what he wanted, so be it. She wasn't talking to him, anyway; she thought to herself stubbornly.

They then walked to the village square, where they found charming tavernas and cafes.

"I think we need a drink and some shade," he said simply, and they sat down at an empty table at a taverna. "What do you want?" he asked her gruffly as a waiter arrived at their table.

"Water," she said sulkily.

"Two large mineral waters please and I'll have an espresso as well, make that a double," then he lit a cigarette and smiled at her, "So, how long are we gonna continue with this charade?"

"What charade? You brought me here?" Here it comes. She thought to herself.

"Come on Bella? You're running hot and cold on me. I have absolutely no idea what is going on in that lovely head of yours. What are you thinking?"

"Honestly? I wish I'd never come on this bloody holiday," she said sulkily.

"Okay great. You're talking to me, that's a start." He smiled, taking a sip of his water, "So, what about us?"

"What do you mean?"

"What are you thinking about us?"

"Nothing?"

"Aren't you curious? Haven't you wondered, if you hadn't been so darned pig-headed and contentious and come to me, instead of listening to Madison, found out the truth? Don't you wonder what might have happened to us?"

"Nothing would have happened to us. Don't you see? All we do is fight. We're at each other's throats constantly. We want to kill each other most of the time."

"We have a love hate relationship. Actually, we're the dynamic duo of love-hate relationships." he said.

"Yeah, you love me. I hate you." She stated.

"That's only because of all the misunderstandings. If we'd been totally honest with each other, more open, you know, like normal couples, maybe things would have turned out differently."

"I don't think so."

"Until all this crap reared its head again, we were getting on fine?" he stated.

"As friends. Then *you* have to spoil things."

"Isabella. We were in love. We could be married with kids by now."

"You don't like kids," she snapped.

"Since when."

"Since forever. You told me you don't want kids."

"I don't remember saying that. *If* I said that, I was being an ass. Look, I need you to be honest with me now."

"About what?" she asked nervously, crossing and uncrossing her legs.

"About us, for God's sake. Are you honestly telling me you don't want this to go any further?"

"Yes."

"I don't believe you." He reached into his pocket and pulled out some Euros and left them on the table. "Come on, you've finished your drink. Let's go."

"Go where? I'm worn out," she was getting fed up with this. They were over. Done. Weren't they?

He took hold of her hand and led her out of town.

"Are you going to tell me where we're going now?" she sighed.

"For lunch."

"Couldn't we have just eaten back there?"

"No. Now stop your whining."

He never let go of her hand as they walked in the withering heat along a scenic walking trail amongst the natural beauty of the island, a hidden treasure tucked away in the countryside.

They came to a lush olive grove, offering panoramic views of the Aegean from its high vantage point.

"What are we doing here?" she asked.

"Looks as good a place as any. Come on, let's find somewhere in the shade to eat."

"Are you crazy? Won't we get into trouble? What are we going to eat, olives?"

"Of course not. There's no one around, anyway. Here looks good," he said, pointing to a spot where he kneeled down under the ancient, gnarled olive trees and removed his large backpack. He then pulled out a bulky blanket, which he lay on the dry ground, a huge plastic box and a now tepid, litre bottle of mineral water.

"What's in the box?" she asked.

"Come sit next to me" he patted the blanket next to him.

"A picnic." She asked, dumbfounded.

"Yep, a picnic."

She knelt down next to him on the scratchy blanket.

He removed the box's lid and inside she could see and smell the fruit bread, olive bread, Greek cheeses and sun-dried tomatoes.

"Help yourself," and he began tucking into the delicious Greek fayre.

"I don't believe you. You had this all planned, didn't you? You said you wanted to talk, not come for a bloody picnic."

"Aren't you hungry?"

"Yes, I'm hungry, but that's beside the point." She said snarkily.

"Look, can we at least have a truce while we eat?" he suggested. "Joe has made us a feast here, and I'm starved."

"Okay," she grumbled and began nibbling a piece of bread and cheese.

So, in the tranquil embrace of the olive grove, with dappled sunlight filtering through the canopy of leaves, they ate in silence. Both eating zealously, the air filled with the earthy aroma of olives; they tucked into the culinary delights.

Sitting next to each other, although neither of them saying very much, a palpable tension lingered in the air, a silent reminder of the unspoken words that hung between them like a delicate thread. Despite the breath-taking beauty of their surroundings, there was a heaviness to their interaction, a sense of unresolved emotions simmering just beneath the surface.

They picked at their food in silence, the clink of cutlery against plates, punctuating the stillness as they avoided each other's gaze. Each bite imbued with a bittersweet flavour, a reflection of the complex emotions that swirled within them; longing, regret and a faint glimmer of hope.

Occasionally, their eyes met fleetingly, a silent exchange that spoke volumes in the absence of words. An unspoken understanding between them, a shared history that bound them together, even as it threatened to tear them apart.

Eventually, the tension between them eased, softened by the gentle rhythm of the olive branches swaying in the breeze.

"At least we have fresh olives," said Jack keenly, pulling one from the very branches that shaded them.

"Jack."

"Here try one?" and he popped a succulent black olive, with the fresh taste of the countryside, into her mouth, before she could resist.

"Mmmm. Yummy," she agreed. This was incredible. One minute they were ready to kill each other, the next they're enjoying a companionable lunch. What was going on?

Slowly, almost imperceptibly, the atmosphere between them shifted, replaced by a quiet acceptance and shared connection.

He removed the lid from the bottle of water and extended it towards her, "Here, drink."

"No, you first," she said.

He relished a long drink and then handed her the bottle. "Bit warm, I'm afraid."

"Thanks, it's okay, anything will do. I'm parched."

"And for dessert …" and he rummaged around in his backpack for the second time and produced two large fresh figs, "For madame."

"Wow, this is remarkable. Joe thought of everything."

"With my instruction. Not all Joe."

She lay back on the blanket and savoured her fig. "I'm whacked," she puffed. She lay there wondering how they were going to get back to shore.

In the afternoon sun, they found solace in each other's presence, their unspoken bond weaving a delicate tapestry of understanding and forgiveness.

The weight of their shared silence lifted as he lay down on his side next to her and rested his head in his palm. "Okay, food's over. Now for the serious stuff."

"Jack." she warned.

"No, damn it. I'm sick of your stubbornness. I need to talk to you. Honestly. No bullshit."

"Great," she said, "Haven't we had this conversation before, like a dozen times?"

"Did you absorb anything we talked about last night?"

"I suppose so," she said, picking at her nails and biting her cuticles.

"You suppose so? Don't you think, with everything that came to light, things have changed?"

"Not really no."

"You're so fucking annoying." He roared, smacking the ground next to him.

"It's your fault." She whined, thinking that he made her feel like the worst version of herself.

"Oh. So now everything's my fault." He laughed. "You truly are astounding." He stood up then and turned his back on her to gaze down at the olive grove spread out below them. She watched him light a cigarette, take a few puffs, then turn around and face her. He sat down beside her again.

"Okay, here goes nothing," he stated. "I've spent the most desolate couple of years of my life. Just when I thought I could put you behind me … Vegas. I decided if I couldn't have you in my life permanently, then I'd make do with your friendship. I honestly thought it was a good idea. But I can't bear it any longer. I've tried to get over you. I really have."

She sat up to face him then. He looked so sad. The sparkle had gone from his eyes and it looked as if he had the weight of the world on his broad shoulders.

"Jack, look …" she sighed.

"Bella, be quiet for a minute, okay?" he sighed. "I brought you here to tell you something."

"Yes?" she whispered.

"I'm as much in love with you today as I was three years ago in Kenya. Nothing's changed. I want to put this mess behind us and start again, I adore you, but I also respect you, so I want you to tell me honestly how you feel," he took hold of her hands and held them tightly, "If you tell me you don't love me, then I'll let you go, once and for all. I despise myself for not finding out the truth earlier. If only you'd told me. I feel we've wasted so much time. But it's up to you. Your call."

"Honestly?" she smiled shyly at him. It felt so good just to hold his strong, coarse hands. Here was the safety she had been craving for so long. He was offering her a future together. He remained perfectly silent, gazing directly into her eyes, readily awaiting her reply.

"Yes Bella. You need to be honest with me."

"Can I have time to think about things?"

"How much time do you need?" he groaned.

"All this, well, everything that's happened the last couple of days. I don't know where my head's at?"

"Okay, but no more games?" he said sadly.

"No more games," and she crossed her heart, "But Jack ... I can't promise you anything. There's not just me to think about now."

"I know Bella," and he stroked her cheek gently, "I know you come as a package deal."

"Jack, look, I need to ..." she gulped.

"Shh. It can wait" and he leaned in closer, as their eyes met, sparkling with desire and anticipation and he kissed her on the mouth. She froze at first, but then as she responded to his lips, his touch, the kiss became more fervent as an irresistible magnetism drew them together. He lay her backwards onto the blanket and continued to kiss her passionately. A moment of pure, unbridled passion, a collision of hearts and minds that reignited the desire within them - years of pent up desire. In a rush of raw emotion and longing, he ran his hands through her hair, over her body, whilst she groaned and wrapped her arms tightly around his huge shoulders and caressed his back. He moved his mouth to her neck, her shoulders, her breasts. He could hardly contain himself, but he didn't want to scare her away. They stayed like that, their bodies pressed together for what seemed like hours, lingering over each other, hands roaming over each other's skin, kissing like a couple of teenagers, as they lost themselves in the heat of the moment. Time stood still as they drowned in the intoxicating sensation of each other's touch, their two hearts beating as one. With every kiss, they poured their love and desire into each other, their passion building with each caress. A dance of lips and tongues. As they finally broke apart, breathless and trembling with emotion, a sense of peace and possibility lingered in the air.

"Hullo, everyone," said Jack, grinning from ear to ear as they returned reluctantly to the boat later that day. They were both looking flushed and sheepish.

"Hi," said Isabella shamefacedly, still a little embarrassed, "Sorry about earlier, everyone. Hello baby" she smiled, giving her son a cuddle as he came to greet her, "Did you miss me? I missed you." She stroked his back and caressed his still damp hair. "Did you have a good day, sweetie?"

"Yes, we went thwimming."

"You did. Did you wear your armbands?"

"Yes, I was a good boy."

"All good here?" asked Jack, sitting down amongst his friends.

"All good thanks mate" replied Harry.

"What happened to you two, then?" asked Ingrid, regarding Isabella and Jack closely. She was dying to find out what had happened, as were the rest of them.

"Ingrid," said David, "Sorry, you two. Here, let's get you both a drink. You looked bushed."

Jess poured them both each a glass of peach iced tea.

"Mm, this is good. I was dying for a drink. So, Teddy's been okay?" asked Isabella, lifting her son onto her lap.

"He's been fine. We've all had great fun. What about you two? Had a nice day?" Harry grinned.

"Yes, thank you" said Isabella.

"So… what did you do?" asked Ingrid.

"We walked, we talked," said Jack.

"Yes," said Isabella, "We went to look around a pretty little village and then had lunch."

"And that's it?" enquired Ingrid sceptically.

"Jack and I cleared the air, if that's what you're asking?"

"Well, that's a good start," said Harry. "Now, can we enjoy the rest of our holiday in peace?"

"Peace? With these two? They have as much chance as Israel and Palestine."

***

CHAPTER THIRTY-THREE

The next day, the skipper set sail to venture around more of the Cyclades. They remained on board, enjoying the sunshine, the sea, and each other's company. Jack didn't press Isabella. He wanted her to come to him in her own time.

They spent the days on the expansive decks soaking up the sun, lounging on the beds, sipping cocktails and enjoying the incredible views. Now and then, they'd indulge in more of the water sports activities.

One day, the men gathered on deck, their excitement palpable as they prepared for some fishing. Equipped with top of the line fishing gear and expert guidance from the crew, they cast their lines into the sparkling blue depths below. With each cast, they eagerly awaited the telltale tug of a bite, their competitiveness clear as they argued about who was going to catch the first and the largest fish–it was hilariously entertaining.

As the morning unfolded, they immersed themselves in the sport, their focus unwavering as they patiently waited for their prey to take the bait.

As the hours passed and Jack caught several smaller fish, he felt a sudden tug on his line. "Quick Teddy, come and help me. I think it's a big one." He sat the little boy between his legs and showed him where to hold the fishing rod. He leant back, muscles straining against the weight. The others crowded round in anticipation, their cheers and words of encouragement mingling with the sound of the wind and the sea. With each tug and pull, the tension built. Finally, the surface of the water broke, revealing the biggest catch of the day as it fought against Jack's line. With a last heave, he hoisted the fish onto the deck, where it thrashed and flopped. Jack then threw it into the bucket of other fish he had hauled aboard the yacht. Teddy found both the fishing and the friendly banter between them all enthralling.

Joe continued to prepare more exquisite meals every day for them to enjoy alfresco, complete with fine wines and decadent desserts. They spent their evenings dancing under the stars and hours sharing stories and chatting away in the lounge areas.

Jack surprised the girls by bringing over some beauty therapists on the tender one day and treating them to facials, massages, and other pampering treatments.

Isabella called Bibi late one night from her stateroom.

"Hey Izzy, how are you?"

"I'm good Bibi. I'm getting so brown and fat. We've eaten so much." She complained in a hushed voice, as Teddy was fast asleep next to her and just in case her voice filtered through into the other rooms.

"You? Fat? I doubt that very much."

"It's been so relaxing. It's wonderful. The last few days have been bliss. The islands are amazing."

"And?"

"I still don't know. I just don't know what to do, you know? Part of me wants to give it another shot with him."

"It's been days since you texted me and told me what happened, what he said. Surely you know by now?" said Bibi, her brow furrowed, concern clear in her tone.

"I keep flip-flopping."

"I'm guessing you haven't told him about Teddy yet either?"

"No. Not since I tried that day. I just don't know what to do? I'm not sure when to come clean."

"Do you love him?"

"I think so. No. I know so. Every time he's near me, I just want to kiss him again. I don't know what's stopping me?"

"Don't you think it could be this huge thing? You must be terrified to tell him. It's something that could really impact your relationship; maybe it's worth considering whether it's fair to keep it hidden any longer."

"Harry keeps on at me too. I know you're both right. It's just ... I'm scared. Scared of losing him, scared of what he'll think of me when he finds out the truth. But I also know that keeping this secret isn't fair to either of us, but I don't want to spoil things just yet. I'll have to tell him when we're home."

"Izzy," her friend sighed, "It's okay to be scared, but remember, honesty is the foundation of any healthy relationship. Look at the mess that you've already made. And if he truly cares about you, he'll understand and support you, no matter what."

"It's all so messed up."

"You're not wrong there."

"What do I say to him about us, I mean?"

"You just have to be honest, Izzy. Tell him you love him too. You belong together, you really do, and I guess what's romance without a little rivalry?"

"We're never alone. I'm not doing it with everyone watching us."

"Make time alone?"

"I guess."

"Just do it, Iz. Sooner rather than later. Tell him how you feel. Then you carry on, date like a normal couple. But put him out of his misery, okay? Wait until you are home to tell him about the other thing, if that's what you want?"

"Okay." Oh God, what a bloody mess. "Thank you for being here for me, for always supporting me, even when things are tough. You're not just my friend, you're my unpaid therapist, you poor thing."

"Of course, that's what best friends are for. And no matter what happens, remember, I'm here for you."

Early the following day, they headed for Tinos another captivating destination and all took the tender to a secluded sandy beach, hidden away from the hustle and bustle of the island's more popular tourist spots, accessible only by a narrow footpath, or like them, boat.

The crew set up some space for them in the shade of some trees. They prepared a brunch for them; there were no facilities on the beach, just sand, sea, and sun at its purest. Similarly, there were no other tourists on the beach that day, so the group was alone.

They lounged around on the crescent of pristine golden sand framed by towering rock formations and the crystal-clear waters. The empty beach stretched out before them, as they spread out and claimed their own private piece of paradise, sunbathing, playing volleyball and making sandcastles with Teddy.

They headed to the water's edge, the soft sand giving way beneath their feet. They took turns rolling down the sand into the water, which Teddy loved and found hysterical. Giving himself into the sheer joy of the moment, he too launched himself forward, tumbling headlong down the sandy slope, limbs flailing and laughter bubbling from his lips.

The tranquil water was perfect for paddling and swimming and the water so clear they could watch the fish; Teddy and Harry spent ages trying to catch one in the net, but without success.

"Come on, let's go back up and eat" said Jack, putting his arm around Isabella's shoulder and leading her out of the shallows, droplets of water cascading from her hair and glistening on her skin, "God you look good enough to eat in this bikini. Your ass is fully on show," he whispered into her ear, grabbing hold of her bare cheek.

"Are you complaining?" she flirted.

"Not at all. I love it. But it's hard to focus on anything else."

"Good idea, I'm famished," said Harry, noticing the

affection between the pair of them. Something had changed over the last couple of days. Yes, obviously the anger had gone, but the friendship seemed to have progressed to something else? The energy between them both was palpable. They were like a couple of honeymooners. Anyone looking in from the outside would presume they were. As he watched them walking up the beach, a myriad of emotions swirled within him. Amidst the twinge of anxiety, he couldn't help but marvel at their connection, the way they lit up in each other's presence, their laughter. As he watched them draw closer, their bond deepening with each passing moment, he rooted for them, silently cheering them on. He wished them all the happiness in the world, however, he knew full well the big hurdle they had yet to cross and boy, was it a big hurdle?

As the sun beat down relentlessly from the cloudless sky, the small group made their way up the beach, their progress slow and laboured under the sweltering heat. The soft sand clung to their feet, each step feeling like a Herculean effort as they trudged forward, not realising how far they had travelled, their destination seeming impossibly far away.

The adults, their faces flushed and glistening with sweat, mixed with seawater, struggled. They exchanged weary glances, silently commiserating with each other as they soldiered on through the oppressive heat. Amidst the group, Teddy toddled along, his chubby legs wobbling uncertainly in the shifting sand. He clutched David's hand, his tiny feet sinking deep into the soft terrain with each faltering step. His rosy cheeks flushed with exertion as he bravely soldiered on alongside the adults.

The air was heavy with humidity, bearing down on them like a suffocating blanket. Each breath felt like a struggle, the breeze offering little relief from the oppressive temperature. Eventually Teddy couldn't manage the walk anymore and David gratefully picked him up.

Finally, after what felt like an eternity, they reached their luxurious set up, collapsing with a collective sigh of relief.

Teddy squealed with delight as he plopped down beside them all, his sandy fingers reaching eagerly for a cool drink. They all sat around the rustic wooden table, a canopy of billowing fabric providing a welcome respite from the midday sun, creating a cool oasis of shade ready for a delightful lunch experience.

As they settled into the plush beach chairs arranged beneath the canopy, a gentle breeze rustled through the palm fronds overhead. The crew had yet again spared no expense in creating a sumptuous feast for them, complemented with ice cold wine and beers. Teddy tucked into some tuna sandwiches whilst sitting on Harry's knee. The attentive crew served them with warm smiles and impeccable service, ensuring that they had their every need met, frequently topping up their glasses with chilled wine or beer.

They reclined in their chairs, satisfied, basking in the afterglow of an unforgettable lunch of grilled seafood, vibrant salads, crusty loaves of bread, and creamy dips and spreads. After the crew had cleared away the last crumbs and they had all savoured a lot of drink, Jack asked Isabella quietly, "Fancy a walk?"

"Sounds good? Let me just get Teddy to sleep in his buggy?"

"What are you two plotting?" smiled Ingrid.

"We're going for a walk. I'm just hoping that Teddy will fall asleep. He's so tired and grizzly," she said.

"Don't wait for that. Just go, he'll be fine with us," said Eva.

"If you're sure?" asked Isabella.

"Come on Bella, let's go." And Jack grabbed her hand and pulled her from her seat.

They walked silently hand in hand for fifteen minutes, happy to just take in the views and walk off their indulgence. Eventually, he turned to face her. He pulled her sharply towards him and kissed her hard on her mouth, taking her head in his hands and drawing her close to him. He took her breath away. After a few seconds, they pulled apart from each other, giggling.

"Oh God. Look, they're all watching," cried Isabella, turning around to face their group of friends.

"Who gives a shit?" said Jack, as they heard the whoops and cheers from back at their table.

"Come on you, let's paddle, the sand's too hot," he said, dragging her into the water.

"That was some kiss," she smiled.

"I've been dying to do that for days," he groaned.

"I've been dying for you to do that for days." She said.

"You have?" he asked.

"I have." She said proudly, "After *our talk* in the olive grove when you kissed me raw."

"Ah yes. *Our talk*," he said, making quotations in the air.

"I've been thinking …" she said hesitantly.

"Yes …" he asked eagerly.

"Well … I, I think … I still love you too," she said in almost a whisper. There was no longer any point in holding back, there had definitely been enough games already.

"You … think?" he smiled.

"Okay, I know."

"You know what, Bella?"

"I love you."

"Louder."

"I love you."

And she pulled *him* towards *her* this time, kissing him ardently, gripping him. He pulled her on top of him into the shallows without breaking their embrace, the gentle waves lapping against them as they lay entwined in the warm sea, the water caressing their skin, as Jack enveloped her in his embrace.

With a trembling voice, she poured out her heart. Her declaration of love carried on the gentle breeze that rustled through their hair.

As they moved into deeper waters, he pulled her onto

his lap astride him and they both spoke of the depths of their affection, the strength of their bond, and the beauty of the connection that bound them together.

As they floated, wrapped around each other, immersed in each other, she silently prayed that their love would weather the storm to come and endure for all eternity. Tears glistened in her eyes as they clasped hands, their fingers intertwining in a silent promise of forever. She pulled away breathlessly after what seemed like forever. "So what happens now?" she smiled, still straddling him, gazing into his beautiful eyes.

He took hold of her hands again, pulling them upwards towards his mouth, and gently kissed her salty fingers. "We take it one day at a time. Slowly. And this time, no secrets. If we've something to say, something on our mind, we say it. That goes for both of us. I want no more screw ups like this one, okay?"

"Okay."

"We start at the beginning and we fall in love all over again."

"Sounds good to me," she smiled.

"Now, come on, let's get back to the others. We've a fair walk back."

"It's all your fault, you know?" she smiled.

"Yeah, yeah, whatever."

As they sauntered up to the group, Teddy ran up to greet them both. Clearly, he hadn't slept yet, "Mummy. Jack," he cried.

"Hello darling boy," she said and crouched to pick him up and nibble his neck, whilst he squealed with delight.

"Hey," said Jack to the others, pulling himself out a chair that had been tucked away under the table.

"So," said Harry, "I take it after *that* display, straight out of *From Here to Eternity*, we're all sorted?"

Jack smiled at Isabella sexily.

"We're all sorted," smiled Isabella.

"And?" said Harry.

"And nothing" said Isabella. She knew what he was referring to.

"One day at a time," said Jack.

"Thank God for that," gasped Ingrid, "You're back together."

"You could say that, I suppose," whispered Isabella, smiling at Jack.

"Yes, that's right" said Jack, looking pointedly at her in return, "But let's get one thing clear here" and he stood up and walked around the table. He stood behind her chair, bending down and kissing her on the head and holding onto her shoulders, "I never intend to let this damned pain in the ass woman out of my sight again."

"At last," cheered Ingrid.

"Too bloody right," said David.

"Oh God," said Harry teasingly, "Fireworks ahead." Eva looked addled and unsure what was going on and Harry shot her a look as if to say 'later'.

"So," said Ingrid, "After all this, do we get to hear why you were both torn apart in the first place?"

Over another round of cold beers, Isabella explained fully, once and for all, to all of them, exactly what Madison had told her that fateful evening in Mombasa.

"You stubborn, hot-headed foolish girl," said Harry, "If only you'd have told us sooner, instead of keeping it close to your chest. *I* could have bloody told you that Jack hadn't slept with Madison."

"And just how would you know exactly?" she asked indignantly.

"Jesus Izzy, you only have to spend over ten minutes in that blasted woman's company and she practically freezes your balls," said Harry.

"Isabella, I can't believe you thought Jack was just a fuck-boy," said Ingrid.

Isabella responded, "Well, that's the impression I received."

"And why lie about going back to Robert and say you were going to marry him?" pressed Ingrid.

"It just felt safer. It was the only reason I could think of to end things with Jack, by making out I'd made a mistake."

"So now this is all out in the open. Can we all hope for this relationship to start anew and without all the tears and tantrums?" asked Ingrid.

Jack removed his sunglasses and looked at Isabella and took hold of her hand, his heart pounding with a mixture of nerves and unwavering devotion and in front of everyone said, "All I will say is, she is the most amazing, annoying, frustrating woman in the world and I love her. I never intend to let her go, no matter what. I will let *no one* or *anything* come between us again, understood?" he said directly to her, "Right, baby?"

"Right," she beamed.

He looked into her eyes, his voice steady yet filled with emotion. "My love. Bella," he cleared his throat. "From the moment we met, the moment I saw you across the room, my life was changed forever," he said, looking into her eyes, his voice steady yet filled with emotion. A soft smile played on his lips as he continued, his voice growing stronger with each word. "With you, I am whole. Without you, I am nothing. You are my soulmate, my everything. I love you."

"You see, Amor vincit omnia," exhaled Harry.

"Whatever he said," said Ingrid, and they all clapped and cheered.

"I always said you'd make a stunning couple," said Eva simply.

They returned wearily to their yacht later that day and, whilst they all had a nap, showered and changed, the captain up anchored and set sail for the nearby Mykonos.

Freshly showered and changed and engulfed in Henry Jacques, *Belle Isabelle* Pure Perfume, Isabella arrived on deck with Teddy, just as the sky was transforming into a canvas of vibrant hues. She was wearing a full-length ethereal gown from Valentino in pure silk and combined with simple, elegant jewellery pieces that added a look of sophistication, she exuded confidence and elegance.

"Wow, that dress looks insane on you Izzy," gasped Ingrid.

"Thank you," she said unassumingly.

"You look and smell divine baby" Jack said, hugging her tightly to him, "Everyone still okay to eat out tonight?" he asked. They all began tucking into hors d'oeuvres and aperitifs as the sun set around them.

"Sounds good" said Harry. The others murmured their agreement.

The evening wrapped around them like a cozy blanket, filling them with a soothing warmth, as they moored in a cove. They took the smaller boat to shore to peruse the beachfront restaurants and settled on a pizzeria. They were all starving after their busy day.

They had a fun filled evening and ate and drank copious amounts before returning to the yacht, where after putting Teddy to bed, all the girls settled in the main salon and lay around in varying states of repose. The men stood at the bar, enjoying a brandy and a cigar.

"God, they stink," complained Ingrid.

"Ok, how about a tune to end the night?" asked Jack. He stubbed out his cigar in the ashtray and walked over and sat at the piano. He lifted the top and tinkled the ivories.

"This one's for you baby" and he grinned at Isabella and began to play and sing *All the Way.*

"*So if you let me love me. It's for sure I'm gonna love you. All the way. All the way.*"

They all clapped and cheered upon conclusion.

"That was so romantic." said Eva, "I've never heard it before?"

"Frank Sinatra," said Harry.

"It's our song," grinned Isabella.

"Yes, baby, it's our song," smiled Jack.

"Oh. The boat!" cried Eva. "Now it makes sense."

"Well, on that note, I'm going to bed," said David. "Coming?" he asked Ingrid.

"Yep."

"Us too," said Eva.

"Okay, let's all call it a night," said Jack and he closed the lid.

The two couples headed off first, then Jack and Isabella followed closely behind, heading to their respective suites.

"Well, goodnight baby," he whispered, pulling her towards him for a deep, passionate kiss.

"Goodnight?" she asked coyly as they parted.

He regarded her curiously.

"Well, I don't know about you, but I'm not tired. I want to be with you, Jack," she said, her tone all sultry femininity.

"You do? What about Teddy?"

"Ted is fast asleep. I've got the monitor and I'll make sure I'm back in bed before he wakes. He'll never know the difference."

"You mean?" he inhaled.

"Come on. Let's go check out your massive bed," she teased. With a mischievous glint in her eye and a coy smile on her lips, she took his hand in hers, leading him to his beautiful suite. Each step filled with anticipation, the air thick with a palpable sense of desire and excitement.

As they entered the dark room, she closed the door behind them with a soft click; the sound echoing around them. With a playful giggle, she pressed a finger to her lips, her eyes dancing with mischief as she beckoned him closer. With a slow, deliberate motion, she reached up to trace a delicate finger along his jawline, through his hair, her touch sending shivers of anticipation coursing through his veins. Her gaze locked with his, drawn and smouldering with desire, as she leaned in close, her breath warm against his ear.

Within moments, they were all over each other, tearing at each other's clothes. Their stifled laughter mingled with moans as they fell naked onto the bed, exploring each other's bodies as if they'd never experienced each other before.

"Ouch. I can't see anything," said Isabella.

"We don't need to see anything," he panted, as their bodies entwined in a passionate embrace as they lost themselves in the heat of the moment. As he finally entered her, gradually at first, then more forcefully, they both got swept away in each other. Each touch was electric, sending waves of pleasure coursing through their veins as they explored each other with a hunger that bordered on desperation. As they came together in a tangle of limbs and desire, their moans and whispers filled the room. Neither of them was aware of anything or anyone except each other. They spent the night making love. With each thrust and sigh, they reached new heights of ecstasy, their bodies moving in perfect harmony as they headed towards the ultimate release.

Time stood still as they lost themselves in the throes of passion, their world narrowing down to the sensation of each other — the taste of sweat on skin, the intoxicating scent of arousal. Their bodies shuddering as they collapsed into each other's arms, spent and sated, napping on and off and never letting go of each other. Rediscovering each other. Loving the taste of each other. Laughing and talking into the early hours of the morning, when Isabella reluctantly tiptoed back to her room.

***

CHAPTER THIRTY-FOUR

The rest of the holiday passed by. Everyone could see that Isabella and Jack were blissfully happy and tried to leave them to their own devices. They were touching to watch as they gazed at each other, tender touches and glances, not leaving each other's side for a moment. All the worries and stresses of the world faded away, replaced by a profound sense of peace and contentment. Harry and Eva were generous in helping to look after and distract Teddy, so they could spend as much time together as possible - he revelled in the attention.

They continued their journey to the mountainous, quiet and most northerly island of the Dodecanese, Patmos. On the first night, they took the tender to the harbour and chief port town of Skala, where a charming blend of traditional Greek architecture, picturesque streets, and stunning coastal vistas greeted them again. They began at the bustling harbour and meandered through the labyrinthine streets of the lively town, with its whitewashed houses, courtyards in full bloom, many tavernas, hotels, restaurants and shops, where they bought handmade crafts and local souvenirs.

They spent another couple of days exploring the rest of the spectacular island's lace-like coastline, great beaches, small coves, busy ports and fabulous scenery.

The highlight of the stay, however, was a visit to the most important landmark and place of pilgrimage; the imposing monastery of St John that dominated the island and also provided them with more magnificent views of the

Aegean from its site atop a hill overlooking the town. None of them were religious, but they spent ages pouring over the fantastic array of priceless religious artefacts and relics, many dating back to medieval times. Nearby, the Cave of the Apocalypse beckoned with its sacred aura and ancient significance, believed to be where St John received visions and heard the voice of God that inspired the Book of Revelations.

On the last evening, as the sun dipped below the horizon, casting a warm glow over the town, they found themselves reluctant to leave, memories of the enchanting streets and welcoming atmosphere lingering in their minds.

However, from here, they sailed past Leros; the coastline and warm shallow waters of Kos; Symni near the Turkish coast and Rhodes, where they spied a pod of dolphins in the dark blue waters, frolicking in the yacht's wake. Their sleek bodies glided effortlessly through the water as they danced and leaped in perfect harmony. The dolphins drew nearer, their sleek forms slicing through the waves with effortless grace, soaring through the air with an elegance and agility that took their breaths away. As they leant over the bow railings, their faces alight with joy and wonder, they watched the creature's playful antics, listening to their playful chirps and clicks echoing across the water. As the pod eventually faded into the distance, they were all left with a sense of gratitude for witnessing these spectacular mammals.

Eventually, they reached their final destination before returning to Athens; Jack's favourite and the third largest island in the Dodecanese, Karpathos. They toured the imposing coastline of cliffs, hidden coves and caves, pristine beaches and secluded bays and swam in the turquoise waters. At night, the island came alive with the sounds of traditional music and dance and they enjoyed more fabulous cuisine and lively entertainment.

They also travelled to the north of the island, where they took in the imposing mountains full of forests and the fertile land. They embarked on a long and tiring 2-

hour hike to a village nestled in the mountains. The village remained isolated for centuries, and its inhabitants continue to speak the local dialect. The women in the village still wore traditional dress. Dramatically beautiful, this backwater village was like entering another world, virtually untouched by tourism.

They visited the relatively quiet capital Pigadhia, where they enjoyed and listened to traditional music in a taverna, whilst they enjoyed sampling some local dishes and wine. Between bites and sips, the friends engaged in animated discussions about life, love and the pursuit of happiness.

After this last evening out, they lingered at their table, reluctant to part ways and return to everyday life. With hearts full and bellies satisfied, they raised their glasses in a toast to Jack. To his hospitality and generosity. To the holiday of a lifetime and finally to friendship.

"You know I'd love you to all come out again next year," he stated.

"Back to Greece? I'm in," said David.

"Well, I was thinking about the Amalfi Coast. The crew are sailing her back to Marina Grande in Sorrento after we leave. Then next summer I was thinking of taking her along the coastline, Positano, Amalfi, Capri. Maybe even head down to Sicily, then across to the French Riviera. Make a longer trip of it."

"Well, David and I are definitely in. I've got a taste of this glamorous lifestyle now and nothing else will quite stack up to this holiday, unfortunately."

The others all murmured their agreement, and the table was soon buzzing with excitement about this potential trip. All chimed in with their ideas for what they'd like to do during their time there, their excitement easing some of their dread about leaving.

On their stroll back to the yacht, whilst pushing the sleeping infant, Harry took Isabella aside. "Izzy, Eva and I were wondering if you would like Ted to sleep with us in our room tonight?"

"Really? Why?" she asked innocently.

"Well, I hope I'm not overstepping the mark, but we wondered if you and Jack would like to spend the night together."

"You mean, you've been wondering if we've slept together?" she smiled.

"Oh God, I know that," he said.

"You do?" she asked suspiciously.

"You don't think we haven't heard you?"

"Oh God," she groaned.

"And haven't heard you coming out of his room in the early hours?"

"Oh God," she groaned again.

"We just thought it would be nice if you could wake up together? Mind you, I don't think there's been a great deal of sleeping going on. *Jack, oh Jack*," he mimicked.

"Don't," she squealed.

"Think about it?"

"I don't need to. I'd love to spend the entire night with him. Teddy would love a sleepover with you two, as long as you're sure."

"Positive. One more thing?"

"Yes, Harry."

"When are you going to tell him?"

"When the time's right."

"You should have told him by now."

"You think I don't know that?"

"Sooner rather than later, okay?"

"I know. I'll do it when I'm ready. I don't know how he's going to react. We've been getting on so well, having such a wonderful time. I don't want to spoil things. There's a lot to consider. We've only just got back together, for God's sake."

"Well, all I'm saying is don't leave it too long, okay?"

"Okay."

"Hey, what are you guys plotting?" asked Jack, coming

over and putting his arm around her.

"Nothing" said Isabella, "Just catching up."

"Hmmm" he sighed, "Sounds ominous."

After a nightcap, the others discreetly headed to bed early. "Shall we have another drink on deck" he asked as they sat alone, finally.

"I'd love to. It's a lovely evening," she smiled.

As they walked outside into the balmy air, he briefly stopped to chat with one of the crew before joining her at the handrail. They peered out across the calm, flat sea, glistening silver in the moonlight, each moment a cherished memory to be savoured and treasured for years to come.

"We've had a wonderful few days, haven't we, Jack?"

"It's been heaven, baby. I don't want it to end. I don't know how I'll be able to let you go."

"I don't know either."

"You know we haven't talked about what happens after?"

"What do you mean?"

"Since our soul searching in Andros?"

"We're okay, aren't we?"

"Yes, of course, baby."

"So, what's the problem? We agreed to take things slowly, one day at a time, remember? It's too early to plan. We both know how we feel about each other. Let's just savour this moment."

"You're right," he said, pulling her towards him, "You certainly know how I feel about you," he whispered huskily, then kissed her fervently on the mouth.

Then, as if on cue, she could hear music beginning to play from the discreetly placed speaker.

"Frank," she smiled, as she looked at him lovingly.

"Let's dance baby," and he grabbed her tightly, and they swayed to *My Funny Valentine*.

"You planned this, didn't you?" She said.

"Naturally."

"You old smoothie."

They held each other and danced for another couple of tracks before they heard the strings of *All the Way*.

"Our song." She smiled and nestled her head even deeper into the side of his neck, as he sang along with the words.

He pulled away after what seemed like an eternity, and they both looked at each other dreamily.

"I've missed you so much," she whispered, her voice almost hoarse.

"Me too," he said, taking hold of the back of her head and pulling her towards him again, before kissing her passionately again. With every brush of their lips, they shared the depth of their longing, their hands roaming freely, exploring every curve and contour of each other's bodies. Fingers tangled in hair, nails grazed skin, as they sought to express the depths of their passion in every touch. As they finally broke apart, breathless and flushed with desire, he took a step back and took hold of her hand, "Come on you, let's go to bed."

They woke up late the following morning, and he looked at his phone.

"God Bella, we've slept in."

"I know." She smiled.

"What about Teddy?"

"What about Teddy? Harry and Eva have him."

"You planned the whole thing?"

"Naturally" she said.

"You little minx. Now come here." And he made love to her again.

They awoke for the second time and made their way down to breakfast gone eleven o'clock. They walked hand in hand, where the others were all waiting for them.

"Good morning." Harry grinned.

"Morning everyone," said Jack, smiling like a Cheshire cat.

"I take it you had a good night?" quipped Harry.

They looked at each other like a couple of love-struck teenagers and burst out laughing. Jack kissed her, then said,

"Wonderful."

Teddy ran over to his mummy and Isabella picked him up and gave him a big hug. "How's my little boy? Was he okay?" she asked Eva.

"Perfect. He slept right through, didn't wake up once, did he, Harry?"

"Good as gold," replied Harry. "So what's the plan now, Jack?"

"We're gonna sail around the base of Crete before heading back to Athens. It'll take at least a couple of days."

"Oh God, then home," groaned Ingrid.

"Don't remind me," said Isabella sadly.

After a few more heavenly days at sea, they finally arrived back in Athens. None of them were looking forward to getting back to the real world, but Isabella was particularly dreading having to say goodbye to Jack, who had to return to the States.

As the luxury yacht docked at port, signalling the end of their journey, they all said their emotional goodbyes to the dedicated crew first and paid their thanks for tirelessly looking after them all so well during their unforgettable voyage. They had become more than just staff; they had become friends; companions on a journey filled with laughter, adventure and unforgettable moments, as well as a few forgettable moments. They expressed their heartfelt gratitude to each member of the crew, thanking them for elevating their experience beyond their wildest expectations, leaving them with memories that would last a lifetime. With a last embrace, they reluctantly stepped off the yacht, each step feeling heavier than the last, the weight of impending separation bearing down upon them as they watched the crew prepare to set sail for their next adventure in Italy.

Boarding their van, they headed to the airport, the mood among them subdued, the air thick with unspoken emotions. As the haunting lyrics and emotive music of U2's Kite played on the radio, with every passing mile, the realisation that their time together was drawing to a close. The bond between them all had grown stronger, sustained by the simple pleasures of good food, superb wine, and good company.

They arrived at the terminal where Jack was flying first to Paris, then on to JFK, just just an hour before their return flight to London. Amidst the hustle and bustle of travellers rushing to their gates, Jack and Isabella stood on the precipice of a heart wrenching farewell. After what had felt like an eternity of separation over the past few years, they had finally reunited, but with departure looming, they were being wrenched apart again. Their fingers entwined, clinging to each other as if afraid to let go. Tears glistened in their eyes, reflecting the pain of impending separation. Words caught in his throat, choked by emotion as he pleaded with her, "Please don't forget how much I love you. I couldn't bear to lose you again."

"I love you too. I'll miss you dreadfully. My heart's breaking at the thought of being apart from you."

"Ditto."

"Can't you come with us?" she pleaded.

"No, I can't, I'm sorry Bella. I'd cancel if I could, but I have to get back to New York. It should only be a week at the most. Then I should be able to return to the UK. We can speak every day?"

"I know, but it's not the same. I've just found you and now you have to leave again."

"It's only a week."

"Promise?" she said as she kissed him long and hard. "I love you Jack."

"I love you Bella. Thank God we have sorted everything between us. No more secrets, okay?"

"No. No more secrets," she said and squeezed him tightly, "Jack ..."

"Yes?"

"Nothing. It can wait?"

"Isabella?" he groaned.

"Really, it can wait."

"Sure?"

"I'm sure. Listen, that was you. They've just made the last call for your flight. You'd better go."

"Okay. I love you Bella," he whispered, as they shared one last embrace, holding on to her with all the strength he possessed.

"Me too. Take care Jack. Call me as soon as you get there, okay?"

"I promise," and then he turned back to face the others, who were patiently waiting for them to say their goodbyes, "Harry, look after her for me?"

"I will Jack. Thanks again for an amazing time," and he hugged his friend.

"Thank you, Jack. It's been fantastic, the trip of a lifetime. I don't know how to thank you," said Eva, giving him a hug. Ingrid and David hugged Eva, and they made promises to stay in touch and plans to reunite soon.

"And little Teddy," said Jack, as he scooped him up in his strong muscular arms and kissed him, "Take care of Mommy, okay?"

"'k."

They said their last farewells before Jack headed to his gate, turning around now and again to steal fleeting glances at her, committing every detail of her face to memory. Isabella felt as if her heart were being ripped from her chest - she already missed his charismatic smile, the sparkle in his eye, the warmth of his touch. She couldn't bear to leave Greece, she couldn't bear to leave him. She wanted to stay there forever. On the boat. On the sea. Why did it have to end? Tears flowed now, tracing down her cheeks as he disappeared into the crowd, the ache of separation already haunting her.

***

CHAPTER THIRTY-FIVE

Jack was true to his word and phoned or Face Timed her every day and sometimes up to four or five times a day from New York. Each time the conversation was more or less the same, "I miss you terribly" they'd both complain, "I can't wait to see you again" and "I love you so much."

She spent the long, lonely, endless nights, sitting in the lounge listening to Frank Sinatra, reflecting on her new relationship with Jack and their aspirations for the future. Longing to see him again. How could she have been such a fool? Why did she waste so much of their lives?

On the night before he was due to arrive, he texted her.

"Arriving early tomorrow morning."

"Fab. When will I see you?"

"David, Harry and I are meeting with some associates near Westminster to go through a new proposal. Should be done, um, about three your time, then I'll be at yours as soon as I can get there, after that."

"I can't wait."

"Me neither."

On the day of his arrival, she kept the day free and made sure all the household chores were up to date, so the house looked immaculate. She made sure every surface was sparkling clean, and every corner was free of clutter. The aroma of freshly cleaned linens mingled with the aroma of her favourite Diptyque scented candles, filling the air with an inviting warmth. Abundant fresh flowers filled the space, and

Isabella diligently put away all the toys that usually made it messy. As she moved from room to room, she hummed with nervous energy, eager to create the perfect atmosphere for his arrival.

Unable to relax, she was tense. She changed outfits several times. She wanted everything to be perfect for him, without overdoing it. This was the first time they'd be meeting in 'normal' surroundings, with her everyday things around them, rather than more exotic locations around the world.

She had also arranged for Bibi and Darysus to collect Teddy mid-afternoon, to take him to their place for the evening, so that when Jack arrived, they could be alone.

The main thing going through her head, and had been ever since getting back from Greece, was when would be a good time to tell him about his son? Now? Or would it be better to wait a couple of days to see how things progressed? All she knew was she was absolutely dreading it. He was so volatile, their relationship still so fragile, and heaven knows what his reaction would be. What if he didn't want him? What if the prospect of fatherhood was too much for him? What if he was so pissed off with her, he wanted nothing to do with either of them?

She prepared a delicious meal with his favourite dishes. The aroma of savoury spices wafting through the air heightened her anticipation, knowing they'd soon be sharing this meal together. She set the table for two and couldn't help but steal glances at her watch, counting down the minutes until his arrival. A good bottle of wine was chilling in the fridge. Perhaps she should have brought champagne instead? Every passing second felt like an eternity, each sound outside causing her heart to race with anticipation, pounding in her chest.

She had just sat down to have a rest whilst she waited anxiously for him, when a BBC News special appeared on the television. *You're watching a BBC News special. Reports of a shooting outside the Palace of Westminster. Outside the House of Commons. A policeman has been stabbed and his apparent attacker shot by police officers. In what is developing into a major security incident outside the Houses of Parliament. These live pictures of Westminster Bridge, where eye witnesses say a car, in the words of eye witnesses, mowed down several people. Some reports suggesting as many as 12 people injured after a car hit them and then ...*

She felt a surge of adrenaline and the room spun as she realised that's where they were. Near there. She felt as if she was going to faint or be sick, or both. The room started spinning, and she felt as if she were going to lose her balance. She had to sit down to avoid falling. Oh my God, what should she do? She didn't know what to do. She couldn't think straight.

She rang his mobile. Straight to voicemail.

She rang again. Still no answer.

She tried Harry. No luck.

The TV continued in the background and she could pick out broken pieces. *Many people are being treated at the scene ...* She texted them both. Repeatedly. She paced back and forwards.

She rang again. Time and time again.

at twenty minutes to three London time.

Her mind was foggy. She didn't know what was going on. She was panicking.

Her phone rang. It was Bibi. "Have you seen?"

"Yes. Oh God Bibi, that's near where they are?"

"What? No."

"I can't get hold of them. Oh God Bibi, what do I do?"

"Stay calm. I'm sure they'll be fine."

"I'll have to go up there?" she sobbed.

"You can't. They've closed the surrounding areas. It'll be chaos."

"I'll never forgive myself. What if he's injured, or worse?"

"You can't think like that. He'll call you soon, I'm sure. Shall we come back?"

"No. No. Stay there. Keep Teddy there. I'd better go in case, in case one of them calls me."

"I'm here if you need me."

She kept texting and phoning Jack, Harry and David continuously, but without success. Glued to the television, she was just watching the same thing repeatedly on all channels. She paced the room and every time she heard a car in the road, she peered out to see if it was him. Compulsively, she kept picking up her phone to check the time and sound notifications.

By 6pm she was nearly insane with fear. Why weren't they answering?

Suddenly, a message pinged through from Harry.

Izzy. Call me. I need to talk to you.

Oh God, Harry.

She rang his mobile, but he still didn't answer. Fuck. she screamed.

Just as she was about to redial, there was a hammering at her front door.

"Coming," she screamed, her heart pounding. God, if anything had happened to Jack, she didn't know what she'd do. Whoever was at the door was in a hurry and wouldn't let up on the banging.

She flung the solid door open wide to see Jack standing before her, riotous and dishevelled.

"Thank God," she screamed, as relief flooded her entire body and she threw herself at him.

His expression was tortured. His eyes were black, the skin around them even blacker. She had never, ever seen anyone so furious. Not even Jack. His rage was almost tangible. It essentially looked as if he were about to combust, to burst into flames. If she weren't so relieved to see him in the flesh, she would have been terrified by his frenzied appearance.

He pushed past her roughly and stormed into the lounge. He absolutely stank of alcohol.

"Jack? What's going on? Were you there? Why didn't you

answer me? Why didn't you text me? What's wrong? Please Jack, you're scaring me," she sobbed.

He threw his jacket on the chair, then just sat down on top of it and put his head in his hands, overwhelmed by conflicting emotions.

"Please Jack, tell me?"

"I wasn't there. None of us were. We heard about it like you did."

"Oh, thank God," and she fell onto a chair near him.

"I need a drink," he stated.

"Of course. What do you want?"

"Anything." He lit up a cigarette.

"Jack, do you mind?"

"Don't you fucking dare," he roared.

"Jack. What the hell's going on?"

"Isabella, just get me a drink, now," he bellowed. Pain etched on his face.

She scuttled to get him a drink and poured him a large whiskey in a tumbler, wondering what the hell had happened to him. Had he been a witness? Was he in shock?

She returned warily to him and handed him the glass of amber liquid, which he poured straight down his throat.

Then he literally stunned her with his outburst.

"Why the fuck didn't you tell me?" he yelled, standing to face her, shoulder to shoulder. He towered over her menacingly. "Come on. Tell me. Answer me?" he thundered, his fists clenched, signalling his intense emotional state.

She thought he was going to hit her. She had never been so terrified of anyone, ever. And then he burst into tears, sobs engulfed his body as he sat back down and wept into his hands.

"Why?" he groaned, "Why Isabella?"

And then she knew. Knew the only thing that could have affected him in this manner. She felt sick to her stomach, queasy, as if she were going to vomit. She thought she was going to pass out. She felt hot, started sweating, her stomach started churning. Her mind was whirling. Her heart felt as if it was going to beat out of her chest. This was nothing to do with the terror attack? How the hell did he find out? Then the reality hit her. Harry's text. She collapsed on the chair behind her and began to sob and sob.

His tears subsided then, and he calmed down a little when he heard her anguish. He wiped his eyes with his hands and ran his hands through his hair. But he was still in a state of sustained rage and he came and knelt down in front of her. He stank of booze and cigarettes and his words were slurred.

"Don't you think I had a right to know? Do you know what you've done? How could you?" the confusion and shock on his face was clear.

"Jack ... I don't know what to say. I'm sorry. I'm so sorry."

"You're always sorry. You're always making excuses. How could you lie to me like this?"

"I was going to tell you, I promise," she wailed.

"Oh, you were? Just three years later? He's my son Isabella," he roared, and he stood and turned away from her to stare out of the window, endeavouring to close himself off emotionally.

"I promise, I was going to tell you today. I nearly told you twice in Greece."

"I can't process this. I can't process that I have a son. A son that I knew nothing about. A son you paraded around in front of me on holiday. The little boy I played with was my goddamned son. My son. God. What have you done, woman?" he roared.

"Jack I'm sorry. I don't know what I was thinking. You must forgive me?"

"Forgive you? Forgive three years of my life wasted. Everything you've done."

"I know. I know. Don't you think I wanted to tell you?"

"So why didn't you? I don't get it? I just don't get it."

"Jack, I screwed up."

"Does he know?"

"Teddy? Of course not."

"Don't you think you've cheated us both? Poor little guy's never had a dad. How could you do this to him? To me?"

She remained silent, taking in the gravity of his words. You could cut the atmosphere with a knife as they both wrestled with the intense thoughts and feelings.

"How did you find out?"

"Harry," he stated simply.

"I knew it. The bastard. He's supposed to be my friend. He knew I was going to tell you," she sobbed, "I wanted to tell you when the time was right."

"Harry's not to blame here, Isabella. It's you. The only person to blame here is you."

"I know. I know. What can I say? What can I do to make things better?"

"I loved you. I loved you from the moment I saw you. But what did you do? You just backed off? Right out of my life," he was shouting again, "What gave you the right to do that to me? To have my child without even telling me. What kind of monster do you think I am? Did I not deserve to know? What kind of woman are you? You're nuts. An absolute fruitcake. Man, I wish I'd never laid eyes on you, do you know that?" he ranted.

"I was going to tell you." She screamed.

"You should have told me," he screamed back, "Do you know how many opportunities you've had to tell me? You could have told me straight away when you found out? You could have told me in Vegas. That night I saw you pregnant in London–Jesus. That was my baby you were carrying. Why didn't you tell me then? Why did you carry on lying to me? This could have all been over years ago. Why didn't you tell me in Greece? No secrets, remember? Ha. Fucking hell," he yelled, his pain tangible.

"Why did Harry do this? Why's he ruined everything?"

"You. You ruined everything." He yelled, pointing at her.

"Oh God," she wailed.

"At least someone had the decency to tell me I'm a dad. I

have a son."

"I was going to tell you." She screamed, now more angry, than upset, her face flushed with the rush of blood and complex emotions. "I thought you were dead."

"What are you talking about?"

"I thought you were dead. I couldn't get hold of you," she screamed.

"I told you, we weren't near the bridge."

"I didn't know that," she yelled. "I thought you were injured or dead. I couldn't bear it. I couldn't bear to live without you."

"Oh Bella," he cried and came to comfort her then. He held her in his arms until their sobs subsided.

He poured them both a large whiskey, then led her to the sofa and took her hands in his own.

"Baby. I don't know if I can ever forgive you. You must tell me why you didn't tell me?"

"It was what you said in Kenya."

"Not that fucking holiday again."

"You told me you didn't want kids. You said they were a waste of time and spoiled things. You said …"

"I don't give a damn what I said. Anyway, I told you I didn't mean it. I don't even remember saying it."

"I do."

"Don't you see? I've already missed so much. His first two birthdays. I've missed his first words, his first steps. Christ, he probably doesn't even know the word Daddy. How can I ever forgive you? Don't you realise what you've done?" he bawled again, running his hands through his unkempt hair.

Amid the chaos, they reopened long, buried and old wounds. Tears flowed as the weight of the truth threatened to crush the fragile bond that held them together.

"What have I done?" she shrieked. "I'll tell you what I've bloody done. I've raised my son. Our son, all on my own, the best I know how. I was alone. Terrified. You and I had finished, or at least I believed so. Do you not think I lay there every night, every day, wishing you were with me? Watching all the other couples in the ante-natal classes. Out shopping. Out to dinner. When all I had was me." She stopped then, sobs once again racking her whole body.

As the argument raged on, emotions reached a fever pitch and there were no simple answers or quick fixes to mend the fractured relationship. Each of them struggled to grapple with the harsh reality of their situation, unsure of how to move forward from the wreckage.

"Oh Bella. What have we done? If I'd have had any sense or even looked past my nose, I'd have known. Jesus, the dates. For Christ's sake, he even looks like me. I should have come after you. You should never have lied to me. So many lies," and he began to cry again, as he held her tightly to his chest, a lingering sense of emptiness and despair as the harsh reality sank in.

"Jack, I'm so, so sorry. I should have told you, but ... but ..." he didn't finish her sentence.

"Shh, baby, I know, I know, I'm sorry."

They sat there for ages, holding each other, comforting each other, soothing the hurt, trying to ease each other's pain and turmoil, leaving a glimmer of hope, a flicker of possibility that maybe, just maybe, they could rebuild what they'd lost and forge a new path forward, together.

"So why did Harry tell you?" she asked, eventually.

"We had the meeting. I thought everything would be over quickly, but they'd laid on a lavish lunch. I was dying to come and see you, but I had to stay to make sure the deal was closed. It was driving me mad. We had a few drinks ... don't look like that Bella ... Anyway, I was mumbling about seeing you and Teddy, et cetera, et cetera, when I made an innocent comment about your ex."

"What about my ex?"

"Well, I said 'what kind of prick was he, that he would leave his girlfriend and baby and not have anything to do with them'. Harry piped up, 'Because he's not the father, Jack'. As soon as the words were out of his mouth, he regretted them. He had been drinking a lot more than me. I said 'What?' I was astounded. I couldn't believe it. So, David asks 'So who is Teddy's father?'. Harry didn't know what to say, he just looked at me kinda sheepishly. I asked him 'Harry, Harry, what's going on here?' A funny feeling came over me. But he didn't have to say anymore. I just knew. Anyway, I just upped and left. I didn't know where I was going. The place was chaotic. The attack happened near to where we were. I didn't know what to think. I was confused, angry, upset, every emotion you can think of. I went to a bar and drank and drank. Tried to blot out the pain. As the truth sank in, I struggled to come to terms with this revelation. My disbelief gave way to a flood of overwhelming emotion. Hurt. Betrayal. I couldn't believe that all this time I had a little boy. My mother died for God's sake, without knowing she had another grandson …" He stopped then. He was too upset to go on.

"Jack I'm so sorry. Can you ever forgive me? Will you ever be able to see past what I've done?"

"Bella, I love with you all of my heart …"

"I love you too."

"But …"

But before he could say any more, they heard the front door open.

"Mummy. Mummy. I'm home." They heard little Teddy call as he burst through the living room door like a cyclone. "Mummy sad?" he asked, concern etched on his little face, as he ran over to Isabella's side, "Hello Jack" he said smiling shyly at his Mummy's friend.

"Hey little buddy," said Jack, ruffling his hair.

"Yes, darling mummy's sad, but I'm fine now," she said, wiping her eyes and her runny nose.

Bibi entered the room and stared inquisitively at her distraught friend and the unkempt but gorgeous man beside her. "I take it you're Jack and you're not dead?"

"No, I'm not dead," he deadpanned.

"Thank God for that." She gasped.

Bibi left them then, and over the next few hours, Isabella and Jack sat together as Teddy played around them, their hearts and bodies intertwined. In the aftermath of the highly emotional afternoon, they found solace in each other's arms, their love a beacon of hope in the darkness of their past traumas. With tears of joy and relief occasionally streaming down their faces, they made a solemn vow to face their future together, united by their newfound understanding and unwavering commitment to each other. A sense of peace washed over them both, knowing they had finally found their way back to each other after so many trials and tribulations. The sounds of Teddy's laughter and chatter weaved amongst them, a reminder of the joys that awaited them on the journey ahead. With a renewed sense of purpose and determination, they were both ready to take each other's hand and take a step forward into the unknown, ready to embrace whatever challenges and adventures life may bring.

***

Epilogue

They had sold her house and bought a substantial contemporary home, set in twelve acres of elevated land perched on the banks of the Thames, near to Richmond.

On a gorgeous late summer's evening, the elegant home and meticulously landscaped gardens were still full of caterers and guests as they all prepared for the upcoming evening reception, following the nuptials of Mr and Mrs Vincent earlier that day.

"Oh Izzy, you looked amazing." Bibi fawned as she watched Isabella twirl in front of a full-length mirror in her beautiful Vera Wang wedding gown in her dressing room with floor to ceiling windows that offered a tantalising glimpse of the tranquil Thames and lush countryside beyond.

"I can't believe I'm married," she stated, fingering her new wedding ring, now sitting next proudly next to her enormous pear-shaped diamond engagement ring.

"We've waited long enough."

Teddy came running in dressed in a little custom Dolce suit and tie to match his daddy's. "Mummy, Daddy said are you nearly ready?"

"I'm nearly ready, darling."

"Come on Izzy, let's go," pleaded Bibi.

"Yes Mummy, come on. Daddy's waiting for you."

Mother and son walked hand in hand down the flower dressed, stunning staircase; the focal point of the grand foyer, with its soaring ceiling and polished marble floor, where Jack was waiting patiently for them.

"You look beautiful, Mrs Vincent, doesn't she Teddy?"

"Yes Daddy. Like a fairy princess."

"Thank you, my loves."

She could hear *their* first song playing in the marquee set upon the manicured lawn.

He looked at her and took hold of her hand. "So, Mrs Vincent, you ready?"

"I'm ready." She said breathlessly, as they walked together towards their friends and family, into a promising future filled with love, hope and endless possibility. At last, their love had conquered all and that love would guide them through the storms that they ahead, the start of their own and their beautiful son's happily ever after.

ACKNOWLEDGEMENTS

I started writing this book when I was pregnant with my eldest son back in 1996, whilst on maternity leave. An avid reader of Enid Blyton as a child, I then progressed to romance books as a young girl starting with the American author, Danielle Steel. I became enamoured with the genre. As I got older, I moved on to Jackie Collins and other fabulous authors. I felt I had a love story in me and the idea started growing from there. Over the years, I have kept returning to, and rereading, All the Way; adding and deleting and updating things - particularly the technology – of course smart phones didn't exist when I started! Eventually, in 2020, because of the COVID-19 pandemic, out it came yet again. This time, I was determined to finish it. It has always had the same title and the main characters have always been the same, but over the years, names have changed and the story has developed. I would like to thank my younger, prettier, sister Kirst (Kirsten) for her ongoing support and love and for being my first ever reader – I'll never forget the day she rang me crying in hysterics at my first attempt at a sex scene. To all my other friends and family, I love you all and I assure you that all characters are living in my head and I see them as if I'm watching a movie or reading someone else's book and none of them are you or me! Thank you to my mum for giving me the passion of books and my late beloved dad, music. But most importantly, I would like to thank my darling sons James and Joe, who taught me unconditional love and showed me the reason I am here on this earth, to be your Mummy. I love you more than words can ever say.

ABOUT THE AUTHOR

Stephnie Conn

Stephnie was born in Easington, County Durham in 1968. She is a mother to two grown-up sons, James and Joe. An avid reader from a young age, Stephnie felt determined to write and publish her own novel, based on her favourite genre, romance. Stephnie currently lives in Surrey, England. As a young child, her father's work took her to first to Zambia and then Kenya, where her love of travel began.

ALL THE WAY

I never knew of a morning in Africa, when i woke up that I was not happy - Ernest Hemingway

Printed in Great Britain
by Amazon